AND THE

As they wa   a's cabin,
the ship th   ⲙⲟ gave a
great sigh, then sank, hissing at her fate.

"Inga, we made it," Nick said shakily. "We're alive."
He pulled her closer, trying to shield her from the
dying horror of the blaze.

As she clung to him, her long-dammed tears at last
broke free. Holding her shuddering body as tightly
as he could, he felt his desire growing. The small,
consoling kisses on brow and cheek became something more. His lips sought her tear-wet mouth,
one arm crushing her to him, his other hand
straying over luscious, forbidden curves that took
his breath away.

He felt her suddenly go very still. Then she began
to tremble again. Her arms came up and around
him, palms pressing against his back, drawing him
down, down. . . .

IN THIS SWEET LAND
Inga's Story

1

That year, the frost had gone deep, and it wasn't until May that the iron-hard winter released its hold on the earth. The planting was late.

From where Inga Johansson stood, she could see across the vast prairie. Her girlhood home with the little steepled church beside it looked like a child's blocks. That tiny dot on the horizon would be her father, Pastor Gustav Lindstrom, founder of this settlement, plowing the good land.

Inga shut her eyes, remembering how the black earth turned, rolling from the plowshare in a curving wave; remembering herself following it, as her brothers and sisters were surely doing now, casting the seed that would sprout, green, then ripen into a golden sea of waving grain.

Her brother Sven, would have been with her, too; Sven, who had run away to join the Confederate Army somewhere in the South and had never returned. Their mother hadn't heard from Sven these last two years. Perhaps, now that the war had ended . . .

Inga sighed, knowing that Sven would not come home. It would be enough, however, to have word that he was safe.

In the meantime, the potatoes must be set in the ground.

She had prepared the plot as well as she could without a plow, hoeing it, turning it. Her husband, Olaf, had hitched their only horse to the cart and ridden into town nearly a week ago. He would be drinking at the riverside saloons, frequenting the bawdy houses, doing all the things a good Swedish Christian should not do.

And nobody ever blamed Olaf Johansson.

Not even Inga's father, Pastor Lindstrom, would point a shaming finger at Olaf in church, or accuse him of pursuing wicked ways. For it was all her fault.

According to the congregation, Inga was a wanton wife who had driven him to his excesses, presenting him with a wood's colt as her second child. A girl, instead of the boy he wished for, and a "heathen Indian" at that.

Inga looked at small fourteen-year-old Jenny, sitting on the back stoop, her skirt hiked up to reveal slim brown legs. The child's hair was raven-black as no Lindstrom's or Johansson's had ever been. Her eyes were huge pools of darkness, her complexion a sun-warmed amber shade.

Inga sighed, pushing back her own flaxen braids with a soiled, work-hardened hand. Married at fourteen to Olaf Johansson, a bachelor in his late thirties, Inga had produced first Kirsten, now fifteen, who looked very like herself—and then Jenny.

When Jenny was born, Olaf accused Inga of unspeakable things. He recalled a time when he had come in from the fields to find a buck Indian in his kitchen. Though Inga had only fed the man, who was hungry, Olaf swore Jenny was living proof that there had been something more between them.

Olaf left Inga, still weak from bearing Jenny, and went to her father with his indictment. The following Sunday, Pastor Lindstrom heaped coals of fire upon her head from his pulpit. Inga was cast out of the church, and no decent woman of their small religious community was allowed to speak to her.

Only Inga knew there had been no other man than Olaf. Where had Jenny, this beloved changeling child, come from?

"Are the potatoes ready, Yenny?" Inga said her daughter's name with the soft Swedish accent that made it sound like music.

Small Jenny, seed potato in one hand, knife in the other, was daydreaming; looking for signs of spring that would deepen into summer; summer, when she would run barefoot through the fields of wild mustard, goldenrod, and fireweed. There should be crocuses soon.

"A few," she said, blushing guiltily, and picked up another potato.

Her mother smiled and filled her apron with the sprouting eyes, then moved back into the garden, poking holes into the soil, dropping a bit of potato in each, moving on.

7

Jenny went back to her work with the best intentions, but was lost in thought once again as she watched Inga. Her mother looked like a goddess, she thought, her thick braids coiled in a coronet, her eyes bluer than the sky. And Kirsten looked like Inga.

Why was she herself so small and brown and ugly?

And why did Papa hate her?

The sound of a trap approaching interrupted Jenny's thoughts. She leapt to her feet, spilling potatoes from her lap, and ran around the house.

It was Oskar Bjorn, bringing Kirsten from the school in St. Paul. When Olaf Johansson's drinking habits had proven him undependable, Bjorn took it upon himself to act as protector to the girl who would one day be his wife.

Oskar Bjorn was a widower in his forties, but he and Kirsten had been bespoken since she was twelve. Bjorn was a wealthy man, a mill owner. He paid for Kirsten's schooling, insisting she be educated so she could handle his books when they married.

Jenny greeted the arrivals as the trap stopped. Bjorn ignored Jenny and helped her rosy-cheeked sister down from his trap. Then he was off.

Jenny ran alongside the hurrying Kirsten to ask what she had learned at school during the week. Later, she and her mother would sit at the plank table in the kitchen, the kerosene lamp turned high, and labor over the same lessons, with Kirsten as teacher.

"Did you see Papa?" Jenny asked finally. Kirsten reddened and shook her head. Though she was closest to Olaf, his forays in town were an embarrassment to Kirsten. But she did not blame him, either.

"Where is Mama?" Kirsten asked.

"We are planting potatoes."

The blond girl yawned, putting a hand to her mouth. "I suppose you should get back to work. I must study."

Returning to her post, Jenny informed Inga that Kirsten was home, and continued her labors with vigor. She couldn't wait until they were finished, until she could sit at the table and absorb the magic of the written word. The job did not take long. There were so few potatoes. The last potato sprout planted, Inga washed her hands at the basin outside the back door and went to milk the cow.

When she had finished, she carried the full pail into the house, poured a cup of milk apiece for herself and the girls, and cut a few slabs of bread. It was still daylight when she brushed the crumbs away and brought out the slates she and Jenny used to write their lessons on.

Listening to Kirsten's soft voice as she explained the day's lessons, Inga gazed at the fair head bent beside the dark one and thought how much she loved them both.

Kirsten had never respected her, for her mind had been poisoned long ago by her father. But the lovely blond girl was her firstborn, a reminder of happier times. And Jenny—Jenny's birth had brought her grief, but she was her light in the darkness.

Jenny's head lifted and she frowned a little, listening. "Someone is coming," she announced.

A cold hand closed around Inga's heart. She and Jenny had been shut away, shunned by the community. No one but her mother dared visit, and then only when her own husband was away. It had to be Olaf coming home.

When she heard stumbling footsteps, a fumbling at the door, swear words uttered in the Swedish tongue, Inga was certain.

Olaf. And he was drunk again. When he was drinking he was not himself. At first it was she whom he abused. But of late, with Jenny near grown up, and becoming more unlike him every day, he had turned his animosity toward her.

Inga folded her arms about herself protectively. But in her mind she was praying: "Don't let him hurt Jenny."

The door finally crashed open, and there he stood; six-foot-six, stout with middle age and too much liquor. His thatch of graying blond hair was sweaty, and his chin, below a red-veined nose, stubbled.

"Where is Yenny," he slurred. "Get her things together!"

He looked around the room, finally focused on the girl, and shambled toward her.

Inga watched him with alarm. "Olaf! What are you going to do?"

"Get rid of that millstone around my neck," he growled. "Out of my way, woman!"

Get rid of her? What was in his drink-crazed mind?

"Olaf—"

He ignored Inga, and moved toward the cowering child. As Inga stepped in front of him, interpos-

10

ing her body between Olaf and their daughter, he swung his arm and swept her aside.

"Come here, Yenny!"

"Olaf!" Inga clung to him, pleading as he gripped Jenny's arms. "Olaf! For the love of God!"

"Do not add blasphemy to your other sins, woman! I have found a man who wants a woman, and does not give a damn if she's a bastard! Do you understand? He will take her without question; get her out of my sight—"

Inga felt a cold chill of terror. She could imagine her husband in drunken conversation, discussing the source of the shame that drove him to drink with someone equally dissolute; a dock worker, a boatman, a gambler, offering to give his daughter away to the highest bidder.

"Olaf, I will not allow you to do this!"

"Allow me? You cannot stop me! Come here, Yenny!"

He yanked at the girl's arm and she whimpered as he twisted it painfully. Again Inga tried to maneuver her body between them. This time Olaf hit out at her, his fist connecting with her mouth; then he threw her down. Inga struck her temple on the stone of the cold fireplace. As she reached out, half-dazed, her fingers closed around something to pull herself up.

The poker!

Olaf was dragging Jenny toward the door. She had to stop him. Getting to her feet, she swung at him. There was a dull thud as the instrument connected with his head. Olaf turned and looked at her, his bloodshot blue eyes wide in amazement, before he took two staggering steps, then crashed to the floor like a fallen tree.

"Papa!"

The word burst from Kirsten's lips as she ran to her father and knelt beside him. When she lifted his head, she could see the blood seeping from his lips and nose.

"Papa!"

Inga pressed the knuckles of her left hand to her bleeding mouth and looked down at the weapon she held. She had no memory of picking it up, of striking out. But her husband, Olaf Johansson, lay at her feet, the back of his fair hair a gory sight. Jenny cowered in a corner, the sleeve of her dress half-torn away, black eyes wide with fright.

And Kirsten, her father's favorite, had risen, staring at Inga in horror and accusation.

"You've killed him, Mama," she said in a voice flat with shock. Then it rose, a terrible keening sound that trembled at the edge of hysteria. "You've killed him!"

2

For a long time, Inga was unable to move. She felt the scene before her would be imprinted in her mind forever. Jenny, pale and mute, cowering against the far wall; Kirsten, kneeling, her mouth open, screams issuing from lips stretched wide with horror—a square cavern in her white face.

Other than the screams that echoed off the walls, there was no sound; no movement, except the slow welling of blood that ran across Olaf's grizzled head to puddle on the floor.

She had murdered her husband!

"Mama?"

Jenny's small, frightened voice brought Inga to her senses.

"Get out of the house," Inga said in a strangled tone. "Hurry! The horse is still hitched! Get in the cart, Jenny! Kirsten! Do as I tell you!"

Handing them their cloaks, she shoved them out the door and turned back. Scarcely knowing what she was doing, or why, she snatched up their few clothes, the bagged seeds from their shelf, her sewing scissors, and shoved them into Olaf's old carpet bag.

Then she reached for the family Bible, but drew her hand back as if it had been burned.

She left the Bible where it was, and began to tremble. Dear God! What had she done!

The bag in one hand, she turned at the door to look at the man with whom she had shared her marriage bed. The lamp on the kitchen table flickered, casting monstrous shadows, and for a moment he appeared to move.

She imagined him rising, coming toward her, that awful bloodied head hunched between his shoulders as he reached for her; imagined him knocking her to the ground, stepping over her, lurching toward the cart—and Jenny—

No, it was a trick of the light! He hadn't moved.

With a strangled sob she ran outside and shut the door, hoping it would look as if there was no one home.

And there was not, she thought dazedly. Nobody who would speak, invite a guest in. Only Olaf, who lay dead on the floor of the room that served as kitchen and sitting room, the lamp casting grotesque shadows that would forever haunt her dreams.

Inga climbed into the cart and took up the reins. Though Kirsten was still crying, her hysterical screams had deteriorated into exhausted, mindless whimpering. Jenny's voice, though it had a hollow sound to it, was steady.

"Where are we going, Mama?"

What could she say? *I don't know? You tell me! Help me—?* She was the adult here. The mother. And mothers were supposed to make decisions in time of trouble. At the moment, she needed her own mother.

"I think," she said, trying to still the quivering of her mouth, "we'll go to St. Paul."

But when they reached the end of the lane, Inga turned impulsively toward her childhood home. Though twilight was falling, her father would still be at work in a far field. The children would be with him. Her mother would be alone.

Birgitta Lindstrom, walking from her chicken pen to the house, saw the cart coming and shaded her eyes against the setting sun. It looked like the rig that belonged to her son-in-law, Olaf Johansson. She had no use for the man. She would send him out to where Pastor Lindstrom was working, she thought sourly.

Going into the house, she set her pail of eggs on the table and began sorting them. Some she would hide in the bottom of the cupboard to sell. Pastor Lindstrom—she had never thought of him by any other name—needn't know about it, just as he had never learned about her butter and cheese sales.

One day, she told herself, now that the war was over, she would take her savings and go south to look for Sven.

All she had of her oldest son was a two-year-old letter. Once in a while she would slip away, mak-

15

ing a furtive visit to the daughter she wasn't allowed to see, and ask Inga to read the letter to her again.

Birgitta had almost memorized the letter by now. Especially the parts about it being always warm, and the sweet smell of flowers and magnolias. Though the dried petal he sent in the envelope had lost its scent, she savored the descriptions, wearing the thought of them like a warm shawl in the frigid Minnesota winter.

There. The eggs were now divided into what she regarded as her husband's share and her own. She went again to open the door, and her jaw dropped in shock as she saw it was Inga at the reins, with the two girls in back of the cart. Something must be terribly wrong for Inga to dare coming here.

Before Birgitta could move, Inga was out of the cart and running toward her.

"Mama," she said breathlessly, her face white as death, "Mama—"

Birgitta looked toward the fields. Pastor Lindstrom should be coming in soon, and he would be angry if he found Inga here. He would not beat her—he was not that kind of man—but he would keep her on her knees in prayer throughout the night. And her knees were swollen enough already.

"Your father . . ." Birgitta began.

Her words fell on deaf ears. A white-faced Inga clutched her arms, fingers bruising to the bone. "Mama . . . Mama, I have just killed Olaf!"

Birgitta Lindstrom began to tremble. Her sins had, at last, caught up with her.

"Tell me," she said.

Inga sketched the evening's events swiftly. Her

16

mother knew how Olaf felt about Jenny, that he refused to consider her his. "But I have never been with another man," Inga said. "Mama, I swear!"

Birgitta closed her eyes against the blue sincerity in Inga's.

"I know, daughter. I know."

Inga rushed on with her story. Olaf was drunk, bent on giving Jenny to an unknown man. She had tried to stop him. Somehow, she'd struck him. It was an accident.

"You know what they'll do to me when they find him."

Birgitta did. And even Inga's father would make no effort to protect her. Her voice, when she spoke, was strangely old and quavering. "Come into the house, child."

Inga entered the house of her childhood, the home she hadn't visited since Jenny's birth. It was just as she remembered it. Everything was worn but clean, the wide board floors freshly scrubbed with lye water. In all this house, everything was utilitarian; there was nothing of beauty.

She watched the figure of her mother, bent from too much work and too many children, as she moved to a row of hooks on the opposite wall to take down her shabby wadmal coat. Inga's eyes widened with surprise. Did her mother intend to go with them?

Birgitta put the coat into Inga's arms, stroking it lovingly as she did so. "This coat is very warm. You will notice the lining is quilted. I want you to take it."

It was clear her mother was giving her her most

prized possession. "No, Mama. I have my coat. You will need it."

The expression Birgitta turned on her was a little sly. "You do not understand. This is a very special coat. Into it I have sewn money over the years. I had thought to use it to find Sven—"

Seeing the sorrow in the faded face that must once have resembled her own made Inga remember her mother, too, had her problems, and she burst into tears.

"I can't, Mama. I can't take it. I'm not what everybody thinks I am, but I've killed a man—"

"I killed him," Birgitta said with dignity.

It was clear the shock of what had happened had unhinged Birgitta's mind.

"No, Mama! I—"

Birgitta's worn hand waved Inga's words away. "I killed him, just as surely as if I'd had that poker in my hand! I destroyed you, your marriage, your little Yenny."

Inga stared at her, eyes rounded, reaching out to touch her mother's bent shoulder. She should not have come here, bearing her terrible burden.

"I have something to tell you," Birgitta Lindstrom said firmly. "I will make haste but I must begin at the beginning . . ."

In a slow, steady voice, she told Inga the familiar story of her marriage in Sweden, to Gustav Lindstrom, a man twice her age. Gustav, a member of a small, fanatically religious sect, had been to America, accompanying Major Steven J. Long on his exploration of the Minnesota and Red rivers. Gustav returned to his own country to gather together a group of like-minded people to colonize this area, and he needed a wife.

Young Birgitta did not really know him, but he was a minister, therefore a good man. Her parents listened to his proposal, and consented for her. By the time they arrived in Minnesota, she had already borne him a son, Sven, and she was desperately unhappy.

A youthful farmhand, Louis Valour, of French and Indian blood, worked for her husband.

"He was . . . kind," Birgitta said. "Pastor Lindstrom was usually away. And one day, when Louis and I were scything wheat, Sven asleep at the edge of the field, we . . . we . . ."

She stopped, her face reddening at Inga's stunned realization of what she was saying, then continued, omitting the romantic details.

"I . . . It happened more than once, Inga. I knew it was wrong, but I could not help myself. Then I found I was in the family way and was afraid. When you were born, with the fairness of our people, I thought all was well, until . . . Until our Yenny."

Jenny! It was not she, Inga, who had been at fault, but her mother! Fate had played a cruel joke, visiting her mother's sin, not upon her, but an innocent child. Pastor Lindstrom was not Inga's father. He was no relation at all. Her father had been a field hand, a half-breed.

Inga's anger rose, hateful words trembling at the edge of her tongue. Then she closed her eyes, seeing a wheat field, a slender blond Swedish girl in the arms of a French-and-Indian lad with Jenny's dark features; imagining the sweet scent of the day, larks singing.

When she spoke, her tone was tinged with love and pity. "Mama, why didn't you tell me!"

"I was afraid," Birgitta said again. Suddenly she looked past Inga, out the door. "Your father is coming. You must go! I will tell him that your husband was here with the cart, that he will be in church with Kirsten on Sunday. When he does not come, someone will go to ask why . . . Inga, child . . ."

"Yes, Mama."

"Go to St. Paul. The Danbergs will take you in."

Inga barely remembered the Danbergs, Helga and John, her mother's friends. Helga had known Birgitta in Sweden, when they were girls together. They moved to St. Paul, and she and her husband had come to visit Birgitta once, but were turned away.

Helga, Pastor Lindstrom had thundered, was a "light" woman, with her fancy clothes and her laughter. Birgitta was forbidden to see her. He did not intend to have his God-fearing family corrupted.

Birgitta had disobeyed him for once in her life. On a day when her husband was laid up with an injured leg, and she had to go into St. Paul for supplies, she drove to the Danberg home.

Small Inga, who was allowed to come along, watched with round eyes as the women hugged each other, weeping. Then the mood changed and they were soon laughing, Birgitta looking absurdly young for a time while the two women recalled their lost girlhood.

As the women talked together, Inga roamed the house, nibbling at the candy Helga gave her—a treat her father would have considered wasteful.

20

The rooms of the Danberg home were filled with pretty things.

But the visit had ended with a quarrel.

"You can't live the way you are," Helga said. "Life's too short!"

"Pastor Lindstrom is a good man," Birgitta said staunchly.

"So is my John! We go to church, we say our prayers. But I don't think God intends religion to be a punishment! Get out of that narrow-minded little community, Birgitta! Leave that man!"

"You don't mean—"

"Divorce? Yes, I do!"

Birgitta's mouth set. "Come, Inga. We are going. My husband was right, Helga. I will not see you again."

Birgitta held true to her word. There had been no further communication between the women. But now she was sending Helga her daughter—a woman with blood on her hands.

"Tell her I was wrong," Birgitta continued now. "Tell her you are leaving a husband who is much like the pastor, that I beg her to help you."

"But we can't stay there!"

"Helga will help you take passage on a steamboat. Use another name. Travel in first class. No one will think to look for you there, if they should find ... find ..." She paused, unable to put words to the horror. "And look for my Sven. You will do this for me?"

"Yes, Mama."

"You will forgive me?"

"Yes, Mama. Oh, yes."

Birgitta hugged her, an unfamiliar gesture, and

21

Inga hurried toward the cart. She climbed up into the seat, then looked down to see her mother had followed.

"Take this with you," Birgitta urged. "It may help you to find him." She handed up Sven's letter, two years old, folded, creased, worn with love and handling. She kept the dried magnolia petal Sven had sent along with the message that he was alive and well. Inga would have no need of that.

Then the cart moved away, and Birgitta stood calling good-bye until they were out of sight. Again her voice sounded strange in her ears—yet familiar.

Birgitta finally placed it. It sounded like that of her own mother at their parting in Sweden, when she knew she was losing her daughter and would never see her again.

Turning the cart onto the main road, Inga whipped up the horse as she passed the lane that led to her and Olaf's home, and felt a chill along her spine at the thought of the secret the house held within its walls.

3

Inga remembered little of the trip into St. Paul. Her mind was filled with thoughts of survival for herself and her family. What if Olaf's body had already been found? Suppose the galloping horseman who passed them a mile or two back was carrying the message into town? She would be stopped, imprisoned, probably hanged. What, then, would happen to her children? Her father might take Kirsten in. But not Jenny—never Jenny.

Her thoughts went around and around like a squirrel in a cage. And at the heart of them was a dead man, his gory head burned indelibly into her memory.

"Mama," small Jenny asked from behind her, "do you suppose someone will find Papa—soon? If they don't—"

If they didn't, the house where Inga had lived,

had borne her children, would become a horror. Inga began to shiver, a trembling she was unable to stop. It was a moment before she could answer Jenny.

"They will find him. Your grandmother will see to it. We ... we mustn't think about that. Right now, we have to get away."

Then Kirsten spoke for the first time, her voice harsh with condemnation. "Where are we going?"

Inga outlined her plan. They were going to the home of friends who would help them find passage on a riverboat. Then they would go down the Mississippi to Tennessee, where Sven had been heard from last. Memphis was said to be a beautiful place, she informed her daughters with false enthusiasm. She would find work there.

"I am not going with you."

"Kirsten, listen to me—"

"I will not, Mama! I am going back!"

"To ... that house?" Inga's voice was choked with revulsion.

"I will go to my grandfather. Or to Oskar Bjorn. You forget that we are to be married."

"Mr. Bjorn is an old man, Kirsten!"

"He has a nice house, land, a mill ..."

Inga shuddered. When Bjorn first approached Olaf about marrying Kirsten, the child had been averse to his courtship. But Olaf had gradually talked her into it. The words she had just uttered might have come from her father's mouth.

"Sometimes that isn't enough."

"What you had wasn't enough for you, was it, Mama? That's how we got our Jenny!"

Inga's hand cracked against the girl's cheek, leaving prints of her fingers. "There will be no more of that, Kirsten! I have never done anything to hurt Olaf."

"Except kill him!"

The girl spoke the truth. Inga felt that awful quivering inside again, a jerking and twitching of nerves that she must overcome in order to survive.

"Yes, Kirsten," she said quietly. "I did. I did it to protect Jenny. I would have done it to protect you. If you wish, we'll go back, but I can tell you this—no matter what my reasons, I will be found guilty and hanged. And you will be the daughter of a murderess, her blood in your veins. Do you think your grandfather will take you in? That Oskar Bjorn will marry you? That they will allow you to remain in that community?"

There was no answer from behind her. Inga drove on.

What blood was in her own veins? she wondered. If evil lived on, as her community believed, what strain had she acquired from her unknown father? Was it an evil taint that had led her to violence?

A small hand reached from behind her, touching her cheek like a butterfly, a reassuring hand that said, "I love you. All will be well."

Jenny.

Inga shifted the reins and laid her work-roughened palm over Jenny's. If blood told, then Jenny's grandfather had been kind and gentle. She wished she could have known him.

But she hadn't. And neither did she know St. Paul when she turned into it in the early dawn. She had not been there since before the birth of Jenny, more than fourteen years. At that time, the

25

town had not extended as far; the streets were hopelessly out of plumb, and there were few people. Now it was a thriving metropolis in her eyes. Most of the houses were dark, but despite the hour, drunken men walked the streets, calling out lewd suggestions to a lone woman with a cart, not knowing that in the bed of the vehicle, her daughters slept.

It seemed hours before she located the address Birgitta had given her. Memory flooded back again as she saw a little house with a blue door set in among other, less modest structures. It was smaller than she recalled, but still looked warm and inviting.

Leaving the girls asleep, she approached the house and knocked at the door. Helga Danberg, in gown and robe, flaxen braids hanging down her back, answered her knock, lamp in hand. She drew in a sharp breath. "Birgitta?"

"Birgitta's daughter," Inga said unsteadily. "I . . . need help."

And then she burst into tears.

Helga Danberg put her arms around Inga, holding her against a warm, maternal breast, her heart aching as Inga poured out as much of her story as she dared.

She was running away from her husband, Inga explained, to make a better life for her children. Her mother had told her to come to Helga.

"Of course," Helga soothed her. "Of course." She was only too happy to do for Birgitta's daughter what she had been unable to do for her friend.

Helga clucked over the girls, who were roused and brought into the house. As she led them to a room with clean, sun-fragrant sheets and soft beds, she noticed that their faces were tearstained and they were emotionally exhausted. No wonder, she thought compassionately. Poor things. They needed love, tenderness.

Inga was led into a homey kitchen, where Helga prepared coffee and little cakes, asking no questions, since it was clear the young woman was at the end of her nerves. As she flitted about, Helga talked of the old times when she and Birgitta had been best friends.

For the first time, Inga was able to think of her mother as a laughing, lovely girl, eyes glinting with a delicate mischief, as Helga told of their pranks. Then she stopped reminiscing and asked, "She still with that man?"

"Yes."

"If I were married to him," Helga said grimly, "I would kill him!"

She didn't see her guest shrink at her words, but a few moments later, realizing how quiet Inga had become, Helga insisted the younger woman go to bed.

Alone in her room in the Danberg house, Inga sat before the mirror, taking down the plaits that crowned her head. She brushed her hair until it looked like waves of summer wheat and thought how lightly time had dealt with her. Only her red, work-roughened hands set her apart from Kirsten. And she thought of her mother, the Birgitta that Helga had known.

Now Birgitta was old, worn, like the coat that hung on a hook behind Inga, a reminder of her mother's love and trust. It was the coat of a poor, hardworking country woman—like me, Inga thought. Today—no, yesterday—I set the seed potatoes in the ground. The soil is still beneath my nails. And now, my potatoes will grow, and there will be no one to harvest them.

She felt a sudden wave of homesickness for the only land she had ever known, the black earth with its swift greening, and swifter ripening; flickertails, meadowlarks; myriads of wildflowers . . .

And then the snows, piling deep around the Johansson house, the wind howling about its corners, prying at the windows, trying to get in.

She had had no love for Olaf. But it had been good there, in those early days, before Jenny was born.

And last night she had killed a man!

She must not think of the past.

She plaited her hair once more, leaving it to hang in braids down her back. Then she went to the coat and took it down from its hook. With trembling fingers she picked away at Birgitta's small, fine stitches, transferring the money to her carpetbag. It seemed so much, her mother's life savings.

"I'll find Sven for you, Mama," she whispered. "If he is anywhere."

She didn't think it likely that he would be. Sven had fallen in love with a girl from New Ulm, a girl whose religion differed from that of his family. Their father—no, she thought, not my father, but Sven's—had importuned him to wait for marriage.

New Ulm had been the scene of a savage attack during the Dakota War. The Indians left a ground littered with butchery, children murdered, men mutilated, women ravished and killed. Sven had gone there, seen the devastation, and found his Sarah's body.

And he had not come home until after the hangings at Mankato, where thirty-nine Indian warriors were executed for the attack. Some others had been pardoned at the intervention of President Lincoln. Announcing that he hated the President, Sven had left with a vow to seek his own revenge. And he headed south to join the Confederate Army, to fight against a system that did not avenge his Sarah.

The last time Inga saw her brother, he was not himself, but a grief-stricken, angry boy, his eyes glittering with madness.

Now Birgitta Lindstrom had lost two of her children.

Inga shook out the coat. The lining had yielded up all its riches, and it was now in rags. She would have to leave it behind. She ran a loving hand over the warm material as her mother had done. Then she replaced it on its hook. When they were gone, Helga would throw it away, never knowing how much love it stood for.

Inga drew the shades against the rising sun and lay down to sleep. She did not sleep long, but came to a sitting position after a few moments, stiff with terror. For she had dreamed. In the dream, she was in her own bed, and there was something beside her—the body of a big man, a horrid stain matting his mop of yellow hair. And in the background, a voice like thunder—Pastor Lindstrom's voice—admonishing her, condemning her to hell.

29

4

Inga was still exhausted when, two days later,
she stood at the railing of the *Ruth*. The steamboat,
a bright new vessel, fresh from the yards, had been
built in a hurry to meet the travel needs increased
by the end of the war.

Normally, Inga and her daughters would have
had to wait in St. Paul for some time, but with
peace returned to the country, river traffic had
picked up. Two vessels had been in the harbor, the
Ruth and a smaller packet. The boats had come
upriver packed with returning soldiers, men who
had left Missouri, Iowa, Illinois, and Minnesota to
follow their country's flag.

Not the flag Sven had followed, Inga thought
with a shiver. That flag was buried somewhere in
the South.

Given a choice between the two boats, Inga had

selected the *Ruth*. Despite the weary, wounded cargo it had brought from battle, it was the most luxurious thing she and her daughters had ever seen.

It looked like a wedding cake, all white, with fancy scrollwork outside. Inside, the main salon, which ran the length of the ship, was decorated in velvet and gold, with mirrors and tinkling crystal chandeliers.

Helga's husband, true to her word, had arranged passage for them—in his own name. They were listed as Mrs. Danberg and daughters. John Danberg was a kind, gentle soul, and Inga felt guilty at deceiving him.

"You are the luckiest woman in the world," Inga whispered to Helga as she hugged the older woman in farewell.

Helga's eyes went to John, misty with love. "I know," she said.

Inga and the girls slipped aboard in the confusion caused by the landing military, and went straight to their rooms, staying there until the ropes were cast off and the vessel floated free.

Only when St. Paul was far behind them did Inga give the girls permission to roam the ship. She was still afraid to venture out, afraid that Olaf's body had been found, that someone would be aboard who could identify her, that her guilt would show in her face.

There was another reason. Inga had seen the ladies in first class promenade the deck in their elegant clothing, twirling their sunshades flirtatiosly, and she knew that she would be conspicuous, even in her best dress. It was a dark blue cotton with a small print, made when she was carrying Jenny and taken in later. It was almost new, since she had had little chance to wear it, but its simplicity would shame her before these people in their silks and velvets.

So she stayed inside the cabin until one morning she could bear it no more. Waking long before dawn from a troubled sleep, she dressed and slipped outside to stand at the rail, sure that no one else would be up. Except for the chuffing of the paddle wheel, there was no sound. She might have been alone in a dripping world of semidarkness.

The deck beneath her feet was damp, and the trees on shore were silhouettes. The air smelled of lush wet earth and fish. And as she watched, under a lightening sky, wisps of fog began to rise from the slate-colored water that turned silver where it caught the light.

She could see, now, that much of what she had thought to be shore consisted of islands. Tomorrow morning, she thought, she must wake Jenny early. The girl should not miss the special beauty of the hour.

She was so absorbed in the view, she didn't hear the man come up behind her, cat-footed on the damp deck, or see him until a pair of large masculine hands closed on the rail next to her own.

"Good morning, ma'am," the newcomer said in a deep voice. Then, seeing her expression of stark terror, he apologized. "I'm sorry if I startled you."

He had, indeed. She swallowed hard. "It is all right. I was just going."

"Nonsense! Stay and enjoy the view. I won't bite."

Inga blushed, and looked up at him. He was a fine-looking man, with a narrow face, expressionless except for one dark brow raised comically as he studied her.

"On shipboard," he said, "it's to hell with convention." He thrust out a hand. "I'm Nick Tremont."

"I am . . . am Mrs. Danberg," she said, blushing at the lie.

"Swedish," he guessed, hearing the lilt in her voice. "Minnesota." With a swift glance at her hands he added, "And you farm."

"Yes," she said, longing to put her hands behind her, but not daring to.

Nick Tremont turned away from her, looking toward the river. "I always try to get out here this hour of the morning."

"An early riser, like me," Inga ventured for want of something to say.

He chuckled. "Wish I was. But the fact is, I haven't been to bed. By the way, where are you going?"

"Memphis," she told him. "Memphis, Tennessee."

He studied her keenly. "Looking for a husband in the service."

"No, a . . . a brother. I am a . . . a widow."

"Bet this is your first trip!"

She nodded.

"Nothing like a riverboat." He began to tell her about the way, prior to the war, the boats had raced along the river, oblivious of the danger to their passengers. For a time, one out of eight vessels had exploded, burned, or sunk, due to some human miscalculation—usually during a race.

33

"Is this boat safe?"

"As safe as any." He shrugged. "It's the ol' Mississipp' that's deadly. When it's low, you've got snags, shoals, and sandbars to contend with; high, you've got sawyers. She's a crotchety old girl, this river, and she doesn't want us riding on her back."

He paused, noticing how pale Inga had become. "I frightened you. I'm sorry. I've been going up and down this river for most of my life, and I'm still alive and kicking." He smiled at her. "There are times when I've been guilty of exaggerating, especially when I try to impress a pretty woman."

Inga found herself blushing again. "I . . . I worry about my children."

His eyes slid over her slender body, her face, in disbelief. "You've got kids?"

"Grown daughters," she said. "Kirsten is fifteen, Jenny fourteen."

"I find that hard to believe! You must have been a child bride!"

"I was Jenny's age when I married," she said, flustered at the warmth of his expression. "Now, if you will excuse me—"

He caught at her hand. "Don't go! I've only just found you. Have breakfast with me."

"No, really. I must."

There was urgency in her voice, and fear. Tremont released her hand and bowed. Inga left him at the rail, her heart slowing only after she secured the cabin door behind her. Was she frightened of the perilous river? Or of a man?

She realized that the words she had exchanged with any male, other than Olaf, during the last fourteen years might be counted on her fingers.

34

For the remainder of the day she caught herself going over their conversation. His gaze had been frankly admiring. He had hinted that she was pretty. She put her hands to her hot cheeks.

The way the gentleman had accosted her—was it improper? Had she erred in speaking to him when they had not been properly introduced? Did he, perhaps, consider her a loose woman?

"To hell with convention," he'd said.

Then, again, he had asked a lot of questions. With a kind of horror, she realized he might be from the police. But his attire—dark trousers, a white silk shirt with belled sleeves beneath an embroidered vest—was not what a policeman would wear.

Unless he were searching for a woman with something to hide! She made a vow that she would not leave the cabin again.

The day was hot and muggy. She was restless, confined to the small room, and she was lonely, with both Kirsten and Jenny gone most of the day.

Kirsten's clothes were passable, and she seemed to enjoy promenading with the elite. Though she was a little pale, and looked at Inga strangely sometimes, she hadn't mentioned her father's death since they came on board. Whether that was a good or bad sign, Inga had no idea. But it was preferable to hysteria and accusations.

While Kirsten preferred to roam the first-class deck, Jenny was all over the ship, from the wheelhouse to the galley. Inga considered stopping her, then, too exhausted to press the point, let her go. No harm would come to her. Let the girls find what enjoyment they could, under the circumstances. Within a week or so they would be landing in an unknown place, practically penniless.

That night, her head aching, Inga forgot her vow and slipped out again to the railing. The air was thick with mosquitoes, but coming from Minnesota, she had grown immune to them. More important, she was alone, and the night was studded with stars. The water looked deep and dark, its rippling surface studded with what looked like small slices of moon.

On the lower deck, a band played softly; someone sang about a girl named Lorena. And occasionally a dancing couple reached the rail, stopping to look out into the wonder of the night.

Inga had never been allowed to dance, but she wondered how anything so lovely could be a sin. Wrapping her arms around herself, she took a few graceful steps, moving as though she were in a dream. And she imagined a partner, a big man in an embroidered vest over a white silk shirt that opened at the throat—

She stopped suddenly. Had she gone mad, like her brother, poor Sven? There would never be another man for her, never.

The music ceased briefly. And from far below, from a pen on the bottom deck, the odd bleating of a lamb drifted upward. Inga flinched and closed her eyes. It sounded like a cry of pain, the sound a man might make when he was struck down by his wife.

She turned away from the music that was sinful, the dancing that was sinful, the magic of the river and the night—possibly evil, too, in the eyes of her father and his congregation—and went inside.

Early the next morning, in spite of her good intentions, she found herself at the ship's rail again, watching the mists rise to meet the sun. And in a little while, Nick Tremont, the man who never seemed to sleep, came to join her. His dark eyes, rimmed with fatigue, brightened at the sight of her.

"I was afraid you wouldn't be here," he said frankly. "I was afraid you'd just disappeared, like a beautiful dream."

"I love the mornings," she stammered.

"I love them too, especially now."

Her lips curved in a reluctant smile, and he touched them with a dark forefinger. "You should smile more often."

A barge passed, its sides glistening with dew, and their attention turned to it. After a time, talk came a little easier. And once, Inga was startled to find herself laughing.

For that moment, she was Inga Danberg, widow, without a dreadful past behind her, enjoying the attentions of a charming and handsome man.

5

Kirsten Johansson maintained her stricken attitude in her mother's presence, but actually she was having the time of her life. Her father—*poor* father, she amended in her mind—had always indulged his elder daughter, so her clothes, though not the best, were not too unsuitable on the first-class deck. She had noticed that a young man had been staring at her as she promenaded.

The boy was usually in the company of his mother, an aristocratic woman—so unlike her own mother. Kirsten could not imagine that lady indulging in an illicit affair, bearing a wood's colt, or killing her husband with a poker!

Kirsten, overlooking the young man's pouting mouth, thought him extremely handsome. He had large dark eyes and black hair that fell in a wave over a tanned forehead.

If she could meet someone like that, marry him, she would be able to live the kind of life Papa wanted her to have. She could be rich and respectable, no longer lumped in with the likes of her mother and Jenny.

She wove a dream as she walked. A dream in which his mother nudged him and said, "Look, son, that is a very suitable young woman, don't you think?"

He would agree. Later, he would tell Kirsten it had been a case of love at first sight.

That, of course, would be after they were properly married and moved into their beautiful home. They would have two children, one boy, one girl . . .

But how to meet him?

Kirsten found her opportunity in the afternoon. The young man's mother, miserable with the heat, had gone to her cabin to rest. He stood alone at the rail, looking moodily out at the water, unaware that the pretty girl he watched had already planned his future for him.

The meeting was accomplished by the age-old ploy of dropping her handkerchief. Kirsten heard a male voice saying, "Ma'am," and turned to look at him.

"Excuse me, ma'am, I believe this is yours." He proffered the lost article.

"Thank you," she whispered, blushing. "Thank you very much."

"My pleasure."

But still he didn't move, riveted by a pair of blue, blue eyes above sun-pink cheeks.

"Please allow me to introduce myself," he said

39

finally. "I am Talbott Todd. We are going south to join my father, General Todd, who will be stationed in Memphis until—"

Kirsten uttered a squeal of delight. "Memphis! That is where we are going!"

Quickly she sketched a past in which her beloved uncle—implying that he was a Union soldier, of course—had disappeared. Her widowed mother, her sister, and she were going to search for him, for the sake of poor Grandmama.

"Perhaps my father can help you."

There was a pretty slim chance of that, Kirsten thought. But she dimpled up at him. "That would be wonderful! So kind! We would be pleased to accept his assistance."

She turned away and felt his tentative touch on her arm. He jerked his hand away, reddening.

"There is dancing on the deck every night. I have not seen you there."

"I'm afraid it would not be appropriate—without an escort."

Young Talbott took a deep breath and plunged in, knowing that this was the sort of thing to be cleared with his mother first. But he could not allow this enchanting creature to get away.

"May I presume to offer myself in that role, ma'am?"

She looked at him with undisguised delight. "How gallant of you! But of course, I must obtain my mother's permission. Shall I meet you here?"

They settled on time and place, and when she had gone, Talbott Todd stood for a moment, bracing himself. He had to face his mother next, and he had an idea it wouldn't be easy. But Kirsten just had to be the most beautiful girl he'd ever met in his life!

As expected, he caught genteel hell all afternoon. But, surprisingly, that night, when his mother met Kirsten Johansson, the older woman seemed to approve.

The girl was not dressed to suit the occasion, of course. She wore the same dress she had worn earlier, pulled down a bit at the neckline to reveal creamy shoulders, a black ribbon tied about her throat. But she had explained that they were traveling light, not expecting to join in any social occasions, with her mother so recently widowed.

"The war," Mrs. Todd guessed.

Kirsten lowered her lashes as if to hide her tears, and went on to explain that they were searching for her mother's brother, a heroic young man who had disappeared in battle. They must either find him—or his grave.

Mrs. Todd blew her nose daintily. There were so many private tragedies. And as the wife of a general, she must do her bit wherever possible. Though this sweet young thing had an odd accent that indicated she was not from an old-line family, still it would not hurt to be kind to her. Talbott was rebellious about this move they were making, and he'd not been the pleasantest of companions. Perhaps this child would take his mind off his problems. And there certainly wouldn't be time for him to be drawn into any kind of romantic attachment.

"I do not think I will attend the dance," Mrs. Todd said bravely. "I am rather tired—this dreadful heat—and I believe I shall retire to my room.

Talbott, watch over Miss ... Miss Kirsten. See that she enjoys herself."

Talbott Todd intended to see that she did just that.

Kirsten was in seventh heaven. One of her classmates in St. Paul, pitying her for her folks' fanatic religious beliefs, had taught her some dance steps. She had secretly practiced them, and now there were night, stars, and music. Kirsten expected that her conscience would pain her, that she would hear the voice of Pastor Gustav Lindstrom thundering in her ears. She was delighted to find she did not feel sinful at all, just as her classmate had predicted. Her grandfather was wrong in this instance. Dancing couldn't be bad, if Mrs. Todd approved!

Despite her lack of experience, Kirsten found herself moving smoothly. She had a natural sense of rhythm, and found all she had to do was keep her feet moving to give an impression of grace.

She succeeded so well that several others asked for permission to dance with her. Talbott Todd watched her whirling in other arms, and then, his pout more pronounced, suggested a walk about the deck.

Kirsten, flushed with activity, and afraid her lack of expertise would be found out, was only too glad to comply.

She learned a lot about Talbott Todd as they promenaded. For one thing, his family was immensely rich; his education was the product of tutors rather than public schools, and he was terrified of joining his father in Tennessee.

His father was very autocratic. And Talbott had

heard the area was peopled by rednecks—people of a lower social status, he explained—and Negroes.

He had no reservations about freeing the slaves, he explained carefully. He only hoped his father did not expect him to treat them as equals. Though he had never met one socially, he was none too certain they were acceptable. He had been told they were untamed, and some roving bands were said to murder, for instance. . . .

Kirsten shivered.

"You're cold," he said remorsefully. "You need a wrap. Let me escort you to your stateroom."

To her stateooom? Mama, who was there now, visiting with Jenny, would answer the door in that awful print dress, and Jenny would probably be sitting like a . . . a squaw, dress up to her knees, showing her bare legs.

"I would prefer to dance some more," she told him.

In the girls' cabin, Inga paced the floor. She had not seen Kirsten for several hours. And she had no idea where the child was.

Jenny finally cracked beneath her mother's concern, though she had learned long ago that where Kirsten was concerned, one did not carry tales and go unscathed.

"She is dancing, Mama."

"Dancing!" For a moment Inga's upbringing rose to choke her. Then she recalled her feelings of the previous night. "Dancing—with whom?"

Jenny shrugged. "A boy."

Inga had assumed that. And she also knew that she had to be content with any information she received from her strange little daughter, who was talkative and taciturn by turns.

Later, Inga went to the railing and looked down. She saw no sign of Kirsten. But the girl had always been self-sufficient, and would not appreciate her concern.

Inga stood for a long time looking out across the water. For once, the beauty of the night and the river could not alleviate the weight she carried on her shoulders. Both of her daughters were innocents when it came to the ways of the world; she herself, not much wiser. Through her own actions she had proven she was not a fit mentor to guide them through the trials ahead. She would just have to trust Kirsten.

At the lee side of the riverboat, enclosed in protective darkness, Talbott Todd touched dry, reverent lips to Kirsten's cheek. It was not unpleasant, Kirsten thought. But neither was it the earthshaking experience her more experienced classmates had led her to expect.

The fault must lie with Talbott.

Somehow, between now and the time they reached Tennessee, Kirsten hoped he would learn how to kiss.

6

Jenny, alone so much at home, had grown up like a small wild thing. And she had an untamed creature's powers of observation, along with an instinct for being almost invisible.

She watched from a distance as young Talbott Todd courted her sister. She was also fully aware that her mother conversed with a gentleman at the ship's rail every morning as the sun rose.

Both situations worried her a little. Mrs. Todd was a dreadful snob, and sooner or later, Kirsten would be hurt. The man with whom her mother visited was a gambler who worked the boats that plied the Mississippi. Someone told Jenny he carried a gun, and was known to have used it. She was surprised her mother would choose him for a friend. Maybe it was because Inga had met no one else. Perhaps, Jenny thought, it was a mistake to have only one friend. She had made a lot of them.

None of them were in first class, it was true. But she knew the pilot, and sometimes he let her steer. Down on the deck where the poorer people stayed, sleeping in the open air, there was a nice man whose wife had died. He was taking his baby back to his mother in St. Louis, and sometimes he let Jenny hold the baby.

In the galley, the ship's cooks were a fat black couple, Tom and Thora, who had two plump toddlers who laughed and played around their feet in the crowded quarters.

Jenny liked them best of all.

She headed there now, pausing on one deck to talk to an old man who always told her about his boyhood. Then on to smile at a young woman who seemed sad, but always smiled back. Finally she reached the magic room that was filled with steam and the smell of good things cooking.

Tom, stirring something at the shiny black range, saw her first. "We got comp'ny, Thora," he boomed. "Our li'l missie done come to visit."

Thora, busy rolling out a pie crust, wiped her black face with a floured forearm and beamed. "Come in, honey. Reckon we kin find you-all somp'n for you hollah laig."

Jenny laughed and joined them, sitting on a high stool to eat the warm cinnamon rolls Thora provided. The toddlers had their share, and were soon sticky; small faces streaked with white frosting.

Finally Jenny slid down. "You wait just a minute," she told the little ones, "and I'll take you out on deck to play."

She began to clean up after Thora as the woman slid a pie in the oven.

"You sho good at neatenin' up, Jenny," she said in admiration.

"Jen—nee . . ."

One of the toddlers said her name! Jenny shouted with delight and scooped the child up to hug her. The little boy tried to butt his woolly head between the two of them and, failing, repeated his sister's word. "Jen-nee."

"I want to take them up and show them to Mama," Jenny said, laughing. "Please, may I?"

Tom looked at Thora, his normally placid face wearing a worried frown. "They don' 'low niggahs on the first-class deck, Jenny. Cap'n don't like it."

"It will be all right," Jenny told them. "Captain Jennings is a friend of mine."

Tom and Thora reluctantly gave their permission, and Jenny headed toward the stairs that led upward, the little ones in tow. Her mother was going to love meeting them!

Someone else had decided it was time to be introduced to the reclusive widow. Talbott Todd's mother had begun to have misgivings about Kirsten. It was clear her son had fallen head over heels for the young lady. Perhaps she had made a mistake in encouraging the relationship. Now she was trying to discourage it, and her gentle questioning was driving him out of his mind.

"We know nothing about her family, Todd. Have you met her mother yet? There is something wrong, dear. Not that the girl isn't quite presentable. Do you suppose she's ashamed of her mother?"

He did not know.

A horrifying thought suddenly struck the woman. Her face crumpled. "Do you think," she asked incredulously, "that the fault lies with us? That a . . . a general's son isn't good enough? Or, Talbott, her husband! What if he wasn't with the Union Army?"

Reluctantly her son promised to investigate the matter.

When the ship tied up to take on wood at a small town in Iowa, Talbott paid several children on shore to gather wildflowers in a field starred with them. Then, impeccably dressed, bouquet in hand, he presented himself at the door of the room Kirsten shared with Jenny.

Kirsten answered his knock and stepped outside, quickly shutting the door behind her. Though Jenny was out roaming somewhere, Inga was in their room doing some mending, and Kirsten did not intend for Inga and Talbott to meet.

She took his arm and led him toward the rail, smiling up at him. "Flowers? For me?"

"For your mother," Todd said quietly. "I want to meet her. If you would announce me, please."

Kirsten took the blossoms, cheeks blazing. "Thank you, but she is indisposed. I will give them to her."

"What is it, Kirsten?" He put a hand on her arm as she turned away. "Why all this mystery? I want an introduction. In fact, I insist upon it!"

"Talbott," she faltered, "She . . . she is not like your mother. She . . . she's different . . ."

At that moment, Jenny rounded the corner, carrying two giggling black children, one under each arm. The ribbon had slipped from her braids, and her hair hung, inky black, to her waist. The days in the sun had burned her brown, and her too-short, too-tight dress was faded and torn at the waist.

A smear of frosting on her mouth accentuated her darkness and her teeth flashed white in a happy smile.

"Oh, Kirsten," she laughed, "Penny just said my name for the first time! And guess what! Then Sammie said it. You should hear . . ."

Talbott Todd stared at Jenny in horror. Evidently this . . . this mulatto was in the Danberg employ, but she should be reminded of her manners.

"You are interrupting our conversation," he said icily. "The young lady is not interested in your . . . your pickaninnies. I suggest you go on about your business."

Jenny was accustomed to receiving her father's abuse. She had always tried to be as unobtrusive as possible, knowing that for some reason he was ashamed of her. Normally she would have bowed her head before anyone who criticized her and scuttled away. But this boy's condescending manner, the look of distaste he directed at the children, roused her anger. She raised her chin.

"I will talk to my sister anytime I want to," she said, tossing her black hair. "Now, if you will move, we're going in to see Mama!"

The cabin door slammed behind her. Talbott Todd stood for a moment, stiff with shock, then mumbled a weak excuse and fled. He left Kirsten standing alone, her arms filled with flowers.

Rounding the corner that led to his own stateroom, he mopped his perspiring brow. He had had a very close call. It would seem that Kirsten's family was not only secesh—but worse!

Kirsten stood still for a long time, anger thudding in her veins. Anger at Talbott Todd—and at Jenny. She had no right to appear like that! To allow him to think . . . whatever it was he thought! And he had been a . . . a jackass to think it!

Kirsten walked to the railing and threw the flowers far out into the water. They drifted away on the brown breast of the river and she watched until they were out of sight.

Her dream was over. And that was all it had been. Only a dream. She had grown up with the knowledge that Jenny's father was not her own, and now her mother was a murderess. They were running from the law. But for a little while she'd thought . . . she'd hoped . . .

It made no difference. What happened today was inevitable. It would have taken place sooner or later. Besides, Talbott Todd wasn't all that great at kissing!

She entered the stateroom to find Jenny weeping in Inga's arms, two puzzled small black children looking on.

Kirsten, who had never apologized in her life, felt compelled to do so now. "It's all right, Jenny," she said. "It's my fault, not yours. Believe me, it's all right."

Inside, she felt a dull ache that wouldn't go away. She supposed it was a part of growing up.

7

While Kirsten languished in the stateroom and Jenny enjoyed the run of the ship, two people aboard wished the journey would never end.

One of them was Inga Johansson, who felt safe and secure here on the river. She loved the tiny, isolated world the ship created. When she stepped ashore, her troubles would begin.

The other was Nick Tremont, who stood beside her in the dawn.

At first, Nick had been a little dismayed at finding a woman standing in his favorite spot at his accustomed hour. Then he had been amused at her delight in the scenery, her naiveté, the wide-eyed interest she took in his exaggerated tales of legendary rivermen: Mike Fink; Tom Leathers, the best "cusser" on the river; Roaring Jack Russell, the best fighter.

He loved sharing his knowledge of the river with her. He pointed out clay shoals, blue hazards lying in waiting shadow; sandbars, golden in the rising sun. The river was at low ebb now. But he had seen it get up and stomp! Seen islands submerged, trees growing from water that looked like plowed ground; he had seen houses swept downriver, bodies swirling in eddies, turning and turning.

He pointed out the wreckage of a steamboat that had careened against the shore. "There are hundreds of such ships sunk into these waters; longboats, keelboats, riverboats—hell, you name it, it's here. The pilots know many of the locations and take them into account, but the Mississippi's a wily old devil, constantly making and remaking her bed."

When Inga shivered, he thought he had frightened her again, and was a little ashamed. He had never been a braggart, but he felt a boyish urge to impress this woman and establish himself as her protector.

He hastened to make amends. Most of the problems were in the past, he assured her. And their present captain was a most capable man.

"Look." He pointed at a riverman kneeling on the lower deck. "They're taking soundings now. Listen."

The gentle rocking of the boat ceased. There was a brief cessation of movement, a grating sound, and the vessel moved on.

"Made it," Nick Tremont said with satisfaction. "Shoal. It wasn't there, last trip down."

Nick had mentioned spending most of his life on the river. Was he employed on the boat? Inga wondered. He wore no uniform, nor did he dress like the ordinary roustabouts. She had seen him only at dawn, never during the day, and he had never said anything about his occupation.

"You . . . you don't own this boat—do you?"

He laughed heartily. "Hardly," he said in an amused tone.

She blushed. "You've never said what you do for a living. You do some sort of work here on the river, I am sure."

"In a way."

Why, he wondered, could he not tell her how he earned his livelihood? With any other woman, he might even have boasted of his line of work, and she probably would have considered it dashing and romantic. It was hardly that, he thought ruefully. But he had always been proud of the way he earned his living, a very lucrative one at that.

Born in the French Quarter of New Orleans to a woman of dubious reputation, Nick had taken to the river early on, first as a shill for a gambling man, then a successful gambler in his own right. His hands were deft. He could make a deck of cards do anything he wished. But most of his success lay in his talent for reading people, a necessary attribute in his profession.

In this particular case, however, he had failed. The young widow Inga Danberg was a mystery to him.

She was undeniably beautiful. That was the first thing that caught his attention. She was a little taller than average, straight-backed, with a coronet of braids that gave her a regal appearance; most definitely a lady.

Yet there was a country simplicity about her, a shyness, a reticence. It was as if she had been out of touch with the world, forgotten how to converse with people. He had a strange hunch that she was running away from something—or somebody. He had seen those blue eyes cloud as she stood in reverie.

And, dammit, he longed to put his arms around her, not to caress her as he had with so many others, but to reassure her.

It was a peculiar sensation for a man who could have any woman he wished along the river. Maybe it was because this was the first one he'd met in years that he really wanted. A pity, since he knew instinctively that Inga would not fit into his disorderly life.

He sensed that she would disapprove of gambling. That she would consider it the devil's work.

"What is your religious persuasion, ma'am?" he asked impulsively.

Her face flushed, eyes filling with guilt. "I do not think you will have heard of my denomination," she stammered. "It is an offshoot of a religion brought over from Sweden. I must confess I have not attended church in some time, however. And you?"

Tremont shrugged moodily, wishing he hadn't brought the subject up. "I suppose the river is my religion ..." He stopped, afraid she would consider his answer sacrilegious.

Looking out over the water that was the great throbbing heart of her country, the gigantic river with its ever-changing whims, Inga said she understood his feelings. Man could not create anything so vast, so allied to the elements.

They had reached a spot where the river was both wide and deep. In the distance, frosted with early-morning dew, a smaller ship steamed past them, going in the opposite direction. A hooting whistle sounded through the dawn; their own vessel answered. And on the other ship's top deck stood a couple, a man and woman, early risers viewing the sunrise on the water.

They stood waving, bathed for a moment in golden light. Then the man put his arm around the woman, holding her close.

Newlyweds?

Husband and wife?

Or lovers?

Nick Tremont's mouth went dry, for he longed to do the same. To hold the girl-woman beside him, to live with her, to love her all his life.

And it could not be. He was a creature of the night, she of the day. He would only bring her unhappiness. He made his excuses and left hurriedly.

Inga stood alone, looking out over the water, trying to sort out her scrambled feelings. She had wanted to lean against Nick Tremont, to have him touch her, wanted it with a need that left her shivering inside.

She had never felt that way before. Never with Olaf. Her sexual experience had been duty, nothing more. She had never loved Olaf, though she had respected him in the beginning. And she did not love this man, this stranger. Yet her traitorous body yearned to be near him.

Now she could understand how her mother had felt, all those long years ago in a summer wheat field.

From that day, Nick and Inga were both conscious of a strong attraction they felt toward one another, and things were not the same between them. Though they met again each morning, they were very circumspect. They stood apart from each other, drawn by emotions neither of them could resist, in spite of their intent to do otherwise.

Nick Tremont's poker face stood him in good stead. The woman who stood beside him would never know the anguish that ate away at him. But then, she wasn't easy to read either. She wore the armor of a woman with something to hide, he thought.

Theirs would be a chance shipboard acquaintance, nothing more, both silently determined.

8

The boat docked briefly in St. Louis, and then moved on. Later that night, it stormed.

The wind came first, riffling the dark waters of the river, finally turning them into a replica of plowed ground. Lightning darted across the skies, and thunder rumbled and growled. Then the rain came, solid sheets of it, destroying visibility.

The captain, a prudent man who loved his vessel as he would a woman, was determined to protect her. They were ahead of schedule and he had no intention of risking his boat in the storm. Since it was some distance to a regular port, he made an emergency stop, tying up at a spot along the riverbank.

There would be no dancing on deck this night, passengers realized. Disgruntled women went to their cabins; most of the men headed for the salon to partake in games of chance.

It was a perfect setup for a gambling man, but Nick Tremont found himself losing steadily. His mind was not on his cards, but on a woman.

Inga, Kirsten, and Jenny retired early, and the girls were already sleeping peacefully. But Inga lay awake, feeling imprisoned, shut in by the storm, by the wooden walls of the crowded stateroom. As it had for so many nights, the enormity of her problem pressed in upon her; the future was an unknown quantity, and she was caged between the two concerns.

The air felt heavy. Rain drizzled against the porthole like tears. Inga ached with the need to escape the stuffy cabin, to slip on a cloak and walk the deck despite the weather, to run away from herself.

There was a sudden dull, booming noise and the ship seemed to lift and shudder. Inga frowned briefly, then dismissed the occurrence as something to do with the storm. It had to be thunder, wind.

She brushed out her long silken hair and began to braid it again.

Down in the salon, Nick Tremont also heard the booming sound and felt the tremor. His hand faltered as he played his hand; then he stood, bowing out of the game for a moment.

Stepping out on deck, he uttered a sharp curse as he saw another ship bearing down on the *Ruth*, turning the rain the color of blood. Men in oilskins were rushing about the *Ruth*'s deck. Someone called out an order to cast off.

"Take an ax to the damned rope," another bawled. "Let's get the hell out of here!"

Tremont's first thought was of Inga. He began to run.

The banging on the door frightened Inga. She rose, throwing a cloak over her nightdress, and opened it to see a man who at first looked like a stranger. Behind him was an odd flickering light. His expensively tailored suit was a sodden ruin, his dark hair plastered to a chalk-white face, his expression grim as he clutched Inga's shoulders in a bruising grip.

"Out of the cabin! Dammit, hurry! Go to the other side of the ship. Jump, if you have to!"

"What is it?" she asked in alarm.

He pointed, and she drew in a sharp breath.

A steamboat making its way upriver had turned into a flaming pyre. It had passed the *Ruth* earlier, but its boilers had exploded and it was drifting backward at an angle that was on a direct collision course. The *Ruth* was finally getting up steam, but there was little time—

There was a second explosion, a third. The burning vessel staggered like a wounded animal. Bits of blazing debris were thrown upward to the night sky, a piece of burning wood landing on the *Ruth*'s deck. Nick ran forward, picked it up with his bare hands, and tossed it overboard.

Inga could see black, twisting shadows on the deck of the approaching vessel, silhouetted against a backdrop of fire. A low moaning assaulted her ears, and she knew the sound had come from human throats; a chorus of the doomed.

She ran to pound on the girls' door.

Kirsten and Jenny appeared, eyes wide with shock as they saw the fiery apparition. Somehow Inga managed to get them into their cloaks and to the far side of the ship where Nick had directed them. They huddled together in the rain, and Inga rounded the deck once more, to look at the fiery juggernaut bearing down on them.

It was a hellish scene, the great boat coming on inexorably, haloed against the night sky, scattering burning bits and pieces of itself as it came, turning the waters around it red.

As Inga watched, a burning figure separated itself from the ship's flames to soar downward toward the river's night-black waters. Arms stretched wide, the body resembled a burning cross.

"Help him," Inga screamed. "Oh, please, God, help him!"

Then she was pulled against a man's deep chest, her face pressed into his shoulder so that she could see no more.

Nick Tremont held her, his eyes on approaching death, a sardonic smile on his lips. If he had to die, this was the way it should be, with the feel of the woman he loved in his arms.

The burning monster moved toward the *Ruth*, fiery arms outstretched to embrace her. Nick could feel the heat burning his face, could smell the scorched paint . . .

Then, by a miracle, the ships passed each other by. The *Ruth*, cut loose from her makeshift mooring, was out in open water, while the flaming boat still wallowed toward the shore.

The ship that had become a hellish inferno heeled suddenly, gave a great sigh, like that of a dying giant, then sank, hissing at her fate. A huge cloud of smoke rose, an exhalation of fetid breath. And she was gone.

"We made it," Nick said shakily. "Oh, God, Inga!"

He kissed her; her lids, her cheeks, her lips.

"We're alive!"

Nick could feel her body in its wet cloak shuddering against him. The blue eyes turned up to him were blank with shock.

"Inga . . ."

He could see she didn't hear him. Her eyes were still fixed on the horror of the burning. He had to get her to her cabin, out of this cold rain.

"Come, Inga."

Gently he led her toward her stateroom door, closing and bolting it behind him.

"You're cold," he whispered. "Here, let me help you."

He undid the clasp of her sodden cloak and noted that the gown beneath it was also soaked from the wind-blown rain. She stood dazed, too numb to protest, as Nick undid the tiny buttons at her throat. And the nightdress slipped downward to lie about her feet.

Nick drew a sharp breath at the beauty that stood before him—Venus, rosy in the glow of shimmering lantern light. Then, lifting her, he carried her to her cot and lay down beside her, to hold her.

Finally the tears that had been dammed so long broke free. Inga wept for those who had died on the burning boat, who probably hadn't deserved such a death; for herself, who deserved it and had gone free.

Nick Tremont, professional gambler, known along the river as a "hard case," found himself smoothing back her damp hair, muttering incomprehensible words of tenderness.

"Don't, sweetheart. Ah, don't . . ." As she clung to him, sobbing spasmodically, he felt his desire growing. The small consoling kisses on brow and cheek became something more. His lips sought her tear-wet mouth, one arm crushing her to his, his other hand straying over luscious forbidden curves that took his breath away.

He felt her suddenly go very still. Then she began to tremble again. Her arms came up and around him, palms pressing against his back, drawing him down, down to her.

How he managed to divest himself of his clothing, he had no idea. He had only the knowledge of silken flesh burning against his own, of the depth of a woman's passion wakened for the first time, intensified by a need for closeness, for consolation.

They came together, ascending to the sun, descending on a sigh, Inga crying and laughing and moaning all at the same time.

Afterward, Nick slept, his dark face pillowed against Inga's ivory shoulder. She, however, lay awake, dreamily aware that she had sinned, but not caring. Somehow those moments in Nick's arms had washed her clean of the past and she was strangely at peace. For a short while, someone had thought her worthy of love.

After a few moments, she slid out of his arms and rose to dress. She was fastening the buttons of her blue print dress when she felt Nick's eyes upon her.

"Inga," he said quietly, "where are you going?"

"Outside, on deck, where I can think."

"Are you angry with me?"

She shook her head.

"Are you . . . sorry?"

She looked at the man in her bed, half-sitting up against the pillows, the sheets dragged down to reveal a muscular, honey-dark body, a body that had shown her what it was to be a woman—for the first time.

"No, Nick. Never."

Inga did up the last button and hurried outside. The rain had ceased, and the day dawned cold and gray. The *Ruth* still lingered in the vicinity of the wreckage, her small boats lowered, searching for survivors.

There were none. There was nothing to see except for shattered remnants of charred timber, a funnel sticking barely above the waterline. For weeks the river would be covered with flotsam and jetsam. And if a bit of debris appeared to be a hand, a foot, gnarled, burned, twisted, no one would recognize it as anything but an old burned twig or branch. The residue would float into nooks and crannies along the river, lodge itself on sandbar and bank, and finally disintegrate to become part of the Mississippi's haunted past.

In a short time, the sinking of a riverboat, exploding, burning, and going down with all hands, would be little more than a legend.

When Nick joined Inga at the rail, he had a cold premonition that their brief affair, like the lost fiery ship, had burned itself out. He reached to touch her hand.

"Are you all right?" he asked.

She nodded.

"Inga, I know you're running away from something. If there is anything I can do—"

"Thank you, but there's nothing."

There was affection in her tone, but nothing else. Yet he had to try again.

"I want to marry you, Inga, take care of you for the rest of your life." He forced a laugh. "Hey, this is me talking! Old hardhearted Tremont, ready to leave the river and settle down."

"You couldn't, Nick. The river's part of you." Inga laid a tender hand on his sleeve. "Besides, I do not intend to marry again."

"Your husband?" he hazarded. "You loved him that much?"

"Let's just say I don't want to be tied down," she told him. "And I don't believe you do, either."

In his heart, he had to admit she was right. He knew he wasn't husband material. He studied his lean brown hands, his only talent. It was best to remain uninvolved. Yet he knew he would never forget her.

"I'm going to get off at Memphis with you," he said finally. "Just to make sure you're settled. It's a rough place these days."

"I would rather you didn't," she told him. "It's better to leave it this way."

They said their final good-byes the following morning, both of them suffering from the yearning ache of lovers who would not meet again.

Nick reached his hand to Inga, then dropped it.

"Oh, hell!" He grabbed her, groaning a little as he held her close, his mouth searching for hers.

His action was unexpected, and she responded with passion.

At the sound of the shuffling feet of a deckhand swabbing the dew-wet deck, Nick pushed her away, his face twisted in pain.

"I will be back," he said hastily. "Do you have any idea where you'll be staying?"

She did not.

He gave her a name, the address of a riverfront business that he often frequented. If she left a message there, it would be given to him on his next trip upriver.

"I will look you up. See if you're all right."

In spite of her polite nod, Nick sensed that their brief idyll was over, that it would end when she stepped ashore at Memphis.

"Well, then, I'll help you when it's time to dock, see you off—"

"No, Nick."

It was clear she meant what she said. He forced a painful grin and raised his hand to his forehead in a mock salute.

Then he was gone.

Inga went to her stateroom, sad that she would not see him again, but convinced there could be nothing between them. Best to make a clean break. The parting hurt. Oh, how it hurt. But she wasn't free. From now on she intended to devote herself to her children. At least Kirsten and Jenny would never learn of her recent folly.

She didn't know that Kirsten had followed her last night, had seen her in Tremont's arms, seen him half-carry Inga to the safety of her cabin.

Kirsten, certain now that her mother's moral

character was exactly what her father said it was, realized that the man with Inga was dark, with Jenny's coloring. Putting two and two together, she came up with a horrifying assumption, something too terrible to think about. She said nothing to Jenny.

9

Kirsten was silent and pouting when the *Ruth* pulled up to dockside at Memphis. Jenny seethed with excitement. Inga did not look back. She feared she might see Nick Tremont, and in her vulnerable condition, terrified of what lay ahead of her, she might turn back.

Nick had kept his promise. He came on deck, but stood back in the shadow of the wheelhouse. The deck was crowded with shipboard acquaintances waving farewell, but Nick was tall enough to see beyond them. Though a number of people left the ship, he could pick Inga out easily. Her coronet of braids shone in the sun like spun gold. He, too, was fighting with his emotions. He wanted to go to her, plead with her to remain with him, get down on his knees if he had to.

There had been many women, but she was the

first he had really loved in a long time, and he was letting her go . . .

A solid blow to his back nearly staggered him. He turned to see a plump businessman, a fat cigar planted in the center of his mouth.

"Be some newcomers aboard tonight, huh?" the man asked jovially. "Let's get up a good game, strip 'em before we get to N'Awlins."

"Sure," Nick said vaguely. "Sure thing."

"I envy the hell out of you, boy," the man continued. "You got yourself a life! Don't have to do nothin' but play for a livin'! Bet you wouldn't trade with nobody."

"No," Nick said, straining to see the last of a slender, straight-backed woman disappearing from view. "I suppose I wouldn't."

The fat man moved on with a feeling of unease. Either Tremont was allergic to his cigar or he just got word that someone died. He'd swear the fellow's eyes were filled with tears.

Nick Tremont went to the cubbyhole where he slept and sat on his bunk, absently shuffling a deck of cards. And then he put his hands over his eyes and wept for what might have been.

Ashore, Inga and her daughters stared in awe at the great city of Memphis. It had once been a bustling center of commerce, but since its occupation by the Union early in the war, it had undergone many changes.

The huge warehouses lining the shore once had been filled with baled cotton. Now they stood empty. The cobbled wharf was filled with soldiers, a few of them Union, most in shabby gray, their boot soles secured with twine. The conquered, from battlefield, hospital, and prison, were still trying to make their way home.

Some could afford to pay to ride the river. Others, scarecrow figures, bearded and bandaged, broken and blinded, surrounded the ship's captain, begging for work.

Inga Johansson was terrified, though she tried not to show it. For one thing, her mind was dazed by the confusion around her. This was a city such as she had never seen. The streets were of boards or cobbles. Looking uphill from the spot where they had stepped ashore, she could see countless tall buildings beyond the warehouse district.

She had no idea which direction to take.

Jenny found the solution.

An old black woman, who was busily frying fish over a charcoal brazier, carried on a brisk business with Union officers. Waiting for a lull, Jenny approached her.

She and her mother and sister were looking for a hotel, preferably one nearby, Jenny explained.

The old woman looked at her dubiously, eyeing the shabbiness of the girl's dress. "There's the Gayoso House," she said. "But it moughty 'spensive. Hear tell it got runnin' water, a ballroom, that kine of fixin's."

Jenny blushed. "I'm afraid that wouldn't do. We'd like a cheap place, preferably for women. We . . . we're looking for work."

White teeth flashed in the black face. "Why did'n yuh say so? You-all wanna go to Miz Fannie's. One street up, two ovah. Jus' say Rosie done send yuh."

The small party toiled up the hill and finally

located the old house. It looked grim on the outside, two stories of gray stone without any trim to alleviate its harsh exterior, only a small cupolalike structure atop the whole. But inside, the furnishings, though nearly all damaged, were luxurious. The huge front room held a rosewood grand piano, in excellent shape except for a few missing ivories.

"Miz Fannie," as the black woman had called her, was a delightful soul. Small and plump, with a bosom like a pouter pigeon's, the old woman was every inch a Southern lady, with an accent like warm molasses.

She welcomed them graciously, insisting on serving tea before showing them her rooms. They drank tea from cracked porcelain cups, ate dainty petits fours from chipped, priceless platters, and listened as the woman talked on, seemingly indefagitable.

They were looking for work? There was always work for three such beautiful women. Like herself, they would do what they had to do, she said, going off into a long rambling discussion. Her family had once been wealthy plantation owners. They'd been burned out by General Sherman. She and her sister had come here, opening this little place, hoping to help other women in similar straits.

At the sound of footsteps on the stairs, she called out, "Sistah! Sistah, come down and meet these young ladies."

Sister was Miz Fannie's opposite in every way. Tall and bone-thin, she had sad eyes and a perpetually lugubrious expression. She joined them and sat in silence as Miz Fannie drawled on, with stories of "Gennul" Lee, that sweet Jeff Davis, with repeated references to "ouah" boys.

"My brother was with the Confederate Army," Inga finally broke in. "He ... we haven't heard from him in several years. We are here to look for him."

Miz Fannie and Sister exchanged startled looks, and then Miz Fannie leaned forward, patting Inga's hand. "Then we-all will be proud to he'p you." She smiled warmly and looked at Sister, brows raised. "I reckon these folks might be happier on the top floor, don't you? The view!"

"My gracious, yes," Sister parroted. "The view."

They climbed a flight of stairs, then a narrow set of steps that led up into the cupola. It consisted of two small rooms, one fitted up with a cook-stove and a cracked marble sink with a tank beside it.

Miz Fannie had hired help, a former slave belonging to her own family. The woman, Tillie, would carry water to fill the tank every morning. She would also empty the chamber pot. Once a week she would bring hot water for the tub. Miz Fannie indicated that facility, also cracked, in its position behind the screen.

They would be just as snug as bugs in a rug up here! They needn't bother theirselves with anything that went on down below! There were steps outside to use if they liked, just across the roof and down. She showed them that the door had a good stout lock, and left.

Downstairs, Miz Fannie looked at Sister with worried eyes. "Ah almost made a mistake," she confessed. "When they said old Rosie sent them—"

"A natural mistake," Sister comforted her. "Perhaps they won't discovah anything."

71

"And if they do," Fannie said, "they'll just have to put up with it, or find anothah place."

Still, she felt a trifle guilty. She should have told them. She'd explained about the war and all, but there were no words to describe how she and Sister felt, watching the burning of a home that had been in her family for a hundred years; the shock two spinsters had endured, being ravished—at their age—by a horde of conquering hoodlums; the struggle to save what they could of their things once the invaders left.

And then the misery of cold and wet, the gnawing pain of hunger . . .

With the help of slaves who had hidden in the bushes, the sisters had dug up the silver buried in the garden, managed to load what they could reclaim in a cart, and come into Memphis, where they had purchased this old stone house.

Now it was a haven for others, young widows, left homeless and penniless, whose only goal was survival; daughters, who had lost their "virtue" during the conflict through no action of their own. In some ways, entertaining the Union soldiers at night was a small price to pay. Loving them, they hated them. And they took their money gladly.

Upstairs, Inga and her daughters inspected the rooms. They were small, but the beds were scrupulously clean, made up with fine old much-mended linens. It was hot and humid at the top of the house; curtains hung limp at the windows; everything gave off a slight smell of damp and mildew. The much-touted view proved to be a disappointment. From the front, a huge mercantile building cut off the light. At one side was a crooked street;

a long structure, its doors and windows secured with boards, across the way. To the right, what appeared to be a rooming house with a saloon below. And behind Miz Fannie's establishment was a cotton warehouse, almost, but not quite, closing off a view of the river.

Shaking out the few things in her carpetbag, Inga felt choked and crowded. She was accustomed to the wide sweep of fields, a far-off sky. She stepped out onto the roof for a breath of air, but found none stirring. Even the sky, darkening now, seemed to press down upon her.

Still, they were safe and secure. They had found a place to stay. And when Miz Fannie appeared at the door with a plate of golden fried chicken, a bowl of white gravy seasoned with sage and sugar, along with fluffy biscuits, Inga was ashamed of her misgivings.

She had to forget that other life, just as she must forget her part in Olaf's death, as she must delete Nick Tremont from her memory.

In spite of her determination, Inga did not sleep that night. It was hot, the sheets wet with damp. Without the gentle rocking of the boat beneath to lull her, she dwelled on the horrors of the past, her precarious hold on the present, and her fear of the future. Where would she find a job? How should she begin to look for Sven? And would she be able to care for her daughters?

Jenny, in her cot wedged behind the kitchen table, slept the sleep of the innocent. But Kirsten, like Inga, was wakeful.

She was thinking of how, this very morning, she had wakened aboard ship to find her mother gone.

She'd peeped through the stateroom window, seeing her at the rail.

And she was not alone.

She was with that man, the same man who had alerted them to the fire. He was holding her in his arms. And, Kirsten thought bitterly, she was enjoying it! She had heard them making plans to meet again, with her father so newly dead—murdered!

Olaf Johansson had not been perfect, but what he had become was her mother's fault. Sometimes Kirsten was upset when he seemed cruel, but then she would remember he had reason.

He would not really have given Jenny away, Kirsten told herself. It was only that he had been drinking and wasn't thinking straight. She had to believe that!

Just as she had had to believe what she had seen this morning with her own eyes. She hadn't recognized the man with Inga. She only saw enough to know that he was dark, with black hair like Jenny's. There could be only two explanations for that intimate scene. Either her mother's morals were so low that she'd take up with the first stranger who came along, or Inga had known the man long years ago, when Jenny was conceived, and they were resuming an old affair.

Kirsten's grandfather, Pastor Gustav Lindstrom, said that a woman, once she had turned bad, was evil incarnate.

It was true, Kirsten thought now, burying her face in one of Miz Fannie's lacy, down-filled pillows. It was true!

10

Inga's first act the next morning was to search for a magnolia blossom. Jenny located one in the front yard of a fine home and cheerfully appropriated it. After all, there were a lot of blooms on the tree. No one would miss it.

Inga placed the bloom in a little box and posted it to Minnesota, to an aging woman who had never learned to read. Birgitta would understand what it meant: they had arrived at their destination.

For the next several weeks Inga searched for work, and for her brother Sven. Through some magical connection, Miz Fannie produced names of Union officers and letters of introduction.

Inga Johansson was always politely received, and as politely turned away. There was usually a vague reference to the Federal Prison, which they would check for her, or to the field at Shiloh, where thousands of young rebels lay buried in three common graves.

Consulting Confederacy sources was almost impossible. Disorganized, with its head—its leaders—lopped off at the top, there was no one in a position to respond. Inga and her daughters laboriously wrote letters to Davis and to Lee, but they received no answer. Either their messages did not reach their destination, or those gentlemen were beset with too many problems of their own.

The women took to stopping Confederate soldiers on the street.

Had they known a young man from Minnesota? His name was Sven, Sven Lindstrom. He was tall, with light hair, and spoke with a Swedish accent . . .

Dull eyes pondered the question. But the answer was always the same. Following the ejection of a stream of tobacco to stain the cobblestones, someone would drawl: "Don't rahtly remember. Don't figgah I did. If you heahed from around these pahts, he mebbe fell at Shiloh."

In every case, their search led to a dead end, though their genteel little landlady insisted they were going at it the wrong way. From time to time she consulted a local preacher who had turned to the occult. She was certain he would help find Sven.

"Good gracious! Didn' he he'p me get through to mah sweet ol' daddy? And when I tole Daddy about my work heah, he gave me his blessin'!"

Inga was none too sure about that. In these past weeks, she had gained a pretty good notion of what Miz Fannie's work consisted of. Sounds of confusion drifted up from the lower floors at night;

stumbling male footsteps, giggling girls, and once a scream, followed by Miz Fannie's voice lifted in stentorian tones.

"Get out of mah house! You-all done betrayed mah hospitality! We only 'low gennulmen heah!"

Once she realized what was going on, Inga was very careful to see that she and the girls were in their rooms before darkness fell, and that the door was securely fastened.

In time, Inga began to grow accustomed to the feeling of failure in her search for work. One would think that, somewhere in this city, there would be a job for a woman who was earnest, not unattractive, willing to work. She sighed. But the place was crowded with dispossessed blacks who, at first exhilarated at the thought of freedom, had swarmed into Memphis.

When hunger began to plague them, those few who still had homes to go to went away. But the great majority were homeless, rootless, finally willing to work for nothing but food and shelter, exploited by their employers, in many cases worse off than they had been before.

"Ain't nobody goin' tuh hire you, when they can get a niggah for free," Miz Fannie said emphatically one afternoon as Inga returned. "You tried findin' somebody wants a govahness?"

Inga couldn't admit to the kindly woman that she and Jenny had no formal schooling, and that Kirsten had little. A governess would need references, and those they could not provide.

"Things get too bad, honey, I can find a little somethin' for you. Mebbe it ain't 'xactly the line you'd choose, but ..." Miz Fannie suggested one day.

"Don't worry," Inga said hastily. "We'll be all right."

She left Miz Fannie and hurried up the stairs.

Inga found Jenny waiting for her, her dark little face shining with pleasure. She had made the acquaintance of some of the other tenants in Inga's absence. "They are so beautiful," she enthused, "and they have such pretty clothes. They must be very rich. One of them has a real ruby necklace a gentleman gave her. Another—"

Inga reddened. "That is enough, Jenny. I do not want you to—"

"Wait, Mama! Listen! The one called Pearlie— she's the prettiest—works for Miz Fannie. Pearlie says she thinks Miz Fannie might give me a job."

"Jenny, this house ..." Inga stammered. "I ... I have decided we must find another place to stay."

There was no money, however. The money she had taken from Birgitta's coat was almost gone. Miz Fannie's rental was low, and she was patient. She would wait until Inga or the girls found work, no matter how long it took.

It was Miz Fannie who heard that Gayoso House was looking for help, a poised mannerly woman to serve as hostess in the dining room.

"Oughta suit you to a tee," she said with enthusiasm.

Though Inga feared it was hopeless, she went to apply, dressed as neatly as possible and determined to charm the manager if she could.

Leaving the girls in the lobby, Inga went to the office, where she met an imposing gentleman who introduced himself as Mr. Williams and looked her over with an appreciative eye.

"Harrumph," he said, fiddling with his watch chain as he lifted his gaze to contemplate the ceiling. "I am willing to give you a try, Miss—"

"Mrs.," Inga told him. "Mrs. Inga Johansson."

His expression changed, and she added hastily, "I am a widow."

He was benevolent again. "Well . . ." He beamed, shoving a paper toward her. "I think we're going to get along just fine. Just fill this out here. You can begin tomorrow."

Inga's fingers trembled as she wrote her name. She had found work at last! And just in time. The man was staring at her bosom as she leaned forward, but it didn't matter. Surely she could keep him in his place.

As she handed the paper back, his hand touched hers. "Maybe you'd like to stick around? Have lunch, learn the ropes?"

She shook her head, saying that she was meeting someone, and escaped as quickly as possible. Her face was bright with relief as she hurried to the lobby. But the light in her eyes faded as she saw Jenny struggling in the grasp of a man in a business suit.

Kirsten had wandered away, and Jenny had been deep in conversation with a porter when the gentleman had approached her, his face wreathed in an anticipatory smile.

"I've read about you little honeys." he said tipsily. "Mulattos, quadroons, whatever the hell you are! Figured I'd try one before I head back north, but

79

you're the first one I've seen. Come on up to my room, sweetie. I'll make it worth your while."

He took her arm and tried to pull her along with him. The black porter stood trembling with fear as he fought with his desire to help her—and with the knowledge that someone would kill him if he tried.

"Let me go," Jenny cried. Finally she kicked at the man's shins to free herself. He grabbed at her again, this time in anger. "You little devil!"

Inga headed toward them and Kirsten returned, coming from the other direction. As Inga grabbed at the startled man, jerking him away from Jenny, Kirsten struck him on the head with her folded sunshade. The man flailed out, grasping Kirsten's arm. She screamed, kicking to get free.

The lobby erupted as curious patrons surrounded the struggle, and the manager charged out from his office to see what was going on.

He found his newly hired hostess and two other young ladies involved in a free-for-all with one of his best bar customers—who was also a friend of the hotel's owner.

Wading into the melee, the manager pushed the gentleman free, dusted him off, and turned to Inga. Her blue eyes were blazing, her cheeks crimson with anger, and his decision wavered for a moment. Then he remembered that he had to keep his job.

"I find your . . . er . . . disposition is unsuited to our requirements," he said, flushing. "Our female employees must maintain their dignity under any circumstances. You are fired."

"I am not sure that I was ever hired," Inga spat. "Come, girls!"

Jenny began crying silently, tears running down

her cheeks as they walked toward Miz Fannie's. She had only been talking to the porter. Then the man came up to her, took hold of her; she couldn't get away.

"It is all right, Jenny," Inga said, and patted her daughter's arms.

"But he called me some strange names. What did he mean?"

Kirsten, burning from embarrassment at the situation, lashed out at her. "He thought you were part nigger, that's what he thought!" The image of the dark man on the boat swam before her eyes, and she glared at Inga. "She isn't—is she?"

Inga's hand itched with the desire to slap her older daughter. But Kirsten had come to her sister's aid. And one scene had been enough for the day. She had found a job and lost it within minutes, and her head ached. One thing she knew. She and Kirsten could search for work, but she would never allow Jenny out on the streets alone again. Not in this town, swarming with a mixture of overbearing Northerners and ragtag remnants of the Southern army.

She told Miz Fannie that the job at the hotel had been filled.

"That's a cryin' shame," the old woman consoled her. "It sounded jes perfect foh you."

"I am afraid," Inga said, her chin high, "that my disposition was unsuited to their requirements."

The next several days were as hopeless as the previous ones had been. Inga and Kirsten called on prospective employers together, leaving Jenny trapped in the hot little rooms at the top of Miz Fannie's house, forbidden to go outside, to talk to the other tenants, and instructed to keep the door latched.

Even if she found work, Inga thought, this sort of thing could not go on forever. Again she considered leaving Memphis. Perhaps she could find a place in the country.

Occasionally she and Kirsten went their separate ways. But if Inga arrived home first, she was panicked until her older daughter came in.

Inga's worst fears were realized one evening when Kirsten arrived, out of breath, her face livid. A man had followed her all day; a Union officer. She didn't say that she had been more than a little flattered at his attention, nor that she had smiled in his direction more than once.

She became alarmed only when he followed her home. Then, outside the house, he had caught her arm, and made an indecent suggestion, saying that he would be back after dark.

"I told him I wasn't that kind of girl," Kirsten wept. "But he said I had to be, or I wouldn't be living here. Mama, those women downstairs—you don't suppose . . ."

Inga flushed. This last incident was the final straw.

"It doesn't matter," she told Kirsten. "We'll be leaving here in the morning."

She locked the door against the outside world and went to bed, wondering where they could go and how they would live without money. For the first time since she had been cast out of her church, fourteen years earlier, Inga prayed for help.

——— 11 ———

Young Lieutenant Whitby hadn't seen any of the active fighting. His father, a wealthy banker, had seen to it that the boy spent his time in Philadelphia as a recruiting officer. He was handsome, wore his uniform well, was regarded as an eligible young bachelor, and cut quite a swath at social affairs. But at the war's end, through some clerical error, Whitby had been transferred to Memphis to replace active personnel, and found himself in a humdrum job that could have been handled by any storekeeper.

Memphis was decidedly not Lieutenant Whitby's cup of tea!

The fine old families closed their ranks, maintaining a solid front against the people who invaded their home territory. Though some of them were secesh, others Union, they were unanimous in their distaste for newcomers: soldiers, riffraff, carpetbaggers, and the horde of blacks that milled in the streets, some of whom were behaving with a new and frightening militancy.

Lieutenant Whitby was an outsider for the first time in his life. The pretty girls from the big Georgian mansions were guarded like treasures, kept far from the contamination that crept into Memphis during the war. And though Whitby was in charge of issuing stores—and making a pretty penny on the side—he missed his social life, and most important, the ladies.

Early on, he had discovered Miz Fannie's establishment, and formed an acquaintance with several of the girls. He especially liked Pearlie, but the relationship was not completely satisfactory. Though she was a little beauty, he sometimes had a feeling that she looked down on him, too, like the other damned Memphians. It also angered him to pay for something he felt he deserved.

Then, only yesterday, he had seen the lovely Nordic-looking blond. She was walking down the street ahead of him when he left Miz Fannie's. He had a feeling she had just left the same building, but he couldn't be sure.

He had followed her, admiring her slender height—she was almost as tall as he; admiring the golden hair that, released from its braids, he imagined, would flow through his fingers like water. Her face was as lovely as the body he coveted, blue eyes, skin like cream painted with rose.

There was a dignity in her bearing that put some of those mincing little Southern belles like Pearlie to shame. He was certain she had noticed him, too. She smiled, and though she looked past him at a child, he was certain that smile was meant for him. Stepping over a puddle in the street, she lifted her skirt, showing him a lovely curve of calf and ankle.

He considered it to be an invitation. When at day's end she returned to Miz Fannie's and started up the walk, he was sure of it.

He raced forward and took her arm. As she turned to face him, he was surprised to find her looking at him with shock and revulsion.

"Let me go!" she said in fury. "Please!" Then, as his hand touched her bosom, "Please, I'm not that kind of girl!"

The hell she wasn't! All day she'd been leading him on. This whole rotten town had been treating him like dirt, and he'd be damned if he was going to be snubbed by a prostitute!

Holding her tightly, a caressing hand moving over her body, he told her that he intended to return, and described in great detail what he intended to do to her. When he let her go, she ran sobbing into the house.

His mouth twisted cynically as he watched her go. It was only an act. She was pretending to be a virginal maiden in order to raise the price.

Returning that evening, already half-drunk, from a bottle of rum he carried with him, the lieutenant asked Miz Fannie about her new girl. He was told she was only a tenant, and unavailable. So he settled for Pearlie.

Pearlie May Allyson Tolliver had been the spoiled daughter of a fine old family in Mississippi. She had hidden in a slave cabin while her home burned and her parents were murdered by a roving band of renegade deserters, shaking with fear as her pampered life tumbled into ruins.

Trained only in music and fine sewing, Pearlie sold the only thing she had left—herself. Still, she considered herself a cut above the others, no matter what their background. And she especially disliked the tenants on the top floor.

They were Northerners, weren't they? And except for the little one, they kept to themselves. It was obvious they considered themselves too good for the likes of Miz Fannie's girls.

When Lieutenant Whitby arrived, still seething over the way Kirsten Johansson had treated him, Pearlie sympathized. Together they emptied the bottle he brought. He spilled out his troubles to her, complaining of the girl who had rejected his advances.

Pearlie had an idea.

Whitby could go up the outside stairs without being seen, and onto the roof. There was a stout lock on the door to the cupola rooms, but the windows were none too secure. Jenny had told Pearlie that she and her mother shared the larger room, the kitchen. Kirsten had a room to herself—that would be the one to the south. . . .

Whitby began to grin. He could see himself, a romantic lover in his military blue, kissing the young lady of his dreams into submission, showing her he was not to be put off!

Whitby left by the front door, and Miz Fannie breathed a sigh of relief to see him go. In her mind, "that one" spelled trouble.

Pearlie went back to her room, feeling a little

guilty as the effects of the rum wore off. It had been a tacky thing to do; she knew that. But after all, that girl was no better than she was, the stuck-up thing!

Lieutenant Whitby carefully climbed the steps at the rear of the building, moving with tipsy, exaggerated care. The cupola was dark, and he grinned with satisfaction.

Moving quietly to the window Pearlie had described, he took out his penknife, cut the screen, and released the hook that held it in place. He was in luck! The window was open, propped in place by a stick.

He climbed in a little clumsily, his eyes fixed on a bed, barely visible against the far wall, and breathed a sigh of satisfaction as he stepped forward.

Behind him there was a terrible crash. He froze. His movement had dislodged the stick that braced the window.

Kirsten sat up at the sound. Then, seeing a figure between herself and the window, she screamed.

Whitby paused for only a second, then flung himself across the room, clapping a hand over the girl's mouth.

"Shut up, dammit," he panted. "I'm not going to hurt you! I just—"

He didn't finish his sentence. Small Jenny, wakened by her sister's scream, burst into the room and flung herself on his back. Though his coat was pulled half-off, imprisoning his arms, Whitby tried to wrestle her away. Then Inga appeared, a cast-iron skillet in her hand. She swung, connecting with his head, and Lieutenant Whitby went down.

When Miz Fannie and Sister reached the cupola, alerted by the noise, they found Kirsten weeping in her sister's arms and Inga Johansson standing over a body, hands clenched about her weapon.

She looked at Miz Fannie, eyes blank with shock. "I killed him," she whispered. "Just like Olaf! I have done it again. . . ."

Miz Fannie took charge immediately. The man wasn't dead, just knocked out. She knelt beside him and, unbuttoning his trousers, removed the contents of a money belt around his waist.

"No point in wastin' this," she sniffed.

Then she called in several of her girls. They were to drag the fellow down toward the docks, leave him in front of the warehouses, a bottle beside him. Maybe he'd forget where he'd been.

When they had gone, bumping the lieutenant none too gently down the steps, Miz Fannie turned to Inga. "That man might remember what happened and try to get revenge. He is, after all, a Union officer. It might be best for you to take the girls and leave the house. Don't you have any place to go?"

Inga shook her head, explaining that there was no money left. That she knew nothing but how to farm.

Miz Fannie bit her lip. There were plenty of homeplaces scattered over the countryside, places to which their owners would never return, many of them having been killed in the recent fray. Some of the plantations and farms had been picked up for taxes, for investments by Northern speculators who were absentee owners, but other places had no owners alive. Inga would have to be careful.

There were still roving renegades, vultures feeding on the tragedy of others; squatters, both black and white, who might kill to protect what they now considered their property.

"Law, honey, Ah reckon that's your best bet. Though Ah hate to see you-all go. My offah's still open. Y'all could work foh me."

Inga put her arms around the old woman. "Thank you, but . . . no, we couldn't."

"Then let's get movin'. Y'all will need some he'p. Sister!"

Within an hour, a decrepit old horse was loaded with axes, shovels, blankets, a small store of food and water, and a bottle of elderberry wine.

"Agin the chill," Miz Fannie said, waving away their thanks. The money she had taken from Whitby's money belt would cover everything.

Miz Fannie's last gift was a shotgun. When she presented it to Inga, she stood on tiptoe to whisper a question into her ear. "Y'all said you killed another fellah. Was he a Nawthener, by any chance?"

"Northerner? Yes, I suppose he was."

Miz Fannie patted her hand. "You done good, honey," she said with satisfaction. "Ah got two of the bastahds mah own se'f!"

12

They walked through the night-dark city, moving away from the Mississippi. Inga donned a shawl and insisted the girls do the same, despite the heat. In their shabby clothing, leading a broken-down horse, they appeared to be nothing more than Negro refugees making their way back to the country. Still, the presence of women at this late hour, no matter what their age or color, brought catcalls and obscene remarks from the drunken soldiers who thronged the streets.

For a time, Inga was unsure of her decision. Miz Fannie had been most explicit about the dangers they would face. And Kirsten, in spite of her recent fright, was dead set against leaving Memphis. She was sure there would be no opportunity for any kind of life for her and for Jenny in the country.

When they finally reached the edge of town,

Inga breathed a sigh of relief. It was good to be in the fresh air again. And though Kirsten sulked and lagged back, the sight of Jenny running on ahead in the pure joy of being free convinced her that she had done the right thing.

As they walked into the rising sun, Inga saw the dew trembling on leaf and grass. The land to either side was good land, much of it cleared, but showing signs of neglect. Still, smoke rose from the chimneys of small houses, attesting to their occupancy.

The road was broad and well-traveled. Inga could imagine armies crossing and recrossing this route. Perhaps Sven had walked here.

They made a brief stop for breakfast of bread and cold beef. Jenny, too excited to sit, foraged while they ate. Finding a horseshoe, she brought it to her mother. "It will bring us luck, Mama!"

Then they were on the road again. A farmer passed them, his cart loaded with hay, evidently bound for the stables in town. He touched his hat. " 'Mornin', ladies. Where y'all bound?"

Inga came up with the only name she could think of. "Shiloh."

He looked at them pityingly, touched his hat again, and drove on. Inga realized that her destination was not unusual, that other women combed the battlefields, searching for their dead.

At noon they took another break. The sun was directly overhead, the countryside simmering around them. They ate, seated in lush grass, their burned faces stinging with perspiration, surrounded by swarms of midges. Inga was tired; Kirsten, her feet beginning to blister, was almost at the point of collapse, but Jenny was full of life and ready to go.

"Damned Indian," Kirsten muttered under her breath.

Inga turned on her, completely losing her patience, fixing her elder daughter with hot blue eyes. "What did you say?"

"Nothing," Kirsten answered.

As they trudged on, Inga thought of the question Kirsten had directed at her about Jenny's ancestry after the episode at the Gayoso. She wondered if she should tell Kirsten what she had learned from her mother, vindicate herself—and thereby, Jenny. She decided against it. It would be a betrayal of her mother, and a shock to Kirsten when she learned that she too was the descendant of an adulterous relationship. The girl was confused enough at the moment, sulkier than ever, nursing some kind of grudge. This was not the right time.

Several times they left the road to avoid small convoys of Union troops. Toward afternoon the skies began to darken with an approaching storm. Thunder rumbled in the distance, moving nearer. Lightning cracked to earth, and a cold wind swept the hot humid air before it with a spattering of rain.

The women looked for a house, a barn, a haystack where they might shelter. But the road was lonely, fringed with trees that ran down to a river on one side, rose to a barren hill on the other. When it began to pour, they found a small depression in the side of the hill and huddled, covered with sodden blankets, shivering until the morning.

Inga woke to a sharp cry from Jenny. Sitting

upright, she saw that the rain had ended. And Jenny's blankets were empty. She tried to rise and fell back again, her limbs, stiff and aching, refusing to comply.

"Mama! Help me!"

The call came from somewhere on the road ahead.

Finally getting to her feet, Inga snatched up the shotgun and ran. Slipping through the muck, she fought her way through thorny bushes that lined the edge of the road, pausing for an instant in horror at what she saw.

A gaunt man in gray had one hand on their horse's lead rope, fending off Jenny's attack with his other arm.

"Thief!" Jenny was shouting. "Robber! She's our horse! You can't have her!"

"Get away from me, you damned little bitch!"

The man gave Jenny a cuff across the face that knocked her sprawling in the mud, then lifted his eyes to stare into the muzzle of a gun, an implacable blue gaze backing it up.

He went pale.

"Didn't know the animal was y'all's, ma'am. Figgahed it wuz a stray—"

"He's lying, Mama! I saw him cut the rope!"

"I ought to shoot you!"

The man began to babble in an attempt to excuse his action. He was only a poor Confederate soldier trying to make his way home to Georgia, where he had him a woman and some little ones to look out for. He had only done what any desperate man would do.

Studying him, his wolfish face, his shifting eyes, Inga sensed he was lying. He was no true soldier, but one of the renegades Miz Fannie had mentioned. Inga gestured with the shotgun. "Go!"

He took a step toward her, hand outstretched as if in supplication, his eyes sly. "But, ma'am—"

"Jenny," Inga said firmly, "go wake your father and your Uncle Sven!"

Jenny's eyes rounded and she opened her mouth to speak, then shut it quickly and scuttled into the brush. Her voice carried to them as she obeyed her mother's command: "Papa, wake up! Uncle Sven! Mama needs you—"

The man who had been willing to try to face down two women wanted no part of it if there were male protectors. He took a backward step, his hands raised helplessly. "I'm goin' . . ."

He started walking toward Memphis, and Inga, on impulse, fired a shot behind him.

He began to run.

At least, Inga thought, the incident had served to alert her. It was possible that the renegade would have second thoughts and follow them, discover they were women alone. From now on, they would have to take greater care. Last night, she had slept too heavily. If Jenny hadn't heard the man . . .

Kirsten, who hadn't wakened until she heard her sister calling for her father and Sven, thought Jenny had lost her mind. At the sound of the gunshot, she managed to get to her feet, but when Inga returned to explain the situation, she promptly sat back down again.

She wouldn't go another step, she insisted, unless they headed back to Memphis.

It was some time before they could convince her

to move on. And the caravan set out again, slipping and sliding in the mud, with Inga keeping a sharp eye behind them to make certain they were not followed.

They paused that night at a small farmhouse where Jenny went forward to peep into its windows. She returned to announce that it was occupied by several rough-looking men, forcing them to go on to sleep in an abandoned barn.

Within the week, they found only one friendly reception. Their food had run out. Kirsten was barely able to hobble. Finally she collapsed in the road near a small unpainted cottage. Inga steeled herself to go to the door.

A big black woman answered, her inquiring expression turning to one of pity.

"Come in, chile! Oh, my stahs! Set down."

The shack was filled with children. Shooing them out of the way, the woman, who said her name was Grace, produced tall glasses of buttermilk and wedges of hot cornbread for her guests. Then she heated water for their swollen feet, and later applied an odd-scented salve that took the pain away.

"Where y'all goin'?" Grace asked as she clucked her tongue over Kirsten's blisters. "Way this chile's feet is, Ah hope it ain't too far."

Inga, too worn to dissemble, explained their plight. There were no jobs in Memphis, and she had a family to support. All she knew was the land. She had hoped to find an old abandoned farm, a piece of land where they might settle for a while.

"Ain't gonna find it on the main road," the woman said wisely. " 'Sides, no tellin' what y'all goin' run intuh. Me, I'd fine me a crick, with a path alongside. I'd follah that for a while."

That night they slept on straw pallets on the floor in a room with wall-to-wall children. In the morning, they were served hot biscuits and a drink of toasted barley, heavy with molasses. They said farewell to their black benefactor, and once more they were on their way.

The load the horse carried had been removed; some of it was left behind with Grace in payment for her hospitality, and the remainder was divided into two bundles. Inga carried the larger one, Jenny the other. Kirsten, who had never worked in the fields as the other two had done, rode astride the horse that had been used as a pack animal. She could walk no farther.

Still, at the end of the day, Kirsten wondered if her feet hurt any worse than the rest of her.

13

Two days later, Inga found her little creek. A small lane, almost lost in weeds, ran alongside it. Jenny was immediately euphoric, longing to explore, certain that something wonderful waited at the end of the path. Kirsten hung back.

They were only getting farther and farther from civilization. She had visions of being hopelessly lost, of starving to death, of dying someplace where their bodies would never be found.

"Nonsense," Inga said briskly, though she was none too sure, herself.

Her confidence was even more shaken when they had walked several miles and found nothing. Both sides of the lane were heavy with underbrush and briar. The trees along the river were taller, casting a blacker shade, and the only sound they heard was birdsong.

Evidently no one had traveled the path in a long time.

That night they slept beneath a sky blanketed with stars and woke to a misty morning filled with rainbows.

"I love it," Jenny cried, dancing from one foot to the other. "Oh, Mama, I love it!"

They went on, following the path, which was even more overgrown. Finally it ended, and Inga realized they would have to retrace their steps.

She sank to the ground, burying her face in her hands. Again she had made some kind of dreadful error. She was tired! So tired! These last few miles she had been staggering, carried along only by the promise that lay ahead. The heavy pack had cut into her shoulders, and she ached all over. Her skirts were heavy with dried mud, her body caked with it.

She pushed her hair back with a weary hand as she envisioned herself and the girls wandering homeless for the rest of their lives, searching for shelter, no matter how poor.

Kirsten sat on the horse, too feverish and miserable to say "I told you so." But Jenny ranged the area, small nose twitching with curiosity.

Suddenly she disappeared, sliding down the bank toward the river.

Inga called her. "Jenny!"

There was no answer. When the girl had been gone for a few moments, Inga got to her feet in alarm. Then Jenny's dark face appeared through the roadside brush, her features white and awed.

"Mama, I found something. You'll have to come and see."

Inga took a step and winced. She followed her daughter, expecting a flower, a bird's nest. She frowned a little when she saw that the girl had found only a continuation of the path.

"We'd better go back, Jenny. There is no point in getting lost."

But Jenny ran on ahead, so Inga groaned and continued in the child's footsteps. Ducking to avoid a low-hanging limb, she suddenly caught her breath at the first sign of civilization they had seen for some time. The creek's tan waters were spanned by a bridge, a delicately arched bridge with some of its side pieces missing. And there, beyond it . . .

Beyond a tangle of weeds and flowering shrubs, a house—no, part of a house—reared two stories into the sky. In the front, smoke-blackened columns reached upward, supporting nothing. Behind them, a spiral staircase leaned drunkenly toward a scorched gallery, a door beneath it. The rear part of the house seemed still intact.

Still farther away, a number of small cabins were clustered like a little town. And in the distance, fields that had once been productive, but were now a tangle of weed and wildflower, stretched as far as the eye could see.

"It's ours, Mama. Nobody lives here," Jenny said reverently.

"How do you know?"

"I just know." The girl shrugged.

Then she was off and running toward the house before Inga could stop her. She raised a hand helplessly, then gave up. Whatever danger waited in this place, they could go no farther.

Inga stumbled up to the road, and taking the

lead rope, led the horse, with her daughter Kirsten astride, down to the bridge and across it, to what she hoped would be home.

As Jenny had said, the place was deserted. Though it was a ruin, the kitchen at the rear of the house, separated from it by a dogtrot, was intact. Inga looked with awe at a monstrous wood range layered with dust. With a good cleaning, it would work.

She would not think about that now. At the moment, she was unable to move. Foraging again, Jenny found a well and a tin washtub in a cabin that had evidently served as laundry. She drew a bucket of sweet water and they quenched their thirst.

Too exhausted to explore further or to think of food, they stretched out on the kitchen floor and slept through the remainder of the day and until the following morning.

Inga awoke to the song of a mockingbird and the saucy answer to its trill, which surely came from young Jenny. Though Kirsten still slept, the younger girl had been up for hours, studying their surroundings.

She led her mother from miracle to miracle.

At one side of the kitchen, steps led down to a dirt cellar. The hooks for hanging meat were empty, but the raiders had neglected to take huge covered crocks of flour and sugar. Whoever had left them there had stored them carefully with bay leaves, against weevil infestation. There were also a few jugs of molasses and honey, now crystallized, but heating would restore them to usefulness.

"And that isn't all," Jenny said mysteriously.

She led her mother to a small kitchen garden. Though a tangle of weeds, it had reseeded itself. There were onions, squash, and melons.

"I think we should call this place Heaven," Inga said, close to tears.

"I found its name," Jenny said.

Inga followed her to the front of the house, where the girl pointed out a sign lying in the weeds. It was made of wrought iron and it spelled out "Sweethom." "It's 'Sweethome,' Jenny said. "I found the E. It broke off, but I can fix it."

Inga believed her. Jenny could fix anything.

Wary of the leaning staircase, they entered the main house through a back door. At the rear was a small serving porch. Through another door was a breakfast room with a bay window, its glass still intact. Beyond was an enormous dining room—draperies torn down, magnificent furniture hacked and scarred, the padded seats of elegant chairs ripped open, legs torn off. A fire had been started there, too, but it had burned out without much damage except for smoke-grimed walls.

It was plain that this gracious Southern mansion had been gutted and vandalized during the recent war.

Across the hall from the breakfast room was a sewing room where there was little damage. Open cupboards revealed dusty bolts of cloth. Though Inga gasped at the sight, the raiders had obviously not considered the materials valuable enough to carry away.

Opposite the dining room, what had once been a library was a shambles. A desk had been tipped, the contents of its drawers scattered. Papers had been trampled, but they managed to find a name: Theron St. Germain.

This had been his home, his chair that was slashed to pieces, his books pulled from shelves, their bindings ripped away, pages strewn. And there had been a woman here. The sewing room attested to that.

The door to the hallway opened under the gallery with its tilted stair, indicating how much of the house had burned. There were still rooms upstairs, over the part that remained, but there was no way of reaching them.

The raid had evidently been a hurried one, a hasty search for items of worth, with the attackers riding off before they had thoroughly accomplished their destruction.

Inga thanked God for that.

They spent the day clearing out debris, washing down walls. Some of the slave cabins had been left open, their interiors destroyed by rats and coons. A few had been shut tightly. They smelled musty, but in them Jenny found three straw mattresses in fair condition.

She slit the mattresses open and spread the straw in the sun, washed the ticks in the stream, and filled them again. Kirsten, unable to walk on her swollen feet, hemmed lengths of unbleached muslin from the sewing room, fashioning sheets.

That night, they turned the library and dining room into bedrooms, where the girls slept sweetly, under a roof at last.

Inga stood in the doorway listening to the ripple of pale brown water below an arched bridge, frogs holding their concert under the stars, night birds sleepily chirping. She felt as if she had come home.

She was the child of her mother and an unknown half-breed; she had killed a man, but that was all behind her. God had been good to her. Here, among the ruins of someone else's life, she would build a new one for herself and for her children.

14

Each day that passed was one of discovery and accomplishment. A small orchard, untended and unpruned for years, almost hidden in thigh-high grass, still bore some fruit.

Jenny found a charred shed filled with tools. The greatest treasure it yielded was a plow. Hitching up the little horse Miz Fannie had given them, Inga turned another garden plot, planting the few seeds she had brought from home. She knew nothing about the climate here, but instinct told her she might be able to raise a fall garden.

Jenny, in her free moments, ranged farther afield. One day she found a rail fence that seemed to mark a boundary. The rich land ended there, and a reddish claylike soil climbed a hill. She went over the fence and up the hill to look down into a small clearing. Below was another tributary to the creek, beside it a little house on stilts. Smoke rose from the chimney.

Her heart stopped beating. Suppose someone who knew Mr. St. Germain lived there? Suppose it was someone who would tell them to get off his land? If they had to go away, she would just die!

She would say nothing about the little house. After all, it was miles away.

Returning to the St. Germain property, she slipped through the trees like an Indian and took a different route home. She came upon a little glade, and smothered a cry of delight. There was a small spring, a pool of water like the clear blue lakes at home. She went toward it, ankle-deep in tall grass and flowers, and knelt to slake her thirst.

Cupping a slender brown hand to bring the water to her lips, she froze. Someone was watching! She could feel it. Body tensed to run, she turned slowly. Her breath caught in her throat.

Through the heavy foliage that surrounded the glade, a monstrous eye peered at her, a rolling eye, surrounded by mottled fur.

Some sort of monster!

The thing gave a peculiar moaning sound, then pushed toward her; a horn appeared, then another.

Jenny began to laugh, a half-hysterical laugh of elation and relief, and walked toward the thing.

"Soo, Bossy," she said softly. "Soo, Boss . . ."

The brindle cow might or might not have been St. Germain's. She had evidently run wild for a long time. In her mind was a dim memory of humans, but she was skittish. None too sure of the slim brown girl approaching her, she bridled and stamped, backing away. Jenny followed, coaxing, her hand outstretched.

And finally Jenny touched her, calming, soothing. The animal twitched and trembled and then stood still.

After a while Jenny took hold of the rope that held a clapperless bell and tugged at it. The animal, now secure in their friendship, followed.

At the edge of the glade, she began to toss her head again, snorting. And Jenny, nausea rising in her throat, discovered the reason.

At the foot of a tree, half-covered with leaves, lay something in the remains of a gray uniform. Jenny drew a gasping breath and swallowed. Bones glinted through a ragged sleeve; a skull looked upward through empty eyes; the tattered jacket showed an officer's insignia.

Backing carefully away, Jenny led the cow along another route.

Inga was overjoyed when she saw them coming— the girl with the animal that could mean so much to their survival. She left the garden and ran to meet them, marveling over the creature, touching it in awe.

"Oh, Jenny, Jenny! Where did you find her?"

Jenny described the glade, but there was something in her face, her voice, that was troubled. Inga looked at her closely, fear tightening around her heart.

"What is it, Jenny?"

"I think," Jenny said solemnly, "that I have found Mr. St. Germain. He's . . . dead."

Inga could not suppress a sigh of thankfulness. If

the man were dead, then their worries were over. They could stay.

Then, hating herself for such thoughts, she asked, "Where is he, Jenny?"

"I'll show you."

They would have to give the man a Christian burial.

Tying the cow in a spot where she could graze, Inga and Jenny took one of their freshly washed blankets and walked across the property. The glade might have brought a cry of delight from Inga at any other time, but now she was intent on her dreadful errand.

"There." Jenny pointed.

"You stay here, daughter. I can—"

Jenny's jaw set. "I will help you."

It wasn't as awful as Inga expected. These were mostly bones and a tattered uniform. Wrapping the remains in the blanket, they carried them home.

By nightfall, the two women had managed to dig a grave at the foot of a tulip tree near the river bridge. Jenny found a flat board among the debris they had stacked for future use, and burned Theron St. Germain's name into it with a poker heated in the fire.

When they lowered the poor bag of bones, covering it, Inga's eyes were wet. She was ashamed that her first thought had been relief that St. Germain was dead and would not return to trouble them. She wept for a man who had built a beautiful home and had to leave it behind. And she vowed that, somehow, she would build it back again.

Kirsten did not attend the simple funeral. The thought of dead bodies, she said flatly, gave her the shivers. And why did someone they did not know deserve the courtesy of a proper burial? Why hadn't they just left him where he lay?

Inga, recognizing her veiled reference to Olaf, turned away, heartsick. There was nothing she could do for Olaf now, anyway. She could only try to repay a debt to an unknown man.

She and Jenny worked all day at the worst of the slave cabins, gutting the interior, washing down the split logs, strewing straw on the floor. When they finished, they had a creditable barn to house the cow.

They were leading her toward it when they discovered they were not alone. A trio of blacks stood watching at the edge of the yard.

Inga, heart in mouth, relinquished the lead rope to Jenny and went toward them.

There was an old man whose hair was white as cotton, as was the stubble on his cheeks. He was gaunt and bent, and leaned on a tree limb that had been fashioned into a cane. Beside him was a middle-aged woman. She, too, was emaciated, the flesh hanging on her bones. She held the hand of a skinny little boy with big eyes and a mischievous grin.

The older blacks looked frightened. They were staring at Inga as though she were what they least expected to find.

"We's lookin' foh Massa Theron," the woman said finally. "We done come home."

Fear caught in Inga's throat. Now they were found out! She forced herself into a calm statement. "Mr. St. Germain is dead. This is our home now."

The woman began to weep, wiping her eyes on

the tail of an apron. The old man put an arm around her, his own rheumy eyes filling with tears.

"Ah's hungry, ma'am. We thought Massa Theron would feed us."

"You hesh, boy!"

The old man, his voice rusty but firm, was already moving away. The others turned to follow, when Inga stopped them.

She had a meal prepared. They were to stay and eat.

The Negroes entered the kitchen timidly, the woman looking with fondness at the big stove, studying the room as if to fix it in her mind.

Jenny had caught two plump cottontails in snares, and the smell of baked rabbit emanating from the oven made the little boy's eyes even bigger. Reserving a small amount for their own meal, Inga set the rabbit before them, along with boiled squash, poke greens, and biscuits.

As they ate, shyly at first, finally giving in to their hunger, they identified themselves.

The old man, Caleb, was the father of the woman, Dinah, and great-grandfather of the boy, who was named just that—Boy. They had belonged to Colonel Theron St. Germain. When he went off to war, the young missus moved to Memphis, taking Dinah with her.

"Missus was allus a puny li'l thing," Dinah said. "Took sick an' died on me."

Boy's parents had headed north, leaving the child with Caleb. The older slaves stayed on until they were scattered when the plantation was burned. Then Caleb, carrying Boy, had walked to Memphis to find Dinah. But there was nothing there for them and they decided to come home.

"You *are* home," Inga said impulsively. "I can't hire you. I don't have any money. But if you want to stay, you're welcome to what we have."

Three pairs of eyes turned toward her, three faces wreathed in smiles.

"We'll work for you!" the woman said fiercely. "We work our haids off, jes to be here! Jes to be home again, praise de Lawd!"

15

The arrival of Caleb, Dinah, and Boy turned out to be a blessing. Dinah knew how to cook and to garden. She milked and churned joyously, singing hymns as she worked.

Boy and Jenny found some half-grown shoats, descendants of those who had escaped at the time of the burning. Using sticks to prod and guide, leaping away from snapping jaws, somehow they managed to herd the creatures home and pen them.

Caleb, too, had talents. Despite his age, he was an expert carpenter. He mended the bridge first, giving it a new coat of whitewash. Then, figuring the tilted staircase might fall and injure someone, he began to shore it up, with Jenny's help. When it was in place, he cautiously checked the planking of the gallery. It was slightly charred in spots, but sound.

Inga, Jenny, and Kirsten were free to inspect what remained of the upper floor.

They found two enormous bedrooms, windows looking out over the magnificent view at the rear of the house. They had been ransacked, mattresses split and spilled, but there was much less damage than that inflicted in the downstairs rooms.

A man had occupied the first room they entered. It was done in rich dark paneling and paper depicting hunting scenes. A cupboard held the remnants of elegant civilian clothing. Several pairs of shabby, soleless boots on the bedroom floor indicated that the raiders had taken what they wanted, leaving their own in exchange.

Across the hall was a woman's room, done in pastel silks and lace. A canopy that once covered the bed had been torn down and trampled. The furnishings were all in white and gold. The mirror of a dainty dressing table was shattered, boxes of powder spilled across the table's surface. An empty jewelry box stood open; drawers of the dresser had been pulled out, revealing delicate lingerie through which rough hands had rummaged; an open cupboard held a few gowns.

Kirsten was ecstatic.

Again Inga was torn between sorrow for the woman who had once lived there and delight in her own good fortune.

"What were the St. Germains like?" she asked Dinah that evening.

"Massa was a hard man," the woman said carefully, "but he a good man. He was fair with us niggahs."

"And his wife?"

A scornful look touched Dinah's face, but it was quickly veiled. "The missus, she a city gal. Don' want no part of this place, don' want Massa Theron, neither. Don' do no work. Jes stay in her room an' pine away."

"I don't blame her," Kirsten said fiercely, looking at Inga. "All those beautiful clothes, and no place to wear them! I can't imagine staying here for the rest of my life! Cut off from everything! I'd just die!"

"That jes whut missus done," Dinah said, scowling at the pale girl who always maintained a distance between herself and the three blacks. "Laid aroun' an' whined till she wore herse'f down to a nubbin! Ain' got no patience with folks like that!"

The look she shot Kirsten was meaningful, and the girl flushed. The nerve of the woman! A . . . a slave, daring to criticize her! And in such a way that she couldn't fight back without admitting that she wasn't carrying her share of the load. She couldn't be expected to. Her feet had only just healed after the long trek—which she hadn't wanted to make in the first place! She took one of the gowns from the upstairs bedroom down, planning to alter it for herself on the morrow. That was work, wasn't it?

Still, when her mother mentioned grubbing the weeds from the front of the house, she volunteered for the job. At least she wouldn't have to be working with the others, with the blacks, on the same level with them!

The next morning Kirsten went out with a grubbing hoe and began her battle with weed and briar. Her face, still peeling from sunburn, burned again. She was certain to get freckles! By evening, scratched by thorns, her hands blistered, she had decided to quit. But when she began to complain, an ominous look from Dinah silenced her. The next morning, she was at it again.

At week's end, a few feet of ground running the length of the house had been cleared. It was beginning to look good. When Kirsten sat for a moment to rest, she looked at the staircase, spiraling to the gallery, imagining herself in a lovely gown standing at the top, looking down. There would be a young man at the foot, his eyes filled with love and admiration as he raised his arms to her.

There were, she thought drearily, coming out of her daydream, only two men on the place. Caleb and Boy. If she were ever to have a life of her own, she must get away from here.

She had had such strange feelings lately—feelings of need, of a kind of hunger that nothing could appease. She had thought of Talbott Todd a lot, her fancies making him handsomer, more heroic, taller than he really was. And in her dreams, he knew how to kiss.

Sighing, she rose and took up the hoe again. Hacking at a particularly tenacious weed, she found it was rooted in several places. She set to work again, using the hoe as a lever, but suddenly it came up with an ease that sent her backward to land on her bottom.

Humiliated, she looked at the house to see if she had been observed, then rose and looked down into the hole.

Something glittered there.

She caught her breath and began to dig again,

oblivious of her blistered hands. Finally she lifted out a broken bag of jewels, and from beneath it, a chest containing silver.

She had found a fortune! Again she glanced toward the house. Then she hastily replaced her find, covering it over again. It belonged, she told herself, to someone else. To whoever buried it there. There was no point in telling the others. One day, if need be, and if no one came to claim it, she might sell it for enough to take her home. Home to Oskar!

She forgot Talbott Todd, since that avenue was closed anyway. In her mind, the aging mill owner was suddenly younger, more virile, his mill larger. He would be waiting for her, reach to forgive her anything when she went back to him.

Her mother wouldn't miss her, she thought scornfully. She had Jenny! Ever since they'd come here, it had been Jenny this and Jenny that! Jenny had found the house, found the cow, the tools, the pigs! But she, Kirsten, had made the greatest find of them all!

She paced off the distance from the house and from the bridge, from a lantana and from the spot where Theron St. Germain was buried. She would have no problem locating the treasure again.

When Dinah, finished with the rest of the chores, came around the house to offer assistance, Kirsten refused it.

She always, she said loftily, completed any job she set herself to do.

That night she worked until darkness fell. When she entered the house for a late meal of bread and milk, her eyes were too bright. She looked feverish, and Inga voiced her concern.

"Too much sun," Dinah commented. "Jes look how her po' li'l face is burned."

Using buttermilk to bathe Kirsten's hot features, Dinah admonished her to use it every night. Then she sat up late to fashion the girl a sunbonnet by candlelight.

Kirsten was impressed. It was a pity the way the war had turned out, she thought, wearing the bonnet as she set to work the next morning. She might have been able to talk Oskar into buying slaves.

16

The gardens flourished in the humid summer weather. By the time frost came, everything edible had been garnered and stored. Dinah's sharp eyes missed nothing; even wild herbs and barks were gathered for medicinal purposes.

"Don' want mah folks gettin' pneumony," she muttered, following her pronouncement with tales of dreadful winters, folks not coverin' their heads proper-like, gettin' their feet wet, coughin' their lifes away.

Inga listened, amused, wondering what Dinah would think of Minnesota weather, the blizzards that howled across the plains, sometimes covering rooftops; temperatures dropping below zero for months at a time.

Despite Dinah's dire predictions, when the cold descended, it was gentle. They rose one morning to a world in which everything was covered with a soft coating of frost. The bridge above the flowing creek appeared to be made of diamond-studded lace; the board that served as headstone over St. Germain's grave looked like glittering marble, the burned-on letters of his name looked as if they had been chiseled there.

Dinah and Caleb announced that it was butchering time, and began building fires under washtubs of water near a frame with a windlass.

"We lucky," Dinah puffed, drawing water from the well. "Some places, they jes thowed daid folks down th' wells. Spoiled the water for drinkin'."

Inga stared at the water in horror.

"Don' worry," Dinah advised her. "Y'all would of knowed it by this time."

Her words were small comfort.

When the tubs were boiling, the hogs were killed, one at a time. They were dipped into the steaming water, scraped, then gutted and cleaned.

Inga was not unacquainted with the process. But in Minnesota the carcasses could be hung and frozen. In Tennessee's chancy weather, a winter might be too warm for meat to keep well. Dinah brought out a hand-cranked grinder, and much of the pork was ground, seasoned with garden herbs, and fried, then put down in crocks, hot grease poured over it. After it cooled it was set in the root cellar, where the earthen walls maintained a constant temperature.

No part of the butchering was wasted. Heads were made into headcheese, and the entrails, stripped and cleaned, were cut into pieces that Dinah called chitlins. It did not tempt Inga's appetite. As far as she was concerned, they fell into the same category as crawdad stew, made with crayfish from the river, and cooter pie, its chief ingredient consisting of turtle dropped live into boiling water.

Old Caleb took charge of smoking the hams. He had his own special "receet." And before long, the hooks in the root cellar were filled with provender for the winter.

He also set Boy to cutting wood. Great stacks of it were lined along the dogtrot that led to the kitchen. At night, fires roared in the fireplace in the sewing room—which had become a sitting room—and the dining room.

Kirsten had insisted on taking Mrs. St. Germain's bedroom, upstairs. She mended the mattress and the canopy. Each night she climbed the circular staircase outside, shivering, But felt it worth it to sleep in such splendor.

Inga and Jenny slept in what had been the library. The dining room had been returned to its original state. Caleb labored over the broken furniture, returning some pieces to usable condition. When it was completed, Inga insisted on a new procedure. And she and Dinah had their first quarrel.

In Inga's childhood, hired hands had eaten at the table with the family. She insisted that Dinah, Caleb, and Boy join them at their meals.

Dinah was horrified. White folks didn't eat with niggers. Massa Theron would turn over in his grave.

"Then let him," Inga said firmly. "The war's over, Dinah! You people are free!"

Dinah sniffed and turned away, but not before Inga saw a smile on the old woman's face.

The first evening of the new regime was an awkward one. Boy and Caleb were almost too shy to eat. Priceless chipped plates were set at every place, bringing back memories of Miz Fannie's shabby grandeur. Dinah, her once-sagging cheeks beginning to fill out, grumbled to cover her discomfort, bemoaning the fact that the utensels were tin, from the kitchen drawer.

"Them scallywags done took the silver," she said angrily.

Later, after she had grown accustomed to the situation, Dinah set herself up as an arbiter of manners.

"Young missie," she said to Jenny, who sat, one foot beneath her, "ladies don' set on they laigs! Miss Kirsten, you holdin' yo' spoon wrong for soup! Miz Inga, don' use that fork. You starts with the one on the outside."

In addition to manners, Dinah worked to improve their appearance. The dress Kirsten had altered from the wardrobe of Sweethome's former mistress was too low-cut, with too many flounces.

"It looked right on Massa Theron's wife, she was a baby-kine of woman, but you look like a riverfront floozy, out man-huntin'. You ought tuh dress mo' like yo' mama. She done got class."

Kirsten looked at her mother, regal in a simple gown she had made herself. The fancy dress she had chosen to make over for herself was, she had thought, the prettiest of the lot, and now she hated it. She was furious with Dinah.

"An' you ladies rub lard on yo' hands, to keep 'em soft," Dinah advised as she went to bring in the dessert. She left, grumbling under her breath.

"Goin' make them wimmen act like ladies ef it kills me!"

When the door closed behind her, Kirsten exploded. "The nerve of that woman! A slave presuming to teach us manners!"

Inga looked at her daughter levelly. "Dinah is not a slave, Kirsten, nor are the others. I suggest you remember that! As far as etiquette is concerned, I think she probably knows more about it than three women off a Minnesota farm."

"I went to school in St. Paul," Kirsten said sullenly.

But her anger was gone. She was imagining herself as Oskar Bjorn's wife, presiding over a long table, dressed with elegant simplicity.

"You have the most exquisite taste, Mrs. Bjorn!"

"Thank you," she would say, dipping her soup spoon away from her, then bringing it to her lips with a graceful gesture that permitted no spilling.

Later, when she went up to her room, she intended to remove the flounces from her new dress and fill the neckline with some delicate lace. And when she had finished, she would rub her hands with lard.

The cold spell held for a while, and then there was a short period of unseasonable warmth. Caleb insisted that there was bitter weather coming. He could feel it in his bones. Dinah, too, returned to her dismal recollections.

"Las' winter I see this happen, it snowed an' blowed. Ol' Maum Sukey got los' on her way tuh de privy; foun' her froze stiff ez a board nex' mawnin'!"

In spite of Dinah's gloominess, the three women

enjoyed the bright blue skies. Even Kirsten, walking in the now cleared yard in front of the house, sun-warmed and dizzy with the scent of sun on fallen leaves, forgot her misery and grievances. The several days of summer out of time were too beautiful to be true.

When the storm hit, as Caleb and Dinah had predicted, it arrived with tremendous force. Black clouds moved across the blue sky. A wind came from the northeast, howling about the house, bringing, at first, huge soft flakes that flew before it like feathers, melting as they hit the ground, then sharp, bitter sleetlike pellets that stung the cheek and blinded the eye.

It stormed all one night, and continued on the next day. Caleb and Boy struggled to the makeshift barn to feed and milk the cow, bringing back a pail of milk that was already crystallizing at its edges.

That night, which was scarcely darker than the day had been, Inga and her daughters sat beside the fire counting their blessings.

They had a stout roof over their heads, and there were many who did not. They thought of those who might be out in the storm, homeless, perhaps hungry, searching for shelter as they had done.

At the front of the house, the staircase creaked in the wind. It might blow down before morning if this weather held, and the steps were packed with snow. It was unthinkable that Kirsten attempt to get to her room.

Jenny generously offered Kirsten her own bed. She would curl up on a blanket before the fire, where she would be cozy and warm.

Kirsten accepted.

When the others had crossed the hall, Jenny stretched out like a kitten, yawning. Then, curling herself into a tight ball, she was instantly asleep. Sometime later in the night, her well-honed instincts brought her instantly awake.

She had heard something! A noise that did not belong. It sounded like the scuffing of booted feet along the hallway. She listened intently, hearing something that resembled a groan, and got to her knees, staring wide-eyed into the darkness as the scuffing sounded once more. It might be a trick of the storm blowing about the wounded house. Yet it sounded more like someone walking . . .

There was a fumbling at the door that led into the hall, and then the door creaked open slowly. The fire leapt up, glinting on an apparition that wore a mask of frost, turning ice crystals into flame.

The creature who stood wavering on the threshold, staring at Jenny with blind eyes, looked like a fiend from hell.

Jenny screamed.

17

Inga, wakened by her daughter's shriek of terror, leapt from her bed. For a moment she was disoriented, still back along the main road, a thief making off with their horse.

"Mama!"

A second panicked cry brought Inga to her senses. The child was having a bad dream, she thought as she stepped into the icy hall.

The front door, under the stairs, had blown open. A blast of freezing wind and snow whipped down the hallway, and the door to the room in which Jenny slept stood partially ajar.

Inga moved to shut off the wind's intrusion, shivering under the sting of wintry weather. She fought the door shut, and turned back, intending to comfort Jenny before she returned to her own bed. Then quickened her steps as Jenny cried out again.

"Please . . . don't . . ."

"I'm coming, Jenny!"

Inga stopped dead in the doorway as she saw the thing that menaced her child.

Small Jenny was crouched in her blankets, staring up at a hollow-cheeked stranger who held a gun.

Inga gave a small cry and the man turned to face her, an odd sound in his throat that might have been either a growl or a sob. She could see now that one sleeve of the tattered rags he wore was pinned up to cover the stump of a missing arm. His snow-frosted hair and beard were shaggy. Lips, split and blackened with cold, were curled into a snarl.

His eyes were what terrified her most. They were dark pools of madness.

Though Inga was trembling, she forced her legs to move and walked toward the intruder cautiously, knowing she mustn't startle him. "What do you want?" she managed in a steady voice.

The pistol dropped for a moment, and the man stared at her in a wild kind of pleading.

"Home," he muttered in a confused, strangled voice. "Home . . ."

"You won't be able to find your way anywhere in this storm. You are welcome to shelter here for the night."

The gun lifted again as the man drew a shuddering breath. "Yankees!" he said. "Carpetbaggers!"

"Sir?"

Inga took a backward step at the hatred in his voice.

"Leave this house," he said in a flat, ugly tone. "Leave this house! Damn you, do you hear me?"

The pistol had settled now, and Inga was its target. There was murder in the man's crazed face as he lifted the gun. And then his eyes went out of focus. His knees bent. He toppled, with a sigh.

Jenny moved quickly, kicking the gun away from his hand with a bare brown foot. Retrieving the pistol, she handed it to her mother and fled through the dogtrot and out the kitchen door. Outside she grabbed the frozen rope that hung from a bell, once used to call slaves in from the fields. She had to swing from it to free the mechanism from its coating of ice. Snow showered down on her dark hair and her fingers stuck to the rope, but she clung to it grimly as the bell rang out its call for help.

When Dinah and Caleb arrived from their quarters, Caleb was armed with a rusty musket he had found. It was broken, and past all use, but he hoped it might serve as a deterrent. They found Kirsten holding a pistol in trembling hands. Inga and Jenny were standing over a ragged figure in gray, while Jenny rubbed the man's only hand in an attempt to restore circulation.

Inga had lifted his head, holding it to the bosom of her white nightdress, and was trying to force elderberry wine past the man's tightly closed lips. The liquid spilled down the front of her gown, leaving a stain like blood.

Dinah took in the scene with horrified eyes. "Who that?" she asked shrilly. "One of them no-good thievin' white trash? Knock 'im in the haid!"

As Caleb moved forward to oblige, Inga held up a staying hand.

"He's sick," she said. "Half-frozen, hungry. He acts like he's out of his mind, but—"

126

Dinah snorted. "Crazy like a fox, you ask me! Lookin' for somethin' to steal! Don' mess yo' han's on the likes of him. Get out of the way an' let me—"

She stopped suddenly, her eyes protruding. "Oh, Lawd! Oh, mah sweet Jesus!"

She clasped her hands to her breast and began to rock back and forth as if in agony. "That's Massa Theron! Our Massa Theron! Oh, mah soul! He ain' daid, is he? He ain' goin' die on us?"

Theron St. Germain? And he wasn't dead—not yet. Then whom had they buried beneath the marker near the bridge?

It didn't matter, Inga thought numbly as she went about obeying Dinah's orders. What mattered was that Theron St. Germain had come to reclaim his own. The home they had built upon the ruins of his plantation belonged to him; the work they had put into it had been all for nothing.

She warmed a blanket at the fire and handed it to Dinah, who was carrying on vociferously as she worked. "Po' Massa Theron! His po' arm! Them damn Yankees, comin' down here, killin', hurtin', burnin', stealin' decent folks' proppity—"

And I'm one of them, Inga thought dully. I'm one of them. Maybe, she thought with a mingling of shame and hope, Theron St. Germain would not survive.

Her shame deepened when, later, as she stirred the thin gruel Dinah had ordered, the black woman came into the kitchen to mix some sort of medical concoction. Dinah's eyes were red, her face sagging in despair.

"Goin' try," she muttered. "That all us kin do, jes try, an' do some pow'ful prayin'."

"Is he . . . bad?"

" 'Fection in that arm, where they chonked it off. Looks like he ain' et in a coon's age. Half-froze. Chest sounds like pneumony. Better keep them li'l missies away from him, case he got somethin' ketchin'."

With a glimmering of fear at the possibility, Inga agreed.

"Now I'se goin' make me up some poultices." Dinah frowned as she surveyed the array of herbs she had gathered for remedies. "This for the arm, I reckon. And a batch of that for his chest."

The gruel was finished. As Dinah mixed her evil-smelling concoctions, Inga returned to the dining room. She had sent Jenny and Kirsten to bed. The man now lay in Jenny's nest of blankets on the floor beside the fireplace.

He should be in a bed, Inga thought. Tomorrow they must find a way to make him more comfortable. Sighing, she realized that she was still thinking of the house as hers, the sick man as the intruder. If he survived, she could be making plans to leave as soon as the weather cleared. They would have to go back to Memphis.

In the meantime, she took her first good look at her enemy. His matted hair, still wet with melted snow, was black. As black as Jenny's. Above the beard there were patches of white from frostbite, but his cheekbones and forehead were red. The man was burning with fever!

She turned away, then back again, noting the way his lashes lay against the dark shadows beneath his eyes. His dark brows drawn together indicated that he felt the pain that invaded his body, even in his unconscious state. He had once been a very handsome man, she thought.

Inga felt a surge of pity, wondering how far this man had had to travel on his journey home. The war had, after all, been over for months. As she watched, Theron St. Germain began to tremble, his dark eyes tortured as he fought to rise.

"Ah, God," he rasped, struggling against her staying hand. "Cunningham! Martin—"

Inga pressed him back down to the blankets, and he sank again into his coma. But it was only moments before he was raving again.

"No," he said. "Damn you, no! I won't tell you . . ."

He broke free of her grip and brought his good arm up, smashing it against the side of Inga's head, dazing her.

Dinah, entering with a poultice, stopped, stricken. "Massa Theron!"

Inga rubbed her aching temple and tried to smile. "It's all right, Dinah. He doesn't know what he's doing."

The black woman's face cleared a little. "He be fine as soon as he knows he home."

Inga looked at the sick man immersed in his private hell. He would be fine, but would they— she, Kirsten, and Jenny? His features, before he collapsed, had been fierce with hatred. If he recovered, they faced a hell of their own.

18

The next morning, the wind had stopped, leaving behind a white and frozen world. The sick man was no better. He still groaned and thrashed with fever, flailing out with his remaining hand at anyone who came near. He did, however, look more presentable. By some miracle, Caleb had made his way up the snow-packed staircase to St. Germain's room and brought down more blankets and a nightshirt of soft white flannel.

Dinah and Caleb managed to bathe the sick man's wasted body and pull the nightshirt over his head.

"Ain' no tellin' whut kind of critters he done pick up in that place," Dinah sniffed. "If he goin' die, he goin' meet his maker clean!"

They washed and cut the shaggy hair until it returned to the soft dark waves of the past. Though the Massa Theron of old had always been clean-shaven, the ragged beard could only be washed and trimmed, for his frostbitten face was too tender to take the razor.

Besides, as Dinah said, the way Massa was feelin', he prob'ly didn' much care.

"He wake up, he goin' be mighty miz'ble, he fine this place belong to y'all," Dinah said as, leaving Caleb with the sick man, they went out to the kitchen. "Goin' bust his heart!"

Inga, watching the man's struggle to live, had done some soul-searching. For months, they'd been living in a fool's paradise. If St. Germain recovered his senses, it would all be over. She would have to tell Dinah of their deception. It was the only fair thing to do.

Her hands fumbled as she tried to fasten her apron; her face reddened. "It does not belong to us, Dinah."

"But you say . . ." Dinah's eyes rounded in disbelief.

"We came here just like you did, Dinah. Looking for a place to live. We . . . we had to leave our home in Minnesota, and farming was all I knew. We'll leave as soon as he's better."

Dinah stared at her, bewilderment turning to understanding. "Lawd he'p us! We done got ourse'fs intuh a fix!" She set her jaw. "Y'all ain' goin' nowhere, missus!"

"But we can't just—"

"Massa Theron wouldn'a had no home to come back to, wasn't for y'all. He be daid, out there in that snow, plumb froze. This place was a mess, missus! Who fix it up nice? Who plant that gahden sass? Who work they fingers to the bone gettin' set up for winter? You stayin', iffen Ah have to hawg-tie that man!"

"I'm certain he won't agree with you, Dinah."

Dinah sniffed. "That's foh sure. But Ah knows that man. His bark is wuss than he bite. Git yo' dander up, honey! He yells at you, you holler back!"

"And I imagine he will tell us to go."

"Y'all go, missus, me and Caleb and Boy, we go with you. One-armed man ain' goin' be able to take care of himself."

Inga threw her arms about the black woman and hugged her.

Dinah backed away, scolding, though her pleasure showed in her face. "Ain' fittin' for a white lady to ack like that, missus."

Inga frowned at her. "When are you going to get it into your head that we're friends! And I shall hug whomever I please!"

She left the kitchen and Dinah smiled after her. It was true. They were friends. The habits of a lifetime, however, were hard to break.

"But I'se gettin' there," she chuckled. "I'se gettin' there!"

She had a feeling Massa Theron was goin' to get his comeuppance!

Taking her stint by the sick man during that night, Inga studied the face that she had now memorized. Even in his desperate illness, Theron St. Germain had a commanding presence. She had a notion few people had ever crossed him.

If he recovered, he would be in for a big surprise.

Dinah was right. She had discovered Sweethome. She had raised it from the dead. And now she intended to fight for it.

Two days later, under a weak sun, Caleb and Jenny hacked away at the snow-covered steps to the upper rooms. They dismantled the bed in the master bedroom and carried it down, piece by piece, reassembling it. Then, slipping and sliding, they managed to get the mended mattress to the ground, down the hall, and into the dining room. Table and chairs were pushed to the wall, the bed set up, and Theron St. Germain's pain-racked body lifted into it.

His taut cracked mouth relaxed, as if his long dream-trek had finally ended. And he slept. That night, his fever broke. Pillows and blankets were soaked through with perspiration.

"Praise the Lawd," Dinah said reverently. "Praise the Lawd!"

He wasn't really conscious yet, but there was hope.

The girls were finally allowed to see him. Warm-hearted Jenny was immediately concerned over his condition. Kirsten, too, though for an entirely different reason. His recovery made a return to Memphis more likely, and there was something she intended to take with her.

"Do you think he will live, Mama?"

"We hope so."

"If he does, what happens to us? Will we have to leave?"

"We will be staying here."

"But if he throws us out?"

"We are staying here!"

Kirsten had noticed her mother seemed to be different lately. There was a strange obstinate look to her mouth when she spoke of staying that indicated nothing would ever move her from this spot.

Jenny, too, would rather die than leave. But Kirsten had other plans, and St. Germain's improvement was scary. She thought of nothing but the cache she had found buried on the front lawn.

What if St. Germain were the one who had hidden it there? Or he might have left instructions for someone to hide it: *If there's trouble, bury the silver and jewelry so many paces from here, so many from there—*

Every night she had dreams of finding an empty, yawning hole, her treasure gone.

Putting on the warmest clothing she could find, and wrapping herself in a heavy woolen cloak she had found in the master bedroom, Kirsten went out into the front yard to check. It was a strange white world, like a blanket filled with humps and bumps, indicating the presence of shrubs. She paced off the distances, pinpointing the treasure, then realized her footprints gave it away.

Crisscrossing the whole lawn in the same manner, she found a spot at a distance, and kicked at the snow with the toe of her boot.

Below the snow's surface was a layer of ice. The ground was frozen. Even if she could manage to dig up the valuables, she would never be able to make her way to Memphis in this bitter weather. She would have to wait until spring.

If the man lives, she thought with satisfaction, he'll still be weak for a long time. And it would take two good arms to handle a shovel, lift the chest. There would be no problem.

Inga, looking for Kirsten, found her older daughter wandering in the front yard, and her heart warmed to her. The girl had always been exempt from the heavier farmwork. But she had cleared the lawn all by herself, and obviously had discovered the satisfaction of a job well done. Now she was probably dreaming of the spring, when the grass, freed of briar and weed, would reappear and the flowers bloom.

19

Theron St. Germain did not rouse the day the fever broke, but Dinah was undaunted, hovering over him like a mother hen.

"Jes look how much better his color is! An' he's breathin' easier. He jes sleepin' now. Lawd, what that man been through, no wonder!"

Inga listened as the old black woman boasted of her master's exploits. Dinah skirted lightly and scornfully over St. Germain's marriage, erasing the vague ghost of his former wife with the sweep of a black hand.

When the war began, St. Germain had gathered his own troop, training them, outfitting them. They had ridden off together. "Didn' take no white trash, neither. Massa Theron had no use for white trash. Believed in stickin' with his own kind."

Inga began to form a picture of a tall, broad-

136

shouldered, autocratic man, master of himself and all he surveyed, contemptuous of weakness. How miserable he must have been in his marriage; how difficult prison must have been for him. And now, having lost a war, his wife, and his status as a Southern aristocrat, what would his attitude be?

Once more Dinah and Caleb took turns sitting with the sick man through the night. Inga took her stint in the early morning; Caleb went to milk, Dinah to prepare breakfast.

The fire on the hearth had been replenished. Looking into the leaping flames, Inga lost herself in her favorite dream, a dream in which Sweethome became a veritable garden. She was certain fresh fruit and vegetables could be sold in Memphis. Caleb had mended a broken cart. They had the horse, less decrepit-looking now that it had fattened on the land. Perhaps they could plant a money crop, haul it to market.

She thought wistfully of the fields that stretched to the horizon. Cotton would be at a premium now. But as Dinah said, it required too many hands, and it was not a familiar crop to Inga. Regretfully she discarded the notion. Perhaps corn?

She turned toward the bed, flushing. Suddenly she felt that St. Germain was watching her, seeing into her mind. But his eyes were closed. It had only been her guilt, she supposed. This was his home. He would make the decisions. Except for one. She would insist upon her share, in return for the work she had done. She would not leave here, ever.

Her gaze returned to the fire and to her dream,

which included building Sweethome back into the mansion it had been.

"Who the devil are you?"

Inga jumped at the sound of a deep male voice with a strong Southern accent, and whirled to face the bed.

Theron St. Germain was awake and alert at last.

He had had a vague awareness of being surrounded by females. He had opened his eyes earlier in the morning to see a strange young woman before the fire, hair wound into a golden coronet atop her head. Certain that he was still dreaming, he shut them again and waited warily. The dream did not leave him.

He put out his one good hand, feeling the wood of the headboard. His bed. Through slitted eyes he cautiously surveyed the room—the dining room at Sweethome.

He had made it, then.

"I asked a simple question," he said again harshly. "Who are you? And what are you doing in my house?"

Inga approached the bed, still shaken by the suddenness of his waking, and tried to smile. "I am Inga Johansson. My daughters and I—we live here."

He hitched himself up on his pillows and looked at her, his eyes menacing in a dark, brooding face. "By whose authority?"

She raised her chin. "My own."

"And what the hell does that mean?"

"It means I found this place, fixed it up, filled the larder, and I plan to stay!"

"A damned squatter!"

"If you want to call it that."

His face was contorted with fury as he struggled to sit up. "I believe in chivalry, but, by God, that is carryin' it a little too far. This is my house! My home! I don't intend to have it cluttered up with trash! Get out, or I'll throw you out!"

She looked at him coldly, her gaze settling meaningfully on his pinned-up sleeve.

"I believe," she said in an icy voice, "you'll find that a little difficult to do in your present condition. Now, if you will excuse me . . ."

She left the room and hurried along the dogtrot to the kitchen and Dinah.

"Your master's awake," she told the old woman, "and back to what I assume is his usual vile-tempered self. I can't remember what I said, but I think I told him to go to hell in a very polite way."

"Uh-oh," Dinah said, her eyes rounding.

Handing the spoon with which she had been stirring the gravy to Inga, she hurried to her master's side, her face set with determination.

What words were exchanged between the older woman and Theron St. Germain, Inga had no idea, but there were no more angry outbursts. Other than that dark brooding look, which Inga assumed was his normal expression, he was scrupulously polite. She sensed a barely concealed contempt beneath his manner, and his occasional sardonic smile was worse than his scowl. When he was introduced to Kirsten and Jenny, his only acknowledgment was a slight inclination of the head. Then he turned away.

Kirsten ignored him, but Jenny was hurt.

"Why doesn't he like us, Mama?" she asked later.

"Don't worry about it. Remember, he isn't well," Inga said. It wasn't that at all, she thought bitterly. The man was an unmitigated snob! He considered them beneath him, and intended to treat them like dirt until he could rid himself of them.

Well, it wasn't going to work. She had lived for years under the domination of a hating man, but her days of submissiveness were over. In this case, Theron St. Germain was in her debt, and it would be he who had to pay.

Within a few days he was sitting up. He had insisted on being shaved, and the removal of the beard revealed a strong jaw, a cleft chin. His mouth, healing now from the effects of his trek through the blizzard, was firm, yet surprisingly tender. Caleb had brought down Theron's robe. Its red velvet, with black accents, set off his dark good looks in a way that finally caught Kirsten's attention.

It was a pity about his arm, she thought. If he were only a whole man—but then, he had been a hero!

Theron ignored the girl, and that in itself was a challenge. She dressed with great care, and insisted on hanging about, dusting the room, poking up the fire, certain that he would finally notice her—and wondering, with a little thrill, what would happen when he did. He was such a strong, silent man.

Kirsten was in the dining room when Inga brought him a breakfast tray. Dinah had made his favorites, scrambling two of their precious eggs. There was ham with red-eye gravy, and fluffy biscuits with fresh-churned butter.

"Massa goin' like this," she had told Inga.

Instead, he picked up a fork and stared at it, then threw it across the room.

"It's evident who prepared this tray," he growled. "Dinah would know better than to send me common kitchen ware."

Inga picked up the fork, wiped it on her apron, and plopped it back on the tray.

"I told you! I will not use these utensils!"

"Then eat with your fingers!"

They glared at each other for a moment; then he said, "Send Dinah to me."

Dinah explained that the silver had disappeared, along with the missus' jewelry and other valuables. She had given Boy's folks, her son and daughter-in-law, instructions to hide it before they ran. But she guessed they didn't have time. It was gone.

Observing the look of pain on St. Germain's face, Kirsten exulted. He knew nothing about the location of her treasure. She needn't be in any hurry to act. She could wait until spring.

Theron looked at the fork with distaste, then lifted a bite of scrambled eggs to his lips, sure they would taste of tin. But he remembered those terrible days as a prisoner at Fort Delaware, stale crackers, bacon green with mold, water filled with organisms, living and dead. Changing his mind, he lifted his eyes to Dinah. "Thank you," he said.

Dinah went back to the kitchen, walking on air. "Mebbe Massa Theron goin' turn out to be human after all."

20

In the days that followed, Theron St. Germain's health improved slowly—too slowly to suit that gentleman. There was an air of brooding about him, and a barely suppressed anger that kept the household in a state of nerves.

He resented his helplessness in a house of women, and especially hated Dinah's new air of independence. She told him flatly that she didn't intend to put up with his ordering her around anymore. Therefore, only Caleb was allowed to wait on him, to help him when he took his first few shuffling steps. The old man was called upon constantly, to fetch and carry, to stoke up the fire, to bring a pillow to put behind the wounded shoulder, to light St. Germain's pipe.

Caleb's rheumatism was aggravated by the cold winter weather. Some days, he was hard put to hobble from his cabin to the house. Seeing the old man, lame himself, tending so slavishly to his master's needs, bothered Inga. She had to admit that her patience was growing a little thin.

Finally, after the invalid sent the black man outside and up the exposed staircase for the tenth time on some unnecessary errand, Inga lost her temper.

"You are to go to your cabin," she told Caleb, "and to bed. I will have Dinah bring you a warming pan."

"Now, see here, Mrs. Johansson!" St. Germain's face was red with anger. "You and your daughters may have forced your way into my household, but I still give the orders to my own slaves!"

"I wasn't aware that you had any slaves," Inga said crisply. "And I resent you giving orders to . . . to my friend!"

"Ah's awright, missus," Caleb said anxiously. "Don' worry 'bout me."

"I *am* worrying," Inga said quietly. "That's why I'm suggesting you go—now!"

Caught between two strong wills, the old man ducked his head in submission. "Yassum. Ah does whut yo' tells me."

He left the room and Theron St. Germain was beside himself with fury. "I need him, dammit! If you think I'm going to let you women look after me, you're a fool!"

Inga's blue gaze was scornful as she glared at him. "And if you can't see Caleb's sick, *you're* a fool! There's no reason for an eighty-year-old man to run his legs off for a . . . a self-centered, self-pitying jackass! Either accept my help or take care of yourself! I'll be in the kitchen."

Two hours later, St. Germain meekly asked Inga for a glass of water. There was no more mention of Caleb, and the old man had a chance to recuperate in the warmth of his little cabin.

When, with the advent of better weather, Caleb was up and about, St. Germain did not request his services again, but was so moody and gloomy that it affected the spirits of those around him. Kirsten languished in her room. Jenny and Boy were out in the woods and fields despite the cold. And Inga was acutely miserable. She was determined to live on here, but life had to be bearable.

She thought with nostalgia of her own home as a child. Her father had been strict, authoritative. But her mother was warm and loving, comforting them with the old traditions she had brought from Sweden . . .

With a start, Inga realized that it was almost December 15, Advent, the beginning of the holidays Birgitta had observed so carefully with rituals that had brightened the lives of her children.

Inga wondered if Jenny would help her to revive those traditions.

On the morning of the fifteenth, Inga rose early, putting on a simple blue-gray gown with a fresh white apron, and hurried to the kitchen. Breakfast was already prepared when Dinah arrived. Caleb brought in a pail of milk and Inga took it from him, laughing as she saw Boy slip past and into Jenny's room.

The milk should be strained, she told Dinah, but

144

it could wait. Right now there was something more important to do.

Inga led the two blacks into the small breakfast room and seated them in their usual places. Then she went down the hall and called up the staircase for Kirsten.

She returned to bend over the sleeping St. Germain, thinking how different he looked as he slept, his face wiped clear of cares. Impulsively she smoothed back his dark hair from his forehead.

"Mr. St. Germain," she said, "wake up. Breakfast is waiting."

He opened startled eyes, to see what looked like the face of an angel bending over him. For a moment a thrill of need ran through him, a feeling he thought he had forgotten long ago. Then he remembered this was not a woman, but a damned Yankee, an intruder in his home.

His face closed against her.

"I shall eat when I am ready," he told her.

"You will eat now. And you are going to come to the table! Sit up!"

She was holding his robe, and he slid his good arm into its sleeve before he realized what he'd done.

"Now, stand!"

"I don't know what the hell you're doing, but . . . Send Caleb to me!"

"Caleb is occupied. Stand!"

He rose shakily to his feet and she lifted his arm around her shoulders. Again he felt an odd sensation, the warmth of her body against his own, the softness of her.

"For the love of God, woman!"

145

"Come!"

He was trembling with weakness—and something more—as she led him to the breakfast room and helped him sit. And there he received a further shock.

"What the devil are the nigras doing here!"

"They live here," Inga said caustically, "just as you do. They take their meals with us."

He turned on her. "If this is your idea, by God—"

"Set down, Massa Theron."

St. Germain's gaze shifted to Dinah's implacable black features, and he obeyed.

He opened his mouth, but before he could speak, Kirsten appeared. And then, behind her, Jenny, a slender dark girl in a white robe, her hair crowned with a wreath of holly, leaves interspersed with candles. She was followed by Boy, his black face split in a grin. He, too, wore a white robe. But on his woolly little head was a pointed cap with stars on it.

"What the hell . . . ?"

"It is our custom," Inga explained. "At the beginning of our Christmas holiday, the youngest daughter—in this case, Jenny—represents Santa Lucia. Boy is a 'star boy.' They will sing for us, and then Jenny will serve our breakfast."

The song they sang was in Swedish, Jenny's clear sweet voice carrying Boy as he stumbled over some of the words she had taught him. But it was a creditable performance. Inga was proud of them both.

As the smiling girl, walking straight-backed to hold the candles steady, placed the meal before them, Inga listed the items, one by one.

"Brod och smor. Pytt i panna. Mjolk. Bakelser."

Bread and butter. Hash with potatoes. Milk. A flaky pastry, light as a cloud.

But Inga's effort to lighten the atmosphere was a failure. St. Germain's discomfort was only matched by that of Caleb and Dinah. The two blacks kept their heads down and ate little.

Finally St. Germain stood, supporting himself on the table's edge. "I think I've had enough! Caleb!"

"Yessuh!"

The old man sprang up with alacrity and hobbled to his master's side, helping him back to the dining room and his chair before the fire.

Later, Theron St. Germain took Inga to task. She had broken one of the most stringent rules of polite society. Slaves did not sit at the table with their masters.

Her face flamed with sudden anger. "I believe we went through all this before, sir! Dinah and Caleb are not slaves! They are human beings! And you're not going to tell me who can sit at my table!"

"My table," he reminded her.

"Your table," she raged, "and my food! I grew it. I cook it, and you eat it!"

She was so beautiful in her anger that he felt the need to justify himself.

"You don't understand. We must conduct ourselves according to Southern custom—"

"And your South is dead! Defeated! It's as dead as slavery! There's no sense in hanging onto something that is dead and gone!"

St. Germain's face was hard, cold, nostrils flar-

147

ing as he gave her a long straight look and turned away.

"I am glad you reminded me," he said dryly. "And it appears you are also hanging onto customs of your own. In case you have any idiotic notions in regard to Christmas, forget them. The South has nothing to celebrate."

That, Inga thought, was his opinion! And she intended to enjoy the holiday season in spite of him. On the long summer evenings, after the chores were done, she had planned ahead, as always, for Christmas, making gifts for her daughters, for Dinah, Caleb, and Boy. They had been completed long ago. But there was still plenty of woolen yarn in the sewing room. She would make something for Theron St. Germain, even if it gave him apoplexy! That night, she began to knit.

During the day, she prepared a feast: cookies, a Christmas fruit cake; molasses taffy. She cooked for days in the kitchen beyond St. Germain's realm. On the night before Christmas, she put a huge ham in the oven over a a low fire. In the morning she would glaze it with preserves.

She and Jenny rose very early to decorate the breakfast room with cedar boughs and winter berries. And then, everything completed, Jenny rang the bell.

"Christmas gifts," Inga sang out gaily, and the others came running. "Christmas gifts!"

Her presents were highly successful, except for one.

Theron St. Germain refused to join them at the table, and looked at the lap robe she had made with distaste. "This is for an invalid," he said. "Which I am not."

Inga lifted inquiring brows. "Indeed? Then perhaps you should try to care for yourself, and not behave like one!"

The master of the household ate a lonely meal at a table shoved against the wall in the dining room, the lap robe over his knees. While from the breakfast room came the sounds of the soft, lilting Swedish and Southern black accents commingled, along with laughter he hoped was not at his expense.

21

St. Germain's disposition did not improve, but after Inga's remarks about his invalidism, he began to take steps to help himself. Soon he was able to walk about the house unaided. His body was beginning to fill out again, and in his regular clothing—restored by Dinah's patient cleaning—he was once again Theron St. Germain, master of Sweethome.

Dinah brought a new problem to Inga's attention. "That gal of yours is sweet on Massa Theron."

"Kirsten?"

Inga stared at the black woman in disbelief. But watching closely for a while, she had to admit that Dinah was right. Kirsten evidently spent most of each night altering the few clothes the man's former wife had left behind. Each day, she wore something different or arranged her hair a different way. The braids she had once worn in emulation of her mother disappeared. Now her golden locks were arranged in a cascade of curls. She also had found a cache of cosmetic aids that belonged to the dead woman. She smelled of scent, and at times Inga wondered if the rosy blush that tinted her cheeks was her own.

It was only natural, Inga told herself, for Kirsten to be attracted to the man. She was at an age when she was beginning to feel urges she probably didn't understand herself.

St. Germain's dark, brooding good looks were enough to turn any woman's head. But St. Germain was older, experienced, maimed. He needed a mature wife, someone who would be understanding, yet firm enough to set him straight when he needed it.

With horror Inga realized she was thinking of herself in that role. She could never marry, not with her great sin on her soul! And if she did, Theron St. Germain would be the last man she would consider! But were her thoughts toward her own daughter tinged with jealousy?

"Massa Theron want his bed moved back up tuh his own room," Dinah said. "Ah wuz wonderin', whut with Missie Kirsten sleepin' up there in the other missus' room, if it wuz propah?"

"Indeed it wouldn't be! She'll just have to go back to sleeping in the study!"

"Ah figgahed y'd say that." Dinah grinned as if she had secret thoughts, and walked away.

Inga looked after her helplessly. Indeed, she was only considering the propriety of having a susceptible young girl in close proximity to a man she admired.

Evidently Kirsten thought otherwise. Informed that she would have to move downstairs, the girl flew into a rage, accusing Inga of wanting the prettily decorated room that had been Mrs. St. Germain's for herself.

"That isn't true, Kirsten! I wouldn't be comfortable there."

"Then maybe you're afraid Theron will look twice at me," Kirsten blurted.

Inga, goaded beyond endurance, slapped her elder daughter. Kirsten burst into tears and fled.

Within an hour, she had her new wardrobe moved downstairs. But she wasn't speaking to her mother.

January passed, fraught with the cold breath of winter. February brought a few warm days, and St. Germain took to walking the grounds at the rear of the house.

There, he could almost believe everything was as it once had been. He could look at the untended fields and dream that, by some miracle, they would be brought back to their original condition. He closed his eyes and saw acres of cotton running to the sky, blacks dragging their long tow sacks, singing as they picked white gold to be baled and taken to market.

Those days of plenty would never come again, for himself at Sweethome, or for any other plantation in the South. With no slaves, no money to hire help, the cotton kingdom was doomed.

The front of the house had always been his favorite place to walk, but now he stayed clear of it as much as possible. The standing pillars, with nothing to support, were a token of Sweethome's ruin. This place was like himself. They were both amputees; part of a house, part of a man.

March brought a greening of the earth, leaf buds shaken into being by a sudden wind, a blooming of crocus and forsythia. One evening, wishing to avoid Inga and the blacks who were working to turn the garden out back, and drawn by what might have been a need to dwell upon his pain, St. Germain rounded the house and walked to the bridge that spanned the creek.

He stood there for a long time, leaning on the rail, looking down into the water that, now high from melted snow, was running deep and fast. He wondered how long a one-armed man would survive in such waters. Or if he could survive. And if he would want to.

His face was still dark with misery as he left the bridge to start back. Then he stopped suddenly, spotting a mound near the tulip tree, a mound that hadn't been there before, with a flat board set into it at an angle, making it look like a grave.

He walked toward it and studied it. Anger welled inside him like a volcano as the words burned on the board were etched into his brain: "HERE LIES THERON ST. GERMAIN."

That damned woman and her daughters! They had been so certain he wouldn't come back!

He returned to the rear of the house with long, purposeful strides, tore the shovel from Inga's fingers with such force that they were numbed, and tossed it to the ground. Then, clasping her arm with his one hand, he dragged her around to the tulip tree near the bridge.

Still clutching her with bruising strength, he inclined his head toward the makeshift tombstone. "What is the meaning of this?"

"I . . . I intended to remove that," she faltered. "I had forgotten."

"Remove it? Why? So I wouldn't find it? So I wouldn't learn how low you would stoop to steal my property? Or should I compliment you on your cleverness?"

"I don't understand."

"You just moved in, set up housekeeping. And you were sure I wouldn't return, weren't you? So you faked this . . . this damned grave, in case anybody came along asking questions."

"Massa Theron, suh, you hesh yo' mouf!"

Dinah, seeing the murderous fury in St. Germain's eyes, had followed them. She stood a few feet away, threateningly, shaking the hoe she held in her hand.

"Them's bones in that grave! An' they wearin' a gray uniform! They found 'im, an' they reckon he you! They lay him down proper-like!"

"Is that true?" St. Germain's eyes were troubled and contrite as he looked at Inga, his temper gone.

But her own had risen. Snatching the hoe from Dinah, she presented it to him, slamming it into his one remaining hand. "If you don't think it is, start digging!" she snapped, and returned to her garden.

That night, unable to sleep for the anger that still boiled inside her, Inga walked the rear of the property, a cloak pulled around her against the evening's chill. The distant fields were a moonscape, the nearer garden a series of braided rows.

Feeling unutterably lonely, she walked toward Dinah's cabin, hoping the old black woman was still awake. She was. She could hear her singing—but it was a lullaby for Boy.

Dinah had lost her children when the young folks had run North. But at least she had someone. And Boy had a grandmother who loved him. Even old Caleb had his family—and his memories.

Her own memories, she couldn't live with. And Jenny was like a wild creature, never to be owned. While Kirsten . . . Kirsten seemed to hate her more each day.

Shaking her head in bewilderment, Inga started back toward the house, then, on impulse, rounded it. She wondered if St. Germain had really dug up the grave, as she had challenged him to do. She wouldn't put it past him!

She reached the tulip tree. The board had been removed and was lying on the grass, but the mound was still intact. Tomorrow she would ask Jenny to make another marker. It would say "UNKNOWN." And perhaps "REST IN PEACE."

Her cheeks were wet with tears. She was crying for a soldier who died alone—perhaps with someone, somewhere, to mourn him—and for herself, feeling alone and forsaken. A dark figure stepped out of the shadows.

"Mrs. Johansson? Inga . . ." Theron St. Germain approached her and put out a wondering finger to touch her glistening cheeks. "Tears? For someone you don't know?"

She remained mutinously silent, and he sighed.

"I'm not the poor devil buried there, but I might have been. And if I were, I would have needed those tears. There would have been no one else to shed them. I'd like to thank you on that man's behalf—and to beg your forgiveness."

Inga looked up at him. His mouth was tender, as it appeared in sleep. The night-dark eyes, in this mood, held an amber light. And suddenly she found it very difficult to breathe.

"Mr. . . . Mr. St. Germain—"

"Theron," he interrupted her.

"Th-Theron . . ."

Once begun, she could think of nothing to say. He said it for her. Leaning forward, he brushed her lips with his own, a contact that made her heart skip, sent the blood surging through her veins until she began to tremble.

"That," he said, "is also on his behalf." He gestured again toward the grave. "In case he had no one to say good-bye to when he died."

Taking her arm, he led her back to the house and to the door beneath the winding stairs. And there he kissed her again, an urgent kiss that burned her mouth and into her very soul.

"That one," he said wryly, finally drawing away, "I cannot explain. Except I did it because I wanted to."

Then he left her. She watched him climb the stair, holding to the rail with his one hand, a tall, imposing figure in the moonlight, the dark and brooding master of Sweethome.

22

Inga's heart was beating so wildly when she went to bed that she was certain she faced a wakeful night. Instead she slept the sweetest sleep she had ever known. In her dreams a man held her close. He had only one arm, but that was quite sufficient.

And in her dreams, his mouth brushed hers in a feather touch that aroused all the yearning in her long-denied body. It was followed by another kiss that left her weak. Floating high above the bed, looking down—

Down upon a woman with flaxen braids, clasped in a dark man's arms. Her mother and the lover of long ago? The man who had been her father? No, no . . .

She woke burning with desire—and guilt. The man's actions had been nothing but a sort of apology. She thought of Nick Tremont, the way she had given herself to him so easily. It had not been love, but need. She knew that, but occasionally the wonder of it had returned to haunt her.

She had never known passion with Olaf, nor realized it was missing from their relationship. Now, love-starved, she was reading something into a simple kiss. At least, she thought wryly, with Theron St. Germain her feelings made little difference. He could have no affection for a woman who was a Northerner, and, if he but knew it, a bastard—and a murderess.

Finally she rose, dressed, and went to help Dinah, only to find that St. Germain had gone.

Dinah was fuming. "He jes took the horse and rode off, say he's goin' to Memphis. Man sick as he been got no business goin' off on a wild-goose chase! They's some woman behin' all this," she said direly.

No doubt, Inga thought, tight-lipped. The aristocratic lord of the manor had had a weak moment last night, and was afraid to face her. Not only had he chosen the coward's way out, he had taken the animal that pulled the plow, just when it was needed most.

"With luck," Inga said bitterly, "maybe he won't come back."

"You don' mean that, missus!" Dinah sounded shocked, and Inga forced a weary smile.

"No," she said, "I don't. Not really."

"Didn' figger you did!"

They finished breakfast and went to their work, planting the ground that was readied. Kirsten pouted in the house. If Theron St. Germain went to Memphis, he could have taken the cart, so she could have ridden along with him. She had dropped enough hints regarding her loneliness here, her desire to see the city once more.

And they could have stopped at night, built a campfire. She envisioned herself standing over it, cooking a meal for him. And afterward . . .

Afterward they would sit by that fire, beneath the stars. Then the evening would grow cool and they would probably have to share their blankets. . . . And then—

"Kirsten!" Her mother's voice broke into her daydream.

Inga needed help. The windlass on the well had broken, and Caleb was repairing it. Dinah, who had stepped on the rake tines, had gone to her cabin to soak her foot. The cow had wandered off and Jenny and Boy had gone in search of it.

"I cleared the weeds in front again," Kirsten said mutinously.

"Yes, but now we have to get the garden in," Inga explained patiently.

"My father said I'd never have to do that sort of work. If I'd married Oskar—"

Inga wiped a dirt-smeared hand across her forehead and straightened her tired shoulders. "If you do not work," she said in a tight voice, "you do not eat!"

Inga left the house and, after a time, Kirsten followed to drag a rake desultorily across the furrows so her mother could plant the seed that would sustain them through the winter.

And Kirsten just might not be there to share it! If St. Germain didn't deign to notice she existed, she would be long gone! Leaning on the rake handle, she drifted into a daydream in which she was surrounded by eligible men, and Theron, realizing what he had missed, was brokenhearted. . . .

The days dragged by in much the same manner. Dinah's foot was infected following her injury. Caleb's rheumatism returned to plague him. Kirsten dawdled through the working hours. And finally Theron St. Germain returned.

The trip had drained his strength. That much was evident, for his face was gray, his eyes dark and impenetrable.

He handed the reins of the horse to Caleb and went directly to his room without speaking to anyone. The expedition had been a nightmare.

Memphis, the beautiful city once a symbol of the South's affluence, had deteriorated under Union occupation. The enormous cotton sheds on Main Street stood empty. Four regiments of black soldiers, numbering four thousand, patrolled the city. And through it swarmed the pseudo-politicians, the carpetbaggers, the grafters, spreading corruption.

St. Germain had seen a white woman, a lady, knocked to the street by an arrogant black man importantly shuffling through a sheaf of papers. As Theron St. Germain moved to the woman's defense, he heard her admonishing her children, "Don't tell Papa. If you do, he will kill the nigra, and the Yankees will hang him."

Even more devastating was the plight of the former slaves who stood about homeless, starving, awaiting the blessings freedom was supposed to bring them. Their ranks had doubled in number. On the fringes were the Confederate soldiers left rootless after the war's end—ragged, maimed, wolfish-looking creatures who slunk into doorways when Union officers passed.

St. Germain wove his way through the crowded streets, making his first stop at the courthouse, where he learned the worst.

Lands throughout this area of Tennessee were being gobbled up, either to pay off debts or because they had been deserted by the men who had gone to war. They were being parceled out to homeless blacks or sold to Union officers with a desire to settle there.

The last purchase Theron St. Germain had made before he went to battle was a large block of uncultivated land that adjoined the front of his property to the west. So many times, he had made his way over the bridge that spanned the river, crossed the lane that separated Sweethome from his newly acquired acres, dreaming of how he would plant that land when the conflict was over, making fields of cotton that reached to the sky.

Now that dream would never be realized. Sweethome was safe, but Marnie Lee, his wife, had not kept up the payments on the other property in his absence. He supposed she had used the money to maintain a Memphis residence before her death.

The land had been sold to someone by the name of Matthew Weldon. Captain Matthew Weldon.

"A Yankee?"

The clerk who provided the information flushed. "I presume so."

"You bastard! You know damn well it's so!"

St. Germain got his temper under control and went to find someone who could help him regain his property. He located his old general, Bedford Forrest, who had recouped his fortunes by housing more than one thousand black women and children on an island—President's Island, which he owned. Confederate that he was, Forrest was still a power in Memphis.

But the general could do nothing for St. Germain. His eyes watered as he explained that he received sometimes as many as a hundred letters a day from his old soldiers and friends, letters telling of injustice and hardship, theft, women being ravished by roving bands of renegades.

Forrest tried to send money when it was needed. But as for St. Germain's problem—land seized for just payment—there was nothing he could do.

Theron St. Germain went home to sit in his room and brood.

Dinah was worried. In spite of her newfound emancipation, she carried hot meals up the winding stairs, limping on her wounded foot. Caleb, too, creaked his way up and down, tending to the man's needs.

"He don' do nothin'," Dinah said. "Don' say nothin'. Jus' sets an' looks out the window."

After three days of such pervasive gloom, Inga had had enough. She wrested a tray from Dinah's unwilling hands and made her way up the steps. Receiving no answer to her knock, she walked in and set the tray down with a bang on a small table.

St. Germain turned from his position at the window, startled for a moment out of his gloom.

"Your lunch," Inga said, gesturing toward it. "And the last one you get unless you pull your share of the load!"

Still shaken, he stared at her, putting a hand to the empty sleeve. "I don't understand. I cannot—"

"You can, and you will! Caleb's plowing an extension of the garden. You can plant."

"Gentlemen," he said icily, "do not work alongside nigra field hands."

She felt a hot wave of anger rising, and remembered her altercation with Kirsten. "Then there is one gentleman who won't eat." She shoved the tray toward the edge of the table. "Enjoy it. It just might be your last meal."

23

St. Germain did not appear for the evening meal, nor for breakfast the next morning. Dinah was extremely agitated by Inga's refusal to allow her to take something to him.

"Men folkses gotta eat," she said, pleating her apron with nervous fingers. "Gotta keep up they stren'th."

"Mr. St. Germain isn't exerting himself," Inga said shortly. She dried the last dish, and they headed for the garden.

They had been working only a short while when Inga became conscious of the fact that someone was watching her. She turned to see Theron St. Germain standing at the edge of the furrows. He finally made his way toward her, his face like a thundercloud.

"Would you care to show me what to do?"

She demonstrated how to plant the corn by dropping the seed into holes a certain distance apart, three grains to the hole, then tamping it down with her foot. Filling his pocket with grain, she went on about her business.

The simple process was slow work for him. He punched the holes with a stick, which he then had to hold under the stump of his arm until he had dropped the seed and could move on. Caleb, who had started at the beginning of the row, soon caught up to him. He said something to his master, and St. Germain chuckled.

Inga looked back to see master and former slave working side by side, indulging in what appeared to be pleasant conversation.

She and Dinah quit early and went to wash up and prepare lunch. When they called the others in, St. Germain took his place with them at the table. His eyes were clear again, with that amber light Inga had seen earlier. Black hair tumbled over a forehead that was smudged with a streak of dirt. He suddenly looked so virile, so masculine, so appealing.

And he was clearly enjoying himself.

"Yes, I remember Maum Sukey," he said to Caleb. "She belonged to my folks when I was a kid."

"Member how one eye look one way, one the othah?"

"I remember."

"Well, this buck niggah, he figgah she got the evil eye. Maum Sukey had these li'l gals, an' he wuz shinin' up tuh one, an' she catched him in the act. He tuk off runnin' thu the yard, wid Maum

Sukey behin' him, yellin', 'Wait, heah's yo' pants.' He run smack-dab intuh de preachah!''

Theron St. Germain laughed, the first genuine laugh Inga had heard from him. It was rich, deep, heartfelt mirth. And for a moment she had a glimpse of the young man he once had been.

Toward the end of the meal, however, he seemed sunk in thought again. The eyes he lifted to those around him were veiled.

"I have to tell you what I learned in Memphis. I've lost the property across the creek. It was purchased by a Union officer."

"Then," Inga said briskly, "we must make do with what we have. Everybody ready to go back to work?"

As the days passed, too quickly for what had to be done, there was a shifting of duties. Kirsten sent old Caleb on ahead and worked beside St. Germain, dimpling up at him as she dropped her seed corn, tamping it with a dainty heel, in the process raising her petticoats to reveal an ankle.

Inga, across the garden, itched to take her daughter into the house and . . . and paddle her. But she could not help noting that St. Germain didn't seem averse to the girl's attentions.

Indeed, he wasn't. Theron enjoyed having the pretty girl, with the flaxen hair and creamy complexion so like her mother's, chattering beside him. It was a pity that she didn't have more of Inga's characteristics, he thought. But Kirsten kept him occupied, kept him from watching the older woman who bent to her work with the grace of a willow.

"You are very quiet, Mr. St. Germain," Kirsten

said. "I'm hoping that the loss of your property doesn't trouble you too much."

"I think that the notion of it falling into the hands of a Yankee bothers me most," he said quietly. "I couldn't have planted it. I can't even plant the acres left to me without slaves. I'd give my soul to be able to rebuild Sweethome, to have it all as it once was."

He paused a moment, looking out over the weed-grown fields, heartache in his eyes. Then Inga approached, bringing a dipper and a bucket of water cool from the well.

St. Germain drank thirstily, then thanked Inga, an expression on his face that irritated Kirsten.

All that gratitude for a drink of water! And he looked like he might be interested in her mother. He couldn't be! Her mother was old! She had had one husband!

Kirsten thought of her father, Olaf Johansson, lying in a pool of blood. Her mother had killed him! She could not forget that. Besides, if anyone could make Theron St. Germain's dreams come true, she, Kirsten, could! She thought of the secret she hugged to herself, the untold wealth buried in the front yard, that only she knew how to find.

That night after dinner, St. Germain suggested Kirsten take her mother's place at doing up the dishes. He and Inga were going for a walk. Inga protested, but succumbed, blushing, when he reached out his one hand to pull the tie of her apron strings.

"Here," he said, handing the apron to Kirsten. "We will see you later."

Kirsten, her hands blistered from pulling on a

167

rake, was now forced to thrust them into soapy dishwater. Anger at her mother swelled inside her brain. And Theron had treated her like a child! Well, she was not one. And she would prove it to him.

Together Theron St. Germain and Inga walked toward the little bridge. As they passed the grave of the unknown soldier they saw three sprigs of forsythia tied with ribbon that Jenny had surely put there.

They walked on to stand at the bridge's railing and look down into the rushing creek. Inga thought with nostalgia of the clear running streams at home. Here the water was much like Theron—dark and impenetrable; one had the feeling it was hiding secrets.

"I would like to tell you something about myself," St. Germain said, as if he had guessed at her thoughts.

He launched into the story of a little boy with a powerful father, a delicate mother, slaves to tend his every whim. He had been brought up by a set of rules: he must remember that he was an aristocrat, not associate with the common class.

"Like me," Inga said.

He touched her cheek with a gentle hand. "Like you," he said, and he made it sound like a compliment.

Theron's parents had died shortly after his marriage. He had known his wife as a child, and they married because they were expected to. It was only later that he learned she was in love with

168

her cousin and that she could not adjust to plantation life.

And then the war.

He told Inga of the horrors he had mumbled of in his delirium, of his men dropping around him like fallen leaves, before he himself was wounded. He had been taken to Fort Delaware, that most terrible of Northern prisons, situated on an island in the river.

There he was interrogated, hammered at, and finally put to pulling carts loaded with stone for repairing the dikes around the dismal prison, working like a beast linked with other beasts, Confederate prisoners, the castoffs of the Union Army—deserters, thieves, bounty jumpers, murderers.

"Our ration was four hard crackers a day," he said quietly, "and one-tenth of a pound of bacon. We washed it down with standing rainwater filled with insect larvae."

The wound in his arm had worsened, and he was unable to leave his bunk. Then one day they had come to carry off the man in the bunk above him. He was dead of smallpox. The surgeon who had come to verify that fact took a look at Theron, too.

"This fellow's in a bad way. That arm's going to have to come off."

Theron began to tremble as he repeated the remembered words, his face suddenly soaked in perspiration.

Inga reached out a hand to him. "Don't!" she whispered. "It's all over. You don't need to tell me this."

He looked down at her with troubled eyes. "I

have to. I can't stand to have you think less of me. I know you see me as a spoiled, incompetent child, and perhaps I have been. It is difficult to have been reared one way, and then to have one's world turned upside down."

And, Inga thought, to come home and find it in ruins, taken over by three women from the North.

"I understand."

"I intend to try to do better," he said humbly. "But . . . help me."

"If you get out of line," she said with a forced smile, "I will try to set you straight."

He chuckled. "Just do what you've been doing. Maybe you'll make a man of me yet." She could see that his eyes were clear amber as he bent toward her. "Inga, may I kiss you?"

She shrank away, fearing that she would be lost if his lips touched hers. "No, please—"

"Then," he said, wryly, "perhaps you won't mind if I hold your hand on the way back to the house. This"—he flexed his one good arm—"has grown so accustomed to working that it feels strange with nothing to do."

She reached out to him, laughing, and he caught her hand. As they left the bridge and walked across the grass—crushing the tender blades beneath their feet, the scent of spring rising around them—their faces had a youthful glow.

When they entered the kitchen, Inga's rosy cheeks and St. Germain's oddly gentle expression did not go unobserved by Kirsten. She wiped the soapsuds from her hands, removed her apron, and fled to her room. She was almost finished anyway! Let her mother do the kettles!

Lying awake in bed, Kirsten began to plan. She would show Theron St. Germain she wasn't a child! She could give him something her mother couldn't! She could give him Sweethome as it used to be.

24

In the morning, Kirsten begged off the gardening work by explaining that she had found a young crabapple tree—a volunteer had come up beside an older gnarled one—and wanted to plant it in the front yard. She knew the exact spot!

"I'll dig the hole foh you, missie," old Caleb said. "That's too hard work foh a young lady."

Kirsten gave him an enchanting smile. "Why, thank you, Caleb. But you see, I feel the front lawn is mine. I've worked at it so hard that I'd like to finish it."

It was true, Inga thought. The girl had taken such pride in her work, she should be allowed the feeling it was her creation. They could manage without her.

Kirsten left the others and rounded the house, shovel in hand. She could find her treasure with her eyes shut. To prove it, she aligned her body with landmarks and closed her eyes to step it off. Finally she began to dig, heart in mouth as she worried that it might be gone. What if someone had come in the night and spirited it away?

Her breath was expelled in a sigh as one more shovel of earth revealed what she was seeking. Lifting out the jewels first, she held them up to watch how they caught the sunlight. On impulse, she put several expensive-looking items in her pocket. Then she replaced the remainder on top of the chest and ran around the house, calling to Theron St. Germain, "Come see what I've found!"

He came, followed by the others, to kneel at the edge of the hole she had dug.

"God in heaven," he whispered, "Marnie's jewelry! The silver! A fortune."

"Guess them rapscallions of mine done did what they was told," Dinah put in.

St. Germain stood, smiling at Inga. "Do you know what we have here? The wherewithal to rebuild Sweethome! To begin again!"

"I found it for you," Kirsten said.

"And God bless you for it!" He slipped an arm around the girl and hugged her, giving her a swift peck on the cheek. "I'll have to go to Memphis to sell this. I'll make up a list of supplies and materials tonight and leave in the morning. I'll hire some help. Dinah, if you and Boy could get a few of those cabins made presentable—"

"I want to go with you," Kirsten said.

St. Germain looked at her in surprise. "That wouldn't be possible. We'd have to spend some nights on the road. I'm sure your mother wouldn't approve."

She began to laugh, a high, humorless giggle. "Do you think Mama is a good judge of what's proper? You're going to take her word for it?"

"Kirsten!" Inga's voice cracked like a whip. "Go into the house!"

"But, Mama!"

"Go into the house!"

Kirsten backed away, then turned and ran into the house. Inga followed her into the bedroom, where the girl stood defiantly, back to the wall.

"Suppose you explain your remarks, young lady!"

"I don't have to! Anybody can see that Jenny—"

"Jenny is my child and your father's."

"I don't believe it!"

"That's up to you, Kirsten. All I can tell you is that I had never been with another man—"

"No?" The girl's voice was drawn out, insolent. "Then who was the man on the riverboat? The one you sneaked out to meet every morning? How long had you known him?"

Inga's cheeks flamed. "If you mean Mr. Tremont, he was only a shipboard acquaintance."

"And do you always sleep with casual acquaintances, let them spend the night in your room? Or only after you've murdered your husband? My father!"

Inga's face was white now, completely drained of blood as she stared at the girl who was her elder daughter. Her hand was drawn back to strike, but she dropped it to her side.

"I'm not going to hit you," she said flatly, "though

it would give me great pleasure to do so. Just don't . . . don't provoke me too far!"

As she turned to leave, Kirsten called after her, "You don't need to think Theron's interested in you! It's me! Me! I found his jewels and his silver for him! And he's not going to forget it. So keep away from him!"

The door slammed against her tirade.

When Inga returned to the front yard, Theron looked at her strangely. "What was the matter with Kirsten?"

Inga shrugged. "She was upset because she wanted to go to Memphis. You know how young girls are."

Actually, Theron thought, he did understand. Marnie had not been as young as Kirsten, but her behavior had been similar. He sighed and put the incident out of his mind.

Inga could not. Kirsten was in such a rebellious mood, Inga feared it was only a matter of time until she went to Theron with her damning accusations. And, suddenly it was very important that he not believe them.

Maybe if she went to him herself, told him her story . . .

But what could she say? She had killed Olaf. And she had slept with Nick Tremont. Kirsten had said nothing that wasn't the truth.

Inga didn't sleep that night, and the next morning, Theron was gone.

Caleb's rheumatism still gave him problems. Dinah's foot was bothering her again so she kept to her cabin with Boy to fetch and carry. The only major chore remaining was that of cleaning the cabins for the help Theron planned to bring from Memphis.

Her mind still whirling with conflicting emotions regarding St. Germain, Inga took that chore for herself. She knew that unless she worked to the point of exhaustion, she would not be able to sleep this night, either.

Jenny offered to help, but Inga had seen the wistful expression in her eyes as she looked toward tree and field. There was no reason Jenny shouldn't have a brief respite, now that the garden was in. Inga told her she'd call if she needed help.

Jenny, set free, wandered far and wide, missing Boy, her usual companion. She visited the spring-fed pool where she had found the body of the soldier they buried. And finally she came to the rail fence that divided two properties.

It wouldn't hurt to go closer to the little house on stilts, now that Mr. St. Germain was home and they couldn't be accused of trespassing on his property.

It never occurred to Jenny to go up to the house and knock on the door. It would spoil the game she played, the game of being an Indian maiden slipping through the wood, seeing but unseen. She had even taught herself to walk as an Indian did, slightly toed in, toes down first, then heels, to avoid the crackling of a twig. Slipping through the border of trees, she moved from one to the next, then froze as she heard a man's voice in the distance.

"Gee-yap! Ho!"

Finding a vantage point in a wooded copse on a

slight hill, she was able to look down and across the fields surrounding the house. There a man was plowing, using an ox to draw the plow. But neither the ox nor the reddish clay that peeled away from the blade, so different from the earth of Sweethome, caught her attention. She could see nothing but the man.

Shirtless, his bronzed body wet with perspiration, gleamed in the sun. She caught her breath at the sight of those magnificent muscled shoulders, the thatch of yellow hair like ripe wheat, the long, strong legs clad in a pair of tight Confederate gray trousers.

Crouched among the trees, Jenny watched until the sun went down and man and ox wended their way back toward the shack and a small unpainted barn behind it. Then she rose and ran silently back to Sweethome.

She had had only the briefest glimpse of the young man's face, gilded with the setting sun as he turned from his plow to glance toward the spot where she lay hidden. But Jenny had fallen in love.

25

For a time, Jenny was unable to return to her surveillance of their neighbor. Dinah was still laid up with her injured foot, Caleb with his rheumatism, and Boy had caught a summer cold. And adhering to the rule that one disaster follows another, Inga, carrying eggs to the house, stepped into a hole and sprained her ankle.

The task of keeping the household running fell on Jenny—and Kirsten.

Jenny, despite her sudden loss of freedom, turned to it with a will, Kirsten grudgingly.

Since Inga spent her time in the kitchen with her foot propped up, in order to oversee the cooking, Kirsten, who avoided her mother whenever possible, left the kitchen work to Jenny.

Trudging through the muddy yard after a night of rain, Kirsten decided gloomily that she had cut off her nose to spite her face. Her skirts were bedraggled, her shoes leaden with mud as she went to the barn to milk the cow.

Milking was one of Jenny's favorite chores. She loved leaning her head against the cow's soft flank, inhaling the scent of warm milk and clean straw. But Kirsten could smell only the barnyard odors. And she always had the strong suspicion she had stepped in something more pungent than mud.

Plopping down on the three-legged stool, she banged the pail to the floor. The animal, which contentedly filled the pail for Jenny, was fractious, refusing to give her milk. It took Kirsten twice as long, and the pail was half-full.

Finally she took the milk to the house, handed it to Jenny at the kitchen door, and made her way to the chicken pen with a bucket of grain. Then it was time for the most detested job of all, swilling the pigs.

Filling a pail with the odorous mixture of discarded slops and grain that simmered in a covered barrel, she tried not to breathe as she slipped and slithered toward the pen. The pigs were squealing and grunting, and she was half-afraid of them. She set her jaw. Jenny said to give them two buckets of the foul-smelling concoction, but she gave them only one. It would hold them, and no one need know!

Suddenly her feet went out from under her, and as she sat down hard, the contents of the bucket spilled on her.

It was the last straw! Rising, she looked down at herself in dismay, suppressing the nausea that rose in her throat. She was through! Finished. If her mother wanted the damned pigs fed, she would just have to find someone else to do it!

Making her way toward the house, blind with anger at her plight, Kirsten didn't see what was taking place at the pen behind her. The animals, deprived of their expected rations, were hungry. One old boar lunged against the side of the pen and knocked it down. In seconds, the horde of half-grown young ones were out, running and squealing in all directions.

"Jenny!" Kirsten screamed. "Mama!"

Jenny was out the door instantly. Taking in the scene, she thrust a broomstick at Kirsten. "I'll take the ones heading toward the fields. You take those that went around the side. You'll have to get in front of them to turn them back."

Kirsten rounded the house. Most of the animals had stopped there and were rooting aimlessly in search of food. One venturesome young shoat, however, had reached the bridge, his small feet clicking on the wooden structure as he crossed it. Kirsten, behind him, waving the broomstick, spurred him on to greater speed.

For once, her petty grudges were forgotten. This was meat! Meat for winter. She didn't dare lose the animal.

It crashed through the brush at the other side of the lane, Kirsten following, briars tearing at her skirts, ripping them to shreds.

As she burst into a clearing, there was a shot. It was close! She froze.

A few yards ahead of her, the young shoat lay on

the grass, blood issuing from its nose and mouth. It was dead.

That might have been me, she thought numbly.

Coming toward her was a man in a blue uniform. She turned, poised to run, but her curiosity as to what a Union officer was doing there was almost greater than her fear.

"Wait," he shouted. "Wait."

She decided she had better obey. He had a gun.

As he drew nearer, she could see that he was smiling, his blue eyes twinkling. He was a very good-looking man; not in a romantic way, like Theron, but . . . nice.

"Hello!"

He paused in front of her to look her up and down. Kirsten was suddenly conscious of her bedraggled state. With St. Germain gone, she hadn't bothered to curl her hair, but wore it in two long plaits down her back. Her skirts were covered with swill, her shoes with mud—or worse. Seeing his nose wrinkle slightly, she leapt to the offense.

"Who are you?" she stormed. "You have no business here! Who do you think you are, coming on people's property, killing their pigs!"

His amused expression tightened. "Your pig? I thought it was wild. I'm sorry. But as to the property, it's mine."

It was the Yankee who had cheated Theron out of his land!

The man's hand was outstretched. "I would like to introduce myself. I'm Matthew Weldon. I've come on ahead to stake out the house I plan to build.

181

The materials are to arrive next week. If you're my neighbor—"

Stamping her foot and giving her imitation of a Southern lady's way of speaking, Kirsten said, "You, suh, will never be ouah neighbah. Youah a . . . uh . . . cahpetbaggah! You will not be welcomed at Sweethome."

Weldon began to laugh. He laughed until the tears came. She watched him, confused, until he got himself under control and wiped his eyes. "I'm sorry," he sputtered. "I couldn't help it. First time I ever heard a Swede with a Southern accent!"

She glared at him, abandoning the drawl. "I'm giving you fair warning. We have no use for Yankees at Sweethome! If you step on our place, you will be shot, just like . . . like any other pig!"

The friendliness went out of his face and he stiffened. "I can assure you that I won't," he said coolly, inhaling with an expression of distaste. "I don't have too much in common with pig farmers."

Kirsten spun furiously and began fighting her way back through the brush, wishing there were a more dignified way to do so. The man was absolutely insufferable!

And when Theron learned how he had insulted her, he would kill him!

By the time she reached the house, Jenny had collected the rest of the escapees. They were busy at the trough while Jenny repaired the pen. A slender, wild-looking, barefoot creature, her hem out, looping above brown feet, Jenny worked with concentration.

She looks like a pig farmer, Kirsten thought, still smarting from Weldon's remark as she went into the kitchen, where Inga sat with her foot up, peeling potatoes.

"Did you get them all?" Inga asked.

"All but one."

Kirsten told Inga only that the Union officer who had purchased the land across the way was surveying his property, and that he had killed their pig.

Inga paled. Everything the plantation produced was precious to her, life-sustaining. She still mourned the eggs she had broken when she fell. Though there were a number of swine, some of them had to be saved for breeding. Every loss diminished the way of life at Sweethome.

Kirsten laughed scornfully. "You forget, Mama. We have money now, thanks to me. I'll talk to Theron. I'm sure he can have your pig replaced."

When Kirsten used St. Germain's first name, and spoke as if she were privy to his thoughts, Inga's hands tightened into fists, but she forced herself to remain calm. "This neighbor, Captain Weldon—what manner of man is he?"

Kirsten shrugged. "Typical Union officer. Arrogant, overbearing, insulting!" Her face reddened and she looked down at herself. "I'm going to change!"

She went into the bedroom, and while she was gone, Inga thought about their neighbor. She didn't dare offer him hospitality, not with Theron feeling as he did, but it would be nice to have visitors. She wondered if the man had a wife.

And then she forgot him completely as Kirsten

reappeared in the kitchen dressed in a blue voile gown, her hair once more arranged in an artful combination of swirls and curls tied with a blue ribbon. She even smelled of perfume. What in the world had gotten into the girl?

26

Kirsten maintained her new obsession with her appearance. In the evenings, she also fell into the habit of crossing the little bridge over the creek and walking up and down the lane. Probably, Inga thought wryly, so that she would be the first to see the master of the house as he came home.

Kirsten had no such notion in her head. She was hoping that the stuck-up young man across the way would get a good look at her as she really was. Then, if he so much as dared to speak to her, she would cut him cold. Unfortunately, she saw him only at a distance, and since she did not intend him to think she had any interest in him or in what he was doing, she couldn't do anything about it.

He has working with a contraption of sticks and twine, constructing what appeared to be some kind of maze. It looked childish, she thought, tossing her head. Whatever it was, she had no interest in it.

Jenny had no such compunctions. One morning Weldon looked up from his work to see a strange young lady standing close beside him, watching him with bright, curious eyes. At first he was taken aback, believing her to be an Indian with her long black braids and simple frock that revealed too much of slim brown ankles. He had not even heard her approach.

"Hello," he said.

"Hello. You're Captain Weldon. I'm Jenny." It was a simple statement. With the formalities over, she edged closer. "What are you doing?"

He grinned at her. "Building a house."

She laughed, a pleasant giggle that charmed him. He had no idea she was imagining him as a spider, a big blue spider, living in a dew-spangled web spread out across the grass.

He explained in simple terms the process of creating triangles which resulted in square corners.

"I could do that," she said excitedly.

"Of course you could."

She surveyed his layout with a judicious eye. "It looks big."

"It will be. Look, here's what I plan." He smoothed a piece of bare ground with his boot, then knelt to draw the outline of a house. It would be similar to one he had seen in Natchez, he explained, full two story, with a wrought-iron staircase sweeping to the upper gallery from the side. He supposed the style would be regarded as Spanish Colonial, since there would be many arches in its construction. For the roof, he had purchased red tile.

"You must be very rich."

He grinned. "Not very. Actually, I inherited the family mills in Pennsylvania. But when I saw this country, I wanted to settle here. So I sold out, took that money and what I saved from my military pay, and here I am. Now, let's talk about you. Where do you live?"

"Across the creek, at Sweethome."

"Indeed?" He studied the girl. She, too, had the slight singsong accent of the Swedish people. But there was certainly no resemblance to the blond young lady whose pig he had shot.

"Do you have a relative?" he asked. "A girl with blond hair?"

"My sister, Kirsten."

"I met her the other day."

"Yes, I know."

"She gave me holy hell," he said ruefully. Jenny's answering grin told him that she'd already guessed at that.

During the remainder of their conversation he elicited the fact that there were three women across the way: a mother, Inga, and her daughters, Kirsten and young Jenny. His brows shot up when he learned that they came from Minnesota and they now lived with Theron St. Germain, a former colonel in the Confederate Army.

"Do you work for the St. Germain family?"

"There isn't a family. Only Mr. St. Germain. And, no, we just live with him."

"All of you?"

Jenny looked at him, perplexed. Why was he so surprised? And it was a pretty dumb question, anyway. Did he think she would live in one place, Kirsten somewhere else, and Mama in yet another?

"All of us," she repeated. Then, bored with staying in one place on such a beautiful day, she made her excuses and hurried home.

He watched her go, wondering exactly what kind of setup they had across the creek. There was something different about Jenny. She seemed unbelievably innocent—trusting, childlike.

And Kirsten, her lovely blond sister who attracted him more than he cared to admit, despite her temper and her dishabille the first time they met, seemed to be two different people. He had watched her walking along the lane on several beautiful summer evenings, dressed in gossamer gowns, and guessed she meant to attract his attention.

Why?

Because she wished to show him she was something more than a keeper of pigs? Or because she was accustomed to the attentions of men?

One Confedcrate colonel and three Swedish women who, according to Jenny, all lived with him. Matthew Weldon sighed. If the arrangement was as intimate as it sounded, Theron St. Germain was far, far more of a man than he!

When Jenny burst into the house, excitedly telling about meeting the new neighbor, and the wonderful house he was going to build, Kirsten's heart sank.

"He didn't see you looking like that!"

Jenny looked down at her too-short frock. "Why, what's wrong with me?"

"You look a mess! The man will get the wrong impression."

Jenny couldn't understand why her sister was so upset. "You didn't look any better when you met him. And you didn't smell very good, either!"

Kirsten, with a small inarticulate cry, fled the room.

"I don't see why she got so mad," Jenny said defensively.

Inga reached out to take her daughter's hand. Lovely Jenny! Her years spent shut away on the farm in Minnesota had kept her a child in some ways. But she was fifteen now, and would grow up all too soon.

"It's her age, Jenny. Kirsten's reached a time in her life when she wants something, and isn't sure exactly what it is. It makes her cross."

"She's only a year older than I am, Mama, and I'm not like that—am I?"

"No, Jenny."

But *I* am, Inga thought. I'm fourteen years older than Kirsten and I still have those longings.

The morning chores finished, Jenny went calling on Dinah and old Caleb. They assured her they were all feeling better and Boy would soon be able to join her on her excursions.

Though she was pleased to hear it, her heart sank at the thought of not being able to go to her secret surveillance of the man with a tanned, golden body and a thatch of yellow hair.

She made her way hurriedly across the St. Germain property and climbed the fence, losing herself in the trees. On the far side of the field the man had been plowing, the trees moved inward to a kind of point, following the tributary of a stream.

She walked Indian fashion, moving effortlessly through summer leaves like a shadow.

When she reached her vantage point, she could see him clearly as he walked along strewing seed. A bird sang in the trees above her and he raised his head to listen. She could see a handsome, boyish face. On impulse, she mocked the bird's call and saw him look up once more.

Stifling a giggle, she shifted position and gave the warbling call again. His startled gaze kept shifting as he tried to locate the source of the sound. Then he shook his head in bewilderment and went back to his sowing.

In the afternoon, as Jenny walked slowly home, there was a strange, trembly feeling in the pit of her stomach. She was beginning to have an idea about what was wrong with Kirsten. She, too, was growing up.

Jenny was so intent on her own thoughts that her usual keen perception of everything around her—the scent of grass and flower, the rustling of leaves, the odd bark of a squirrel—was dulled.

Heading toward the house, she was surprised to see someone working at the cabins. They were all clean now, whitewashed, with fresh calico curtains— except for the one at the end of the line.

And sure enough, there was Inga, dragging out a ruined mattress to burn. Stepping from the trees bounding the property on that side, Jenny called out to her, "Mama—"

The word choked off as a hand closed over her mouth, and she was bent backward against a body that smelled of horse and sweat. Jenny tried to scream, but managed only a whimper.

Inga looked up to see Jenny struggling in a man's arms. Then the sight was cut off as a group of horsemen thundered into the yard with a rebel yell, firing at everything in sight.

Inga snatched up a hoe leaning against the side of the cabin, and ran, limping, to Jenny's defense. She swung wildly at one of the riders, who turned his mount sideways, shouldering against her to stop her flight. He reached out and snatched her weapon, tossing it to the side, then slid from the saddle. "This one's mine!"

Inga backed away from the gleeful lust in his eyes, and he put out a dirt-grimed hand to snatch at the bodice of her gown, ripping it to the waist.

For a moment he faltered, and she followed the direction of his eyes. Kirsten had come out of the kitchen. She was dressed in the blue voile again, her hair arranged into careful ringlets.

With a sound like the yapping of a wolf pack, the renegades made for her.

"Kirsten!" Inga screamed. "Kirsten! Run!"

But the girl's figure was blotted from view, and Inga had her attacker's attention once more. Another man stood behind him.

"When you're done," he said, his lip lifting in a wolfish leer as he spat a stream of tobacco into the grass, "by God, it's my turn."

27

Theron St. Germain left Memphis at the head of a train consisting of three wagons laden with building materials. Sitting atop the wagons were a dozen black men, only one of them with building experience. But the rest were willing to learn, and they were as glad to leave Memphis as St. Germain was.

Within a short time the power structure of the city had turned, the bottom level rising to the top, the "first citizens" disfranchised. The Irish from the slums called Pinchgut on Catfish bay, once employed only for labor that might kill valuable slaves, ruled the city from mayor to fireman. They hated the blacks, and the feeling was reciprocated.

The four thousand black troops who had for a time kept a semblance of order were mustered out. For several days, still armed, but without authority, they roved in wild bands and were particularly insolent to the city's Irish population. On May 1 the situation escalated into all-out battle between black ex-soldiers and Irish police.

Within three days forty-six blacks had been killed, many of them innocent; whites dead numbered two, with seventy-five wounded. There had been five rapes, a hundred robberies, ninety-one houses burned, four churches pillaged.

The Klan, a group of whites formed to terrorize strangers and blacks, entered into the fray. Skulls and crossbones were painted on fences. And the local papers carried KKK notices, worded in mysterious fashion:

"The moon is on the wane."

"You will scatter the clouds of the grove."

"The dark and dismal hour grows nigh."

"By order of the Grand Cyclops, GCT."

It was said that St. Germain's old friend Bedford Forrest was involved in much of the agitation against the blacks.

Theron sighed in despair. Good God, what had this war done to them all! In his experience, the blacks had been good, gentle, loving people like Dinah and Caleb. Though he had to admit that he had never really regarded them as human until he had worked beside them.

He owed Inga Johansson a great deal, he thought soberly. Then his dark brows drew together in a perplexed fashion as he thought of the errand she had sent him on.

Inga had asked him to deliver a cured ham to a house near the riverfront, to a woman known as

Miz Fannie. He did so, and spent a pleasant hour at tea in the company of that lady and her sister, only to learn later that the place was a brothel. What the hell did those people have to do with his Inga?

He sighed again. At least he was nearly home. The slow-moving wagons had traveled at a snail's pace. They had spent too much time on the road. He turned the spirited horse that was his first purchase and rode back to check the status of his loads. He gave the driver of the lead vehicle instructions so he could go on ahead. The others would follow at their own pace.

He spurred the horse forward, and the animal, given his head, raced down the road, his great heart exulting in the freedom. And Theron exulted with him as they pounded down the lane that led to Sweethome. Soon they were over the river bridge, heading toward the tall free-standing pillars that welcomed them. This time, Theron St. Germain thought, I've come home in triumph!

At the sound of a scream, he jerked on the reins, pulling the animal to its haunches.

A whistle—a rebel yell—guns firing. And over it all, the sound of Inga's voice: "Kirsten! Run!"

Sweethome was being attacked—Inga was in danger—and he was not armed!

At the rear of the house, Inga fought for her life. She gouged at the eyes of the man who held her. Swearing, he struck her with his fist, and she went down, her last conscious thought of Jenny and Kirsten.

Jenny fared better. Biting through the hand of

the man who held her, she pulled free. If she had run into the woods, she might have escaped. But she raced toward the man assaulting her mother. Landing on his back, she clawed at him, only to be pulled away, locked in iron-hard arms against a filthy uniform.

"Let me go," she screamed, kicking out at her captor.

The man swore. "You damned little wildcat!"

Jenny kicked him again. He grabbed at her braids and wrapped them about her throat, strangling her into submission with her own long dark hair.

Kirsten managed to get inside the door before the horde of savage, shouting renegades reached her. She barred it, but with the repeated assaults from outside, it began to splinter and give. Soon there was a hole big enough to reveal a bloodshot, leering eye and part of a whiskered face.

"Just wait, girlie, we'll get there!"

Kirsten cast frantically about the kitchen for a weapon. Snatching up a boiling pot from the stove, she aimed it straight and true. The man disappeared with a shriek that was accompanied by hooting laughter from his companions.

And the battering began again.

Dinah had come limping out of her cabin after shoving Boy beneath the bed, admonishing him to stay there. When she saw what was happening to her beloved missus, she grabbed up a sickle and charged. She ripped down one man's arm before she was overwhelmed.

Two men held her while another tore at her

sturdy cotton dress. Black or not, old or not, she was female.

Caleb, too, had come outside, his old face fierce with anger, his rusty musket at the ready.

"There's a niggah," someone yelled. "The bastahd's got a gun! Shoot 'im!"

A squinting renegade lifted a pistol and shot.

Caleb went down.

Tearing free from her captors, Dinah ran toward the old man who was her father, fell to her knees beside him, and took his bleeding body in her arms.

There was a moment's uneasy silence; then a mounted man, obviously the leader, spoke. "Shoot the bitch. Hell, she's just anothah niggah. They's enough wimmen to go around."

As the pistol was raised, a shout rang out.

"Ten-*hutt*!"

The renegades had once been Confederate soldiers—the dregs of a lost war, but they had been trained to obey commands. The call to attention stopped them in their tracks. They stood staring at a man on a huge black horse, who had come charging into their midst. A big man, with tousled black hair, his face set like granite, his eyes filled with the fires of hell.

A man with one arm.

St. Germain looked over the rabble before him. Only one of the wolf pack was still mounted. His uniform was in rags, but he wore the chevrons of a sergeant on what was left of it.

"Sergeant!" St. Germain roared. "Prepare your men to mount and disperse! By God, sirs, you do no credit to the uniforms you wear!"

The sergeant spat a stream of tobacco and wiped his mouth on his sleeve. "A damned officuh," he said contemptuously. "Ah kin smell 'em a mile off. Tyson, shoot 'im."

The pistol that lifted toward St. Germain wavered a little. Tyson was still under the spell of the man's powerful, authoritative presence.

Suddenly a well-placed bullet sent the pistol flying from Tyson's hand. Another caught the mounted leader directly between the eyes. A voice at the side of the house barked orders to unseen troops: "Hold your fire, men. Cover me!"

A Union officer stepped from behind a shielding shrub, gun at the ready.

"We have you surrounded," Matthew Weldon said crisply. "You have two choices. Surrender your weapons and disperse, or . . . take the consequences."

With hangdog expressions, the renegades obeyed. Leaderless now, they had lost their bravado. One by one, weapons were tossed into a pile on the ground.

"Mount up!" Weldon ordered.

He called back to his hidden companions, "Keep to the trees. They're coming through. If there's any trouble, fire on the bastards!" Then he turned back to the surly rebels, once more on their horses. "My men have their orders," he said coolly. "But if I were you, I'd ride like hell for a day or two, in case they forget."

They needed no reminder, and within minutes the yard was cleared of their ragtag presence."

Theron St. Germain knelt at Inga's side and tried

to cover the beautiful bared breasts with one trembling hand. There was a purpling bruise that disfigured her face, but she was breathing.

He knew that if anything had happened to her, he would die.

His breath caught on a harsh, gasping sob. "Inga, sweetheart," he said over and over. "Oh, sweetheart . . . I love you!"

Averting his eyes from the sight of a grown man crying, Matthew Weldon went to Jenny. The girl was sitting up, still gasping for breath.

"I'm all right," she whispered. "Mama . . . Kirsten . . ."

Weldon assured her that Inga was in good hands, and went to search for Kirsten, terrified at what he would find. When he had first heard the shooting, his immediate thought had been for her safety.

The door to the kitchen, pounded off its hinges, had fallen inward. Kirsten crouched in a corner of the room, her eyes wild and frightened. She fended Weldon off as he tried to touch her. Then, recognition finally dawning on her, she collapsed into his arms, sobbing her heart out.

He held her while she wept against his shoulder; feeling the softness of her slender body, its warmth; feeling desire building inside him.

That was something he had wanted to do since he first saw her, he thought as he kissed her tear-wet upturned mouth. Despite the way she had looked. He smiled, recalling the mud-covered creature who smelled of pig swill. Damnation, but it was hard at a time like this to remember that he was engaged to be married, that Martha waited for him back home.

Finally he got himself under control and disentangled himself from Kirsten's clinging arms. She was all right; he had to see what damage had been done.

"Don't leave me," she wept. "Please don't leave me . . ."

"I'll be back," he said. "I'll be back."

He and St. Germain helped the still-dazed Inga and Jenny into the house, then went to Dinah, who sat on the ground holding her father's head to her bosom, rocking back and forth and making a keening sound.

Old Caleb, who had tried so bravely to protect his loved ones with a rusted, useless weapon, was dead.

Weldon picked up his small frail body and carried him into the cabin St. Germain pointed out. Theron comforted Dinah, his arm around the shattered old woman.

"Ah got tuh tell Boy," she whimpered.

"I'll tell him," St. Germain told her. "Dinah, Inga and the girls may need you—"

"Sweet Jesus," Dinah said, "ef them men done hurt mah missus . . ." She hurried toward the house; imprecations mingled with her sobs.

St. Germain went to Dinah's cabin to find Boy. Weldon, wanting to go back to Kirsten, yet feeling that the house at the moment was no place for a man, began to clear the yard. There was much to do, graves to be dug, but he had reached a point where he had to wait for instructions.

Finally he went to Dinah's cabin, glanced into the open door, then turned away. For the autocratic St. Germain, officer and Southern gentleman, was sitting on a homemade cane-bottomed chair, a little black boy held close; the man's eyes were wet with tears as he comforted the child.

Weldon, feeling instinctively that St. Germain wouldn't want his enemy to see him at such a moment, returned to the yard.

"I suppose," St. Germain said reluctantly when he finally joined Weldon, "I am indebted to you. But I don't understand why you let those bastards get away! Why the hell didn't you order your men to fire?"

"What men?" Weldon asked quietly.

St. Germain stared at him. "What men? You mean there weren't . . . ? You didn't . . . ?"

Weldon shrugged in answer.

Theron St. Germain's dislike of Weldon was tinged with a touch of admiration. There had been no backup, then. It was all a colossal bluff. The fellow was a damned Yankee, they would never be friends, but he had to admit, by God, that the man had courage!

Weldon offered to help dig the graves for the two dead men, Caleb and the unknown renegade. St. Germain refused.

He had help coming. His newly hired workers would be there within the hour.

It was quite clear to Weldon that, though he had done a service for Sweethome, he was not welcome. So when Dinah, her face still swollen from crying, came out to announce that all was well with the women of the house, he took his leave.

"Them gals wasn' hurted a-tall, ef you knows whut Ah means."

They knew, and Weldon saw his own relief reflected in St. Germain's face.

All was well—except for Caleb, who would never potter around his beloved Sweethome again.

The two men, Confederate and Yankee, parted.

They did not shake hands.

28

The wagons of supplies and workers arrived shortly after Weldon's departure. Though the newcomers were dismayed at the scene confronting them, they viewed it stoically. Things had been much the same in Memphis, and here, at least, they would have food, a roof, and a protector.

St. Germain's first action was to distribute the confiscated weapons among them.

John, the man he had appointed foreman of the crew, scratched his head. "Niggahs ain' 'lowed to have guns, suh. In Memphis, it git us kilt."

"This isn't Memphis," Theron said shortly. "This is Sweethome. And while you are here, it is your home. I expect you to protect it."

John nodded.

Under the foreman's direction, two men were set to digging a grave, several others to salvage what they could from the carcasses of slaughtered animals; the rest unloaded building supplies.

At dusk, the gray-clad renegade was laid to rest beside the other unknown soldier at the foot of the tulip tree. Perhaps, Theron thought, the uniform was all the two of them had in common.

The next morning, there was another funeral.

Dinah had washed old Caleb's body and dressed it in a black suit he had saved for his burial. The foreman, John, handy with tools, had made a box from some of the fresh-smelling new wood brought to rebuild Sweethome. It was lined with velvet from the sewing room.

Caleb, in death, knew more luxury than ever in his eighty long, hardworking years.

Six of the new workers carried Caleb's coffin to the small slave cemetery beside the St. Germain family graveyard, a grassy little knoll with markers lost in the lush spring grass. The group that followed Caleb on his last journey was a sad one. Inga, her ankle injured again, insisted on attending.

She leaned on Theron's arm, her face purple with bruises and stained with tears. Kirsten and Jenny were still numb from all that had happened. Dinah, her face swollen and eyes blind with grief, held tightly to the hand of a sobbing Boy.

Behind them came the remaining workers, hats to their sides in respect for the man they had never known but who was one of them.

At the graveside, Theron stepped forward. "We are here to pay our last respects to Caleb," he said solemnly. "To my knowledge, Caleb had no last name. I owe him a great debt, therefore I would like to share my name with him. He was my faithful"—Theron paused to look at Inga—"my faithful friend."

He bowed his head. "We commit the body of *Caleb St. Germain* . . ."

Inga sobbed, and felt a warm comforting arm go around her.

"Everything goin' be awright, missie. Caleb goin' be fine. Goin' set on the Lawd's right hand an' sing with the angels."

As if Dinah's words were a signal, the brief service ended and the black workers began with a soft sweet humming sound.

Swing low, sweet Chariot
Comin' foh tuh ca'y me home

The volume increased, becoming jubilant, triumphant. Inga looked up through her tears, and the sun seemed to radiate outward in concentric circles, until it became a chariot of fire.

They returned to the house, where Kirsten collapsed. She still had moments of hysteria, waking from dreams of a door being battered in, of an evil eye staring at her, framed by splintered wood. She declared passionately that she never wanted to see a man again.

"Not that gal," Dinah muttered under her breath. "She got her mind set on Massa Theron. She layin' in there lookin' foh attenshun!"

Dinah was only partially correct. Kirsten, certain that Theron would come rushing to her bedside, had insisted on wearing a fine lawn bedgown, with blue ribbons laced at the neckline. With her hair loose around her face, she knew she made a fetching invalid. But he hadn't come.

It's odd, Kirsten thought, when she tried to escape in daydreams, the face she conjured up was not Theron St. Germain's, but Matthew Weldon's.

St. Germain was having his own problems. He remembered kneeling beside Inga, babbling out his love for a moment, her blue eyes opening, then closing again.

He knew now that what he had said was the truth. He did love her! But there was the question of her relationship with Miz Fannie. He had gleaned nothing from his conversation with the old woman in Memphis, except that Inga and her daughters had once lived there—in that house.

He could not imagine Inga being involved in Miz Fannie's business. But he could not dismiss the question. He had been reared like a young prince. If his eye wandered in his youth, he was immediately pulled up short by his aristocratic family. That girl has no social graces, they would point out. Another's people, though nice enough, did not have the proper background. One girl's grandparents were immigrants . . . One by one, his parents eliminated them, steering him gently toward Marnie Lee—and a marriage that was disastrous for both husband and wife.

Inga would never have suited his family, and they would not have suited her. The life of a pampered Southern lady would stifle her. The fresh air of the country perfumed a complexion that had never known creams or artifice. She worked with her hands. Yet, as he had watched her in the garden, sans bonnet, the sun gleaming on her coronet of braids, making it into a golden tiara, he saw a Nordic goddess.

If Inga had not been there when he stumbled in

from the blizzard, he would not have survived. He realized it now. But for a time he had only seen that much of his house lay in ruins. How many months did he sit and brood over his losses, while Inga had taken what was left and made a home of it, planted a garden, stored food for the winter. He would not have known where to begin.

Nor did he know how to begin with the rebuilding of Sweethome. He hoped the carpenter he had employed to serve as foreman would supply that knowledge. But he soon learned that John's talent extended only to saw, hammer, and nails.

Together they paced off the distance. One corner had been there before the building was razed, another here.

Jenny viewed the stakes they set with a critical eye, and decided that Sweethome had been built all wrong in the first place. The lines would not be true. Theron and his overseer watched as the girl worked magic with stakes and twine, talking of footings, foundations, and base plates. Where had she learned to do such planning? Theron asked.

Jenny knew St. Germain would not be pleased that she had visited with the Yankee across the way, and so kept her source a secret. "I saw someone do it once," she mumbled.

She couldn't know that it was another blow to the master of Sweethome's pride. St. Germain was dismayed that even a young girl was more adept at construction than he was.

When the house began to take shape, John, the carpenter, was able to take over. Jenny watched closely, slipping across the river occasionally to ask a question and return with an answer.

Matthew Weldon's house was going up at a rapid rate. And it was going to be beautiful. Though he had been expected to run the family mills, Weldon claimed, his real interest had always been architecture. He showed Jenny the plans he had drawn to scale, and was proud of overseeing the job himself.

He always stopped to visit with her, and it wasn't long before she learned that his conversation eventually turned to Kirsten.

"How is your mother? Your sister, Kirsten, is she well? I haven't seen her in some time. Please give her my regards."

Sensing his interest, Jenny tried to hint to Kirsten: "You should see the house Captain Weldon is building."

"I couldn't care less."

"He asked about you today."

"Did he?"

"I think he's sweet on you, Kirsten."

"Oh, for heaven's sake! As if I'd look at him twice!"

Kirsten flounced away, and Jenny was sorry she had brought up the subject. Maybe, Jenny thought, Kirsten was still upset by what happened when those raiders came. For a time, Jenny too had been nervous, not wanting to remember what they tried to do to her, to her mother and sister. She was more afraid of men now. Except for St. Germain and Weldon, of course. They were known to her, and she thought nothing of their presence.

But when she came upon one of the new workers unexpectedly, she would feel a shiver of fear run through her body. That fear had kept her from her game of spying among the trees on the next property. The man there was an unknown. Suppose he should catch her ... She shivered again, but this time she wasn't certain just why.

She stayed close to home, helping Dinah cook for the workers, harvesting the vegetables that grew now in great profusion.

Inga began to worry about her younger daughter, who had become much too quiet. Jenny was no longer the laughing wild creature she had always been. Inga often found the dark-haired girl in the garden looking across the fields with a yearning that Inga did not understand.

And on the property adjoining the rear of St. Germain's land, which had once been known as Belle Terre, Jesse Norwood, sharecropper's son, was afflicted with the same ailment.

He started at every bird call, and looked vainly for the flicker of a red petticoat, the pixie face of a small girl peeping from among the leaves.

29

As summer deepened toward fall, the heat and humidity intensified. Bees droned lazily among the crape myrtle and rose of Sharon. The progress of the building slowed as St. Germain's workers felt the effects of the enervating weather.

Then the unforgiveable happened.

The second story of the Yankee intruder's house rose higher than the trees that lined the river. It was visible from Sweethome, the conqueror looking down upon the conquered.

Face dark with rage, St. Germain redoubled his efforts. The construction moved toward completion at a rapid pace despite the weather. Jenny ran from garden to building site, handing up nails, steadying ladders. She got to know the black workers well, and they no longer frightened her.

Kirsten, however, seemed to be in a perpetual

pout. Theron was busy, too busy to say more than a word in passing. And if he smiled at anyone, it was her mother. He had forgotten, she thought miserably, just who it was who had found the treasure that made his building possible.

Dressed in her favorite blue gown, her hair freshly washed and gleaming, Kirsten wandered around the side of the house one day, hoping to attract his attention.

A ladder leaned against the wall with a black man atop it. She skirted it carefully, recalling that walking beneath a ladder brought bad luck. The worker, hearing the rustle of a woman's garments, thought she was Jenny and called down to her. "Theys a li'l bitty board leanin' 'gin the wall, honey. Yo' hand it up to me?"

Kirsten's face reddened with anger at his familiar tone. "I will not! And I suggest you remember your place! I don't have to take orders from Negro hands! You're working for me!"

"I was under the impression that I hired this man."

Kirsten turned to see an angry Theron St. Germain standing behind her. "And I was also under the impression that you live here too. It's as much to your advantage that we finish here before winter as it is to mine. Hand the man his board!"

"But—"

"Hand him the board!"

Kirsten obeyed, frightened at his grim expression.

"Now," he said, "I would suggest you get into something more suitable for work and either help out here or assist your mother and Jenny with the canning."

Kirsten did neither. She fled across the little bridge, her cheeks flaming. She intended to walk up and down the lane, but catching sight of the mansion going up across the way, she gasped in astonishment and moved nearer in order to get a better view.

She was sure it would be the most beautiful house in the world when it was completed. Its doors and windows were graceful arches. A handsome staircase led up to a gallery that would provide a view for miles. The whole was being painted a gleaming white. It took her breath away.

"You like my house?"

Matthew Weldon had come up behind her. Kirsten turned to look into smiling blue eyes that viewed her with approval.

"Yes," she whispered. "Oh, yes!"

"Come. I'll show it to you."

Offering his arm, he led her into the structure. There were parquet floors, a staircase that rivaled that of Sweethome with its glowing, hand-rubbed wood, and the whole gave an impression of space and light.

When they climbed to the upper gallery, she could see that it looked down on Sweethome.

Theron wasn't going to like that! And for some reason, she felt satisfaction at the thought. Setting out to be her most charming to this Yankee who had bested St. Germain, she smiled and flirted.

One of the upstairs bedrooms especially took her fancy. That section of the house had been completed and the walls were being covered with pale blue watered silk. The room seemed planned for a woman.

For the first time, it dawned on her that Weldon might be married. She felt an incomprehensible pang.

"Will you be bringing your wife here?"

"When I have one."

The pang eased and she blurted, "Do you have someone in mind?"

He smiled, thinking of his boyhood sweetheart waiting for him at home. "I do."

The pang returned.

After the tour was over, he led her outside and to a spot some distance from the house.

"Getting tired of all that hammering," he confessed.

He seated her on a stump and sank down to the grass beside her with a sigh.

"Now, to what do I owe the pleasure of this visit? I can't think that you're here with St. Germain's approval."

Kirsten tossed her head. "I don't need his approval! As to why I'm here, I ... I ..." She searched for a reason. "I wished to thank you for the pig."

Several weeks before, one of Weldon's servants had appeared at Sweethome, driving an enormous brood sow before him. From her appearance, she would soon produce a litter of little ones. Inga was beside herself with delight, for she felt it gave her a chance to recoup their losses from the raid. She hadn't mentioned the sow to Theron, because she knew he wouldn't notice its presence, and that if she told him he would be stiff-necked about it and insist she return the animal to its giver.

"You ... you needn't have," Kirsten told Weldon.

He shrugged. "It was a replacement for the one I shot."

Kirsten thought of the scrawny little shoat she had followed to his property. It was not an even trade. But she said nothing more.

The day was too beautiful to talk about pigs. The sky above them was like the blue watered silk in the house's upstairs bedroom—the room she coveted. Though it was hot and humid, the day was not unpleasant. A heavy scent of wildflowers perfumed the air, and in the distance, a lark sang.

Kirsten demurely spread her skirts around her, tipped her head toward him, and listened as Weldon talked of the house and his plans.

Finally, after a long silence, he asked, "Miss Johansson?"

"Kirsten," she said, shaking a playful finger at him.

"Then . . . Kirsten, forgive me if I sound like I'm prying. But I don't understand the situation at Sweethome. Are you, your mother, and sister perhaps related to St. Germain?"

At the mention of Theron's name, the memory of her recent humiliation returned. She would be damned if she would tell this man that they had come here ragged and starving or that since St. Germain had returned, they were only there on his sufferance!

"Sweethome is ours," she dimpled. "But of course we do not press the point. When the former owner returned wounded, ill, we took him in, nursed him back to health. He had nowhere to go. What else could we do?"

"That was very commendable of you," he said.

His gaze was so straight that she blushed and looked away. "I had feared . . ." He caught himself and amended his words. ". . . had thought there might be a romantic interest involved."

"I . . . I cannot say there is not," she said, lowering her lashes. "At least not on his part. But of course, he is much older than I am."

The look of alarm on Weldon's face was like balm to her wounded ego.

"Kirsten, promise you won't let him press you into anything. Good God, the man's a tyrant!"

Kirsten stood, shaking out her skirts. "I'd better go," she said softly. "I must help my mother and Jenny."

Then she was gone, flitting across the grass like a butterfly, a creature made of sunbeams and dreams. Weldon watched her go, his brows furrowed.

Jenny had told him the property belonged to St. Germain. Kirsten had put forward an entirely different story. And neither of them had any reason to lie to him.

He certainly hoped the young lady had no involvement with that bad-tempered reb. She was far too young; so delicate and lovely . . . And so unlike his own dear Martha, with her sturdy down-east forebears.

He felt a moment of guilt as he realized how attracted he was to this Swedish girl with her soft blue eyes and errant sunlit curls. He would have to watch his step where she was concerned. Tonight, he must write to Martha and reaffirm his love.

When Kirsten crossed the little bridge on her way back to Sweethome, she was smiling with satisfaction. She was certain that if Weldon had a bride in mind, he had forgotten her today. His admiration for Kirsten herself had been apparent in his eyes, in his every movement.

Not that she was interested in him, really. But she could use his attentions to bring Theron St. Germain to heel, playing one off against the other.

And if all else failed, she still had Theron's wife's jewels that she had held back. They should bring enough money to take her home to Minnesota.

There was always Oskar Bjorn and his mill.

30

The new facade of Sweethome was finally completed. The columns no longer stood free to remind St. Germain of what his home had once been. The structure was not as large as the one across the way, but it had regained its former charm. There was, however, no way to furnish the house, because once Theron paid off his workers, little money remained.

John, the man who served as overseer, came to Theron with a proposition. He turned his cap in his hands as he spoke for himself and the others. His fellow workers were former field hands and there was nowhere for them to go. None of them had made more than ten cents a day since the war's end—not enough to keep body and soul together. And they all had families to feed and care for.

With the master's permission, he and his coworkers would like to stay on, to send for their wives and children. They would work for free, asking only for food through the winter. Next spring, they would plant the cotton fields; their women would put in gardens so they wouldn't be a burden. They, too, were good workers—they could cook, sew, clean, and pick cotton.

"We don' need no pay, suh. We's willin' tuh work for our keep, like before the war."

Theron looked out over the sweeping fields, now gone to weed and bramble, seeing them as they had once been—white with cotton to the skyline. Without help, life would be held to mere subsistance. With it, he might be able to rebuild his world once more.

Deferring his answer, Theron called a conference with those to whom it would also matter.

Jenny was delighted with the idea. She loved the black people, and the thought of the cabins teeming with their families made her happy.

Kirsten was indifferent.

Inga was pleased, but she insisted that it was not fair for the workers to return to voluntary slavery. If they planted and harvested, they should be entitled to a certain percentage when the crop was sold.

"But you don't understand, Inga. These people have nothing anyway."

"And they never will have!" Her eyes sparked blue fire. "Not when there are people like you to take advantage of them!"

Theron bowed to her decision, amazed once more at the changes one woman had effected in his way of thinking.

Within the next few weeks, the sow farrowed, producing a number of sturdy piglets. There was a frantic scramble to glean the garden thoroughly. A light frost caused the leaves along the creek to turn. The wagons, driven into Memphis by several of the workers, returned spilling over with women and children, who shrieked with delight as they saw their new homes.

Then it frosted again. The weather cooled until it was right for butchering. With the new piglets, there was no need to hold any grown stock back for breeding, and the others met their ordained fate.

Now there were many hands to help, to handle any chore that came up.

"Yo' don' do that, missus! That my job!"

Or, "Run 'long, li'l missie. This heah ain' white folkses wuhk."

Inga, freed from her outside labors, spent most of her time in the sewing room preparing gifts for Christmas. Kirsten had taken to slipping over to Matthew Weldon's.

Dinah, though she still grieved for old Caleb, was in what she referred to as "hawg heaven." The other black women deferred to her, the resident of long standing.

"Ah's the boss-lady," she told Jenny, grinning. "When Ah says jump, they says 'How high?' Sho' do give me a pow'ful good feelin'!"

St. Germain spent most of his time with John, the black carpenter, planning how items of furniture could be repaired or replaced. Jenny, who liked the smell of varnish and fresh wood, sometimes made herself useful by picking up chips and sweeping out sawdust.

Boy was so delighted with his new companions that he almost forgot Jenny existed.

"Want to go for a walk, Boy?"

"Not now, Miz Jenny. Me an' Tom an' Ish, we plans tuh git in some fishin' 'fore the crick's fruz over."

Jenny wandered lonely as a cloud amid the confusion, the autumn woods calling to her with their songs of scarlet and gold.

She walked across the fields, hating the shoes Inga insisted she wear in this weather. They seemed to hold her back, to tie her to the ground. She wished she could run barefoot, free even of the long dress and petticoat she wore in the name of propriety.

Why, she wondered, had clothes ever been invented? She had seen little black children rolling on cabin floors, playing, giggling, naked as jaybirds, and nobody seemed to notice.

She yanked her skirt free from a briar, ripping it. Mama would scold her, but it was not her fault! It was the fault of what she was wearing. Perhaps someday things would change. And women would dress more like men, not all tied up in cumbersome garments that caught on things!

She reached the glade where the spring bubbled into its clear pool, and stood there for a long time, inhaling the sharp fall air, listening to the sound of running water, memorizing the colors of the leaves that would soon be gone.

As always, this hidden spot had revived her spirits. But today, on her first visit in a long time, something was missing. The hollow, lonely feeling she had experienced several times lately had returned to plague her, a nervous sensation that refused to let her soul be still enough to absorb the beauty around her. It was a need—like being hungry or thirsty—but somehow different.

She sighed and turned back toward Sweethome. Then she turned again and headed toward the boundary of the next property, wrinkling her nose in mischief. Kirsten was always accusing her of acting like a child. And perhaps she was. But it wouldn't hurt to play her spying game once more.

As she made her way through the trees, she remembered the raiders that had attacked her last time she was here. For all she knew, the man who lived in the little house might be one of them.

But he hadn't seen her before. Why should he do so now, when bright splashes of foliage would help conceal her? And if she saw him coming toward her, she would run home.

Her heart was beating much too fast when she reached a point where she could look out over the little shack amid surrounding fields. Smoke poured from the chimney in a thin column, rising straight into the sky, but there was no one in sight.

She tried to imagine what it was like inside that house, sensing it would be small and cozy and warm, something cooking on the stove, things all jumbled around in a homelike way.

Jenny had known only two houses well. The one where she was born in Minesota, with high ceilings and rag rugs scattered on bare cold floors, had always smelled of damp and of harsh lye soap. Then they had found Sweethome, with its quiet elegance. Even in ruin, it had been a place of wonder to her. But the scent of cooking never penetrated the big house, and it seemed wrong somehow, a little less than friendly.

Sweethome was the home of Theron St. Germain. Jenny never felt as if she really belonged.

Yet here . . .

She wove a dream of what it would be like, herself seated in a rocker, mending a man's sock over a darning egg. The fire roaring up the chimney, a kettle of soup simmering over the fire. The man of the house sitting opposite her, doing something with his hands. Whittling? Fixing harness?

Jenny suppressed a giggle. In her daydream, he was shirtless! And in the wintertime! She had never seen the man who haunted her dreams with a shirt on. She might not even like him that way!

Where was he? She studied the landscape: the house; a pile of wood; an ax, its blade buried in the stump he had used for a chopping block.

A new thought struck her, a frightening one. Suppose he was sick, or hurt? Whenever she had watched him, he had always been alone.

In her concern for the man who had not appeared, she had forgotten to watch or listen. The crack of a twig behind her brought her head up in alarm. Jenny turned to flee, and ran directly into two arms that folded around her, pressing her face against the rough texture of a woolen shirt, smothering the cry that rose to her lips.

"Gotcha!" a man's voice said with gleeful amusement. "I gotcha!"

31

Jesse Norwood had been in the wooded area examining a dead tree he planned to fell when the girl approached. Grinning to himself, he remembered the constant watch she had maintained earlier, the teasing bird calls she had uttered to attract his attention as she moved like an Indian from one spot to another.

So, seeing her today, he decided to beat her at her own game. In the army, he had been a scout. His eyes and ears were keener than most, and big as he was, he walked cat-footed. He was known as one who could hide himself behind a blade of grass.

He decided to slip up on the girl and grab her. But, to his surprise, it was like having a wildcat by the tail.

He reached up to halt her clawing fingers, then

let her hand go in order to cover her mouth. Dammit, she was breakin' his eardrums. But he couldn't let her go now until he had explained he didn't mean any harm.

"Dammit, gal," he roared, "hesh! I ain't goin' to hurt you!"

She bit his hand.

Swearing, he picked her up and slung her over his shoulder like a sack of meal. Her legs, imprisoned by her long skirt and encircled by his arm, were helpless. She beat against a broad back with both fists, screaming all the while as he took long strides toward the little house on stilts.

He thrust open the door, and when they were inside, he set her down hard in a rocking chair before the fire.

"Now," he said, "yell all yuh want. An' when you're done, tell me what the hell got intuh you!"

Her screaming stopped and she stared at him, mouth open. Beneath the shock of yellow hair, his eyes were the color of gray velvet. She had a notion they would be kind eyes, but at the moment they were only mad—and a little scared.

Down his right cheek were four deep bleeding furrows. And his hand was bleeding.

"I'm sorry," she whispered.

"Sorry, hell!" He went to a cupboard and pulled out a clean dishtowel to mop at his face and then wrap around his hand. "You was up theah spyin' on me all last spring, sneakin' around like a fox. Then, when I try to play the same game—"

"You saw me?" Her voice was incredulous.

"Hell yes I seen you!"

But not really, he thought as he put the teakettle

to boil. He thought he'd seen a kid. It wasn't until he got his arms around her, feeling her softness pressed against him in that moment before she began to fight, that it dawned on him that she was woman-growed.

That wasn't important now. The important thing was to get her hushed up, calmed down, and on her way back to wherever the hell she came from.

Jenny sat cringing in the rocker while he made a pot of sassafras tea. Handing her a cup, he poured the remaining water into a basin, to which he added a generous splash of whiskey. Then he sat in a chair opposite her, soaking the injured hand.

"I'm Jesse Norwood," he said shortly. "Now, who the hell are you?"

"Jenny," she said in a small voice. "Jenny Johansson."

"Wheah you from?"

"Sweethome," she told him quaveringly.

He nodded his head. From her appearance, she was probably the daughter of an overseer. He had been wondering if Sweethome still stood. He had planned to go over to see if the plantation still existed—not that he'd be welcomed if it did—but he had been too busy since he got home. After he was mustered out of the army, he had returned to find the house at Belle Terre burned, the owners gone, his own folks dead, brothers and sisters scattered. He needed some thinkin' time, and he figgered he would do it here. With nothing better to do, he fixed up the house his family had occupied and put in a crop.

"Now"—the gray eyes were fixed on her again—"why were you watchin' me?"

Jenny shrugged, wincing a little. She seemed to have sprained her shoulder in the struggle. "I don't know. I guess, as you said, it was a game."

She looked so small sitting there. Her hair had slipped from its braids and spread around her shoulders. Her gaze was level and sincere. He took pity on her.

"I didn' go to skeer you."

Though his way of speaking was odd, uneducated, his voice was so soft, so friendly, that Jenny's eyes filled with tears.

Haltingly she told him of the raid on Sweethome, what she had thought when he grabbed her.

Norwood cursed himself. He remembered hearing the shots that day, but he had assumed someone was hunting and had gone on about his business—while innocent women were being terrorized.

He didn't blame this girl for feeling as she did, a strange man taking hold of her like that! When she asked about his hand, he told her that he figured he got what was coming to him.

In the conversation that followed, she told him all she could without betraying her mother. Her father was dead, she told him. The rest of the family— she, her mother and sister—had come here from Minnesota. They were looking for her Uncle Sven, who had joined the Confederate Army. They had settled at Sweethome; then Mr. St. Germain came home, but he was letting them stay.

Jesse pursed his lips in a low whistle, revising upward his estimate of the girl's social status. That didn't, however, sound like the St. Germain Jesse remembered. He had been a tall, autocratic young

225

man on a black horse, come to chide his father for not keeping his fences up. There was no point in mentioning that, he decided.

They talked companionably until the daylight began to fade. Then Jesse Norwood walked Jenny home. He did not go up to the big house, but paused at the edge of the trees to watch her as she went on alone.

"Jenny . . ." he said softly to himself. "Jenny . . ."

He had known other girls, but never one like her. And, like a damned fool, he had scared the wits out of her. Now, he supposed, he would never see her again.

She was out of his class, anyway, living in that big house at Sweethome. And she was educated good. She would have no time for an overseer's son who couldn't read or write.

Sighing, he turned back to the property where he lived as a squatter.

Jenny watched as the red-shirted shoulders disappeared among the trees, still a little dazed. The interior of his house had been much as she had imagined in her daydream. She felt she belonged in that rocking chair . . .

She flushed as she thought of the way she had attacked him. His face would probably be scratched for weeks, and it would take a long time for his hand to heal. He was probably glad to get rid of her.

That night at the dinner table she asked about Belle Terre. The owners had given up on it, St. Germain told her. When they were burned out during the war, they moved to Memphis.

"I met a man named Jesse Norwood," she ventured cautiously.

Theron considered the name; then his brows raised. "That would be old Frank Norwood's kid. Norwood was an overseer, made whiskey on the side. Did you meet him on this property?"

"No, I . . . I'm afraid I was trespassing. He lives in a little house—"

"Don't go over there again," St. Germain said decisively, "and don't associate with him. The man's a damned redneck."

Jenny had no intention of obeying his command. St. Germain had no right to choose her friends for her. But she had learned one thing. She now knew what a redneck was, and if Jesse Norwood was an example, she thought they were very nice.

32

Jenny had been unable to conceal her adventure from Inga. She downplayed it, saying that she had been watching the shack—just for fun—and Jesse Norwood had come up behind her and frightened her. To make up for it, he had asked her in— not mentioning that he'd hauled her in over his shoulder— and given her a cup of tea.

Inga was shaken. Her younger daughter had always been too loving, too trusting. What Jenny had done had been a very dangerous thing. In the first place, the man was a stranger. In the second, a lady did not spy, nor did she go unaccompanied into a house where a man lived alone. Jenny was not to go there again.

Jenny, though something of a wild creature with a mind of her own, had never been disobedient. She went to the spring-fed pool several times during the next few days and waited. In her conversation with Jesse Norwood she had mentioned that it was her favorite place, and she had a vague hope that one day he would be waiting there. But he did not come.

She went farther afield, though still on St. Germain property, and spent hours leaning against the fence that separated Sweethome from Belle Terre. Watching the smoke that rose from his chimney, and listening to the sharp sound of his ax, she felt unutterably lost and lonely.

If he were feeling as she did, he would guess she was near, she thought. Sometimes she wondered if he couldn't hear the beating of her heart.

Finally the urge to see him took precedence over her conscience; she would just watch him. She did not have to go near.

The decision made, she drifted through the trees like a wood nymph until she reached her favored spot. She saw him clearly, saw the red wool shirt strain across his massive shoulders as he brought the ax down.

She could also see that he favored the hand she had bitten. And it made her feel terrible. He paused to wipe his face.

"Well, Jenny?"

The sound of his voice, soft but carrying, made her jump. He had caught her again.

Shyly she stepped out of the cover of brush and tree.

Jesse Norwood came to meet her.

"I wasn't really spying," she whispered when he reached her. "I was just . . ."

Just what? She couldn't tell him that she had

to see him once more, just to know he was there. Her cheeks were rosy, and she couldn't meet his eyes.

"I waited in the glade," she blurted finally. "I thought maybe you would come."

Jesse took her hands in his work-roughened ones, wondering how to begin.

"St. Germain don't hanker to have folks runnin' ovah his property, Jenny. An' he damn sure wouldn't figger I was good enough to associate with you. He's too proud to deal with the likes of me, an' I'm too proud to go where I ain't wanted."

"Then I'll come here," Jenny said stoutly.

Jesse sighed heavily, seeing a world of love in her eyes. He had guessed from the beginning that they felt the same way about each other, and it frightened him.

"Could be the man's right, Jenny. You don't know the South. There's three classes here. There's gentlemen, like him. Then there's blacks and rednecks. I dunno which comes first. But you an' me ain't right for each other."

"Do you want me to go home?"

"Gawd, no!" The soft gray eyes were filled with painful sincerity. "But I don't want to make no trouble!"

"Then let me take a look at your hand!"

Soft-spoken, easygoing Jesse Norwood knew he was no match for this strong-willed girl. He also knew that he had nothing to offer her except himself. If he didn't keep the situation under control, they would come to grief, sure as God made little green apples.

He didn't invite her into his house, but sat down on a stump and proffered his hand. She unwound the soiled bandage and studied his injury. Though it had been aggravated by his wood-chopping, it was healing nicely, but it needed bandaging again.

He told her where some clean cloths were and remained outside. She found the material and knelt to tend the wound. Looking down at her hair with its straight part dividing thick braids that swung around her face, he wanted to loosen it, to feel it twine around his fingers . . .

"Hold still," she said sternly. "Your hand keeps shaking."

Lord in heaven, didn't he know it!

They sat and talked for a long while, steering away from anything that might heighten the magnetic current that ran between them.

"You told me you were born here," Jenny said. "Tell me about when you were a little boy."

It sounded like a safe topic to Jesse. So he talked about fishing in the creek, helping his mother with the younger children, his father with planting and seeding. He had never had any schooling, he told her.

"Neither have I," said Jenny. "Not really."

"Don't make no never-mind with women. Men, it's different. Cain't read and write, they never amount to nothin'."

"I can teach you, some," Jenny said. "I'll bring a slate tomorrow."

There must be no tomorrow, Jesse thought. He knew what Theron St. Germain was like. The thought of someone who lived under his roof associating with an overseer's son would be a personal affront to St. Germain's pride.

Well, dammit, Jesse had his pride too. He had no intention of pushing in where he wasn't wanted. Besides, he had plans of his own. Returning here had been a sort of pilgrimage, a brief return to his childhood. He had decided to stick around awhile, put in one last crop before he moved on. But he had a place to go. His old captain, Sam Whitman, had a ranch in the Magdalena Mountains of New Mexico. Sam was an educated man, a sort of country lawyer. And on nights around the campfire, he had spun tales of the haunted mountains, lost mines, high grassy meadows where the cattle waxed fat.

"I'm a lazy son of a bitch," Sam always ended his tales. "That's why I'm always onto young Jesse here. I need a partner to handle the ranch while I fiddle around."

The prospect was pleasing to Jesse, and he planned on heading out as soon as winter was over. But he had a notion a ranch would be no place for a woman, especially one who had known the advantages of Sweethome. He couldn't offer Jenny any future, and he'd better stop right now, before it was too late.

He stood and reached down to raise the girl from where she had settled beside the stump.

"I think you better go home, Jenny. And I ain't sure you oughta come back."

Her black eyes suddenly glistened with tears; her mouth quivered.

"Jenny," he said uncertainly, "Jenny—don't!"

Then, before he could stop himself, he caught her against him, kissing her hair, her damp cheeks, groaning at her willing compliance, at the silken touch of her melting into him, wanting her.

Finally he pushed her away.

"Come on, gal," he said sternly, "I'm takin' you home to your maw!"

As they walked toward Sweethome, he told Jenny of his plans, making it quite clear that she was not included. When they reached the rail fence, he picked her up and set her across it.

"I'll see you again," she said. It was more of a plea than a statement.

He shook his head. "No, Jenny."

Theron St. Germain was out walking his fields, shotgun under his arm. Once he had been able to hunt, but the restrictions imposed on a one-armed man were irritating to him. Steadying a shotgun against his shoulder was almost impossible. Holding the gun butt under his arm could lead to a broken trigger finger. John had worked with him and helped him modify a weapon so that the weapon's recoil did no damage. But it was a question of relearning, and he was slow at it. A rabbit jumped almost from beneath St. Germain's feet and ran off. Swearing, Theron walked on.

Then he saw the couple at the property fence— Jenny and that damned redneck clodhopper! It looked like they were holding hands.

At his shout, they sprang apart. He advanced on them, dark eyes flashing, face like a thundercloud.

"Jenny, get home! And you"—he pointed his loaded gun at Jesse—"damn you, sir, if I ever catch you speaking to this girl again, I'll blow you full of holes."

Without waiting for an answer from the stunned Jesse, St. Germain turned Jenny about and headed her toward Sweethome.

33

By mid-November the carpets St. Germain had ordered arrived. So the great new drawing room downstairs, the small parlor, were lush underfoot though still unfurnished. That would have to wait. During the long winter months, John would construct new furniture, but in the meantime, everyday living was limited to the dining and sewing rooms, the study, breakfast room, and kitchen.

The beds and chests for the upstairs bedrooms were completed, however, and Inga and each of the girls had chambers of their own.

Kirsten insisted that she wanted her former quarters, the lovely room that had belonged to St. Germain's wife. Inga was adamant. It was unseemly, she said. Kirsten would occupy one of the bedrooms that looked out on the bridge and the creek.

Kirsten pouted. The chamber she was given was not as sumptuous as the other. The walls, however, were a soft blue, the carpet a deeper shade. The bed, though it lacked a canopy, was comfortable enough. The room had an additional advantage: Kirsten found she could see all the way to Matthew Weldon's plantation. The property even had a name—he called it Eden.

Weldon had been away from some days, but when he returned, Kirsten intended to visit him again. She would tell him about her view, that if he came out on the upper gallery, she could see him from her window.

It was a most romantic thought.

In the evening, she drew blue velvet draperies to make a frame for herself, and in her nightgown, carelessly opened to show a bit of pearly flesh, sat by the window, lamp beside her, chin on her hand. She wondered how far Matthew Weldon could see at night, and blushed at the notion.

Not that she was interested in the man, Kirsten told herself. She still was set on capturing Theron's attention. And, in a way, she had. Theron had been watching her lately. If she so much as attempted to take a walk, he always managed to stop her.

"Where are you going? Your mother needs you."

She had managed to escape his eyes only once. And that time, Weldon wasn't home. She didn't intend to let Theron keep her a prisoner here, but was flattered to think he was jealous. She intended to fan that jealousy a little further.

Jenny, too, was thinking about a man.

Sitting cross-legged on the bed in her own room, she surveyed it with satisfaction. The carpet was the rich soft brown of earth, the wallpaper the colors of autumn leaves and flowers. There was a small fireplace, and a little rocker John had constructed especially for her. The room was almost as good as being out-of-doors—in the woods, watching Jesse.

Her longing to see Jesse Norwood was almost more than she could bear. She thought of him swinging an ax, the red shirt straining across his muscular shoulders, the little house in the background beckoning to her.

He had said he was going far away, going west. He might even be gone now.

She wished she might go to see if he were still there. But St. Germain's eyes when he had aimed the gun at Jesse told her he meant what he said. She could not risk Jesse's life.

The next morning, while St. Germain still slept and Inga was busy at work in the kitchen, Kirsten put on a blue velvet cloak that had belonged to the former mistress of the house and slipped away. Hurrying across the river bridge, she made her way toward Eden.

Matthew Weldon sat with his boots stretched before a roaring fire, his silk shirt open at the throat. His breakfast sat on a small table beside him, and he was congratulating himself on his good luck. He had gone to Memphis to select furniture and there had happened upon his former aide, Johnson, whom he had immediately employed as a butler-valet. He had also found an excellent cook, a black woman named Callie. The two of them comprised his indoor staff and were already efficiently attending his needs.

Eden was truly Eden, he thought. All he required was an Eve. But he was reluctant to fetch Martha just yet. He seemed to have forgotten her face. It was Kirsten Johansson who haunted his dreams.

As if those dreams had materialized, Kirsten appeared in the doorway. The blue velvet cloak accentuated her sparkling blue eyes. Behind her stood Johnson, a sly look of amusement on his wooden features.

"Miss Johansson, sir."

"Kirsten!"

Matthew was instantly on his feet.

"Matthew!" She swept into the room, reaching warm fingers to touch his.

"L-let me take your cloak," he stammered. "Johnson, set another place."

Weldon seated Kirsten in a soft chair, where he had often imagined her. He watched her eyes light as they roamed curiously about the room, studying the graceful furnishings, the glow of polished wood, the grand piano at the far end of the spacious room.

"Everything's beautiful, Matthew! You've finished it!"

She jumped up and went to the piano, reverently touching a key. A mellow note chimed through the house. Her face was mirrored in the shining surface of hand-rubbed rosewood.

Watching her, Matthew Weldon forgot Martha completely. The gown Kirsten wore delineated high firm breasts; its skirt that swept away from a trim waist would conceal slim, rounded thighs. He trembled as he thought of their inner softness, and when he spoke her name, it sounded like a groan.

"Kirsten—"

"The lady's breakfast, sir." Johnson's voice behind him brought Weldon back to his senses with a jerk.

Sipping his coffee, Weldon watched Kirsten as she ate, daintily but with good appetite, wrinkling her nose with delight at the scent of real coffee, savoring it as she drank. His heart was pounding in his chest and his mouth went dry as he thought of holding her, touching her . . .

"Sweethome is finished too," she told him. "I chose a room that looks out on Eden. Do you know, if you stepped out on the upper gallery, I would be able to see you?"

"Indeed? Then I shall!" He flushed. "Have you ever read Shakespeare? The story of Romeo and Juliet? No? Let me lend you my copy."

He rose and left the room, returning with a leather-bound book. "Please, let me read you a little."

He skimmed through the beginning of the play about the ill-fated lovers whose families kept them apart, and read her the entire balcony scene.

Kirsten was enthralled. Imagining herself as Juliet, she even shed a tear as he finished.

"I must go," she said in a pathetic small voice. "St. Germain would be furious if he knew I was here."

Matthew did not call Johnson, but brought her blue cloak himself, arranging it around her shoulders. His hands paused, lingering for a moment; then he spoke in a choked voice. "I would like to show you the upstairs rooms, how I have furnished them, if you could spare a moment more."

She could, and did.

Each room brought a cry of delight to her lips. But when they entered the last, she was speechless. The elegance of the canopied bed, the French funiture of white and gold, the shimmering blue walls, and the occasional touches of rose made it seem the room of her dreams.

"Do you like it?"

"Oh, Matthew!"

The face she turned toward him was glowing, the blue eyes clear as limpid pools, moist pink lips that called for kissing. With a sigh that seemed to tear his body apart from his soul, Matthew Weldon stepped toward her.

"Kirsten . . . ah, sweet love!"

As his hands cupped her flowerlike face, the velvet cloak slid from her shoulders and slithered to the floor, like an invitation. Then his arms were around her and his lips were on hers, turning her soft mouth to fire.

So *that's* what kissing is like, Kirsten thought wonderingly. And then she ceased to think at all.

She was scarcely aware of masculine hands that fumbled at buttons and laces, of her own hands going involuntarily to help him. The gown rustled to the carpet to join the cloak, and her fingers worked at his shirt as he traced the softness of her breasts. Finally, the room a swirl of rose and blue about her, Kirsten braced herself, her hot palms against his bare chest as he removed his lower garments.

Weldon paused. Something told him that he should stop there. The conscience that had forced him to keep a tight rein on his emotions surfaced momentarily, battling with his need, but passion won.

He lifted Kirsten in his arms and carried her to the bed, and there he took her.

He tried to be gentle at first. Her eyes closed suddenly in a wince of pain, then opened wide with pleasure.

"Matthew—"

There was no need to be tender now. The dam of Weldon's enforced years of celibacy, his determination to remain true to Martha, had been breached. He ravished her with the savagery of his pagan ancestors, and she answered with that of her own.

When it was over, he lay spent for a moment; then, rising, he drew on his trousers and went to the window that overlooked Sweethome across the lane. Feeling another touch of conscience, he remained at the window.

Kirsten, drowsy and fulfilled, stretched like a kitten. She had finally won out over that little ninny Matthew was going to marry, she thought triumphantly. Though she hadn't intended to let it go that far.

At least she had done nothing her mother hadn't done!

As she looked affectionately at Matthew Weldon's broad bare shoulders, her passions began to build again.

"Matthew," she said seductively, "come back. Hold me . . ."

When he turned to look at her, his expression was grim. "You'd better get dressed, Kirsten. I'll help you."

Buttons were buttoned, laces were tied. And finally he bent to put her dainty slippers on her feet.

What could he have been thinking?

The eyes that raised to Kirsten's were tortured. "I didn't mean to do that, Kirsten. I'm sorry. I think you'd better go home."

Her faced paled. When he stood, no more than a breath between them, she swayed toward him and he took her in his arms.

"Dammit, girl, what are you doing to me!"

"Just loving you," she whispered. "I'm going now, Matthew. But I'll be back."

"No—"

The sound of loud voices burst upon their ears. Now it was Matthew's turn to pale. He snatched at his shirt and pulled it on, then stepped out on the balcony and looked down. Johnson was barring the front door, trying to stop someone from pushing past him.

"What is it, Johnson?" Matthew asked, hurrying down the stairs.

Johnson was flung to one side as an angry St. Germain entered. He caught himself and tried desperately to regain his equilibrium. "A gentleman, sir. He says he's come for Miss Johansson."

Kirsten, on Weldon's heels, caught her breath as she looked down into Theron St. Germain's furious eyes. Black and murderous, they bored into her own. Beside her, Matthew stiffened.

He walked toward the door and extended his hand to St. Germain. "Come in, sir. Kirsten was just leaving, but surely she won't mind waiting until you've had some coffee."

St. Germain's eyes were like black pits of frozen

hell as he glared at Weldon. "I had made a vow, sir, never to step on this property again. But the wanton behavior of my . . . my ward has forced me to break that vow. I assure you it will not happen again, and I suggest you extend me the same courtesy. Come, Kirsten!"

"Now, dammit, St. Germain, see here! The girl's done nothing—"

"Come, Kirsten!"

She stumbled forward at the menace in Theron's voice, and he took her arm in a bruising grip. Calling back a farewell to Matthew, Kirsten tried to maintain her dignity as she was dragged along by saying, "I'll see you soon."

She didn't manage to jerk free from St. Germain until they reached the bridge. They stood face to face, St. Germain black with fury, Kirsten terrified but equally angry.

"You had no right—"

"I want to remind you that as long as you are part of my household, you will respect my wishes. The people of Sweethome do not consort with Yankees—or white trash!"

"And if we do?"

"Then you will no longer be part of my household."

He propelled Kirsten toward the house and into the door, ignoring the white-faced Igna, who stood at the foot of the stairs.

"Go to your room and stay there!" he shouted.

"Theron," Inga said, stepping between him and her daughter, "what is this? What's the matter?"

The anger drained from St. Germain's face, and

suddenly he looked gray and old. "Nothing," he said somberly, "that I can't handle."

Her anger flared. "Kirsten is my daughter, and if there is a problem, I will take care of it!" She turned, and lifting her skirts, hurried up the stairs behind the sobbing girl.

Theron went into his study and sat brooding. The relationship of Jenny and Jesse Norwood had been nipped in the bud. But Kirsten and Weldon— good God, they had been upstairs together! And if he had ever seen a man look guilty, it was Weldon!

Maybe he didn't have a right to discipline Kirsten as he had, but someday he hoped to prove himself man enough to ask Inga to marry him, and Kirsten and Jenny would be his daughters.

He had a deep affection for both girls, but he would not accept a redneck or a Yankee for a son-in-law.

The question was, what in the hell was he going to do about the girls? He reached for his accounts and looked at the totals. There was one solution. If he could swing it.

34

For several weeks, relationships were strained in the St. Germain household. Kirsten remained at home, and Theron set a watch on the bridge, under the pretext that he'd heard there were raiders in the area.

Jenny wandered like a pale little ghost, dreaming that Jesse would come for her and carry her away.

And Inga was cold and silent. The sight of Theron dragging Kirsten into the house by force had brought back memories of Olaf. Theron did not tell her the circumstances in which he had found both girls, but said that they had been in the company of men he didn't trust.

Though she agreed her daughters had been thoughtless, she was certain they had done nothing wrong, that Theron's autocratic attitude was merely a form of snobbery and dislike of the men involved.

What if Weldon *were* a Yankee? The war was long over. And if Theron considered Jenny's friend ignorant white trash, then what was she, Inga, daughter of a poor farmer in Minnesota? The girls were her responsibility, and she intended to teach them that all people were equal and worthy of regard.

The tension in the household eased a little when St. Germain suggested a trip to Memphis, ostensibly to purchase supplies, bolts of cloth, and shoes as Christmas gifts for their unpaid workers. He broached the idea several days after he dragged Kirsten home from Eden.

At first Kirsten considered the trip to be his way of making up, of saying he was sorry he had behaved in such high-handed fashion—an offering to appease her hurt and anger.

But the longer she thought about it, the madder she got. It was more likely that he considered this a way of keeping her and Matthew apart. And she was convinced that she didn't want that. Her newly awakened body cried out for Matthew. Her sleep was haunted with dreams of him, the beautiful house at Eden, and the thing that had happened there.

Surely he wanted to marry her—and she would not refuse him. She would enjoy being the mistress of Eden—and looking down on Sweethome!

She sulked all the way to Memphis, with Jenny equally silent beside her. The journey was not a pleasant one.

When they checked into the Gayoso Hotel, Inga was relieved to see there was a new manager.

Kirsten forgot her fury, forgot everything but the magnificent structure that surrounded her. The hotel was reputed to have two hundred and fifty rooms, its own waterworks, gasworks for lighting, bakeries, wine cellar, sewer and drain system.

She had been there before, of course, but only with her mother, seeking employment. Now that she was a guest, she saw it with different eyes. The lobby seemed filled with important-looking people. She longed to linger there, watching the beautifully dressed ladies and gentlemen who frequented the place, but Theron hurried his entourage to their rooms.

He had business to attend to, and there were still enough hours left in the day to handle it. Tomorrow they could do their shopping.

In the evening, when he returned, they dined in the luxurious public dining room—delicate china, fine silver, starched linen cloths and napkins, a menu with unknown, exotic foods with unpronounceable names.

As St. Germain ordered for them, Kirsten decided that they made an attractive picture: Theron in an impeccable suit, his pinned-up sleeve indicating he had been a war hero; herself in a gown of silk and velvet. Even her mother and Jenny, she thought generously, didn't look out of place. If only Jenny wouldn't pesist in looking so miserable.

Jenny was.

Immersed in thoughts of Jesse Norwood, certain that he would be gone when they returned, Jenny hardly noticed her surroundings. She had grown thin and pale and so terribly quiet.

Inga watched her daughers and worried. The

unhappiness of one daughter, the lofty, sullen attitude of the other, were beyond her understanding.
She was certain they were both coming down with
something.

Jenny added to her concern by running a slight
temperature the next morning. Inga insisted that
Jenny must stay abed. To Inga's surprise, Kirsten
elected to remain with her. There was no pleasure
for her in purchasing mundane gifts for the black
workers, and the hotel was more exciting than old
stores with dusty shelves.

Inga felt a wave of relief. The rest would be good
for both girls. And she would be free to go with
Theron, just the two of them, making their purchases like any married couple from the country.

The day was as wonderful as Inga had hoped.
Jenny, who knew the new workers well, had helped
her to prepare the shopping lists. Zada, John's
young wife, had never had a red dress. So Inga
bought a bolt of turkey-red calico. Clem and Delta
had a new baby, they would need a bolt of soft
white flannel in addition to clothing for themselves.

Inga moved through the dry-goods department,
holding each piece of material to the light, pinch-
ing it between her fingers to determine its quality
as she bought prints and plains, adding a length of
cotton lace here and there for trim.

As St. Germain watched her, he thought of his
dead wife, Marnie, who didn't care about such
things. She would have been off in a whirl of
social activity and left the buying to him.

"Got some shirt material your husband might
like, missus," the storekeeper said. He spread out
a length of white patterned silk.

Inga blushed and opened her mouth, and Theron touched her arm.

"I might, at that," he said in an amused voice. "We'll take a bolt."

Inga was still rosy when they moved on to the men's department, where they bought overalls. Finally Inga submitted a series of tracings of the workers' bare feet to the clerk, who measured them for size and filled the order.

By the time they had finished with their purchases of dry goods, overalls, and shoes, it was evening. They would have to buy their staples—salt, sugar, flour, and kerosene—the next day. But instead of turning the wagon toward the hotel, St. Germain drove to a bluff that overlooked the Mississippi River.

Inga looked down at the river road on which she and her children had traveled so many long miles, running away from horror. The memory of what they had left behind them came back to her in a rush, and her expression grew pained.

"What is it, Inga?" Theron asked gently.

"It is nothing," she managed. "Just . . . tired, I suppose."

"I should have been more thoughtful. But I wanted to talk to you. It's about Kirsten and Jenny. I know you think it is none of my business, but—"

He saw her stiffen defensively.

"Dammit, Inga, listen to me! Hear me out!"

For the first time, he told her the story of how he had found Jenny with Jesse Norwood. It was obvious that there was more than friendship between them, though he didn't think it had gone too far. But Jenny was innocent, a child. Anything could

249

happen, with trash like Norwood. He hoped he'd put the fear of God in the fellow, but—

"Jenny wouldn't—"

"But Kirsten would," he interrupted, and told her how he had found Kirsten coming out of an upstairs bedroom with Matthew Weldom, still adjusting her gown. "They both looked guilty as hell," he added.

"Just because he was a Union officer," Inga said hotly, "you're ready to think—"

"Because he's a man, Inga," Theron said gently. "And your daughter would be hard to resist."

Inga thought of Kirsten's pursuit of Theron, her obvious bids for his attention, and began to tremble. It was true. She could see it in his eyes.

Tears began to streak her checks, and he put his arm around her.

"What can I do, Theron? Oh, God, what can I do!"

"I've checked my finances. We can send the girls here to Memphis, to school. Give them a chance for an education, and time to grow up a little. I looked into it yesterday."

School! An education! It was what she had always wanted for her daughters. They would be safe here. Jenny was so sweet and loving, an innocent. She mustn't be hurt. And Kirsten didn't know her own mind. She was apt to do anything on the spur of the moment.

Theron was right. They should be removed from temptation.

But she couldn't let them go! She couldn't! A new thought suddenly struck her. "If we did what you suggest, I couldn't stay at Sweethome, Theron."

"I have the answer to that, too. Inga, marry me."

She had known those words would come, and still she wasn't ready for them. Her heart longed to say yes, oh, yes. But before her she could see the river, a river that began in a clear stream at its headwaters in Minnesota, opaque and muddy when it reached Memphis, with the wreckage of dead ships along the way. It was like her life, once clean, untouched, now soiled, with hidden horrors beneath its surface.

"I can't, Theron. Please—"

But the arm that held her pulled her close, his lips touched her own with a tenderness that brought more tears to her eyes.

"I won't take no for an answer," he said. "But for now, let's do first things first."

She sat in dazed silence as they drove back to the hotel, the feel of his mouth still warm against her own, burning with the desire to reach out and touch him, to tell him she loved him.

Maybe, she thought numbly, it might be better to take her daughters and move on, hide. . . .

Hide from Theron St. Germain, the dark, brooding man at her side—and from herself.

35

The girls had spent an uneventful day. Jenny stayed in her room moping, and Kirsten promenaded the length of the hotel. Aside from the admiring glances of several young officers and a leering fat man in a business suit, there had been no excitement. In addition, it had dawned on Kirsten that if she had insisted on going, Inga might have stayed with the ailing Jenny, and Kirsten would have been alone with Theron.

Of course, she wasn't too sure she wanted Theron anymore, but it would have been nice to turn him down, to watch him suffer. She would see to it that she accompanied him tomorrow.

The next day, to Kirsten's dismay, St. Germain insisted they all go with him. The staples for the plantation were purchased quickly, so they could get to the business he had in mind. He drove them to a four-story brick building that looked prisonlike and grim. Stepping down first, St. Germain helped the women from the wagon, silently.

Kirsten read the words on the building's facade: "MEMPHIS FEMALE COLLEGE." She looked at Theron in sudden dread.

"It's a surprise," he said, forcing a smile. "I was here earlier this morning to see about enrolling you and Jenny. The headmistress insisted on meeting you first."

Kirsten looked at her mother. Inga was white as a sheet. Her mouth had a blue cast to it. Jenny appeared to be in shock.

Kirsten's voice, when it came, was like a thin scream. "I won't! You can't make me! I won't!"

"Nobody's making you, Kirsten," Inga said quietly. "But I think you should go in—see what the school is like. This is a wonderful opportunity, and you should thank Theron for it. You were happy enough to go to school in Minnesota."

In Minnesota Kirsten had been happy for the chance to get away from home. Now she only wished to return to Sweethome—and Matthew Weldon.

"Come," Inga said. It was not a request, but a command.

Numbly the girls obeyed. In the building, Theron led them to the office of the headmistress and introduced them.

"My wards, Mrs. Pickett. The young ladies I discussed with you yesterday."

Mrs. Pickett peered through her glasses at Kirsten. She saw a rebellious young woman in a gown too adult for her age, and hair done in elaborate curls too fancy for the occasion.

"All our students will be required to wear uniform clothing," she said over Kirsten's head, speaking to St. Germain. "Black skirts and white blouses buttoned to the throat. We encourage modesty here."

Then Jenny was subjected to her piercing gaze.

Vanity, Mrs. Pickett was accustomed to. This child represented the opposite. Her black hair was disheveled, her short gown revealed scratched ankles. She was dark enough to be a Gypsy, and seemed to be poised for flight.

"As I told you, Mr. St. Germain, this school is for young women of a certain class. Your wards, you told me, have little prior education, and no social background, an important prerequisite here. If you can give me any information on their ancestry—"

"I have told you, they are Swedish."

"Indeed?" The woman's eyes returned to Jenny again. "I have also told you," Theron said angrily, "that I will vouch for them! If you choose to doubt my word—"

Suddenly the vinegar was mixed with honey. "Of course, Mr. St. Germain. Everyone knows that you come from one of our fine old families. If you say—"

"I do," he said shortly.

"Then I will explain our system of teaching. As I told you, this is a four-year program. The young ladies will learn reading—the classics, of course; enough arithmetic to do household accounts; fine sewing and watercolor; and the social graces.

"There will be no involvement with young men, except for our annual ball, which will be well-chaperoned, and none of our girls will be allowed to leave the premises without a chaperon. Unfortunately"—she smiled—"there will be no openings in our student body until January. They may enroll than, if that is satisfactory."

"It is," Inga said before Theron could speak. They had a reprieve.

Both girls were silent on the way back to the hotel. Kirsten was still stunned at the turn of events. Now she realized that, contrary to her hopes and dreams, Theron wished to be rid of her. Not only that, he intended to keep her far from Matthew Weldon, too!

Jenny was thinking of Jesse. If he went in one direction, she in another, they would be lost to each other forever.

It was a glum group that started out for Sweethome in the heavily laden wagon. St. Germain held the reins and Inga rode beside him. The girls were seated uncomfortably amid the boxes and barrels in the back. There was no conversation. Inga had tried to explain that Theron's motives for sending them to school was only that he wanted them to be educated as young ladies should be.

Her voice trailed off as they turned away from her, and she felt a deep sense of guilt. Had she wanted this to happen so that she would have Theron all to herself? She wasn't sure.

They bounced along, not speaking to one another on the road or at their nightly stops—a group of strangers traveling together, all of them sunk in unhappiness.

The sky, as they neared Sweethome, seemed to reflect their misery. Clouds formed above them, fat and puffy, gray and heavy, gradually blotting out the sun. By the time they pulled across the bridge, the wind had begun to blow. Dead leaves, scurrying across the lane like live things, spooked the horses. Before they reached the house, the sky was black and it was raining, an icy rain that froze on ground and tree, a rain that, later, would turn into blinding sleet.

After they ate the hot meal Dinah prepared for them, the girls went to their rooms.

Kirsten stared out of a window blank with coated ice, unable to see Matthew Weldon's house. Finally she took out the small pouch she had hidden beneath her clothes in a bureau drawer, to look at the jewels she had held back. It was ironic that the buried treasure she had found—and shared with St. Germain—had given him the means to pay her tuition, to send her away.

She didn't intend to acquiesce quietly. She had until January. Before then she would either force Matthew to propose marriage or she would leave Sweethome.

Jenny had donned a flannel nightdress and gone right to bed. The trip had been long and tiring, and she was soon asleep. Then she woke thinking she had heard the sound of Jesse's voice. He was calling her. . . .

Rising, she paced her room. This was the second time that she had a feeling he needed her. The first had been two days ago. What if he were sick? what if his hand had not healed, but had become infected? She was sure Jesse needed her.

Everyone thought she had gone to bed, and no one would suspect that she'd go out on such a terrible night, Jenny figured.

She removed her nightdress and pulled on a dress and coat. Later, tiptoeing through the house, she felt a sense of urgency that terrified her. She ran out into the night, not noticing that the door didn't catch, but blew open behind her. Sleet stung her face like a multitude of tiny daggers, and her lashes were soon frosted; the ground was slippery underfoot, but she forged ahead.

Inga lay awake until after midnight, listening to the wind howl about the house, sleet slap against the windows. She felt trapped, frightened.

She loved Theron St. Germain. But she couldn't marry him. He was a man of fierce pride and many prejudices, and she could be no one but herself. They might be happy for a while, but one day he would think of her as he did Jesse Norwood—not good enough. She couldn't bear that.

As for the girls, he was right: they should be sent to school, given time to grow up a little before they chose their mates. But the big brick building had frightened Inga. Jenny would die there, like a wild bird trapped in a cage. She couldn't let her go. Nor Kirsten!

The best course of action was for all of them to leave Sweethome, to set out and find another place for themselves, but that would be impossible in the winter. If the girls could endure the school until spring, if she could control her emotions until that time, they would leave.

Suddenly she needed to talk it over with someone. With Jenny.

She rose, without bothering to search for a robe, and slipping down the hall to Jenny's door, tapped gently. "Jenny?"

There was no answer.

Puzzled, she opened the door. A candle burned low; the bed was rumpled, but Jenny was not in sight. She peeped into Kirsten's room. Jenny wasn't there, and Kirsten was asleep, her golden hair spread out on her pillow.

Finally she went downstairs. Maybe Jenny couldn't sleep and had gone down to fix a cup of tea. Inga hoped not. It was freezing downstairs, as if someone had left a window open.

She hurried down the hall, past the dining room, the breakfast room, to find the back door standing open. A blast of sleet caught her full in the face. Jenny would not have gone out in this! Not unless someone had forced her . . .

But she was nowhere to be found.

Finally, terrified, Inga raced up the stairs to batter on St. Germain's door.

"She's gone! Jenny's gone!" Inga cried, eyes wild with fright.

Unable to make sense of her babbling, Theron put his good arm around her and coaxed her inside. Seating her in a chair, he knelt beside her. "Now, what is it?" he asked. "Tell me calmly."

Kirsten, down the hall, had heard the noise. Dazed with sleep, she opened her door and saw her mother and Theron St. Germain in their nightclothes, his arm around her as he drew her into his room and closed the door.

36

Jenny paused for a moment as she neared the slave cabins, wondering if she could possibly reach Jesse's house in such weather—and what she would do if he were not there. The hood to her cloak had blown back, and her hair had slipped from its braids, its ends coated with ice. The bottom of her gown first got wet, then froze stiff as a board and banged at her ankles. The ground was covered with ice, and she could only manage to stay upright with a gliding walk, like skating.

She leaned against a cabin wall to clear her eyes of sleet, then glided on.

When she crossed the frozen fields, there was no protection and the wind swirled around her, whipping her hair into her face, blinding her. Once, she fell. For a moment she only wanted to lie there, to never get up. Finally she rose and went doggedly on, praying to reach the trees.

It was not much better there; limbs and trunks were coated and glistening. It was like being in a forest of glass. Saplings that had been supple had become barriers; dry twigs, sharp and deadly weapons. It was hard to believe that summer had ever been, that flowers ever bloomed here, birds ever sang.

Then she was out of the trees, brittle grass breaking beneath her feet, moving ahead on instinct. Again she stepped on a patch of ice. Again she fell.

Reaching out a hand to help herself up, she touched something—metal so cold it froze to her fingers, tearing the skin.

Jesse's ax! Not thrust into the stump as he usually left it, but lying on the ground. Rising, she stumbled on until she saw his cabin looming before her. She struggled up the steps and pounded at the closed door with a fist that felt as if it had frozen and would splinter away.

There was no answer.

She opened the door cautiously, to be met by air only a little less frigid than that outside.

Then he had left.

She did not cry. If she did, she feared, her tears would be frozen.

Now there was nothing to do but save herself.

Moving toward the fireplace, she stubbed her freezing toes against a piece of firewood. A few steps farther, she discovered another. Working in the darkness, she laid them on the hearth and felt around until she found the kerosene can. Dousing the wood, she ran icy fingers along the top of the mantel until she located the matches. She lit one and touched it to the wood. It burst into flame.

After she found the lamps and lit them, she looked around in confusion.

Evidently Jesse had walked off and left everything as it was, even a pot of something that had been cooking on the stove. It had boiled down until there was nothing left on the now cold stove but a leathery, scorched mess.

Jenny held her lamp high. The door to Jesse's lean-to bedroom stood half-open, a yawning darkness. She approached it, her heart beating in terror. For there, on the wide board floor, just outside the bedroom, was a bloody footprint. She felt dizzy as she pushed at the door and it creaked open.

She could see a tumble of blankets, a dark, still form beneath them, and she stopped in horror.

Then she heard her name, just as she had in her dream.

"Jenny . . ."

She rushed to the bed, holding up the lamp to illuminate features that were gray with cold. Jesse's eyes were glazed. She shook him.

"Jesse, what is it? What's wrong with you?"

"Leg," he mumbled. "Ax . . ."

Stripping back the blankets, she uncovered a shivering body. He was fully dressed except for one boot. The other foot, bare and somehow defenseless-looking, was wrapped from ankle to knee in a dish towel, caked and hardened with dried blood.

Somehow she had to get him out of there and to the fire.

First she carried his blankets in and laid them

before the fireplace, then returned to get him up. His injured side to her, his arm around her shoulders, she pulled him out of bed. It was a slow process, but she was able bear his weight and guide him to the pallet, where he passed out from exhaustion.

She hated to leave him even for a moment, but she knew she needed to get something hot inside him. Going out again into the storm, she found more chunks of stove wood, which needed the ice knocked off them before she could bring them inside.

She found a small amount of kindling beside the cookstove, and soon had a fire going. Taking water from a pail with a thin frozen film atop it, she filled the teakettle and set it to boil. When it was hot, she made a cup of tea and held it to Jesse's lips until she was able to get a few drops down him.

Then she filled a basin, and setting the lamp close, began to remove the bandage that seemed cemented to his leg. Beneath it was a nasty gash. The slash seemed to have missed tendons, but had gone to the bone, breaking it. And infection had set in.

Trying to recall where Jesse kept the whiskey his father had made, she searched until she located it. Then she washed his wound and rebandaged it as well as she could.

He must not get cold again, she thought, and worked to build up the fire. Finally she stood before it until her gown was warm and dry, and then lay down beside Jesse, cradling his head against her bosom.

He turned toward her with a sigh, and slept. Only then could Jenny give in to her tears.

"Get well, Jesse," she whispered. "Please . . . for me . . . get well."

37

At Sweethome, St. Germain held Inga's trembling body against his own. Though his alarm was as great as hers, he tried to soothe her. Perhaps one of the workers was ill, he said, probably one of the children. Jenny might have gone out there. He would dress and check.

Inga looked down, and remembering she was in her nightdress, fled to do the same. She was ready when Theron came from his room, and followed him down. His comforting words had done nothing to calm her. Running off and leaving the door open, the sleet blowing in, wasn't like Jenny.

As Theron stepped outside, his boots slipped on the icy steps and he went down. Unable to catch his balance with his one arm, he struck his head.

Inga knelt beside him, trying to stanch the blood that flowed from his injury with her petticoat.

Finally she remembered the yard bell. It rang out its call for help, and candles in the cabins beyond flickered on.

Kirsten heard the bell as she crossed the icy bridge, but told herself it had been activated by the wind. She forgot it in fighting for survival, clinging to the railing for support. Her hair had whipped loose, and her cloak, the remaining jewels in its pocket, swirled around her as she fought doggedly on.

To think, all the time she'd been pursuing Theron St. Germain, the two of them had been making a fool of her, slipping around behind her back! Laughing! To hell with them all!

She intended to nudge Matthew into declaring his intentions tonight. Then let them laugh!

Her face was sparkling with frozen tears when she reached the house called Eden and raised her hand to the knocker. She stopped. The noise would probably wake everyone in the house. Johnson would answer the door, and she couldn't face him! She couldn't face anyone but Matthew. She drew her hand away and tried the knob. The door opened.

Kirsten found a candle on the table inside the door, lit it, and tiptoed up the stairs. She knew where Matthew Weldon slept, just across from the room she had wished could be her own.

At his door she listened. Hearing the sound of his even breathing, she turned the knob and entered. There was a fire in his fireplace, and flickering flames lit the room, gilding the brown head on the pillow, burnishing a smooth boyish face with gold. The blankets were dragged away. It was clear that

Matthew was a man with two good arms and a strong body.

Kirsten felt a sinking sensation in the pit of her stomach, and turned from the sight. Seeing him like that made her feel strange, confused. She had to be able to think, and she must stop shivering.

She set down the candle, shrugged out of her ice-encrusted coat, and went to warm her hands at the fire, fluffing out her hair so that it would dry.

What was she going to say to him? That her mother was sleeping with St. Germain, and she refused to stay under the same roof with them?

No! She would tell him that she'd dreamed of him! That she realized she couldn't live without him. That she'd come to him, through the storm raging outside, with her love.

Her lips curved into a smile. He couldn't refuse her.

A framed picture above the mantel, a portrait of a young woman who seemed pleasantly pretty and self-contained, caught her eye.

That would be Matthew's Martha.

Kirsten stuck out her tongue at the smiling face, and going to Weldon's bedside, bent to touch his cheek.

"Matthew?"

His eyes opened to meet a blue gaze inches from his; he was entangled in a silken tent of golden hair. He felt a small hand slide down his body, caressing, exploring.

"Kirsten!"

"I had to come," she whispered. Then whatever she intended to say was suddenly lost. His eyes were different, their blue darkening. His hand came up to cup her chin, and she couldn't escape that hypnotic gaze that made her all shivery inside.

"You know you shouldn't be here," he said.

"Do you want me?"

"Yes ... No ... Kirsten, for God's sake!" The caressing hand had moved lower, and he groaned. "You don't know what you're doing to me!"

"What am I doing, Matthew?"

"You're driving me insane! Dammit, get away from me! Let me sit up! Give me a chance to think!"

She moved back immediately, and he swung his legs to the floor, staring at her, seeing the hurt in her eyes, her quivering mouth. He buried his face in his hands.

Matthew Weldon was an honorable man. He had pledged his heart to Martha Cabot, and had remained true to her until his brief encounter with this enchanting, disturbing girl. The last few days, upset by feelings of guilt and self-hatred, he had finally come to terms with his conscience by making a vow. He would put all memories of that magical morning with Kirsten from his mind. He would go to fetch Martha as soon as possible. And he would not see Kirsten Johansson again.

Yet here she was, her face glowing from her walk through the storm, a passionate she-devil with the face of an angel.

And he could not help himself.

"I was wrong to come," Kirsten breathed. "I'm sorry if I—"

She didn't finish her sentence. He took her hands and pulled her toward him. Together they fell backward on the bed, and his hands moved freely, roughly, hurting.

"Do you know what you're doing, coming here?" he panted, his eyes flickering with hot blue flame. "Tell me, Kirsten, do you know?"

Her lips curved. "Yes, Matthew, I do."

His mouth captured hers with a passionate greed that set every nerve in her body screaming for more. Hands began to undo buttons and fastenings, his hands, and then her own to help him, and finally there was the pulsing of one body against another, striving to become a single entity.

"Yes," she whispered. "Oh, yes!"

She had won, she thought triumphantly as she felt an ecstasy she had only dreamed of. She had won!

38

The sound of the bell at Sweethome brought its workers slipping and sliding over the ice. Two of them carried St. Germain inside and placed him carefully on a couch in his study.

"He goin' to be jes' fine," one of them assured Inga. "Haid hurt when he wakes up . . ."

There was less optimism when she told them that Jenny had disappeared. She had not come to the cabins, they said. But she might have attempted to, and bypassed them in the heavy curtain of snow. If so, she was probably wandering in the fields beyond.

Jenny was their little missie, their friend. Lost in this storm, she wouldn't have much chance of survival. They would find her. But the bell had called them out unprepared. They returned to their cabins to wrap their boots in rags—to help them keep their footing—and to get lanterns. Finally, clothed properly and wrapped in blankets, they set about dividing Sweethome into sectors, and went out into the howling night to search for her.

Dinah hurried up to the big house. With Jenny gone, and St. Germain hurt, the missus wuz goin' need some help.

Inga, who sat sponging the blood from Theron's temple, was never so glad to see anyone in her life.

"Bes' thing, we puts ice on it." Dinah, half-fozen, peered down at St. Germain's injury.

Inga's breath caught on a hysterical giggle. Ice? They had more of that than they needed. The giggle turned into tears, and Dinah put her arms around her.

"He goin' be awright, missus. And them men, they goin' fine our Jenny!"

They did not. From time to time they reported in, half-frozen, to partake of the coffee Dinah kept boiling on the stove, gray-faced, afraid to look Inga in the eyes.

Unless the girl had found some shelter and was holed up somewhere, they knew they would not find her alive.

Inga, aware she could add nothing to the search, sat beside Theron throughout the night. For all she knew, he too was dying. She forced herself into a false calm, blotting her worries from her mind.

When Theron opened his eyes, it was nearly dawn. He lifted a trembling hand to his head. "It hurts," he whispered.

"You fell," she told him.

"There was something . . . something . . . I was going to do something . . ."

270

"It has been done," she whispered. "Now sleep."

With a smile that ended in a grimace of pain, he closed his eyes again.

Throughout the morning, it kept snowing. The workers arrived every few hours to report: Jenny had not been found.

Inga was aware that Kirsten had not put in an appearance at breakfast, but that was not unusual. When she was sulking about something, she remained abed. And she'd been so upset about the school.

The school!

Inga wished she had put her foot down! Told the girls it was their decision! If that had been the reason Jenny went out into the night . . .

She mustn't think about it, not now, not until Jenny was found. Let Kirsten sleep. Soon enough she'd find out her sister was lost. At least she hadn't had to endure the helplessness of these last hours.

When Kirsten did not appear at noon, however, Inga began to worry. Leaving the sleeping Theron, she made her way upstairs and rapped on Kirsten's door.

There was no answer.

Inga felt a choking senation in her throat. It was all happening over again, just as it had with Jenny. Her hands shaking, she pushed the door open.

Kirsten's bed was empty. She, too, was gone.

And they had not gone together. When she discovered Jenny's absence, Kirsten had been asleep. Now her nightdress lay tossed across the bed, the door to the clothes cupboard open, several gowns draped on a chair. A frantic search revealed that

Kirsten's favorite gown was missing as well as her best cloak, a blue velvet that had belonged to Marnie St. Germain.

There were no clues to Jenny's disappearance, but Kirsten's had been planned.

Inga went back downstairs. Dinah, seeing the white face of her mistress, knew that something else had gone wrong.

Inga spilled out her story, and the old woman shook her head. "That Kirsten! Needs her backside smacked. Where you reckon she done went?"

"I . . . I don't know," Inga faltered.

"I believe I do."

St. Germain was trying to sit up, his face as white as paper. "You don't need to concern yourself about Kirsten. I'm sure she's found herself a roof! It's Jenny . . . Jenny! You haven't found her, have you?"

Inga pressed him back to the pillows. "The workers are looking for Jenny. There's nothing we can do at the moment. Just rest."

He put a hand to his head. "How long ago did this happen?"

"Not long," Inga lied. "Just minutes."

"But how many minutes!"

It was evening before Theron was thoroughly rational. Inga, sitting beside his makeshift bed, had drifted into an uneasy sleep. She woke to find him trying to pull on his boots with his one hand, his face as white as the bandage above it.

"I'm going to find Jenny," he said. "I think I know where she is. That damned redneck—"

"Jesse Norwood? She wouldn't have gone there! Not in such a storm. Not in the middle of the night!"

"We'll see," he said grimly.

"If she did," Inga said, her voice leaden, "she would never have made it that far. We'll have to wait until daylight, Theron."

What she said made sense. And if the girls were where he thought they were he would never forgive them for what they had done to their mother. As for the men involved—he intended to kill the bastards, to blow them straight to hell!

Inga and Theron left the house the next morning, heading for Eden across the way. Kirsten first, Theron said, since they were almost certain to find her. Then Jenny.

Wincing at each step, he strode ahead of Inga, who slipped on the icy terrain as she tried to keep pace with him. The wind and sleet had stopped, their fury diminishing to a soft haze of fine snow.

When they reached Weldon's house, St. Germain turned the knob and walked in.

"Theron, please . . ." Inga was appalled.

He ignored her, and going up the stairs, threw open a door to reveal an empty room. He moved on to the next. And there he found them.

Kirsten lay beside Matthew Weldon, cuddled in the crook of his arm, her fair hair spread out across his shoulder. She sat up, suddenly defensive as she saw her mother's shocked white face and Theron's angry one. For the first time, she realized what she'd done.

But they had driven her to it! It was their fault! Their fault! They had no right to condemn her for behaving as they did. Besides, she loved Matthew!

Clutching the sheet that covered her, she looked to Matthew for help. She had never seen a more

273

uncomfortable man in her life! Tell them you love me, she pleaded with her eyes. Tell them we're going to be married.

"It was a mistake," Weldon said hoarsely. "I am engaged to a girl back home. I had no intention of ..." He stopped, seeing Kirsten's shocked eyes. His voice trailed off weakly. Whatever he said seemed to sound wrong. He had to get his wits together.

"Of course, I intend to do the right thing by Kirsten," he said in an unconvincing tone. "I will marry her."

Kirsten flinched at his tone, her eyes beginning to spark. "You don't have to, Matthew, if you don't want to!"

St. Germain shouted her down. "You're damned right you will!" He choked on his words. "Because I intend to see to it! And then, by God, I don't want either of you stepping foot on Sweethome again!"

Again Kirsten looked to Weldon. "Matthew—"

"Keep out of this, Kirsten, this is between St. Germain and me."

Kirsten felt a hard knot of anger in her chest. She was a grown woman, not a child to have her life ordered for her.

"You're not telling me what to do, Matthew Weldon!" She whirled on St. Germain. "And neither are you! Or you!" She glared at her mother. "You're not so damned pure yourself! I know what you and Theron have been up to, sneaking into each other's rooms at night!"

Inga turned white. "That's enough, Kirsten!"

Once begun, Kirsten couldn't stop.

"Is it? Or should I mention the rest? Anybody can see Jenny's not my real sister! Maybe I should mention the man on the boat, the man you were having an affair with! A long-standing affair, I would think! What happened to him? Didn't he want you after you killed your husband?"

Inga made a small wounded sound, and Kirsten continued to pour out her fury. St. Germain moved toward Kirsten, murder in his eyes, but Weldon was already shaking the girl.

"Stop it," he ordered. "Stop it, Kirsten!" Finally he slapped her. "You don't know what you're saying!"

She shrank back, teeth bared. "But I do know! And don't you touch me again! I hate you! All of you!"

"Colonel St. Germain," Weldon said quietly, "I will ask you to wait downstairs in my study until I can get dressed. Then we can discuss this on a more equal basis."

Theron bowed and took Inga's arm. She stumbled along beside him like a sleepwalker. When they located Weldon's study, he seated her in a chair and went to a window. Drawing the draperies aside, he stared out at the sifting snow. Now was not the time for conversation.

In the bedroom, Weldon put on his clothes, then turned to look at Kirsten. "I'm not sure I understand what's going on—why you came here, what the problem is between you and your mother—but I'm going to try to straighten things out. About . . . what happened, all I can say is, I'm sorry."

Kirsten closed her eyes. Was he saying he was sorry he loved her? Or sorry they were caught at

275

it? Whichever way he meant it, she knew that what they had between them was over.

Within a few minutes Weldon was downstairs, his shirt half-buttoned, feet thrust in slippers, finger-combing his brown hair into position.

"I feel like hell about this situation," he told Theron. "To be honest, it wasn't the first time. I didn't intend for it to happen again, but when Kirsten showed up in the middle of the night . . ."

St. Germain nodded grimly. He could imagine what had happened.

Weldon stopped, grinning wryly, and made a helpless gesture with his hands.

"Do you love her?" St. Germain asked.

"Yes," he said, frowning a little, trying to put the thought of sweet, dependable Martha from his mind. "Sometimes I find it hard to *like* her . . . but, yes, I suppose I do."

St. Germain sighed and put a hand to his temple. It was throbbing like the very devil, and there were other things to do.

"Then I suggest you find a minister. I'm asking for your word as an officer and a gentleman that you will look after the girl properly. Her mother has other problems. Jenny is missing—"

"Jenny?" Weldon's eyes flashed with sudden concern. "Good Lord! Does Kirsten know that?"

St. Germain shook his head.

"But Jenny can't be out in this storm."

"The property is being searched. They haven't found her. I can think of only one place . . ." Theron paused and sighed, then taking Inga's arm, said, "Come, we've found one of your daughters. Now we have to find the other."

"I will look after this one," Weldon said firmly.

He had no idea, at the moment, that he would be unable to keep his promise.

Kirsten, despising all of them, had pulled on her clothes and run from the house. She had almost reached the bridge when she heard her mother and Theron coming behind her. They were not going to stop her, she told herself fiercely.

She turned and slid down the creek bank, trusting to the ice to hold her. But the water beneath the bridge was not yet frozen solid, and she stood ankle-deep in it, shuddering with cold as they crossed the bridge above her. Chunks of ice, dislodged by the movement, rained down upon her.

She hated them, hated Matthew, and most of all, she hated herself.

What had happened between herself and Matthew had seemed so beautiful, so right. Lying in his arms, she felt she'd erased his feelings for Martha, that she would be mistress of Eden. But now she knew that he'd only taken what was so freely given.

Damn him!

And damn Theron St. Germain!

Damn them all!

They'd had a little private meeting to decide what to do with her life! As far as she was concerned, they could all go to hell!

Her feet were numb as she fought her way up the icy creek bank. Inga and St. Germain had disappeared. They would have gone in by the front door, she thought, and that served her purpose. The jewels she had found in the pocket of her cloak. Now all she needed was a horse from the stable.

She rounded the house and froze. Inga and Theron were still in the yard, moving toward a shadowed figure.

"Ain't found nuthin' yet, Mista Theron," the worker called.

Kirsten's lip curled. Evidently they'd set the blacks searching for her before they came to Eden. She wondered what explanation they would give for calling off the search!

She hurried to the stable.

A few minutes later, she led a saddled horse across the arched bridge, the sound of its hooves muffled by the falling snow. Then, reaching the lane, she swung herself into the saddle and rode toward Memphis.

39

Gray dawn peeped through the windows of Jesse Norwood's shack, and he opened puzzled eyes to stare into the fire. *He had made it, then!*

Slowly his memory came back to him. It had been a clear bright day with a chill to it. He knew it was the kind of day Jenny loved, and while he was chopping wood, he thought he saw a flicker of red among the trees. Distracted, he grew careless, and the ax came down in the wrong spot, deflecting off the wood and cutting into his leg.

He remembered crawling to the house, removing his boot, trying to stop the flow of blood. Then he had passed out, waking later in a cold room rank with the odor of burned stew. How long he lay there too weak to move, he had no idea. But he remembered being cold, dragging himself to the porch, to find the weather had changed. Pelted with sleet, he managed to get several logs inside, and tried to roll them to the hearth, but couldn't finish the job. Finally he'd crept to his bed, to lie shivering until his blood slowed and he felt nothing more.

Now he stared into the hypnotic flames, feeling their warmth melting through him. He had survived. Somehow he had also been able to get the cabin warm. Then he realized the cook fire was set; something simmering on it sent out a delicious aroma. He swallowed and lifted his head.

Jenny!

The girl stood stirring something on the stove, her dress open at the throat, sleeves rolled to the elbows revealing slim brown arms, dark hair hanging down her back.

Either he was delirious or he had died and gone to heaven.

Jenny, sensing his eyes on her, turned to look at him. With a small cry, she shoved the kettle to the back of the stove and ran to kneel at his side, bursting into tears of relief.

"Jesse," she wept. "Oh, Jesse . . ."

He raised a hand wonderingly to her cheek, tracing the tears that flowed so freely. "It *is* you! Oh, Jenny, love—"

Then she was in his arms and kissing him.

Holding her tightly, feeling the rising of his desire, knowing at last that this was not a dream and that he was still alive, he kissed her again and again. Ardently he pulled her down beside him.

Jenny rose and backed away, her face pink. "Your broth," she said. "I don't think you've eaten for a long time. I'll get it."

He tried to raise himself to watch her as she got a cup from the shelf and ladled something into it. Then the blanket slipped from his bared shoulders, and he realized he didn't have a stitch on beneath it. She had cut away his bloodied clothes.

Jenny returned to sit beside him, sliding an arm behind him as support, and held the cup to his lips.

He sipped at it slowly, as she directed. And with every sip, his strength returned, and with it, his senses. He looked at the window. The day was beginning to brighten. He stirred uneasily, gesturing for her to take the cup away.

She didn't rise, but set it on the floor beside her.

"How long you been here, Jenny?"

She blushed. "Since night before last."

His gray eyes were filled with concern, because he knew how the situation would look to someone like St. Germain, and it would cause trouble for Jenny.

"St. Germain know where you are?" Her face told him that he didn't. "He's gonna be madder'n hell!"

Jenny tossed her head, her lips set firm. "I don't care!"

"Oh, Jenny, Jenny . . ."

He drew her down to him again, kissing her forehead, her eyelids, her wonderful, gentle mouth. Jenny, with a sigh, cuddled close to him, running her hands across his broad, muscled shoulders.

"I was afraid you'd already gone, Jesse."

"Should of," he said. "Guess I kept hangin'

around, like a damn fool, hopin' I'd see you again. Prob'ly got you in a mess of trouble to home—"

"I don't care," she said again. "Jesse, don't leave me!"

He held her tight, savoring her sweetness. He would have to go, just as soon as he could walk, for Jenny's sake, if not his own. But there was no point in thinking about that now. Not when she was so close, so dear.

Oh, hell! He ached with his need for her, but he had to stop this, get her out of the house some way, before—

His thoughts halted as the door slammed open. Theron St. Germain and a woman stood framed in the doorway.

"Jenny!" Inga's cry was torn from the depths of her soul. She seemed to shrink into the circle of Theron's arm.

"Get up, Jenny!" St. Germain's voice had no menacing edge. He sounded weary and old. As Jenny rose, backing away, he said, "I think you owe your mother an explanation."

"It ain't like it looks," Jesse Norwood said weakly. "Reckon I'd of died if Jenny didn't find me. We didn't . . . we ain't—"

"What we walked in on seems to refute your statement, sir! Jenny, get your cloak!"

The girl stared at him mutinously. "Jesse's hurt. I'm not leaving!"

"The hell you're not!" Theron strode toward her, gripping her arm, dragging her toward the door. To Inga, it was like the replay of a nightmare. "Theron, stop it!"

St. Germain turned to look at her.

Her eyes snapped, red spots on each cheek betraying her sudden anger. "It's quite obvious the man is ill, Theron. Jenny often tends the sick in the quarters. I see no difference—"

"Well, by God, I do!" Theron glared at the injured man. "If she were my daughter—"

"But she isn't, Theron. She's mine. And I trust her."

Theron looked as if he'd been slapped, but he persisted in his fury. "Trust her! Alone with that . . . that redneck trash? Especially after Kirsten—"

It was Inga's turn to flinch. "Jenny isn't Kirsten, Theron," she said quietly. "And the man is sick. I suggest we take him to Sweethome, where he can be cared for properly."

Jenny's eyes lit up, but St. Germain's black brows drew together, his jaw jutting. "I will not have that man in my house! As far as I'm concerned, he ought to be horsewhipped!" He paused, trying to calm himself, shaking his dark head in bewilderment.

"You're young, Jenny. Too young to understand that this is a . . . a compromising situation. I'm not going to drag you home, but I'm asking you, for your mother's sake, to come along."

Jesse, his face livid with fever, hunched himself to his elbows. "I don't like the bastard, Jenny. But he's right. You shouldn't be here. I can take care of myse'f, honey."

"No." Jenny's face was implacable.

I'm losing her, Inga thought. She moved to stand beside her daughter. "She's staying, Theron. I'll stay with her."

Theron sighed heavily. "Then suppose you

283

women get the hell away. I'll take a look at that leg."

They obeyed, moving to stand silently at the stove. St. Germain threw Jesse's blankets back, scowling at his unclad body. "You might at least have had the decency to put on a nightshirt."

"Don't own one," Jesse said.

"I'll send one over," Theron said grimly.

When he unwrapped Norwood's bandages, he drew in a sharp breath. It was clear the boy was in no shape to be a threat to a woman's virtue. Unless someone watched it, he might even lose that leg.

Theron felt a sympathy pain in the stump of his arm.

He stepped over to join the women. "You can stay, Jenny," he said quietly. "But only during the day, and only until he's on the road to recovery. I'll have one of the men take over at night. Is that acceptable?"

Jenny's eyes filled with tears, and she scrubbed at her face with her sleeve. "Yes," she said in a small voice.

Theron turned to Inga. "Let's go. You and Dinah will have to prepare some medications. I'll have John bring them over as soon as possible."

"Thank you," Jenny whispered. "Thank you."

Theron didn't answer, but walked away. Jenny looked at Inga and said, "Thank you, Mama, for understanding."

"Theron didn't mean the things he said," Inga told her. "He's a good man."

"And so is Jesse."

Inga hurried to catch up with Theron, her mind

in turmoil. She had already lost Kirsten, and Jenny was growing up.

Why did it hurt her so?

She and Theron walked back across the fields. The snow had stopped, and the sun was shining, turning everything around them into a fairyland. Dry grass sparkled in icy fronds; bare ground depicted frozen ponds; trees were sculptured in glass.

Inga saw none of it as Theron led her toward the house.

The workers were told Jenny had been found, that she had gone on an errand of mercy. Inga helped Dinah prepare the necessary poultices and herbal teas, and John was sent to deliver them.

Through it all, Inga was silent, her face as pale as death. Theron remained apart from her, unable to cope with her grief. Finally, when Dinah insisted she go to her room, Inga obeyed her orders. She needed to be alone.

That night, Theron sent two of his hands to the shack on Belle Terre. One was to remain there until morning, the other to fetch Jenny home. As he headed back to the house from the cabins, a dark figure emerged from the shadows.

"St. Germain . . ."

Matthew Weldon!

Theron stopped short, then strode forward, his one hand clenched. He had told the man not to step foot on his property, and by God, he meant it. But his anger faded as he got a closer look. The man was gray with fatigue, his eyes red, his hair disheveled.

"What the devil are you doing back here?"

"I didn't want to go to the house," Weldon said hoarsely. "I didn't want to upset Mrs. Johansson . . ."

St. Germain glowered at him. "Don't tell me you've changed your mind, that you don't intend to do right by the girl?"

"It's not that." Weldon swallowed. "Kirsten's gone."

"What the hell . . . ?"

"I was hoping maybe she'd come home."

"She has not."

Weldon put a hand over his eyes. "Oh, God!" he breathed. "Oh, God!"

St. Germain stood silent as Weldon told him how he had not gone up to Kirsten after St. Germain and Inga left, but remained in the study, trying to come to terms with the events that had changed his life.

"I was engaged to be married," he said raggedly, "to a girl back home, a girl I've known all my life. I was trying to think of the best way to tell Martha that it . . . was over. I suppose I just sat there thinking for an hour or more.

"Then, when I went to Kirsten, she was gone.

"Johnson and I searched the house and property. I came here earlier, but you were not in. Then I rode toward Memphis, farther than she could walk in a day. But I didn't find her."

"Mista St. Germain . . . ?"

Both men turned at the sound of a voice. It was Clem, the stableman, turning his hat in his hands.

"Didn' go to interrup' you gen'men, but they's a

horse missing from the stable, suh. I wonder if you knowed who tuk it."

Theron St. Germain felt a tremor run through his body. He knew. It all added up to more grief for Inga. How was he going to tell her?

Late that evening, Theron entered Inga's bedroom and sat down beside her. Taking her hand in his own, he studied her tearstained face. It looked oddly shrunken, her regal beauty gone. But he knew that it would return, and that beauty meant nothing. It was what was inside that counted. She opened her eyes and looked toward him, and he blurted out his feelings without any preliminaries.

"Inga, I want you to marry me. To be my wife."

The tears began again, slow, bitter tears that seeped from beneath her closed lids.

"I can't. I'm not your kind, and you would hate me for it someday."

"No, sweetheart! Never!"

"Besides," she said dully, "I think Kirsten told you why."

That spate of horrible accusations? A childish tantrum! He'd forgotten it.

"But *you* haven't told me."

She sat up, staring at him, her eyes wild with pain. "Don't you understand I did it! Oh, Jenny was Olaf's child, just as Kirsten was. Their ... their difference can be explained. The man on the boat meant nothing. But my husband, Olaf—I killed him, Theron!"

The words jolted him, but he managed to keep his wits about him.

"There must have been a reason. Was it an accident?"

"He was going to give Jenny to one of his drunken friends!" she explained, and described exactly what had happened and how they had run off to St. Paul. "It's my fault," she said drearily. "I've failed with both Kirsten and Jenny, too."

"Don't," he whispered. "Don't blame yourself. And don't think about the past. In the war, I killed a lot of men. Sometimes I can't sleep, remembering. We can help each other. . . . Inga, I love you."

She turned to him, burrowing her head against his shoulder, and he let her cry it out. This was the woman he'd thought was so strong, who had helped to rebuild Sweethome, who had shamed him into becoming a man. And she *was* strong, but not made of iron.

Her strength had been used—used by a bullying husband, by two daughters who had taken from her until it suited them to do otherwise. And, yes, by God, by Theron St. Germain himself!

Now all he wanted was to take care of her.

As if she sensed their reversal of roles, she drew away from him, and wiping her eyes, managed a watery smile. "Yes, Theron. I'll marry you. If you want me."

"Want you! Inga!"

At the moment, however, she needed time, she explained. Time to recover from the blows she'd been dealt today. She felt dead inside. "If you don't mind waiting until spring?"

"If I have to, I'll wait forever."

Holding her, kissing her sweet mouth, feeling her warm, tender curves beneath his hand , he knew he had to leave the room before he lost his self-control. There would be other days, other nights, when they could come to each other as man and wife.

He'd be damned if he'd use her anymore!

It wasn't until he left her that he remembered he hadn't told her about Kirsten.

40

A few days later, Miz Fannie opened her door to a bedraggled, mud-covered creature she did not recognize. Another unfortunate, she was certain, come to join the ranks of those who came to her for help—and a way to earn a living. This one, however, looked more done in than most. Miz Fannie's heart went out to her in pity.

"Theah," she said comfortingly. "Y'all jes come with Miz Fannie. My gracious! You look like you could use a nice hot cup of tea."

Kirsten pitched forward into her arms.

"Oh, mah goodness!" said Miz Fannie.

Half-carrying the fainting girl from the doorway, she led her into the parlor, where, hastily snatching some doilies for the back of a chair, she seated her. The poor child needed immediate attention.

She went to the stairway and called, "Sister!"

Within minutes Sister was downstairs with a basin of water while Miz Fannie clucked over their newest guest. The girl was sick. It was clear she had a fever. And she would not allow Miz Fannie to take her cloak, but clutched at it frantically.

"Neares' Ah can figgah," Miz Fannie told Sister, "she done run off from some man that didn' treat huh good. Keeps sayin' he mustn' find huh."

"Men!" Sister said.

"Yes, indeedy!"

The two spinsters had never had much use for men, except for their daddy and brother, whom they adored. But even they had their "needs." On their plantation, the girls and their mother had turned a blind eye, trying to ignore the passel of multicolor pickanninies running around the quarters.

In their eyes the business they carried on now was divine justice. If a man wanted a woman, he paid, and everybody was happy.

Together the women finally wrested the cloak from the girl, marveling at the bedraggled gown beneath it. It was clear she was from a good family.

When they began to gently wash her mud-streaked face, they were shocked to find familiar features beneath the dirt.

"I declaih!" Miz Fannie said, falling back. " 'Membah those ladies come heah some time back? Miz Johansson an' huh daughtahs? This heah's one of 'em!"

Finally they came up with her name. The little one was Jenny. This was Kirsten, the one that young Union devil had taken a shine to. That she had been accosted in their own house had been an

291

embarrassment to the genteel women. It would be a pleasure to be able to do her some service in return.

There was, however, a problem. It was clear that she was too ill to make sense; she had a fever, and there was no telling what ailed the child. In these days, with cholera rife in the city, the knowledge of a sick person in the house might cause a general exodus, and be bad for business. Even worse, they might be put under quarantine.

They decided to keep her presence a secret, at least until they had a clean bill of health from a doctor they paid to be discreet.

Miz Fannie put a finger to her chin and cogitated. "We'll put huh in mah bed," she said finally. "Ah'll sleep on the couch." When Sister attempted to remonstrate, she waggled a finger at her. "Don' ahgue the point! Mah mind's made up!"

Within a short time, Kirsten was clean, her hair brushed and braided by loving hands, and she was clad in a long flannel nightgown, tucked in a soft bed between clean sheets. The two elderly women looked down at their handiwork fondly.

"Looks lahk an angel, don' she?" Miz Fannie said. "Wish Daddy could see huh . . ."

Then, recalling Daddy's propensities, she was glad he couldn't.

They returned to clean the chair, and Sister picked up the cloak. The fur trim was torn from its moorings, but there was a chance that it could be salvaged. She reached into the pocket, to find a small pouch. Curious as to its contents, she emptied it into her hand and gasped.

Miz Fannie echoed the sound. "Mah stahs! Those

ah real! Mus' be wuth a fohtune! Sister, you don't think that they were stolen?"

Sister didn't.

They decided to put them away for safekeeping.

That night, they sent for Dr. Gillis, whom they kept on a retainer. If any of the girls were sick, he treated them, and checked them periodically for what Miz Fannie referred to as "man diseases."

After he examined Kirsten, he was able to set their minds at rest. The girl was suffering from lung fever and exposure to the elements. With bed rest and good care, she would recover.

Miz Fannie clapped her small hands. "Then maybe she'll join ouah happy little family," she said joyously.

The normally stoic physician grinned at her. "In that case," he said, "kindly put my name at the top of the list!"

The doctor hadn't counted on Kirsten's constitution, and the girl felt better in a day.

Though she suffered from exposure, her main problem was sheer exhaustion. She had ridden day and night, without sleep, on roads that, thawing, turned to mud. A few more miles, she had kept telling herself as she held grimly to the saddle. A few more miles.

By the time she reached the outskirts of Memphis, however, her strength gave out. Dazed and confused, she'd thought of Miz Fannie.

How she found the house, she had no idea. And she had no recollection of collapsing in the woman's arms. Yet she was here.

And she had to concoct a reason for it, some story the two old women would believe. She feigned

293

sleep, her mind working rapidly. And finally she opened her eyes.

Miz Fannie was delighted. "Mah goodness! Sleepin' Beauty decided to wake up!"

And then came the inevitable questions. Where was her mother? What was she doing so far from home alone? Was there a problem they could help her with?

"Sometimes it he'ps jes tuh talk it out."

The women were shocked as Kirsten told her story.

In her tale, Theron St. Germain was a cruel, autocratic man. His apparent kindness in taking them in proved to be a sham when Kirsten discovered his real reason. He regarded her as a ... a possession, and her mother, fearing they would lose their home, encouraged him in his unwelcome attentions to Kirsten.

"My land," Miz Fannie gasped, fanning herself. "Ah nevah would've thought it!"

As Kirsten's story continued, Matthew Weldon came into the picture. He had asked her to marry him, and though she didn't love him, she might have done so to get away from St. Germain. But St. Germain had threatened to kill him.

To prevent a murder, she had run away, taking the jewels Theron St. Germain had given her. "He owed them to me," she said, blushing.

"Ah should think so!" Miz Fannie's eyes were filled with righteous wrath. "You poah, poah thing!"

Going into the next room, she whispered the story to Sister, who was equally indignant.

"Ah told you it was man trouble," Miz Fannie said.

"Men!"

"Indeedy!"

When Theron St. Germain appeared at their door later that week, Miz Fannie did not invite him in. In fact, she had to struggle to keep from slamming the door in his face. She had no idea where Miss Johansson was, she told him, the warm-molasses quality gone from her voice.

She closed the door and leaned against it, eyes shut, asking her departed daddy's forgiveness for telling a lie.

Within a week, Kirsten was able to move about Miz Fannie's room; in another, she had regained her strength completely. Finally she confided her plan to sell the jewelry and return to Minnesota to stay with her grandparents.

Though Miz Fannie was sorely disappointed that Kirsten would not be joining her happy little group, she could see the sense in the girl's decision.

"Huh granddaddy's a preachah," she told Sister. It was good to know Kirsten would be looked after by a man of God.

Miz Fannie used her connections to sell the jewelry and helped Kirsten to purchase a new wardrobe, but it was some time before they were able to obtain tickets on the crowded riverboats heading north and west.

Six weeks had passed, from the time Kirsten left Weldon's house to hide shivering under the bridge, until she stood on the steamboat deck waving goodbye to her two good friends.

Miz Fannie touched a lace handkerchief to an errant tear and waved genteelly back. "Ah'm worried about that child," she confided to Sister.

That very morning, as she completed her packing, Kirsten had felt sudden nausea. Later, as Miz Fannie applied cool compresses to her forehead, Kirsten blamed it on nerves and excitement. But Miz Fannie had been around girls too long not to recognize the signs. She would bet her bottom dollar that the girl who waved farewell to her now was in the family way.

41

Kirsten's disappearance was the final blow to Inga. She rose from her bed, walked, talked, but there was no life in her blue eyes, no laughter in her face. Daily she grew thinner.

"That chile's goin' jes fade away," Dinah said worriedly.

St. Germain shared her fears.

There was nothing more they could do. Weldon had searched his property for Kirsten. There had been another search at Sweethome. Theron had ridden to Memphis, checking trains, riverboats, stages; even going to Miz Fannie's on a hunch.

Kirsten seemed to have disappeared from the face of the earth.

Inga appeared to have built a shell around herself, Theron thought grimly, so she wouldn't be hurt again. He tried to draw her from her worries, to surround her with the warmth of his love, but it was like trying to court a woman through a pane of glass. He reached out and could not touch her. He could wait. But could she? He sensed something was dying in pain behind that cool facade.

And when there was no life in Inga, there was none at Sweethome.

Jenny was there, of course, in a fashion. She left for the shack at Belle Terre early in the morning and returned late at night. Any mention of Jesse Norwood and her feelings toward him were carefully avoided. It was like having a stranger in the house.

Christmas was approaching, but Inga made no move toward creating the kind of festive atmosphere she usually insisted on. Remembering last Christmas, when she had made a joyous occasion of it, despite his role of skeleton at the feast, St. Germain was even more concerned. Finally he went to Dinah to suggest that she decorate the place a little, plan a holiday meal.

"Miss Jenny, she say she won' be here. Goin' spend Chris'mus with that man." Dinah's eyes watered and she blew her nose loudly. "Don' seem no use without them chillun heah."

"Then, dammit, do it because I tell you to!"

"Yassuh," she said. "Yassuh."

It still wasn't the same, he thought morosely as he surveyed Dinah's efforts. The greens hung limply. A small tree she had had a workman cut sat lopsided in a corner, its needles already turning brown. The kitchen was not the cheerful place it had been before.

"Ain' no use cookin' up all dat stuff foh two," Dinah said.

Finally he could stand it no longer. He had to get out of the house. He walked morosely across the fields, cheeks tingling from the cold, seeing only the dead winter world around him. When he reached the fence that divided his property from Belle Terre, he paused for a moment. There was only one way to get Jenny home for the holiday, and as much as he hated it, he intended to do it.

He climbed over the fence and continued on.

He could see the little shack on stilts, smoke rising from its chimney. And he caught sight of a small figure in a man's heavy coat, many sizes too large for her, entering the barn.

Good!

He speeded up his steps, and entered the house without knocking.

Jesse Norwood, his wounded leg stretched out in front of him, sat in a chair before the fire, a pile of harness that needed mending in his lap.

Jesse had filled out, regained his strength, and except for the leg, which was still splinted, he was whole again. And he was a happy man. Jenny had filled his life with warmth and sunlight.

Now, seeing the black-browed, one-armed man who filled the doorway, he was suddenly afraid—not physically, but filled with a fear that somehow Jenny would be taken from him.

He reached for the crutch he had fashioned and tried to struggle to his feet.

"Sit!" St. Germain barked.

He sat.

"I do not like you," his uninvited guest said with an expression of distaste. "And I imagine the feeling is reciprocated. But I have come to ask a favor."

Jesse watched him quietly, certain he knew what was to come.

"You know that Jenny's sister is gone."

Jesse did. Jenny had wept in his arms after she learned of Kirsten's disappearance.

"Her mother, naturally, is upset. But I would like for Inga to enjoy the holidays as much as possible," Theron continued. "I would like to suggest . . ."

His face darkened and he slammed a fist on the table. "It is not a suggestion," he roared. "It's an order! You and Jenny will be at Sweethome on Christmas Day! I will send a conveyance for you, around by the road. Is that understood?"

"I don't want to come where I ain't welcome," Jesse said stiffly.

The two men glared at each other in mutual dislike.

"Her mother and I are going to be married," Theron said roughly. "Jenny won't come without you. Inga's happiness is very important to me, Norwood."

Theron's voice broke a little on that last sentence, and Jesse could tell by his eyes that the man was suffering.

He cares, he thought, amazed. He really cares.

The door opened behind him and Jenny dashed in, her face scarlet with cold, her eyes laughing. "Jesse! Guess what! I just—"

Her laughter died away as she saw St. Germain.

300

She seemed to shrink inside the huge man's coat she wore, her eyes filling with fear.

And that hurt Theron more than he could have believed.

"It's all right, Jenny," he said quietly. "I came to discuss something with Norwood. A Christmas present for your mother. He can tell you about it after I've gone."

When Theron walked back across the fields, he was struggling with a multitude of emotions. Perhaps he had done what would make Inga happier, what was best for Jenny, but he wasn't sure. Everything in his upbringing rebelled against the action he had just taken. He recalled that when he had played with a white overseer's son as a child, his father had taken him to task. Some people were born to be better than others. And they must keep to their place, rather than sink to a lower level, his father had insisted. It was Theron's duty to maintain the quality of life they had provided for him.

The overseer's son had later proved to be a thief. And Theron's father had used the boy's behavior as a lesson. Rednecks and Negroes were to be cared for, tolerated, and disciplined, but never to be treated as equals.

When he reached the house and told Dinah Jenny would be there on Christmas Day, with Jesse Norwood, Dinah was as upset as he. She, too, had been reared to know there were different classes and that they did not mingle.

"Ain' cookin' for no white trash," she said darkly. Then, seeing Theron's expression, she grudgingly agreed that she would. "But I ain' goin' tuh like it."

301

In the shack at Belle Terre, Jesse put his arms around Jenny and told her of St. Germain's invitation. She drew away and looked at his face, sensing that it had not been couched in polite terms.

"You don't want to go there, do you?"

"D'ruther not," he confessed.

"Then I won't go!"

"Ah, Jenny!" He buried his face in her long dark hair. "Jenny!"

What could he say to bring this girl to see that she should forget him, that she was far too good for the likes of Jesse Norwood?

"St. Germain is worried about your mother," he said. "She needs you, Jenny."

"And I need you," she said, wrapping her arms about his neck, her soft mouth touching his, her kisses growing more ardent until he pushed her away. "I know," she said wryly. "We mustn't do this. My mother trusts me."

He had said those words time and again, until it became a joke between them. The major problem, he thought, was that he couldn't trust himself. With his returning strength, it was growing more difficult every day.

Jenny was loving and giving. She had no idea of a man's driving needs. It would be so easy to take advantage of her.

"We'll go to Sweethome for Christmas," he told her. "Both of us."

She was in his arms again, hugging him. Beyond her, he could see the kitchen table covered with oilcloth, the rickety wood stove, the ragged curtains at the window. It would be a good thing to accept St. Germain's invitation. Seeing Jesse in her own home might bring Jenny to her senses.

In the meantime, he ached with wanting her. The master of Sweethome, he thought wryly, might be surprised to know that even a redneck could be as honorable as a Southern gentleman.

42

On Christmas morning Jenny stood with Inga and Theron as they parceled the gifts out to the black workers. Her eyes were shining as she saw their pleasure in what they received. Zada was almost in tears at the turkey-red calico; it would make the red dress she had always wanted. Delta was excited over the warm flannel for her baby. All the women ran covetous fingers over the cotton lace, a luxury they had never known.

Though Jenny joined in their pleasure, she was concentrating on listening. Listening for the wheels of the carriage John had driven to pick up Jesse.

She had not gone down to his cabin this morning, but had waited here, donning the red dress she wore when she first met him. Over it she wore a lacy white shawl, a gift from Inga.

Her gown was too short and a little faded, but

she had chosen it for Jesse's sake. He had nothing to wear but the red shirt that she had washed and mended for him, and his rather threadbare trousers.

Theron and Inga had dressed up for the occasion, but Jenny wanted Jesse to feel at home.

She forced her mind back to the gift-giving. "Here you are, Ceph," Inga was saying. "A happy Christmas to you. And to you, Clem, Tolie . . ."

Theron St. Germain watched Inga worriedly. She had grown so thin. The rosy bloom of health was gone from her cheeks; her hair looked lusterless. But at least, with her beloved Jenny at her side, she was smiling again.

Then there was a whir of wheels on the bridge, and Jenny jumped up to go meet the trap. John climbed down, and easing the injured Jesse to the ground, handed him his crutches. Jenny danced around him like a child.

Theron and Inga went to meet their guest. It was an awkward moment, and set the tone for the day, which was stiff and uncomfortable.

Jenny led the crippled man on a short tour of Sweethome, trying to share its wonders with him. She didn't know that his heart sank as he looked at the luxury around him—the stable with blooded horses, the house, stately once more in its pillared simplicity.

All Jesse could think of was that he could never give his Jenny anything like this!

Long festive tables had been set up for the workers in the barn; Dinah and Zada made trip after trip to the house, loading the tables with platters of ham and candied yams, steaming succotash, baked squash, sweet pickles, and a multitude of pies.

Jesse was uncomfortable when he realized he was to eat in the house with the family.

If the riches outside seemed awesome, he was overcome by Sweethome's interior. He had never been inside one of the old mansions before. The dining table was set with bright linen and crystal that glimmered until he was blinded to the fact that the plates were cracked, the linen old and mended, that the eating utensils were just tin.

Except for an arrangement of holly, the table was bare of decorations.

St. Germain pulled Inga's chair back for her and seated her. Watching, Jesse did the same for Jenny. There were only the four of them.

This time, Dinah had insisted on serving. She would join the others outside later.

Jesse had never been so miserable in his life. In spite of Inga and Jenny's attempts to chat, most of the time passed in awkward silence. There was a plenitude of food, but Jesse tasted none of it. He was wary of the array of forks and spoons by his plate, conscious of his fork clanging against china, of Dinah's dark disapproval and St. Germain's animosity.

The meal seemed to drag on forever; then Theron spoke directly to Jesse for the first time.

"It looks like you're getting along pretty well," he said. "You ought to be able to manage by yourself, before long."

"I suppose so." Jesse had been expecting him to mention it.

Theron pushed his plate back. "You will have to, soon. I suppose Jenny has told you she's going away to school after the first of the year?"

She had not, and it jolted Jesse. His hand jerked, brushing a crystal goblet. It shattered into tinkling bits, water running across the tablecloth and into Inga's lap.

Dinah rushed to her mistress's side and wiped at her skirt with a napkin. But Inga was too upset to notice her gown was wet. She had thought the school business was over and forgotten. And to bring it up at such a time . . .

Jesse was on his feet, reaching for his crutches, his face white. "I suppose I ain't as well as I thought I was," he said with an attempt at a grin. "If y'all don't mind, I'll see if John'll take me on home."

Jenny stood. "I'm going with you," she said.

"It ain't necessary, Jenny," he told her.

"I agree," Theron added.

Jenny shot St. Germain a furious look and followed Jesse through the door.

Inga leapt to her feet. "I'm going to stop them!"

Theron reached out and took her arm. His voice was gentle now. "No, Inga. Don't you see? The boy knows he's not in Jenny's class. If he really loves her, he won't want to condemn her to a life of poverty. I mentioned the school to show him—"

"To show him you're an insufferable snob," Inga spat. "Don't touch me!"

When she reached the yard, the trap was already pulling away. She stood forlornly, watching it go.

Jenny and Jesse did not speak as John drove them back to the shack. It was necessary to travel some distance by road, moving past the ruins of the burned-out Belle Terre from the other direction. The journey seemed to take forever.

But finally they reached their destination.

John helped Jesse into the house, into his chair, then went on his way. Still Jenny and Jesse did not speak. Jenny knelt to build up the fire in the fireplace, then stood, looking at Jesse, who was watching her.

"We're home," she said with a heartbreaking smile. "I'll make some coffee."

"I'm home," Jesse said. "But you ain't, Jenny. I reckon you better run 'long back to your ma."

Jenny tossed her head. "I won't. You can't make me!"

Jesse sighed. "Come here, Jenny."

She came to sit on the floor beside him, her face burying against his knees. He tangled his fingers in her hair absently as he spoke to her.

"I don't want you to git me wrong, honey. It's been real good havin' you here."

He nearly choked on his last words. It *had* been good. At first, he had been weak as a baby, and she tended him like one. Then he had been a child, fretful at being caged in the house. She'd scolded him, given him a slate, taught him, his tongue between his teeth, to write his name and to cipher. But now he had become a man again. Wanting her. Their kisses had gone beyond affection, beyond love, trembling on the edge of passion.

These last few days, he had been arguing with himself. One moment he was certain he could make Jenny happy; the next, he was telling himself that he wasn't much, just an ignorant poor boy who had no right to ask a girl to marry him until he had something to offer.

Today had pushed him into a decision. He was

heading west. Maybe the ranch in New Mexico was what Sam said it was and maybe it wasn't—Sam was an interesting talker, and some of his conversation consisted of "windies," calculated to amuse his audience—but it was time to find out. Instead of moving with Sam, Jesse had come home for a while, to think it over. What if the ranch was one of Sam's tall tales, and consisted of a couple of cows and a windmill? Well, the only way to know for sure was to go and see. And he had to go alone.

"You are not going to send me away, are you?" Jenny looked up at him, pushing her mass of dark hair aside, her eyes huge and pleading.

"I have to, Jenny." His voice was filled with pain. "Guess I got a good look at myself today. I ain't nothin' much—"

"I love you, Jesse."

"Ah, Jenny! Jenny . . ."

Then she was beside him, her arms around his neck as she kissed him, moving against his body as she strove to get closer.

He could feel the heat of her against him, throbbing, as he put his hands to her slim hips to press her to him.

Damn! What was he doing?

With a massive effort he brought his hands upward, disentangling her arms, pushing her away.

The face that had been dazed with love, mouth swollen with passion, changed in front of him, its softness disappearing as it grew small and cold. She smoothed her skirts, pulling them down.

"You don't want me."

"I do," he whispered. "I do. But—"

"But you want me to go home."

"Yes, Jenny. Please . . ."

She caught up her lacy shawl and headed toward the door.

"Wait, Jenny!" He struggled to his feet and hitched toward her on his crutches. "I can't let you go like this. . . . Jenny, I love you! I love you too much to let you settle for nothin'! But I'm goin' west, and I'm goin' to make somethin' of myse'f! Ain't comin' back until I can stand up an' look St. Germain in the eye an' tell him I am somebody.

"Then I'll have somethin' to ask you," he continued.

He caught her to him in a paroxysm of pain, holding her, his hands memorizing her fragile bones, kissing her as if he were saying good-bye forever.

Both of them were trembling when he let her go.

"Go back to Sweethome," he said hoarsely. "Run, don't walk. It's best if we don't see each other again until I come back for you."

For a brief space, night-black eyes searched velvet gray ones, and then she was gone.

Jesse limped back to his chair and sat with his head in his hands.

Theron St. Germain, at Sweethome, was as miserable as Jesse Norwood. Inga had avoided him all the remainder of the day. And now that it was ending, he didn't blame her. He'd been too hard on the boy, but the fellow just rubbed him the wrong way.

Inga accused him of being a snob. That had hurt. Dammit, he might have liked Norwood if it weren't for Jenny. Instead, he had the animosity of a father for a young man he didn't consider good enough for his daughter. He supposed that was natural. Except that he and Inga weren't married yet. The way things were going, it seemed they might never be. He had to find some way to justify himself.

He searched for her, needing to talk to her, to make amends. She seemed to be nowhere in the house, and he began to fear that she, too, had left. Then he heard someone sobbing.

He finally traced the sound to the sewing room. Through the partially open door he saw Inga. She was sitting on the floor, holding a lacy blue shawl to her face—the shawl she had made for Kirsten's Christmas.

He longed to go to her, but decided against it. She had to have her time of grief. As he made his way up the stairs, his mind spinning with his problems, he heard the back door close.

Jenny had come home.

43

As the riverboat took her steadily north and west, Kirsten had a hard time keeping up her spirits. In Miz Fannie's establishment she had been cared for. In a place where love was a commodity, to be sold, she'd lost her feelings of guilt. Now, among strangers, her guilt returned to haunt her. She felt certain that it showed in her face, her bearing, that the other passengers stared at her covertly.

And so they did, but for a different reason.

Dressed in the ladylike clothing Miz Fannie helped her to choose, she seemed mysterious—a strickingly beautiful girl, something of a recluse, blue eyes shadowed with sorrow. There was a great deal of speculation about her. It was possible that she had lost a young husband or fiancé in the war.

More than one young gentleman longed to comfort her but feared to approach her.

The journey that had seemed so desirable as an escape from Sweethome was now a frightening reality. The riverboat took her inexorably toward a destination that each day lost more of its romantic appeal.

Her grandfather knew, of course, that his daughter was a murderess. What would his attitude toward Kirsten be? He was a great believer in bad blood passing down, generation to generation. He might even forbid her his house. But if he did, there was still Oskar Bjorn.

Kirsten sighed. The younger, more handsome Oskar she'd created in her mind had disappeared. In his place was the older, possessive man she had been betrothed to. And was he really wealthy? Or was it just that he had more than the others in their small community? Her dreams of presiding over a table of important guests seemed vague and farfetched now as she remembered Oskar's reputation for being "near." Would he expect her to scrub and clean, to work in the fields as her mother had?

It would be no more than she deserved.

She chided herself for her negative thoughts. She was still having attacks of nausea—a combination, she was certain, of the ship's wallowing progress as it fought its way upriver and her own nervous tension. She had too much time to think, to frighten herself.

The trip was a miserable one, the days gray, the river the color of slate. The decks had begun to ice over as they headed north. And finally the captain was forced to tie up at times when curtains of blowing snow obliterated the river.

Worst of all, she found she was homesick, missing her mother, Jenny, even St. Germain.

Mostly she missed Matthew Weldon; at night she had dreams in which she lay in his arms, crying his name, begging him to love her. She always woke hating herself, sick with shame and anger.

There were other dreams, dreams in which her grandfather, Pastor Gustav Lindstrom, pointed his bony finger at her, her sinfulness apparent to his all-seeing eyes.

She knew now how Inga must have felt— No, she must not compare herself to her mother! What she had done was different.

Different in what way?

She didn't know!

Kirsten kept to her cabin, enduring the dreary days of the journey, the wakeful, nerve-tortured nights, trying to remember her hate for those at Sweethome and Eden, and to expiate herself.

When she stepped ashore at St. Paul, she was relieved to see that although the temperature was freezing, the skies were clear. Dirty patches of snow lined the roadways, but the sunny weather seemed a good omen.

She went to the livery stable, where she rented a horse and buggy.

The proprietor peered at her and asked, "Ain't I seen you afore?"

He couldn't have, she told him. She was from the South.

"You a stranger in town?"

"Yes."

"Visitin'?"

"Yes."

"Who you come to see?"

"Some folks who live out in the country," she answered vaguely.

Unable to elicit any information, he finally gave up, warning her that he'd heard there was a blizzard on its way, to be careful.

As Kirsten drove through St. Paul, her fashionable garb attracted curious glances. And again she was jittery, nerves on edge, wondering if they could tell that she was a "fallen woman." She lifted her chin and drove on, wishing it were night so she could travel in darkness.

"The night belongs to Satan," her grandfather had said.

Perhaps she was a child of the devil.

She thought she would feel better when she reached the outer limits of the city, but she was even more frightened at what lay ahead of her.

She had to decide what her story would be. It would be to her advantage not to be known as the daughter of a murderess. She would say that her father had fallen, striking his head; that Inga, fearing she would be blamed, had run away, forcing her daughters to accompany her. Kirsten had not been able to get free and make her way back until now.

That sounded plausible enough.

She also had to make up her mind where to go first—to her grandparents, or to Oskar.

Recalling Oskar Bjorn's face clearly, she remembered the long white hairs growing out of his nose, the bald spot he carefully combed his thinning locks across, his dry red skin . . . She would go to her grandparents, give herself time to consider her actions.

Occupied with her thoughts, she woke to the fact that she had forgotten how early evening came in northern winters, or that her grandparents lived so far from St. Paul. She seemed to have been driving for hours, and everything was strange and unfamiliar.

As she wondered if she had missed the lane that ran to her grandfather's home, the storm struck with the force of an explosion. Within a matter of moments the road before her was obliterated by snow. Memories came back to her, memories of grown men lost in such blizzards—sometimes between their houses and barns. She remembered times she, Jenny, and her mother had fought their way to the woodpile, clinging to a rope.

The curtain of snow parted, revealing a drive of some sort. There would be a house at the end of it—maybe even her grandfather's. Kirsten turned into the lane, and the snow curtain closed behind her.

She drove on, eyes and nose filling with snow no matter how fast she brushed it away. The landscape was blotted out. She had to trust the little horse to keep to the road.

What if there was no house here at all? What if the lane was only the entrance to a field?

"Please, God, don't let me die," she found herself praying.

And then she whispered, "Mama, help me! Mama . . ."

Finally she caught a glimpse of blurred light—and the dim shape of a building that appeared and disappeared, ghostlike, ephemeral. She was unable to recognize its outlines, but whoever lived there would give her shelter, would be one of Pastor Lindstrom's flock.

Climbing down from the buggy, sinking ankle-deep in a drift, she made her way up the steps, almost blinded, to knock at a door.

It opened to reveal an almost slatternly young woman. She stared dully at Kirsten in her finery, pushing back hair that hung in wisps. Her soiled gown revealed a heavy figure. In the background a baby was crying.

"I . . ." Kirsten gasped, "I think I am lost. The snow . . ."

The woman beckoned her in. Kirsten took one step and stopped. She was reliving a nightmare.

The house that smelled of diapers and sour milk had once smelled of soap and woodsmoke. And the last time she had been there, there was a dead man on the floor!

Her father!

44

Kirsten stared at the spot before the fireplace, nausea rising in her throat, expecting to see . . . him.

She felt suddenly faint and grabbed at the door frame. Then the young woman took her arm and led her to a chair.

"Are you all right, miss? Just set a minute. I'll see to your horse."

"No," Kirsten whispered. "No . . ."

"No trouble at all. I must do it for my husband when he comes home."

The woman snatched up a coat and went out into the night, leaving Kirsten alone at the scene of a nightmare. She was shaking uncontrollably, with cold—and with something else, her mind at the edge of horror.

It seemed an eternity before the woman returned.

Again she asked, "Are you all right?"

Kirsten jerked back to the present. "I ... I am sorry," she said shakily. "It is a shock to find I have come to this house. "I once lived here."

The woman's protuberant eyes were suddenly filled with suspicion. "I think you have made a mistake. This is my husband's home place. He built it. Nobody's lived here but him—and his first wife and children, of course. But they are dead."

"Maybe," Kirsten stammered, "maybe I was wrong."

But she couldn't be! Though the place was a mess, diapers drying over every chair, the blue plates on the shelf had been her mother's. The rag rugs on the floor—Kirsten had knotted the strips, winding them into balls for her mother to crochet. And she could recognize the materials in the patchwork quilt. That deep blue had been her best Sunday dress when she was ten! The curtains at the kitchen window, now soiled and bedraggled, her mother had made from her own wedding gown. The family Bible was in its accustomed place on a little table.

The crying baby in the other room had reached the point of hysterical sobbing.

"She is wet," the woman explained. " 'Scuse me while I change her."

She left the room, and Kirsten moved toward the Bible as if hypnotized. She opened it to the family records her father kept so painstakingly. The date of his marriage to Inga Lindstrom. The date of Kirsten's birth—and death.

Jenny's birth—a harsh black line was drawn

through the name of the child Olaf Johansson had rejected.

Then Inga's death was inscribed in Olaf's own hand. It was followed by the date of his marriage to Jane Thorsson, two months after they'd gone away. And nine months later, the birth of Pia, the baby crying in the other room. . . .

Kirsten barely made it back to her chair before her knees gave way. The woman returned, carrying a fretful child with sticklike limbs and the swollen belly of hunger.

"It is the milk that makes her cry," the woman apologized. "I cannot feed her now, and the cow went dry. Mr. Johansson will see to things when he gets home."

"When do you expect him?" Kirsten asked, her mouth dry.

The woman's eyes slid away, and she shrugged. "Usually he comes home on Monday, but with this storm . . ." She pushed the baby toward Kirsten. "Would you mind holding her while I build up the fire?"

Kirsten held the child close to her breast. It was her half-sister, this poor mewling little thing. She watched as the woman fed the fire with bits and pieces of wood, scraps left from a diminished woodpile, and remembered . . . Remembered Inga going out in the bitter weather, gleaning everything that could be burned; remembered the way she turned withered carrots and turnips into a delicious soup; remembered her mother's rough red hands that cracked and bled . . . And remembered her father coming home with presents for Kirsten and for no one else; Kirsten, his ladylike daughter, who would marry the rich mill owner.

"Mrs. Johansson," she said, her lips stiff, "you mentioned your husband's first family. I think I might have known them. How did they die?"

Again there was that look of suspicion, but she told Kirsten they had drowned when a riverboat sank.

"A riverboat?"

"It burned," her hostess said tersely. "There were no survivors."

Kirsten recalled the fiery inferno that had drifted toward them one night on their trip to Memphis and began to tremble. The ship that burned had been bound upriver. Surely its identity would be known by now. Somewhere, there would be a passenger list—which Olaf Johansson evidently had not bothered to check. It suited him to believe they were dead and gone.

The woman came to take the child, and offered: "I would be pleased to fix you some supper. It won't be much. Until my husband returns with supplies . . ."

Kirsten stood. "I really have to go."

"I can't let you go out in this weather," the woman said in alarm.

"It's all right," Kirsten said firmly. "I'm not going far. But thank you for letting me come in and get warm." Reaching into her purse, she drew out a handful of money and pressed it on the woman, who backed away in alarm.

"I was glad to have company," she said, flushing. "That is not necessary."

"It's for the little one," Kirsten told her. "And you never can tell when it might be needed."

She wanted to add that it might come in handy in case she ever brained her husband with a poker.

45

The snow had eased up a bit, but intuition told Kirsten that before the storm was over, it would get worse; much worse. Still, she was thankful for the respite as she drove on to find the lane that led to the Lindstroms' house.

Reaching it, she paused for a moment. She must brace herself to confront her grandfather, who had never seemed as formidable as now. Fortunately, her grandmother answered the door.

Birgitta seemed to have aged tremendously since Kirsten had seen her last. Numbed by a life of hard work and childbearing, Birgitta had the face of one to whom life offered no surprises. It crumpled at sight of Kirsten, but only for a moment.

"Come in, child," she said, as calmly as if she'd seen her only yesterday. Kirsten obeyed.

Birgitta Lindstrom's antidote for any emotional

situation, be it wedding or funeral, was food. She shooed her younger children from the kitchen and seated Kirsten near the cookstove, pouring a cup of toasted barley coffee and placing a plate of bakelser before her.

She waited in silence until the girl stopped shivering, then said, "Tell me about my Inga."

At the fleeting expression of pain in her grandmother's eyes, Kirsten could not hold to her fabricated story.

"My mother is alive—and well."

"Ah!" Again that brief crumpling of her features as she digested the news. She had never felt that Inga and the girls were dead. Olaf's story of how Inga took his daughters and ran off with a stranger, that it was the stranger who struck him down, had not been true. So when he told her husband that he'd received news his wife and children were dead shortly before marrying the Thorsson girl, Birgitta had not believed him then either.

"I think it is best we do not speak of this to your grandfather," she said slowly. "He is of the opinion that it was God's will. That Inga has paid for her sins."

"And you?" Kirsten said. "Did you think that?"

Birgitta's usually placid face was suddenly bitter. "If that were true, Olaf Johansson would have been struck down. He would not be making life a misery for another woman!"

She rose and poured some more of the coffee in order to regain her equilibrium. Then she asked, "Did you find any trace of Sven?"

She listened quietly, her features resigned as Kirsten described their fruitless search. And finally she asked, "You, Kirsten, why did you return?"

"Why, I . . ." Kirsten stammered, "I was homesick. And there was Oskar Bjorn. I . . . I am promised to him."

"Oskar Bjorn is dead, Kirsten. He left behind a young widow who sold his mills and moved to St. Paul."

Kirsten was numb with shock. For many years Oskar had been a constant in her life—the rich man that she would one day marry. She had counted on him being here, wanting her.

Now what was she going to do?

"Did you love him very much, Kirsten?" There was compassion in her grandmother's voice.

She stared at the old woman, wondering what she would think if she told her the truth—that she'd only thought of Oskar's money, and that now she wasn't certain where to turn.

She didn't have to answer Birgitta's question. For at that moment Pastor Gustav Lindstrom came in from the barn. He stamped the snow from his boots in the doorway, then pulled off cap and work coat and hung them carefully on a nail behind the door before he turned to look at his visitor.

Kirsten reddened under his scrutiny, even as she had as a child. She had forgotten how he made her feel guilty even then.

"It is our Kirsten," Birgitta said shakily. "Through God's help, she survived. She has returned to us."

"Why has she come here? She belongs," Gustav Lindstrom said harshly, "in her father's house. Her mother, if you recall, flouted her marriage vows, went off with a man who struck Olaf down.

They left him, not knowing if he were alive or dead! Kirsten is guilty of complicity in the affair."

His glacial eyes swept over her, noting the fineness of her clothing compared to that of his parishioners. "She does not seem to have fared too badly."

"She—they made me go," Kirsten said. "I came as soon as I could."

Gustav Lindstrom turned away and went to the fireplace to warm his hands. "I do not want the daughter of a harlot corrupting my children," he said sternly.

Birgitta interrupted him, her voice small and timid. "She will go to her father as soon as the weather permits, husband. In the meantime, she will benefit from your good influence."

Lindstrom stared at his trembling granddaughter for a long time. Then he said, "On your knees, Kirsten, Birgitta. We will pray."

He prayed for more than an hour, sonorous phrases sounding through the room as he listed Inga's sins before the Lord and asked that Kirsten's soul be free of wickedness.

Finally Kirsten could no longer hear his words. Her knees were bruised against the cold, splintered floor, her whole body screaming at her to rise. The only thing that held her in her place was the thought that Birgitta, old and arthritic, must be in worse condition. She cast a glance at the older woman from beneath her lashes, and saw no sign of misery on the worn face.

"Amen," Lindstrom said at last. "Now, wife, I want my supper."

Birgitta struggled to her feet and filled a plate

from a kettle at the stove, slicing huge chunks of bread and cheese to go with a savory stew. Gustav Lindstrom ate voraciously, head down, clearing his plate almost instantly. Then he stood, reached for his coat and cap, and headed toward the door.

The cow was calving. He intended to spend the night in the barn in case there was trouble. "I expect you to lead the children in evening prayers, Birgitta."

"Yes, husband."

When he had gone, Kirsten was suddenly able to breathe again.

The children—eight of them, all her aunts and uncles—were called to the table; the remainder of the stew was divided among Kirsten and the others. Birgitta did not eat, explaining that she had little appetite. Kirsten was painfully aware that she had probably eaten her grandmother's share.

When the children had recited their prayers and gone to their beds in the unheated rooms above, Kirsten helped Birgitta do up the dishes, washing, drying, putting them on the long shelf against the wall. Outside, the wind howled around the tall, narrow house, occasionally swooping down the chimney to wrestle with the flames in the fireplace.

The old woman was silent for a long time. She recalled that Kirsten was her father's child, and had often taken his side against Inga. Even now, there was a slight bitterness in Kirsten's tone when she mentioned her mother and Jenny. It was a certainty that they still had their differences.

It was also evident Inga had not told Kirsten the true story—that Jenny's coloring was due to Birgitta's sin, not her own. Kirsten should know the truth, but could she be trusted with it?

The girl did not seem to be herself; there was such a sadness in her eyes.

"Kirsten," Birgitta said slowly, "I do not believe it is wise for you to stay too long in this place. Mr. Lindstrom is a very godly man, but ...."

Her words trailed away, and finally she began again. "I fear his attitude toward your mother will color his feelings toward you. He will expect you to return to your father, which you may do if you wish. But I do not believe Olaf to be a forgiving man. If you have another choice ..."

Kirsten saw suddenly that the old woman was crying, slow, dreary tears that didn't alter her expression. "I have lost Sven," she said. "And I have lost Inga. Except for Sven and young Paul, my sons are growing in their father's image; my daughters can expect nothing more than a life like my own. This would not be my wish for my children—or for you, Kirsten."

Kirsten impulsively put her arms around the old woman. Birgitta stiffened against her. It was evident she wasn't accustomed to gestures of affection, but finally she sagged in Kirsten's arms and wept for a long time.

I will tell her the truth, Birgitta thought when she managed to pull herself together. But not tonight.

Later, Kirsten went upstairs to bed. Bed was a pallet that covered most of an upstairs room, to be shared with three little girls. As Kirsten searched through her bag to find her warmest gown, she could see her breath frosting the air. When she climbed in beside the children, she was shivering. More accustomed to the cold than she, the small ones slept like little mice, curled in against themselves.

Kirsten was cold all night. Both outside and in, she thought uncomfortably. It had been a mistake, returning to Minnesota. With Oskar Bjorn dead, she had run out of options. She could not remain here, she knew. Nor would she go home to her father and his new wife, who, though she was probably unaware of the fact, was not a wife at all.

The children were up when Kirsten woke. She rose, her bare feet sticking to the icy floor. At least the frigid weather provided one blessing. She did not feel nauseous this morning.

She dressed in haste, then went to look out the windows. The skies were gray. The snow had drifted to the second story of the house. To the rear, though great drifts rose on either side of the house, there was an almost clear path to the barn.

She hurried down the narrow stairs.

Gustav Lindstrom stood in the midst of his own personal flock, wife and children on their knees before him. Though he frowned at Kirsten's entrance, he continued with his prayer. She slipped to her knees beside the others.

When his conference with his God ended, he glared at Kirsten. She knew he was studying the richness of her clothing again. Unfortunately, she had nothing plainer. He would probably want to know the source of her apparent affluence. What would she answer?

Evidently he intended to save that for another time. "You have missed your breakfast," he said icily. "You are to receive nothing until noon. It is one of our disciplines. And now . . ." He opened a Bible. "Now I shall read to you from the First Epistle of Saint Paul to Timothy, chapter two, verses eleven through fifteen: " 'Let the woman learn in silence, with all subjection . . .' "

The feeling of nausea that Kirsten thought she had conquered this morning suddenly returned as she knelt with the others to contemplate her sins.

46

Kirsten was to recall the next several days as if they had been painted in shades of gray; there was no warmth and color, as there had been at Sweethome. The children, her young uncles and aunts, were quiet, subdued, shy of her. Each had his own outside chores. They went about them obediently, despite the bitter weather.

This was the house her mother had grown up in, this place lacking warmth and love.

When the snow finally stopped, it was intensely cold. Huge drifts sparkled under a wavery white-eyed sun. The snow was both blessing and curse, drifting across the roads to town. With the roads closed, Kirsten was unable to leave the area—and Olaf Johansson was trapped in St. Paul.

Kirsten knew that she had to be gone before he returned. Olaf Johansson had lied, his male pride refusing to admit that a woman had struck him down. He had lied again, saying that Inga was dead, to be free to marry. And Kirsten knew that he had lied. He would not forgive her for that knowledge, even though no one would take her word against his in this small, isolated religious community, where the men of the house ruled.

All Olaf Johansson had to say was that she was a troublemaker, and no one would listen to her. Gustav Lindstrom would back him in his words, preaching against the sins of Eve from his pulpit, and she would be shunned, as hopeless a prisoner as Inga had been.

Though Kirsten had been her father's favorite, she recalled his fierce drunken rages directed at Inga and Jenny and knew they would now be turned on her.

She had to make her escape, and without her grandfather's knowledge. If he had any notion she was thinking of leaving, he would consider it his duty to stop her.

Birgitta agreed with her. And together they made their plans.

Birgitta's fourteen-year-old son Paul was taken into their conspiracy. Paul, the oldest boy left at home, had become an accomplished trapper, an occupation of which Gustav Lindstrom wholeheartedly approved. It put meat on the table and gave the boy small pelts to sell in St. Paul.

Therefore it was not unusual for Paul to don snowshoes and range across the fields throughout the day, setting his traps, checking to see if they were sprung.

Birgitta instructed him to keep an eye on the

condition of the road, which was being cleared by members of their small community, and on the Johansson house as well. He was to tell her when Olaf Johansson came home.

In the meantime, Kirsten did everything she could to help her grandmother. Once she had caught her sitting, feet up, skirts hiked to reveal limbs swollen with edema. Birgitta hastily snatched them down, but Kirsten, in her anger at her grandfather, determined to spare her grandmother as much misery as possible.

Kirsten hauled the water from the well each morning, carrying it in with frozen fingers; she scrubbed the splintered floors while Birgitta sat at a table peeling potatoes.

"I do not know how I got along without you, child," Birgitta said, a trace of a smile illuminating her tired face. "I have not felt so rested in a long time."

Luckily, except for morning and evening prayers, Gustav spent his time either helping to clear the roads or at the barn. The cow that birthed the calf had developed complications. He hovered over the animal, dosing her each morning and night.

He treats her better than he does his wife and children, Kirsten thought as she carried a bucket of slops to the hogs.

The errand brought back memories of another time, of the day she had first met Matthew Weldon. She smiled, seeing the humor in that meeting at last. Then her mind moved on, recounting their meetings up to that last morning when she'd gone to his bed. Kirsten sighed, remembering the feel of Matthew's body, the heat of it as he filled her with the knowledge of what it was to be a woman. For a time that knowledge had been enough—enough to drive thoughts of her mother and St. Germain from her mind, to make her forget her real or imagined grudges.

Then, when her mother and Theron came and found her in Weldon's arms, her guilt drove her to rebel more forcefully than she had intended. She had said unforgivable things to Inga.

She had been too busy, as a child, seeing herself as the family princess, blaming her mother's indiscretion for her father's drinking, his absences. Now she saw Inga's life in a different light. She understood her at last. And it was too late to tell her so.

Like a child, she had run away, determined to make a new life with money that was not her own, compounding her sins with theft.

She was suddenly terribly, unutterably homesick. But she could never return to Sweethome, that place of burgeoning spring and long hot summers, of honeysuckle, wisteria, and magnolia.

The sight of her grandfather emerging from the barn jolted her out of her thoughts and she bent to pick up the bucket of swill. Suddenly the nausea that had been absent the last several days overwhelmed her, and she was violently, wretchedly sick.

When she finally straightened, her head still reeling, Gustav Lindstrom stood before her, face livid with anger, towering in his indignation as he pointed a bony finger at her.

"Harlot!" he roared. "Slut! Jezebel! An abomination to my house!"

She stared at him fearfully, too dazed to answer,

and he grabbed her arm in a bruising grip and dragged her toward the house, where he shoved her to the floor.

"On your knees," he thundered.

He began to pray, a terrifying exhortation that hammered at her brain with scattered words. Adultery! Fornication! Wicked! Evil! True daughter of a whoring mother! She, too, would bear the fruit of sin! It was some time before his words came together to make a sense that wiped the expression of fright from Kirsten's face, replacing it with horror.

A baby! He was saying that she was going to have a baby!

She toppled over in a dead faint.

She revived to find Birgitta washing her temples with a wet cloth. Birgitta's face was white, her mouth working oddly.

"You must hide," the old woman said. "My husband has gone for Olaf. And Paul says your father has come home at last. Hurry, child!"

Birgitta opened a chest that had come with her from her native Sweden, and urged Kirsten into it as the stamping of snow-laden boots sounded on the porch. Kirsten could hear Gustav Lindstrom's voice.

"I will not have the woman in my house," her grandfather was saying. "One rotten apple spoils the barrel! She is your responsibility. You are her father."

His words were followed by the familiar slurred tones of Olaf Johansson still more than a little drunk. He was saying that he intended to take a whip to the girl, work her until she dropped.

"I was too gentle with Inga and the girls," he said in a maudlin voice. "The devil finds work for idle hands."

"True," Pastor Lindstrom said. "True."

Kirsten heard a door slam, and her grandfather asking as to the whereabouts of the harlot. When her grandmother answered that she had gone, his rage seemed to vibrate throughout the room. Kirsten, trembling, put her hands over her ears. Then she heard a sound of tramping feet as the men went through the house, searching. At any moment, she thought, they would lift the trunk lid and find her.

She lay in a cramped position for what seemed hours, biting her lip to stop the whimper trapped inside her. When the lid was raised, it was Birgitta's face she saw. In her hand the old woman held a bundle of Paul's clothes—pants, shirt, coat, and knitted cap.

Mr. Lindstrom had gone to Olaf Johansson's home. Paul had been ordered to alert the congregation to meet there to help look for Kirsten.

Dressed in Paul's clothes, riding his horse, she would be mistaken for him as she rode by. But they must hurry!

Kirsten dressed hastily and Birgitta handed her a burlap bag containing her own clothing. Paul's horse was saddled and waiting. For a moment the two women, grandmother and granddaughter, looked at each other sadly, aware they would never meet again.

Kirsten knew Birgitta would bear the brunt of her husband's anger. And for what? For a sinful

granddaughter, bearing a child without a name!
She burst into tears.

"I . . . I am sorry," she sobbed. "I didn't know—"

"Perhaps it will help you to be kinder to your
mother," Birgitta said, looking at her strangely.
"Though, where Jenny is concerned, Inga was innocent of wrongdoing. She . . . I . . ."

The old woman paused to consider her brood
who stood watching with rounded eyes. This was
no time to confess her sins. It would be difficult
enough to convince them that they must answer
their father's questioning with half-truths.

"Go," she said to Kirsten. "Go to my friend
Helga, as you did before. And God go with you."

47

The faithful of Pastor Lindstrom's flock ranged up and down the countryside helping their minister look for his granddaughter. Lindstrom himself rode into St. Paul. He found Paul's horse in a livery stable. A boy had been paid to deliver it, along with a bundle of Paul's clothes, to the Lindstrom farm. At the same time, the boy said, he was to pick up the hired horse and buggy the lady had driven there, since she had told him she was leaving the city.

Fuming, the old man left to check out the transportation going in any-direction. He studied the roster on every riverboat leaving St. Paul in the next several days, but found no trace of her.

Finally Pastor Lindstrom returned home to threaten his family with the fires of hell. Someone

338

had helped the girl escape. He turned his angry gaze on Paul.

Paul claimed he was guilty only of leaving his horse saddled and waiting while he changed out of snow-wet clothes into drier ones. He had dropped the damp ones on the floor outside the door of the room he shared with the boys, and when he had found them missing, he had assumed his mother had hung them to dry.

Lindstrom did not believe him, nor did he believe anything Birgitta said. He interrogated the younger children in turn, with no better results. He had a feeling that they stood aligned against him, and was near to exploding with frustration.

His only recourse was to prepare a sermon for Sunday that would be long remembered. In it, he lumped whoring women, unfaithful females, wives who did not obey their husbands, and children who did not honor their fathers into the same category, sentencing them in a voice of thunder to a future of enternal hellfire and damnation.

Olaf Johansson, with his new wife, Jane, and little Pia, attended church for the first time in months. He had two reasons for doing so. First, he was the center of sympathetic male attention. Second, he had much to be thankful for. The girl was gone. And though he figured he could counter any accusations she might bring against him, his present wife's father was a suspicious old devil and quick with his fists.

At the moment, the girl who had inspired Gustav Lindstrom's raging sermon was tucked between clean sheets in Helga Danberg's bright guestroom. The frantic ride into town had affected her physically. She arrived at the Danberg residence white-faced, bent double, her hand to her front.

"I . . . I think I'm losing my baby," she gasped.

The competent Helga took over. Within minutes, Kirsten was abed, Helga propping her up to sip from a sedating drink. And within those minutes, Kirsten had concocted a story.

She had married in Memphis. Her name was now Mrs. Matthew Weldon. She had come home to visit her grandmother, but then her father appeared and she had been forced to escape. He would be looking for her. She must get back to Memphis.

"You're not going anywhere for a while," Helga said practically. "For one thing, the boats are not running at present because of the ice. For another, you are in no shape to travel. If Olaf Johansson shows up, John will take care of him!"

The thought of big, gentle John Danberg facing down Olaf Johansson was amusing. Luckily her father would never think of coming here.

In the meantime, it was nice to lie abed, to be coddled and pampered. Helga had never had a daughter, only unmarried sons, now grown and working away from home, and she poured out her stored-up love on Kirsten.

Kirsten must have a brown egg every day for breakfast. It would make her baby strong. She must think only good, happy thoughts in order to have a happy baby. She must take great care for the next months, with trouble this early in her pregnancy.

She had no idea that losing the baby would be the answer to her young guest's problems. At the moment, Kirsten thought of the child she carried within her not as a tiny creature who would one day live and breathe, but as a burden, a thing that would thicken her waist, make her ugly, give her an additional responsibility when she needed to be free to make a life of her own.

"There you go again," Helga scolded. "Your face is flushed. You're still worrying about the baby! I promise you, everything will be all right."

She would never know that Kirsten, pounding at her door, had been concerned about her own life, terrified at the cramping sensations she was experiencing. That she wished the baby would just go away!

In the days that followed, Kirsten was able to forget her concerns to a degree. John Danberg treated her as a daughter; Helga doted on her.

"You look so much like your grandmother as a girl," Helga kept saying. "She was the prettiest girl in Granna, always laughing, joking, dancing." Helga's eyes filled with tears. "But all these years of working, living with such a man, child-bearing . . ."

She saw Kirsten go white, and hastened to reassure her. "It is different with a good husband, a man who loves you."

What happens, Kirsten wondered, when one has no husband at all?

Kirsten recovered, but still she lingered on at the Danbergs' insistence. She explained that her husband did not expect her to return for several months.

Helga said Kirsten might as well stay and visit until spring weather made traveling easier. She would make her some more comfortable clothing, a christening gown for the baby.

Kirsten, facing an uncertain future, agreed. It was the happiest time in her life. Helga, despite her maternal admonitions, was bright and girlish, an amusing companion. She and her husband John had a wonderful marriage and did not hide their mutual affection for each other.

Some nights they played games the Danbergs remembered from their childhood in Sweden. On others, John brought out his fiddle, and he and Helga sang folk songs. They taught them to Kirsten, whose home had not been filled with music.

On such a night, with the land thawing, the icicles that hung from roof and porch weeping themselves thin, the front door burst open to admit a towering young man who filled the doorway. He wore heavy boots, a sheepskin jacket, a blue stocking rakishly askew on a mass of shaggy red hair. Laughing blue eyes surveyed the room, widening at the sight of Kirsten.

"Holy yumping Yesus!" he boomed.

Helga flew out of her chair right into his massive arms, crying: "Karl!"

John dropped his fiddle and joined them, grinning and clapping the newcomer on the back with blows that would have felled a lesser man.

Kirsten watched, not without a touch of envy. The man was Karl Danberg, their youngest, the one Helga referred to fondly as their naughty boy. He had been working as a logger in the north woods.

"What are you doing here, Karl?" Helga finally asked, halfway between laughter and tears.

He grinned at his mother with affection. He sure as hell didn't intend to tell her of his affair with the mill owner's wife, the little escapade that led to his firing.

"It's been a long hard winter," he teased. "Guess I came home to get warm." He looked over Helga's head, his gaze directed toward Kirsten.

"And it looks like it's going to be warmer than I thought. Who is this beautiful lady?"

Kirsten blushed at the admiration in his bold blue eyes as they were introduced.

From the moment of Karl's arrival, the Danberg home had a different atmosphere. Helga tended his needs, happily cooking all his favorite dishes. And he was much too big for the little house—the power of his boisterous personality made it seem crowded.

Everywhere Kirsten went, he seemed to be there before her, flirting outrageously.

He was handsome, boyishly charming, and great fun, like a teasing older brother. Except it was obvious that his intentions weren't brotherly at all.

Kirsten couldn't help flirting back.

Finally, one day Helga caught the two of them in the kitchen. Karl's big arms surrounded Kirsten, pinning her against the wall. He was attempting to kiss her, as she laughed, turning her head from side to side.

Helga's heart sank. She knew her son where women were concerned. Secretly rather proud of his charm, she was sure nobody would be able to resist him. And Kirsten was the granddaughter of her friend, a married woman, expecting a child.

She dispatched Karl to cut some wood for the stove, and turned to Kirsten, her color high. "I was speaking to John last night. He says the boats are running again. In fact, the *Ruth* will be in dock tomorrow or the next day, and she'll be heading back downriver.

"I wonder if you'd like him to book passage for you. I'm sure your husband misses you."

Kirsten paled. In the warm welcome of Helga's home, she had almost forgotten she didn't belong. She was being rejected again, and this time she guessed why.

"Yes," she said. "And thank you."

She didn't see the tears in Helga's eyes as she turned away. Helga was losing a daughter, but it couldn't be helped. Kirsten had been hers for only a little while, but Karl was her son.

A few days later, Kirsten stood at the rail of the *Ruth*, looking out over the churning water. It was early dawn, and she had been unable to sleep. Her cloak blew in the wind, and it was cold, so cold she shivered. But then, she was no colder outside than in.

She would be warm where she was going, she supposed. On the passenger roster she had been listed as Mrs. Matthew Weldon, destination New Orleans.

It should have been listed, she thought miserably, as Kirsten Johansson—with no place to go.

48

On a lower deck, in the men's salon, Nick Tremont folded his hand. It had not been a lucrative night. Most of the men aboard were ordinary travelers trying to get from one point to another. The well-heeled ones who combined business with pleasure would come along a little later, when the weather was warmer.

But Nick Tremont wouldn't be there.

He looked at the faces of his cardplaying companions, barely visible in the haze of smoke. "That's it for tonight."

Two of them were too drunk to understand him; the third, putty-gray, wore the numbed expression of a loser.

Nick shoved his chair back and went on deck.

Almost two years ago, the zest had gone out of his gambling. And all because of a woman.

He had gone on with the *Ruth* to New Orleans, and boarded her again when she turned back upriver. This time, he was determined to find Inga Danberg, marry her if he had to carry her off by force.

He knew she was not to be found in Memphis, where she and her daughters debarked. He had set his friends searching there, and then in the little towns along the river, but had come to the conclusion, finally, that she had been traveling under a false name.

Whoever she was, he still wanted her.

His days had deteriorated to a dreary grind of tramping the streets when they were ashore, and struggling to keep his mind on his game at night. This would be his last trip, he had decided.

He had purchased a small card parlor in the French Quarter in New Orleans. Maybe, away from the river, he could stop dreaming of Inga.

It was cold on deck, but there was no point in going to his room. He knew he wouldn't sleep. He climbed the stairs to the upper deck as he had so many times before, irked at himself for doing it. He had the strange feeling that one day she would be there waiting for him. He would stand in the same spot, put his hands on the railing she had touched, and try to summon her face to his mind.

He stopped short. Damn. Someone stood there now, a cloaked figure barely discernible in the dim light. Then the morning sun broke through, the hood blew back, and golden hair was touched with a finger of light.

"Inga!"

Kirsten turned at the glad cry, to be enveloped

in a man's arms, a mouth seeking hers. She made a whimpering sound, trying to push her attacker away. Then he was standing back, staring at her with startled eyes.

"You are not Inga! You are . . ."

Kirsten backed from him, able to see him for the first time. And she recognized him. He was the man her mother had had an affair with on the first time downriver. The man with dark hair and eyes, who just possibly might be Jenny's father.

"I am her daughter Kirsten," she said sullenly.

"Is Inga here? Is she aboard?"

At her "No," the light went out of his eyes. When he inquired about her mother's whereabouts, she felt a hateful need to punish him.

"She's living with a wealthy gentleman on a plantation," she said sweetly. "Of course, I do not approve. But—you know how Mama is."

His first reaction was one of shock, followed by a sort of sad acceptance. Inga had been alone, with the responsibility of her daughters. If she'd found a safe haven, he could not blame her. He only hoped she was happy.

As he turned away, he noticed that Kirsten was shivering in the wind, her teeth chattering, lips blue. He reached a hand to her.

"Come with me," he said. "Thora always has a pot of hot coffee in the galley. And I need company."

The good-natured cook, Thora, not only had coffee, she served it in the main salon, delighted to find that Kirsten was little Jenny's sister. After a barrage of questions, Thora retired to the galley to complete preparations for the ship's breakfast hour.

Nick Tremont leaned forward. "Tell me about Inga."

Kirsten was silent. Meeting the man she knew to be her mother's lover brought back all the hatred and animosity she had felt earlier. She tried to quiet the devil inside her that made her want to lash out, hurt someone, whenever Inga was mentioned. She sat staring out a misty window as the sun began to rise, trying to come up with a noncommittal answer.

"Mama is happy where she is. She . . . found what she was looking for."

And while she was finding it, Nick thought grimly, he was going crazy looking for her.

"I didn't see the name Danberg on the passenger list," he said suddenly.

Kirsten looked down at her hands. "Our name is Johansson."

"Then why . . .?"

"Mama used a false name. She was running away from my father."

Then Inga had not been a widow!

The coffee Nick Tremont held slopped over onto his pants. He swore under his breath and dabbed at the offending liquid. At least, he thought, it gave him a chance to recover his equilibrium. "There's no Johansson on the list, either."

"I made up a name too," she said in a whisper. "The man Mama's living with—he . . . he liked me. I didn't want to hurt Mama, so I ran away. I went back to my father, but he didn't want me . . ."

Nick was quiet for a while, trying to digest the sordid details of Kirsten's story. "What are your plans now? Where are you going? What do you intend to do?"

"I don't know," Kirsten said dully. "I just don't know."

She had finished her coffee. She put the cup down and rose to her feet.

"Thank you," she said sweetly. "Now I think I can sleep. I'm going to my room."

He started to rise, and she held up a staying hand. "I can manage by myself." Then she was gone.

Nick Tremont sat nursing the hot cup in his hands, staring down into its steaming depths. He was completely and utterly confused.

He had put Inga on a pedestal, had fallen for her widowed-mother act, had acknowledged the responsibilities she had for her children. He had dashed around like a schoolboy trying to find her. And she had lied. Keeping her true name from him. All the time, she was searching for someone who could give her more than he.

She'd made a fool of him. It was her daughter he was sorry for, the poor little girl, so like her mother in appearance, but sweet, virginal, with no one to care for her.

In her stateroom, Kirsten stood before a mirror and tried to span her waist with her hands. There was some difference, but not too much yet.

It was still nice to see a look of admiration in a man's eyes, in spite of her knowledge about him and her mother. Besides, she was younger than Inga, so Nick would certainly consider her more desirable. It wouldn't hurt to lead him on a little— just for fun.

That evening, the weather changed. It got much warmer. The sharp wind died and the riverboat slowed for the night, seeming to drift on the moon-silvered water.

Nick did not go to the gentlemen's salon that evening. He hadn't slept well, and playing cards with one loser and two drunks was not his cup of tea. It was like shooting fish in a barrel, he told himself.

He found Kirsten once more at the rail, and moved quietly to her side, not wanting to frighten her. She jumped a little, anyway, with an expression of guilt in her face.

"A penny for your thoughts," he said.

Kirsten had been planning her campaign. She looked out over the water, trying to think of something to say, and came up with an inspiration.

"I was wondering . . ." She faltered, her lips quivering a little. ". . . what it would feel like to drown. I think it would be peaceful—"

Tremont's face turned white, and he caught her by the shoulders, shaking her a little. "Don't you ever," he said in a fierce voice, "don't you ever, ever think of anything like that again!"

With a muffled sob, Kirsten crumpled against him. In his arms, she felt like a grown woman. She felt like Inga.

49

From that morning at the ship's rail, Nick Tremont's life was turned round-about. He had always been a creature of the night, plying his trade in the hours of darkness, sleeping during the day. Now he hated leaving Kirsten alone for a moment for fear she would drown herself.

He always tried to be at the railing to meet her when she rose at dawn, so they could watch the sun rise and have coffee together. Nick, exhausted, due to the change in his sleeping habits, began to find it difficult to separate the daughter from the mother.

The way she turned, the curve of a cheek, the wide blue eyes. He tried to quell his growing interest, to tell himself that Kirsten was only a child. There were more than fifteen years between them. He was old enough to be her father.

He was determined to be paternal as they walked the decks together. He had no idea that the sun and the clear fresh air made him more attractive every day. His face darkened to a copper shade that complemented his black hair and eyes. He flushed, a thin line of red accentuating his cheekbones, as he caught Kirsten staring at him, and put a hand to his face. "Is something wrong?"

"I was thinking how much alike you and my sister, Jenny, are in coloring."

"Indeed? I'm not sure I ever noticed her."

If he was lying, Kirsten thought, he was doing a good job of it.

At another time she asked, "How long did you know my mother?"

"I met her just as I met you, at the rail one morning on your voyage downriver."

"I don't know why," she said, "but I had the feeling you might have known her before."

She turned away from him, pointing out a barge, its peeling white paint tinted in rose and blue by the sun. "It's beautiful, isn't it?"

"Yes," Nick agreed. But he wasn't looking at the barge, he was looking at the girl.

He had no idea that her mind was elsewhere, busily planning a future for the two of them. It had dawned on her that her baby needed a father. And Nick Tremont would do as well as anyone.

Her lips curled mirthlessly. Wouldn't Mama be surprised!

The days drifted by, and in Nick's mind Inga became Kirsten and Kirsten became Inga. The girl volunteered no more confidences, but Tremont found himself lying awake at night wondering why

Inga had taken up with a ... a no-good bum, a man who would try to force himself on her own daughter. He also wondered about Kirsten's father in Minnesota. What kind of man would turn his own child away when she went to him in her trouble?

Somehow Nick felt responsible for her, but he was helpless. He wondered if fifteen or more years of age between a man and a woman made all that much difference. It probably did. Kirsten was too young to marry and too old to adopt. He could hardly show up in New Orleans with an unattached female. But Kirsten needed someone to take care of her.

Thora, watching the two of them together, had her own ideas about the relationship.

"That Kirsten girl got that man plumb fooled," she told her husband, Tom. "An' he ain't got sense enough to see it!"

"Don' see nothin' so bad about that," Tom said mildly. "Nick ain't got nobody. She's a good-lookin' little lady."

"Good-lookin', mah foot!" Thora spat. "Looky here!" She took down a porcelain cup, used only for special travelers, like governors and such. "See this? Hold it up tuh the light. See how it shines through? Now, looka this!"

She reached for another cup of blue enameled tin. "This here's purty too, till it gits a chip knocked off. Then it ain't worth nothin'.

"That's how Miss Kirsten is. All show on the outside, jes plain tin on the inside."

"You ain't givin' her a fair shake, Thora."

"Ain't I? She's after that man. I'm tellin' you!

353

And I'm tellin' you this! He ain't gonna git there first! She's already got somethin' under her apron, or I done gone stone blind!"

Tom looked shocked. "Naw," he protested. "Na-a-aw! Whatever give you that idea, Thora?"

"I got eyes," she said indignantly. "I kin see! It's somethin' about her face."

Tom burst into a hoot of laughter and smacked his wife on the bottom. "Git on with peelin' them taters, woman. It'll keep you outta trouble."

"You'll see," she said direly. "You'll see."

Each day, the weather grew warmer. From the shore, and from the small islands around which the Mississippi swirled, gentle breezes carried a breath of spring. The relationship between Nick Tremont and Kirsten Johansson deepened.

The fatherly kiss he bestowed on her cheek each night before he left her turned into something more. But Kirsten was unable to shake the armor of Nick's honorable intentions toward Inga's daughter. She was growing a little desperate.

Nick, too, was struggling with his emotions. On the night before they were to reach Memphis, he knew he and Kirsten had to discuss her situation. She hadn't mentioned her future plans at all.

"Are you going to get off at Memphis, Kirsten?" he asked. "Are you going to go home to your mother?"

She began to tremble and covered her eyes with her hands. "I can't, Nick."

"Would it help if I went with you? Had a talk with this man?"

"No," she said in terror. "No! It would spoil

things for Mama. And when you left, he'd be after me again."

"Then what are you going to do?"

"I don't know, Nick!" She was weeping now. "I just don't know."

"Kirsten, look at me!"

He put a hand beneath her chin, looking down into her drowned eyes.

"You aren't thinking of doing anything ... desperate, are you? Kirsten, promise me ..."

She shot a look at the muddy, roiling waters and shivered. Then she threw herself in Nick Tremont's arms. "Don't leave me alone tonight, Nick! I couldn't bear it! Oh, God, I don't have anyone—"

"Kirsten, don't ..."

She was sobbing loudly, and he could see a couple approaching, rounding the deck. Quickly he led her to her stateroom door, stepped inside with her, and closed it after him.

"We'll work something out."

"Oh, Nick!"

Her arms twined around his neck, pulling his head down. And then her lips touched his and he was kissing her passionately.

Kirsten, after a brief triumphant thought that she'd solved her problems, forgot everything except that this was a man who wanted her for herself and that she was burning with desire.

"I need you," he whispered hoarsely.

And she replied, "Yes ... oh, yes!"

Neither of them would remember exactly what transpired between that passionate embrace and the moment they moved like sleepwalkers to Kirsten's bed.

Nick managed to pull himself together then, but only for a moment. Kirsten was a young, virginal girl. He must be gentle. . . .

Then he forgot himself as they moved together, blindly, mindlessly, intent only on their need, moving to the brink of climax. Nick, driven beyond conscious thought, groaned aloud. "Inga," he said. "Inga . . ."

He had no idea that he had uttered Inga's name. He knew only the body beneath him had suddenly become cold to his touch. His ardor cooled and he came back to his senses. He gripped her bare shoulders and shook her. "Kirsten!"

"Yes, Nick." Her voice was flat, ominous, but at least she was alive.

"I didn't mean to do that, Kirsten. I'm sorry!"

"Why?" Her tone was icy, venomous. "Wasn't I as good as my mother?"

He felt a wave of guilt as he recalled the night he'd spent with Inga. Evidently Kirsten had known about it all along.

"Listen, Kirsten, let me explain."

She sat up, the moon through the window gilding her curves in the darkness. "There's nothing to explain," she said. "You are just exactly what I thought you were! Get out of my room."

"Please, Kirsten," he said coaxingly. "Whatever was between Inga and me is over. I want to take care of you. As for what just happened—"

"You want to make an honest woman of me?" she said mockingly. "Well, you can go to hell! I wouldn't have you if you were the last man on earth!"

There was no reasoning with her. She crouched

on her bed, her eyes like cat's eyes in the moonlight, pouring out a wave of vituperation against him, against Inga. Finally he thought of something that had lingered at the back of his mind. Kirsten was not the inexperienced, innocent child she had pretended to be. She had come to him too easily. There had been no flinching away, no sharp little cry of pain, only the joining of two bodies eager for the same release.

He had no idea why she had encouraged him, nor what had really caused her anger, but she had turned into a howling bitch, and he no longer felt any need to look after her. He hurried to dress and leave.

Once the cabin door closed behind Nick, Kirsten burst into tears.

She was certain now that Nick had fathered Jenny. Her mother's name had come to his lips so easily. In his mind, Kirsten was only a substitute for Inga. Kirsten wanted none of her mother's leftovers!

She felt like screaming out her frustration to the world, throwing things at the walls. But she forced herself to be calm, cold, calculating.

She was through with Nick Tremont. And Matthew Weldon was to blame for the child she carried within her. She intended to see that he paid!

The next day, she walked off the shp at Memphis and made her way to the house where Miz Fannie plied her trade.

50

At Sweethome, Inga had been forced to resign herself to the loss of Kirsten, though they had searched for her everywhere.

As far as Inga knew, Kirsten had no money. She had been in a terrible state when she left. She had taken only the clothing she was wearing, and the weather had been dreadful. She could have wandered off the road, to die of exposure, or she might have met up with a band of murdering renegades.

But Inga refused to believe that anything too terrible had happened to her daughter. Kirsten had always been one to land on her feet. One day, she was sure, there would be a letter from her. Or she would come home.

This particular morning, however, Inga had come close to breaking down. She had gone for a short walk after breakfast, across the little bridge. And there, in the lane, Matthew Weldon was waiting for her, his face drawn and set in worried lines.

"I need to talk to you, Mrs. Johansson," he said in a troubled voice. "Have you heard from Kirsten?"

She had not.

"Then you have no idea where she is?"

"No."

He wanted Inga to know he had written to Martha, the girl he had been engaged to at home. He planned to go to Pennsylvania sometime in June. When he returned, he would be bringing his bride with him.

"I don't want you to hate me," he said gently. "I don't want to hurt you."

It shouldn't hurt, but it did. She supposed their affair had been a passing thing, that the man had not loved Kirsten, but his marriage to someone else seemed to be the first handful of earth tossed into a grave.

"I wish you every happiness," she had said, and hurried back to the house.

Now, standing in her garden, she tried to count her blessings, smiling at the girl who worked beside her.

Jenny was home. And according to Theron, Jesse Norwood had moved on.

Gradually Inga and Theron had made peace. Theron admitted that the way he'd handled the situation with Jenny and Jesse was wrong. But it had all turned out for the best, Inga thought. Jenny needed time to grow up.

She was very quiet these days, her dark eyes even larger in her small face. There was a waiting look about her. She didn't range the woods as she had before, playing games—dangerous games! But she didn't seem unhappy.

Nor was Inga, except for her worries over Kirsten. Her eyes left the face of her daughter, and she gazed out over the fields.

Spring had come gently to Sweethome. The balmy winds of March had melted the mists of winter and shaken budding trees into leaf. April brought a sweet scent of rich turned earth and flowers.

A field hand's son burned off the brittle winter weeds in a patch behind the stable. Further afield, the black workers were busy with the duties of planting time. They sang as they worked, knowing that this time part of the harvest would be theirs.

Dinah, guessing at what was in Inga's mind, stopped for a minute, leaning on her hoe. "Look at that," she said. "Jes lissen tuh 'em. Like old times, 'cept Massa Theron out there workin' with 'em."

Inga smiled to herself. Theron had managed to change, more than Dinah ever would. She had tried to eliminate the word "Massa" from Dinah's vocabulary, but it was too deeply ingrained.

Her smile faded suddenly as she lifted her head, sniffing the air. There was a smell of burning wood— not just weeds—a thread of black curling upward through white smoke; the frightened neighing of a horse split the atmosphere.

The stable! Tolie had let the fire get away from him.

Jenny, who was closest to the stable, raced toward it.

Inga ran to sound the bell, and Dinah stripped the wet wash off the line. As the two women hurried toward the stable, Jenny was already leading a wild-eyed horse away from it, and a small shed at the rear went up in flame, igniting the stable wall.

"Don't go back in, Jenny," Inga called. "Help us here!"

Without pausing, Inga rushed to the back of the burning building, beating at the fire with wet sheets. Coughing, she was enveloped in smoke. Dinah carried buckets of water from the horse trough, but the fire was out of control before the workers arrived.

Theron appeared suddenly at Inga's side to drag her away from the smoke. "Let it go," he yelled. "We can't save it! Where's Jenny?"

Inga, blinking smarting eyes, saw another horse bolt from the stable as a portion of the roof caved in in a shower of sparks.

"Jenny! Oh, God, Theron! She's in the stable!"

As Theron sprinted toward the stable entrance, Inga tried to follow, but Dinah caught her in a pair of strong, unyielding arms.

"You goin' stay right here, missus. That man got all he can han'le without him worryin' 'bout you!"

Inga lunged, trying to break away, without success. Finally she sagged against Dinah, eyes filled with horror and despair as another roof section fell and a cloud of greasy black smoke mounted to the sky.

Then two figures appeared in the doorway, silhouetted by the flames. Theron was leading Jenny, half-supporting her.

Dinah's arms relaxed their grip and Inga ran

toward them, catching her daughter to her in an agony of love.

Jenny had freed all the horses. The last one, crazed with fear, had shouldered her aside, knocking her to the floor. A beam had fallen, pinning her foot, and she'd been unable to get free. The beam was burning when Theron reached her, though the flames had not yet touched her. He had burned his hand as he lifted it away to pull Jenny out.

He didn't mention the hand as he stood with Inga and Jenny, watching his stable burn until there was nothing left but an area of charred and smoking ruin.

They walked back to the house together, a family discussing their loss and planning to rebuild again.

A family!

That was what stuck in Inga's mind as she carefully bandaged Theron's hand in strips of cloth soaked in strong tea. For months she'd held herself apart from him, blaming him for his attitude toward Jenny and Kirsten. But today he'd gone into the fire to save Jenny, risking his own life.

Dear God, they had wasted so much time!

That evening, as Theron and Inga sat quietly on the veranda, she touched his arm. "Let's go for a walk," she said, averting her eyes from his. "There is something I want to ask you."

He followed where she led, across the scented lawn and to the center of the arched bridge. There, in a myriad of leaf shadows, the sounds of running water and night birds surrounding them, she looked up at his questioning eyes.

"Theron," she said, a quiver in her voice, "I'm

ready to set a date for our wedding—if you still want me."

"Want you!" It was a joyous whoop that sounded more like a victorious rebel yell.

He pulled her firmly to him with his one arm, pressing her against the railing until her body fitted into his. "Want you?" he said again, more gently. "Oh, God, Inga, I've waited so long!"

He kissed her, his mouth throbbing against hers. And there, on the arched bridge between water and stars, Inga's hurts healed, and she became whole.

Within the hour, a tapping at her door brought Jenny from her dreams. Slipping on a robe, she answered to find Inga and Theron standing there, their faces glowing. She read their secret in their eyes before they spoke. They told her their wedding was set for the first of May. She hugged them both. "I'm happy for you," she whispered. "So happy."

They would never know what her loving words cost her.

The next morning, Jenny rose early and made her way across the fields and through the trees for the first time since Christmas Day.

Though torn curtains still hung at the windows of Jesse's little house, it was empty. She forced herself to go on, climbing the steps, forcing the creaking door open. The furnishings were still in place, but the big room smelled of dead ashes, mice, and mildew.

There was nothing of Jesse there. She wished she had not come.

For a moment she stood with her eyes closed,

trying to bring back memories: Jesse on his pallet before the fire, burning with fever; Jesse in his chair, crutches at his side, smiling at her; Jesse at the table, his mouth twisted, tongue between his teeth as he laboriously learned to write his name. The vision was so real, she caught her breath.

He had left his slate behind.

She walked to the table where it was placed exactly centered, and choked on a sob.

He had drawn a heart on it, and below the heart, in awkward letters, he'd written "Jesse."

He had known she would come.

51

On the morning of May 1, 1868, Inga woke to find Dinah in her room with an early breakfast on a tray. Dinah had come to give Inga her orders for the day. She was to stay right where she was, and not leave the room.

"It bad luck for the groom to see the bride before the weddin'. You don' want no bad luck, do you?"

Inga did not. She'd have enough of that.

From the yard below, sounds of activity drifted upward: the workmen moving about, laughing, singing as they prepared the front lawn for the festivities. Inga had suggested a simple ceremony with just herself, Theron, the minister, and Jenny present. It seemed wasteful to go to so much trouble for a small wedding, without guests, without friends.

Theron insisted on more. He wanted this to be an occasion to remember. Jenny and Dinah agreed with him. Affectionately they bullied Inga, telling her she had no choice in the matter. They were, after all, the bride's family.

Inga thought of that first wedding, when, little more than a child, she had stood trembling before her father's congregation. Olaf had worn a lumpy black suit, and Pastor Lindstrom, scowling from the pulpit, spoke at great length.

He instructed the bride-to-be in her duties, and stated that Inga, as a woman, was an inferior being in the sight of God, that she must subject herself to her husband's will, that it was Olaf Johansson's duty to watch over her, keep her from her sinful ways. It had not been a wedding, but a formal contract of slavery.

The past was gone forever, with all its bittersweet memories. Now she had to make herself face the future. She walked the floor feeling as if her body were filled with butterflies. How could Theron possibly love her?

If she could just see him. Talk to him.

"Set that table here, John."

She heard Theron's voice in the yard below. Without thinking, Inga ran to the window and lifted a corner of the drapery.

"Git away from that winda!"

Inga whirled and blushed guiltily as she faced Dinah. The old woman, her arms akimbo, face like a thundercloud, stood in the doorway.

"I done told you, missus! You worse than a chile! You goin' behave youse'f, or do I have to stay here an' keep a eye on you?"

Inga, feeling absurdly young, made promises and Dinah left, still grumbling.

The hours dragged. Noon brought a light lunch and the news the preacher had arrived. Immediately after lunch, Dinah and Zada came, carrying a huge tub which they filled with buckets of hot water, scattering savory herbs from the kitchen on its surface.

Inga bathed amid the fragrance of mint, rosemary, and dried rose petals. Then, slipping into a robe, she let Zada braid her hair into its usual coronet—except this time, a blue ribbon was woven into it.

Then Jenny came to help her don her wedding gown.

It was a simple dress, with an underpetticoat of deep blue, an overgown of palest blue silk that hugged her waist and bosom, sweeping into a train behind her. With it she wore dainty satin slippers Theron had purchased in Memphis.

"Mama," Jenny said reverently, "you look like a queen!"

The two women, mother and daughter, hugged each other. Jenny was sincerely happy for her mother's sake. One day, she thought, she would have a wedding of her own.

At two o'clock Inga descended the stairs to meet John, the black foreman, at the foot. He wore a suit of Theron's that the women had altered to fit him, and looked very impressive as he extended his arm and led her toward the open doorway.

Inga stopped, unable to believe her eyes.

Before her, framed by the house's pillars, was a white arbor, its lattice enlaced with leaves and flowers, and beneath it, Theron, waiting for his bride.

To one side, long tables laden with food and drink had been set up. At the other, the workers and their children stood silent, dressed in their best, their faces wreathed in smiles.

And the music began: Ceph with a dulcimer, its notes scattering to the sky, splintering into the air like stars, Clem's homemade fiddle holding the melody tune.

Jenny, in a new dress the color of roses, led the way. Then Inga walked to meet her groom—the autocratic Theron St. Germain, master of Sweethome, former slave owner—on the arm of a black man, his employee and friend.

Theron watched her coming. She looks like the Goddess of Spring, he thought. She would be his love, his wife . . .

His mind went back to another wedding in another time. It was held in a sumptuous drawing room. The bride was a vision in white, with wide hooped skirts, flowing veils, a bodice seeded with pearls. There had been a full week of celebration—music, dancing, champagne, fireworks on a parklike lawn.

But it had not been a marriage, ever.

Not like this.

Standing together before the minister from Memphis, they took their vows. And Theron St. Germain bent to kiss the bride, still marveling at the miracle of her.

She was getting no great bargain. He was missing an arm, his plantation was depleted—but he was more of a man than he had even been before.

It had taken a war—and a woman—to make him whole.

Following the ceremony, the newlyweds moved among their black friends, dizzied with blessings and congratulations. Then the feasting and dancing began, a celebration that was to last all night.

It was dusk when the happy couple slipped away, unnoticed.

Theron had a trap waiting, the horse tethered down the lane a short distance. Inga hastily kissed Jenny good-bye and she and Theron hurried toward it, laughing like children at their escape. Theron helped Inga up, then took his place in the driver's seat. Though she had wanted to spend their wedding night at home, he said he had plans of his own. It was his secret—and Jenny's. And he refused to divulge their destination.

"You are too far away," he said.

Blushing, she slid closer to him, resting her head on his shoulder as they drove through the fragrant night.

Several miles down the road, Theron turned into a lane that led past the ruins of Belle Terre. When they reached the fence that separated the two properties, he tied the horse and helped Inga to alight. "We'll have to walk from here, sweetheart."

Then she knew. The glade, of course!

They went together, hand in hand, across the soft grass, skirting trees until they reached the spot that would always be their own.

Inga caught her breath in surprise.

A little summerhouse shone white in the darkness near the pool, like something out of a fairy tale. Wind bells chimed in the gentle breeze. It was almost too beautiful to be real.

"Jenny helped me restore it," he said, suddenly shy. "She said to tell you it's a wedding present."

"Oh, Theron!"

"Do you like it?" he asked huskily.

"Like it! It's . . . it's beautiful!"

He put his hand to her shoulder and turned her to face him. "With most people, everything is romantic at first," he said in his soft Southern drawl. "Then they move on to practical things. We've managed to do it all backward. But tonight the romance begins. And I promise you, it will never end."

He pulled her close to him, kissing her. Far off, from Sweethome, the sound of music drifted faintly on the air.

Inga's mouth caught fire from his. And suddenly kissing was not enough. She trembled as Theron led her toward the little structure and up the steps. There was a soft bed beneath its roof, a low table set with glasses and a bottle of Dinah's homemade wine.

Theron left her and went to the side walls to release a fall of netting that enclosed them, setting them apart from the world. As he turned back to her, her face was flushed, her heart thumping, with both hope and fear of what was to come.

"Do . . . does anyone know where we are?"

He laughed. "Only Jenny. And she won't tell."

His hand went to her hair, loosening it to fall in a golden rain, then moved down to the fastenings of the soft blue gown.

Inga stood with her eyes closed, her head thrown

back, shivering at his touch, as one by one the confining garments fell away.

He caught his breath at the beauty of her—a Valkyrie, a goddess, pale marble in the moonlight.

"Open your eyes," he commanded. "Look at me!"

She did. A blaze of blue meeting the warmth of amber.

Then he led her to the bed, where silken sheets covered a mattress filled with sweet dried grass; silken sheets for a woman whose first experience at marriage had been an insensitive attack in a soiled and rumpled bachelor's bed.

"Lie down," he whispered.

Inga obeyed.

As Theron undressed, she began to tremble with wanting.

Then he came toward her, his body dark against the netting, and lay down beside her, pulling her to him. His hand moved over her, tracing the secrets of her body, rousing her to a passion she didn't know was in her, that set her pleading for release. His mouth was hot against her lids, her mouth, her throat, and moving down. . . .

"Theron," she whispered, "please . . ."

Then she felt the hard length of him against her and rose to meet him with a little cry.

They came to the consummation of their love with childlike wonder, marveling as if the miracle had been created just for them. This total fulfillment was new to both of them: the woman who had known only brutality from a domineering husband, a brief and healing experience with a riverboat gambler; the man who had catered to the whims of a selfish, frigid wife.

When Theron finally slept, Inga lay still, able to think of her children at last. Of Jenny, sweet, generous Jenny, who had been deprived of her love, yet took such pleasure in her mother's good fortune.

What did life hold in store for her? Or for Kirsten, if, in fact, she still lived?

Slow tears began to seep from beneath her lashes.

As if he guessed she needed him, Theron woke and reached for her drowsily. She turned to him, finding forgetfulness in his passion, in knowing that the two of them belonged to each other forever.

All night, the wind bells whispered, an accompaniment to the waters of the spring. And in the morning they woke, drowsy and sated with love, to find the walls of netting sparkling with dew. Their wedding bower had become a canopy of diamonds. It would be there for them always.

52

The marriage of Inga and Theron St. Germain seemed to bestow a secret blessing on their surroundings. Sweethome burgeoned. All hands—men, women, and children—worked in the fields from dawn to dark, taking pleasure in the work that would bring them profit, and in the fact that the man they had once called "Massa" worked beside them.

Dinah handled the housework and cooking, Inga the garden. Though gardening was harder, she enjoyed being out in the open air, being able to see Theron in the distance, knowing that he turned occasionally to seek her out, the bond between them as tangible as if he touched her.

One day, when she had been weeding since breakfast, she paused to study the terrain. Jenny, in her too-short red dress, worked beside her. It was very hot, and Inga's gown was unbuttoned at the throat; her braids had slipped away from their tiaralike coil and hung down her back like those of a child. Her face was smudged with dirt and perspiration.

Standing, hand pressed to the small of her back, she looked ruefully down at her soiled gown, at the bare feet peeping from below its hem.

"It's almost lunchtime, Jenny. We'd better clean up a little."

But Jenny wasn't listening. Her eyes were fixed on something behind her. Inga turned at the sound of Dinah's voice. "There she is, suh, ma'am. That the missus, and little missie."

The couple who had followed Dinah to the garden were staring at Inga in amazement, as if she were some sort of creature they did not recognize. The man recovered first, bowing. "You are the new Mrs. St. Germain?"

There was a note of incredulity in his voice, and Inga flushed as she nodded assent.

"I'm Will Osborne," he said in a thick Southern accent. "This is my wife, Melanie."

The woman in crisp pink dimity, a matching parasol held in her hand, forced a smile, and her husband continued.

They were the owners of Belle Terre. They had been living in Memphis since the war, but now they were considering returning and rebuilding their home. They had driven out to assess the damages, and thought perhaps St. Germain might put them up for the night.

"Of course." Inga extended a welcoming hand, then drew it back when she saw how grimy it was.

Not before noticing, however, that Melanie Osborne flinched and pulled her skirts aside to avoid contamination.

Inga stiffened a little, then introduced Jenny. "My daughter," she said. Than, defiantly, "Our daughter."

"Theron and I are old friends," Osborne said hastily. "His first wife and Melanie were like sisters. We all grew up together, shared the same tutors, ran in the same circles socially."

And I didn't, Inga thought. That's what he's telling me!

She turned to Boy, who had returned from carrying water to the workers. "Run and call Mr. St. Germain," she said sweetly. "Tell him we have company."

Their obvious shock at meeting Inga was mild compared to what they showed when they saw Theron. They had watched blankly as Boy scooted toward the fields, approaching a man in overalls, indistinguishable from the others at a distance.

"That can't be Theron," Melanie gasped. "Not working in the fields with the niggers."

"These are different times, Melanie," her husband said. "I've told you that if we come back to the plantation—"

"You won't catch me doing slave work," his wife sniffed, taking a meaningful look at Inga's soiled hands. "I was reared to be a lady!"

Inga said nothing, her color heightening.

When Theron dropped his hoe and headed toward them, Melanie Osborne gasped audibly, and her husband's jaw dropped. It was evident they

375

didn't know about the loss of Theron's arm. But Inga was sure that didn't stun them as much as his appearance. Theron was burned brown by the sun; his shirt was open, revealing black curls glistening with perspiration, and his hair was plastered to his forehead with sweat.

"Will Osborne," he sang out as he extended a callused hand. "And Melanie! I'll be damned!"

Now it was Osborne's turn to flinch.

"They're thinking about moving to Belle Terre," Inga said. "Won't that be nice?"

Theron suppressed a grin. He could tell from his wife's tone, from the flush on her cheekbones, that it wouldn't be "nice" at all.

He clapped Osborne on the shoulder and insisted that he walk around the property with him to see what they'd done with it, and leave the women to get acquainted.

"I am sure," Inga said, "Mrs. Osborne would like to rest and refresh herself before dinner. Jenny, would you please take Mrs. Osborne to the . . . the blue room?"

The room that had belonged to Marnie St. Germain would probably suit her!

Then Inga went to her own room to wash away the effects of her gardening and don a cool gown of batiste trimmed in delicate lace. Her hair brushed and coiled again into its coronet, she hurried back downstairs, to find Jenny dressed in her best, her cheeks pink with irritation.

It was clear Jenny didn't like the visitors either, but was determined to put her best foot forward for Theron's sake.

Dinah, in a clean, crisp apron, her hair tied in a

white cloth, had set the table with fine mended linen and was busily preparing a company meal. She had seen the way that high-tony female looked at her missus, and she was determined to put her in her place.

The dinner was delicious, the service suited to an elegant occasion, but Inga watched Melanie's face as she assessed chipped plates and tin cutlery from the kitchen. It did not help that Osborne couldn't keep his eyes off Inga and Jenny. He drank too much of Dinah's homemade wine and kept slapping Theron—now impeccably dressed—on the back, telling him he was a lucky fellow.

Melanie pouted, and was barely civil throughout the meal.

When the men took themselves to the study for brandy and cigars, the atmosphere improved. Melanie confided that she was happy in Memphis among her friends—her type of people—and that she didn't want to move back to the plantation. It was all Will's idea.

She fanned herself nervously. Perhaps Inga would intervene on her behalf, tell him the work involved was just too much for a delicate female.

"I do not find it so," Inga said demurely.

At last the men joined them and they retreated to the front porch to catch the evening coolness. The trickle of the creek could be heard in the distance, frogs croaking along the grassy banks, fireflies glinting against the trees. And everywhere, the smells of summer filled the air.

It was a beautiful night, but it was lost on their guests. Melanie complained of mosquitoes and Will tipsily kept returning to the same subject. A St.

Germain working alongside niggers! He couldn't believe it!

Theron explained that times had changed. It was necessary for everyone at Sweethome to work together. Inga handled house and garden, he did what he could to help in the fields.

And these blacks were not slaves, but partners, in effect, who would be paid when the cotton crop was in. Whatever he could add to their efforts was to his advantage. If Osborne were to rebuild Belle Terre, he would face the same situation.

Melanie was suddenly exhausted. She and her husband opted for an early night.

As Inga and Theron lay close after a whispered session of love making, they could hear voices raised across the hall. Theron chuckled. "Sounds like old Will is catching hell in there."

There was a long pause; then he said rather embarrassedly, "Funny thing. I used to really like Will. But he's changed."

No, my darling, Inga thought. You've changed. Then she was surprised at the intensity with which her husband reached to pull her tightly against him.

"Do you mind if I tell you how proud I am of my wife?" he asked fiercely. "Thank God, I was lucky enough to find you!"

Inga smiled to herself as she rested her cheek against his shoulder. She was glad, now, that the Osbornes had come. It had been a kind of test, and their marriage had not only survived it, but was strengthened. Her fears that Theron would one day look at her and find her wanting disappeared.

Tomorrow their guests would return to Memphis. She was sure they would not move back to Belle Terre. And one day, Kirsten would come home, and then this happiness would be complete.

eral ladies' private matters were much too
laborious to teach. It did not appeal those
things, plus music and small talk, and had
her in constant of these hopes.

53

At the moment, Kirsten Johansson was making
her own plans.

She had left the boat and gone once more to Miz
Fannie's, where she had been treated like a long-
lost daughter, coddled and cosseted even more,
once they knew she was pregnant. To their minds,
she was a poor innocent girl taken advantage of by
a dirty man!

They assumed that she wanted to become a member of their little family, one of their young ladies,
though of course they would not allow her to work
with the others while she was in a family way.
And they were pleased that she hadn't taken any
steps to rid herself of her little burden prematurely.

That was definitely immoral!

Miz Fannie and Sister still had important social
contacts, people who, though they knew of the

genteel ladies' present business, were much too mannerly to mention it. And it was among those friends that Miz Fannie and Sister distributed the results of any . . . unfortunate consequences.

"When they adopt one of ouahs," Miz Fannie beamed, "they know theah gettin' blue bloods! Chillun of theah own class."

At present there were several prospective parents on Miz Fannie's waiting list. And they were willing to pay good money for a little one.

Kirsten wanted more than money. She wanted revenge—a father for her child, and Eden along with it. She had bided her time, waiting until the baby was nearing term. She intended Matthew Weldon to see the consequences of his own acts. He would have to marry her. He owed it to her. This time, it wouldn't be at St. Germain's insistence, but her own.

That particular spring day, Kirsten wandered to the window, pulled aside the lace curtains, and sighed.

The setting never seemed to change. The front yard was a small patch of scraggly grass with several flowering shrubs in unhealthy condition. Miz Fannie tended them constantly. Too constantly, Kirsten thought. Sometimes the woman's persistent kindnesses left her feeling smothered, too.

At least she was safe here. It was going to be difficult to leave.

Across the road, two small children played in a dusty yard. They were ragged, unkempt, and ill-mannered the way they kept shoving at each other. A boy and a girl.

Nose pressed to the window, Kirsten thought of

the little one inside her. For the first time, she realized it was a small human being. Quickly she pushed the image away. She mustn't think of it that way, but as a tool, a lever to get what she wanted.

Miz Fannie's voice intervened. "I've brought you a nice hot cup of tea."

Kirsten mentally estimated the number of "nice hot cups of tea" she'd had this day. Five. And five multiplied by the number of days she'd been there produced an astronomical figure. But she tried to smile as she accepted the cup from Miz Fannie's plump little hands.

Miz Fannie arranged herself on the sofa, spreading her skirts decorously around her. "Kirsten, Ah've been thinkin'. Me an' Sister ain't too suah you'll be happy heah. We been wonderin' 'bout youah baby's daddy. He married?"

Kirsten flushed. "No."

"He know y'all are in a family way?"

"No."

"He got money?"

"Yes."

Miz Fannie clapped her small, pudgy hands. "Theah! Theah's youah answer! He marries up with you, or you make him pay! It's only faiah!"

Kirsten listened to Miz Fannie's idea of genteel blackmail, suppressing a smile. The old woman's reasoning so closely paralleled her own.

"Do you really think I should?"

"Cose Ah do! Damn men, runnin' around killin' an' rapin'! Somebody's got to keep 'em in line!"

Rape? Kirsten blushed, remembering that it hadn't been that at all, but it served her purpose to let the woman think so.

At the end of the week, Kirsten set out on the last miles of her journey. She wore a soft turquoise gown with an oversmock that Miz Fannie and Sister had stitched for her. It made her look like a little girl. And that was its purpose. Just let that man see what an innocent child he had ruined.

Miz Fannie helped Kirsten into the horse-drawn trap—her own, lent for the occasion. She sent a young black girl, Pansy, along too, to look after Kirsten.

Kirsten was to wear her braids down, Miz Fannie reminded her. It made her look younger. And before they arrived, she was to dampen this bit of blue ribbon—when wet, it faded—and rub just a teeny smudge of blue beneath her eyes, to show what she'd been through.

As the trap moved off, Kirsten wasn't sure she would need those last instructions. Though she'd said nothing to Miz Fannie, she wasn't feeling well at all. The baby wasn't due for a month, however.

It must be nerves. . . .

54

As they set out on the journey, Kirsten trembled inside. Her mind whirled with possibilities.

Matthew would be glad to see her and come to meet her with open arms. She would go into them gladly.

Matthew would be shocked, appalled, but he would marry her to give the baby his name.

Matthew would greet her with icy coolness. After all, she had come to his bed uninvited. What assurance did he have that the child was his?

She tried to shut all thoughts of her arrival at Eden from her mind, focusing instead on the familiar road before them, recalling the time she had first traveled it with her mother and Jenny.

Here they had met a farmer, his cart loaded with hay.

There the rains had caught them. A renegade

soldier tried to steal their horse. Mama and Jenny ran him off at gunpoint.

They had spent the night in that abandoned barn, which was almost unrecognizable since it was being rebuilt and painted.

That small shack near the road . . . Grace, that was the woman's name.

"Pull in here," Kirsten told Pansy.

The black woman who had offered them hospitality still lived there with her many children. She remembered Kirsten.

"You is that po' chile with the huhted feets," Grace said, welcoming her. "An' jes look at yuh now! Done catched yuh a man!"

Kirsten nodded and forced a smile as the woman insisted they "come in an' set," pressing them to eat and stay the night. They were given cornbread and buttermilk, and Kirsten shared the remains of the food Miz Fannie had sent with them.

Later, on a pallet in a poverty-stricken little shack, Kirsten slept better than she had in weeks. She was feeling better the next morning as they continued on their journey, exclaiming over the beauty of the trees, the sight of a squirrel streaking across the road in front of them, to scold them from a vantage point high in an oak.

By noon the landscape was simmering, leaves drooping in the midsummer heat. Kirsten, her euphoria of the morning gone, aware that they would reach Eden by nightfall, was beginning to feel the effects of the trip. Enervated by the sun, she sank into an uneasy sleep as the horse plodded on, the wheels of the carriage creaking in a kind of rhythm.

The sky was growing dark when suddenly she awakened, a pain gripping at the small of her back bringing her upright.

She suppressed a moan and sat stiffly still until it passed, leaving her pale, her face wet with perspiration.

Pansy, eyes big in her dark face, looked at her suspiciously. "You awright, missie? Ain' goin' do nuffin, is you?"

"Don't worry, Pansy. I'm just fine."

And she was, for more than an hour. Then the pain came again, this time with greater intensity, spreading through her, back to front. This time she doubled over with an audible gasp.

When it had gone, Kirsten wiped her streaming face and studied her surroundings. They were in a heavily wooded area, trees and foliage at either side. She did not intend to bear this child in the middle of a dusty road!

"Whip up the horse, Pansy," she said, her lips tight. "We're going to have to hurry."

With no idea of what was shortly to descend upon him, Johnson, aide to Captain Matthew Weldon, took off his shoes and settled into Weldon's big chair, a glass of the captain's brandy in his hand.

Johnson was not in the habit of occupying his master's place, nor was he a drinker. But this night was different. It had been, he told himself, one helluva day, and he deserved a rest.

Weldon had been gone only a week when the stablehand, Mose, was kicked in the head by a fractious stallion. The two men dispatched to take him to the hospital in Memphis, had not returned. The overseer and his wife had come down with some undetermined fever the following day. Then, last night, one of the cabins had burned down. It could have been a grease fire, though the workers were all terrified, certain it was the work of the Klan.

Hell, maybe it was! After what had gone on today, Johnson was willing to believe anything could happen in this godforsaken country.

With the stableman gone, the overseer and his wife laid up, jobs had had to be reallocated. The boy entrusted to feed and water the horses had left the gate open, and the beasts had bolted.

Most of the creatures were surplus, purchased after the war. And where would animals with a circled "U.S." branded on their rumps choose to go but onto the property of the rabid Confederate officer across the road!

When Johnson had gone to retrieve them, he had run into the master of Sweethome. And the fellow had given him holy hell! He hadn't been read off like that since he dropped Weldon's best rifle in a creek as they rode into battle.

Swirling the brandy in his glass, Johnson looked into its smoky depths and thanked God Weldon would be back before long. It wasn't possible for much more to happen between now and then.

A violent pounding at the front of the house doused his optimism. Those damned horses again?

He searched for his shoes, and finding only one, arranged his face in its usual wooden expression and went, in his stocking feet, to the door.

He opened it to find a white-faced woman and an ashen black girl behind her.

"Help me," the woman gasped. "I'm having a baby! Johnson, help me!"

Matthew...

55

Johnson had been a brave soldier during the war, but courage under fire was one thing. This was another.

He was fully aware that his captain had committed an indiscretion. And now his chickens, so to speak, had come home to roost. There was going to be hell to pay!

"Matthew..." Kirsten gasped. "Matthew..."

Johnson drew himself up. "The master is away, madam. He is bringing back his bride. I have been charged with keeping things in order."

"Bride?" Kirsten said numbly. "Bride?" Then she doubled over again with a sharp cry.

At the moment, Johnson was certain of only one thing. Though he was sorry for the young lady, he had to get her out of there, and quickly. He looked beyond the fainting girl to the trap in the driveway.

"You can't come in," he said firmly. "Go to Sweethome, across the lane."

The little maid, Pansy, looking in the direction of his pointing finger, saw only a dark line of trees against the night skies. "Don't see nuffin, suh. I'm scared to go in there."

Kirsten moaned and sagged against the door. Johnson felt a fine sweat break out on his forehead as he pondered his predicament.

"Oh, hell!" he said frantically. "Hell!"

He reached for Kirsten, drew back as if she might explode, then summoned his courage and propelled her toward the trap. Pansy followed, whimpering and wringing her hands. Lifting Kirsten into the seat, Johnson climbed in beside her and took the reins.

"Get in," he snapped at Pansy.

He might as well be shot for a woman as a runaway horse, by God! He would take them there himself!

Sweethome was dark when he drew up in front of it, the occupants already abed.

At least somebody was getting sleep, Johnson thought sourly. He would dump the girl on the doorstep and leave. But he knew it was not going to be that easy. The young lady was doubled up and moaning. Between his fear of facing Theron St. Germain and helping a woman have a baby, he chose the lesser of two evils and ran for the house.

Theron, wakened by a frantic pounding on the door, pulled on a robe and reached for his gun. Sweethome had few callers, and none at this hour.

Whoever it was, he would put the fear of God in him.

Inga, frightened for her husband's sake, crept down the stairs behind him, standing to one side as Theron flung open the door to reveal Weldon's man, Johnson, from across the way.

Johnson flinched as Weldon brandished his weapon, but stood his ground. "I need help, sir."

"If it's those goddam horses again—"

"It is not the horses, sir!"

"Then get the hell off my property!"

"I intend to do that, sir! I have only returned something that was trespassing on our property. I believe it belongs to you."

He turned and walked away. St. Germain, dumbfounded, lowered his gun. "What the devil is this?" he asked.

Johnson gestured toward the trap. "I suggest you see for yourself." Once he reached the safety of the trees and was out of sight, he ran like the wind back to Eden.

Theron approached the trap cautiously, weapon at the ready, Inga behind him. Hearing the cry of someone in mortal agony, he speeded up his steps, then stopped short, dropping his gun to the ground. He put a hand out to slow Inga. "Wait!"

But Inga had already seen.

"Kirsten!" she screamed. "Kirsten! She's ill! Oh, Theron, help me—"

"It's awright, missus," said the small, relieved black girl beside Kirsten. "She ain' sick. She jes goin' tuh have a baby."

Inga drew in a sharp breath, and Theron put his

391

hand on her arm. She shook it off. "I'm all right. We've got to get help."

Again the bell rang out at Sweethome, urgent and compelling, calling for help.

Big John, the foreman, carried Kirsten up the stairs to her own room. There Dinah and Inga removed her perspiration-soaked clothing and helped her into a nightgown. Jenny stood by, for once startled out of her new, too-adult composure.

"You don' b'long in here, Jenny," Dinah scolded. "Ain' no place for a young gal like you to be."

"I'm staying," Jenny said stubbornly. "She's my sister!"

Kirsten closed her eyes against them all. For a moment the dreadful cramping stopped, and she was in full possession of her senses. She had waited too long. Matthew was bringing back a bride. And she was right back where she started.

Pain struck again, and her eyes opened, wide and terrified. Her fingers clutched Inga's wrist. "Mama!"

"It's all right," Inga soothed, trying to quiet her.

But it was not all right. Nothing would ever be all right again. The ordeal lasted through the night, with Kirsten twisting on her pillow, and crying out. Dinah, at her wits' end, tried to stop the labor with every concoction she'd ever heard of.

"This chile's goin come afore its time," she predicted dourly.

Inga hushed her, but Kirsten sat upright. "I don't want it," she screamed. "I don't want a baby! All I want is for this hurt to go away!"

"You don't mean that," Inga told her.

"But I do! I do!"

The long night of pain dragged on. It was nearly dawn when Kirsten arched with a cry that tore Inga's heart. The girl sagged back against her pillows then, and her eyes closed in exhaustion.

"Baby's here," Dinah announced in a peculiar voice. "You fix its ma, so she rest easy. I'll han'le this here job."

"Is it . . .?"

Dinah wagged her head sorrowfully, and Jenny choked on a sob.

Together Inga and Jenny tended Kirsten, changing her gown and bedding. Before they had finished, Dinah had washed the little body and wrapped it in a soft towel.

Kirsten, though her eyes were closed, was now fully awake, and could hear Jenny weeping, as well as the whispers of the others at a distance.

"Never breathed one time," Dinah said. "Po' little mite."

Inga's voice, choked with tears, cried, "A little girl. Oh, Jenny, she's the image of you!"

"I want to see her."

Kirsten's voice cut through their conversation like a knife. Cold. Implacable.

"Kirsten," Inga said, "do you think—?"

"I want to see her."

Inga, carrying the still little form to Kirsten's bedside, pulled back the towel that covered it. Kirsten looked at the baby.

She looked at it for a long time. This had been her enemy, this tiny creature that she had wished away. She had thought she would be free now, but she would never really be free again.

"Would you like to hold her?" Inga asked softly.

Kirsten shook her head. "Just take her away."

All she wanted to do now was sleep and never wake up again.

56

Kirsten lay still and quiet, not speaking, but her mind was working on two levels.

She was at Sweethome. The sound of hammering in the distance meant that John was building a coffin. A tiny one.

They would be burying the baby soon. It would be out of sight, but not out of mind.

As long as she remained in her shell of silence, there would be no questions, no recriminations. She could just lie there surrounded by love and the sympathy she didn't deserve. She had come close to breaking only once, and that was when Theron St. Germain came to see her. Holding her limp hand, he told her to not worry, she was home.

Inga was with her much of the time, fluffing her pillows, smoothing her hair. Jenny, in her turn, carried on a one-way conversation, filling her in on what had happened during her absence—the planting, the wedding.

So Inga had married Theron St. Germain.

The old rebellion rose inside Kirsten for a moment, and she quelled it. She realized she always wanted what belonged to someone else. It was something in her nature. Something ugly that she recognized for the first time.

On the fourth day, Inga marched in and opened the draperies, letting the room flood with sun. Kirsten turned her face away from the light. But her mother wouldn't leave it at that.

Inga, pulling the girl up and forward, stacked the pillows behind her back. "You've got to snap out of this, Kirsten. Nothing happened to you that hasn't happened to others!"

Kirsten wanted to rail at her, to tell her that it didn't happen to *her*! That she had been safe with *her* little affair! But she bit back the words as Inga sat down beside the bed and took out one of Theron's socks from a basket of mending she'd brought with her.

"I have a feeling you need to talk, Kirsten. And I intend to sit here until you're ready." She inserted a darning egg into the toe of the sock and began to mend in silence.

"Mama . . ."

She lifted her eyes to meet Kirsten's. "Yes?"

"Why did my baby look like Jenny?"

"Why shouldn't she?"

Kirsten flushed, opened her mouth, and closed it again.

Inga sighed and returned the sock to the mending basket, folding her hands in her lap. Kirsten was grown now. She had borne and lost a child. She might as well learn the whole story.

Inga told her daughter the summer idyll between her own mother, Birgitta, married to a stern older man, and a young hired hand of French and Indian blood. Though Gustav Lindstrom was not aware of it, Inga was not his daughter. Kirsten and Jenny were true sisters, born of Inga's marriage to Olaf Johansson.

Kirsten listened openmouthed. Gustav Lindstrom was not her grandfather! He was no relation at all, in fact! It was Inga who was the bastard, not Jenny! Her own suspicions that Nick had been Jenny's father were unfounded. All these years she'd been wrong!

"Then that's what grandmother was trying to tell me," she said in a small voice.

Inga was on her feet, socks spilling to the floor. The darning egg rolled under the bed. "Mama! You've seen her?"

"Yes."

"Oh, Kirsten, how is she? Tell me! Tell me!"

Inga was crying as though her heart would break, and Kirsten realized at last what leaving her mother in Minnesota had cost Inga.

"She's fine, Mama," Kirsten lied, remembering the pathetic old woman Birgitta had become, the days filled with work, the long hours spent on her knees on an icy floor. "Grandmother is just fine."

"Tell me everything! Tell me about Olaf. What happened?"

All her life, Kirsten had felt vengeful toward Inga. She had considered her own life ruined because of the scandal about Jenny. She had hated her for striking her father down, for her involvement with Nick, with Theron, for loving Jenny more. And now she had a weapon in her hands! With a few short words, just telling her that Olaf still lived, that she, Inga, was involved in a bigamous marriage, Kirsten could destroy her mother.

"Grandfather thinks a stranger hit Papa," she said carefully. "And that you went off with him. He didn't talk to me much. Grandmother and I—we mostly talked about you . . . and Uncle Sven."

Sven! Inga gave a little cry. In her happiness with Theron, she'd almost forgotten him.

"Inga . . ."

Theron's voice sounded in the hall and he peered in the partially open door with an expression of relief. "There you are!"

"Did you want something, Theron?"

"No," he said. "I just wondered where you were. I couldn't find you."

Seeing them together, Inga blond and lovely, Theron handsomer than ever, did something to Kirsten. She couldn't bear the loving look they exchanged, excluding her. They had each other and she had no one. It wasn't fair! Her tight voice nudged itself between them. "You asked me if I wanted to talk to you, Mama. And I do. I think it's even more important now that Theron's here. I know you've all been thinking Matthew Weldon was the father of my baby. Well, he wasn't."

She certainly had their attention now, and she savored it.

"Then, who," Inga began in a choked voice, "Who . . . ?"

"A man I met on the riverboat," Kirsten lied. "His name was Nick Tremont."

Inga paled and grew as stiff as a woman sculptured in marble.

Theron didn't notice her agitation as he moved toward Kirsten's bed, his face set in a worried frown. "Who is this fellow, Kirsten? Where can I find him?"

Kirsten smiled crookedly. "It doesn't matter now, does it? It's a little ... late. Besides"—her eyes went to Inga, a glint of spite showing as she said— "he's probably found himself some other foolish woman by now."

Inga fled, and Theron followed her with his eyes as he absently patted Kirsten's hand. "She seems upset. Maybe I'd better go see what the problem is."

Kirsten watched him go and lay back against her pillows, closing her eyes. She had held back on the news about Olaf. But she'd made Inga pay for that humiliating night when Nick Tremont, making love to her, had called her by her mother's name.

57

The name of Nick Tremont was not mentioned between Inga and Kirsten again. Inga wasn't sure that Kirsten's story was true. Maybe it was born of her pride when she learned that Weldon had married someone else. Nick was too old for Kirsten, and though he was a riverboat gambler, he was an honorable man. Inga was sure he would never take advantage of a young girl.

Inga remembered those heartbreakingly beautiful mornings with him, the sound of water sheeting from the paddle wheel, a sun through mist tinting the landscape with translucent watercolor. The river was a place for lovers.

Inga resolved to ask no questions. There was no point in probing old wounds. What was done was done. Kirsten's disposition seemed vastly improved, and she even seemed to be thinking of others besides herself these days.

"That girl has certainly changed," Theron said one night as they readied themselves for bed. "You wouldn't believe what she suggested today."

Inga stopped brushing her hair and went to him, putting her arms around him. "Try me."

He grinned down at her. "You know, I believe I'll do just that!"

She backed away, blushing. "I meant, what did she suggest?"

"She thinks I ought to take you to Shiloh. Said if your brother died there, it would help you. You'd feel that you had done something for your mother."

Inga's eyes filled with tears. "What a sweet thought. I would like that, Theron."

Reaching out, he tangled his fingers in her hair. "We," he said in a lordly manner, "will discuss it later. Right now, I have other plans."

Later, Inga nestled against her sleeping husband and thought how very blessed she was. She had Theron, and now she had both her daughters.

Thinking of the girls, she recalled Kirsten's suggestion about Shiloh. The search for Sven had been fruitless, but those she'd asked thought he was most likely buried at Shiloh. On the chance that he was, she would visit the graves. It might be the only way she could repay her mother.

But when they discussed the idea in the morning light, Theron had reservations about it. One of the bloodiest battles of the war had been fought at Shiloh. There had been more than nineteen thousand casualties. It was a haunted place.

"Are you sure this is what you want?" he asked in a troubled voice.

Finally, with three women badgering him, Theron

gave in. Within a week he and Inga set out at dawn to make the journey.

Dinah, Jenny, and Kirsten were up to see them off. Kirsten still looked pale and fragile in the morning light. She kissed Theron's cheek and hugged Inga as if she might never see her again.

"Good gracious," Inga laughed, flustered at the unusual show of affection. "We're only going to be away a little while! We'll be back in a couple of nights." She turned to Dinah and Jenny. "Be sure that Kirsten rests."

They promised that they would.

Jenny and Dinah returned to the kitchen. They intended to spend the day canning and preserving.

But Kirsten stood watching until Inga and Theron were out of sight. Finally she went into the house, entering not her bedroom, but Theron's study.

She knelt to open a hidden drawer at the base of his desk, reached her hand toward the back, and withdrew a cigar box. She had seen Theron taking money from it several times. There was some left. She counted the remainder. It would be enough.

Reluctantly she put it all back, closed the drawer, and went to her room to lie on the bed and stare at the ceiling.

Pansy, the little maid Miz Fannie had sent with her, was meeting one of the workmen from Eden secretly at night, down the road. Pansy told Kirsten that Matthew Weldon and his bride, Martha, were expected before the end of the week.

And Kirsten would not stay here! She knew she would not be able to stand the thought of another woman living with Matthew just across the lane, making love to the man who was the father of her dead baby, enjoying his wealth.

It had been difficult enough these last several weeks, watching Inga and Theron like lovebirds in their cozy nest.

So she had devised a plan. And the first part of it was under way. She had managed to get Theron and Inga out of the house, and now she needed money.

She couldn't make herself take Theron's money. She had no idea why, but it was important to leave them thinking well of her. There had to be some other avenue, but there wasn't much time.

Suddenly she smiled. There *was* a way.

When the clock reached a decent hour, she dressed in her best and left by the front door. Walking slowly, like a recuperating invalid out taking air, she crossed the yard and stood for a time on the bridge. Finally satisfied that she hadn't been observed, she continued on across the lane.

At Eden, Johnson answered the door. Caught in Cook's apron, with a feather duster in his hand, he flushed with embarrassment, then paled as he recognized the caller.

What in the hell was she doing here? It could only mean trouble.

"The master has not yet returned," Johnson said stiffly.

Kirsten dimpled at him, her blue eyes shining. "You are the one I want to see," she said. "May I come in?"

Flustered, he stepped aside and she entered. Two black women were on the stairs polishing the curving banister with lemon wax. Kirsten stood for a long time looking upward, recalling the time she'd spent in Matthew's bedroom, in his arms.

When she turned, her eyes were hard. "We need to speak in private."

Johnson led her into his master's study and gingerly closed the door. He knew that the young woman had lost her child. News traveled fast through the servants' grapevine. It was a pity, of course, though a blessing for his master. He was at a loss as to what to say.

He chose to adopt a businesslike attitude. "If you will state your business, madam . . ."

"I've come to ask you for money."

He stared at her, his eyes protruding. "I owe you nothing, madam."

"Forget it, then." She moved toward the door and smiled sweetly at him. "I understand Matthew will be home soon. I'm sure he and his bride—"

Johnson leapt in front of her, blocking the doorway. "This is blackmail!" he said hoarsely.

"Is it? I had thought to trade something for it. My absence, and Matthew Weldon's reputation."

He put his hand to his head and groaned. "How much?"

"Two hundred dollars will do nicely."

Johnson excused himself and returned with a long leather purse from which he painstakingly counted out the money from household funds, averting his eyes as the girl thrust it into the bosom of her gown.

"How do I know you will keep your word?" he asked as she prepared to leave.

She only shrugged in answer.

He couldn't know, she thought as she crossed the bridge to Sweethome. But her word would be kept, not because of a sense of honor, but because she did not intend to come this way again.

Seeking Pansy out, she told the girl they were returning to Memphis, that they would leave in the middle of the night when Sweethome slept. The girl, knowing she would have to part from her lover, began to cry.

"Nonsense!" Kirsten said. "The world is full of men!"

Everything was working out well. She was certain Miz Fannie would take her in again for a while. Then she would book passage on a boat heading downriver.

That evening, when her clothes were packed, Kirsten left the house on a final pilgrimage. For the first time, she went to the graveyard where a tiny body was interred. She stood there for a long time, tears streaming down her cheeks, then wiped her eyes and headed toward the house.

The past was behind her now. It was time for a new beginning.

58

Inga, seated by Theron in the trap on the way to
Shiloh, didn't worry about the daughters she had
left behind. The early-morning atmosphere was
soft with mist, the leaves dripping with dew. When
the sun rose, burning the damp away, scarlet birds
flashed through climbing vines, and butterflies
drifted against a backdrop of lush green.

To Theron and Inga, lost in their private mystery of love, no single item of beauty stood alone.
It was all a part of the whole, a beautiful world
that belonged, at the moment, to the two of them.

They reached a small inn before darkness fell
and spent the night in each other's arms. Then
rising before dawn, they went on to the battle-
ground.

Shiloh was eerie in the dim light of morning, a
place of fog and blasted trees. Mists swirled around

a ruined church like the spirits of the dead engaged in ghostly battle.

Alighting from the trap, they walked to the church to stand among the rubble. The remains of the old stone walls were black with damp. Inga shivered.

"Are you all right, sweetheart?"

She was. But was he? His hand gripped hers too tightly, and she knew that coming to a scene of past battles had brought back memories he wished to forget. Perhaps she had been wrong to insist they come here. But she had been so sure she would find a hint of her brother's presence.

Oh, Sven! Sven! Where are you?

She drew in a painful breath as a spectral figure appeared in the mist.

"You a Reb or a damn Yankee?" the figure asked.

The voice sounded hollow as the apparition moved toward them. It was a moment before they were able to make out the speaker, a ragged man in Confederate gray, thin, emaciated, looking as if he might be one of the dead himself.

He carried a rifle.

Inga shrank against Theron, who put a protecting arm around her.

"Reb," Theron answered.

"Name, rank, and serial numbah," the man snapped.

Theron complied with the information and the intruder relaxed. "Cain' be too keerful," he admitted. He advanced, looked at Theron's pinned-up sleeve with approval, and saluted. "Sahgent Cunnin'ham, repohtin' foh duty, suh."

Inga's knees went weak with relief as she listened to their conversation.

"Didn' have no place tuh go home to aftah the wah," he told Theron. "So Ah figgahed Ah'd stay around, keep caiah of my men. All mah frien's is heah."

It was clear the man was unbalanced, but not dangerously so. Inga's eyes filled with tears.

"Did you know a soldier named Sven? Sven Lindstrom?"

"No, ma'am, don' reckin Ah did. Ah was with Pat Cleburne's brigade. We lost a thousand men. They's so many boys heah—so many many ..." His voice broke.

"But don' y'all worry, ma'am. Ah'm watchin' ovah 'em, watchin' ovah them all."

As he talked on about the war, commenting on his dead friends as though they still lived, the sun broke through, turning the mist into rainbow veils that shimmered and finally disappeared. The light revealed that the devastated trees had put forth new leaves to cover their wounds, that grass grew green over pocked and cratered earth. A bird sang, a single long sweet trill.

The battlefield of Shiloh was healing itself. But seeing the face of the soldier, Cunningham, in the sunlight was a shock. He was little more than a boy, despite his sunken features and mad, burning, eyes. Nothing healing there.

"We all are real proud you an' youah lady is payin' us a visit," Cunningham said politely. "How 'bout Ah show yuh around?"

"We would like that," Theron said. "Lead on, Sergeant."

"Yes, suh!"

Sergeant Cunningham led Inga and Theron to what he considered the main spots of interest. There, in that area of splintered stumps, where small seedlings rose from lush grass, was where the Peach Orchard assault had taken place, pink petals drifting down upon the bodies of the dead.

Here, General Albert Sidney Johnston died, killed by a barrage from the sunken road thay'd called the Hornets' Nest. They carried him over to that ravine—there, where those blue flowers are—to die.

He led them to Pittsburg Landing, where Buell's troops landed in support of Grant's forces, turning the tide of battle.

Then, at last, to the graves.

The Confederate soldiers had been interred in common graves, three long trenches mounded up, already covered with lush grass—heroes and cowards, brave men and frightened little boys, unidentified.

"Miller's here in this'n," Cunningham said. "Taylor's ovah in the next. Should of been in the same place. They was buddies."

"How do you know where they are?" Inga asked.

The soldier looked at her in surprise. "They tolt me."

He was so natural with it all that Inga felt he was hearing words they didn't hear, seeing things they didn't see.

"Could be youah brothah's heah," he said cheerfully. "Ain't met him yet, but Ah'll keep a eye out fo' him."

Inga said a silent prayer that Sven was happy

wherever he was. There was nothing more she could do.

It was time to go home.

They said good-bye to Sergeant Cunningham, who extended a polite invitation to come again, and returned to their trap. As they drove away, Inga looked back to see the gaunt young man with a face like a death's-head watching after them.

When she looked again, he was gone, melting into the shell-shattered trees like a ghostly spirit. A living dead man, looking after his friends.

"That gun he had," Inga asked Theron, "suppose he hurts someone?"

Theron laughed, a laugh without humor. The rifle was broken, he said. It lacked a trigger.

Somehow the visit made her understand her husband a little better. And she had kept her promise to Birgitta to the best of her ability. She had searched for Sven among the living and the dead, and she had prayed for his soul.

The field of Shiloh slept in peace behind them, but the future waited ahead, bathed in golden sunlight.

When they arrived back at Sweethome, they found Jenny crying, unable to speak.

Dinah, her face like a thundercloud, handed Inga a note. "Don't worry about me, Mama," it read. "I'm going to Nick. Love, Kirsten."

"Shall I go after her?" Theron asked.

Inga shook her head. "No," she said. "Kirsten's a grown-up now. It's about time I grew up, too."

But that night, when they had gone to bed, Inga turned to him, her emotions giving way at last. "Hold me," she sobbed. "Oh, Theron, hold me!"

They had slept together, faced life and death together. Now, for the first time in their marriage, they wept together.

As long as they had each other, they would survive.

This chile goin have some schoolin," she said positively.
"Yes."
"He sho' gwine— her hand flashin, ...
...
...
...
...

59

The days passed, and Matthew Weldon brought his bride to Eden.

The year moved into harvest; then came the frost, turning trees along the river into bursts of flame. The leaves blazed and burned, then trembled under a chill wind and finally fell.

They were followed to the earth by a gentle snow, huge flakes falling softly like stars. They mounded over the fallow fields, over a small mound in the burying ground.

At Sweethome, it was the resting time.

In the old slave cabins, a free people sat before the fires, fires that roared in the chimneys, spreading warmth. They did not talk together of the past, with all of its woes, but of the future.

For the first time, they had a future.

Zada tossed her baby high, laughing with her.

"This chile goin' have some schoolin'," she said positively.

"Yes!"

"This chile goin' have two pair of shoes!"

"Yes!"

"This chile goin' walk with her haid high!"

"Amen!"

The cotton crop this year was good. Next year, it was going to be better.

In the big house, Jenny had gone early to bed, the better to hug her secret to her.

Only yesterday she had received a letter written in a crude but legible hand. Jesse's friend Sam was teaching him to write. And the ranch was everything he had said it was. He would be coming for her someday soon.

She went to bed to dream.

Downstairs, Inga, mending in her lap, was also dreaming. She gazed into the fire, her hands idle for once. This was home, she thought, looking at Theron.

This was home.

She had lost Kirsten, perhaps, but she was not alone.

Kirsten Johansson, at that moment, walked along a street in the French Quarter of New Orleans. She had just stepped off the boat from Memphis, and looked in awe at the fairytale city around her.

The buildings on the narrow cobbled streets towered above her, improbable colors of faded pink and blue, fronted with iron lace. The streets were crowded, hucksters of peanuts and pralines calling out their wares; beautiful women, blacks, quadroons, stood on street corners exchanging laughing comments with gentlemen of certain wealth.

There was music, gaiety, an aura of carnival, of excitement, such as Kirsten had never seen before.

New Orleans was her kind of place!

She located the narrow shop she had been looking for. "NICK'S CARD PARLOR," the sign read.

She stopped for a moment to prepare herself, to go over the story she intended to tell him. He was the father of her child, which she had borne in Memphis, penniless and alone, losing it prematurely.

He would not dare turn her away.

Summoning tears to eyes that had been carefully shadowed with a fading ribbon, she opened the door to Nick's Card Parlor and went in.

Kirsten had reached the end of the River Road.

In Minnesota, at its beginning, a blizzard was blowing. Snow had drifted to the upper window. Pastor Lindstrom was in the barn seeing to his chores, and old Birgitta snatched a moment for herself.

She opened the marriage chest that had come with her from Sweden, and took out a small packet.

It contained two dried magnolia blooms.

One had come from Sven.

The other from Inga.

She held them tenderly, thinking of her children, of a warmer clime she would never have a chance to see.

Then, reluctantly, she returned her treasures to their hiding place.

Pastor Lindstrom would be coming in soon.

It was almost time for prayers.

About the Author

Aola Vandergriff, born in Le Mars, Iowa, spent her formative years in Oklahoma City, OK. Her credits include a book of poetry, more than 2500 short stories and articles, and 18 novels published worldwide and in several translations. Home is the adobe hacienda which is located in a haunted canyon above the village of Le Luz, Alomogardo, New Mexico. Though she travels extensively to research her novels, she is active in political and civic affairs. She is the mother of six children.